D1505087

This Cursed Light

Emily Thiede

WEDNESDAY BOOKS
NEW YORK

First published in the United States by Wednesday Books, an imprint of St. Martin's Publishing Group.

www.wednesdaybooks.com

The Library of Congress Cataloging-in-Publication Data is available upon request.

ISBN 978-1-250-79407-9 (hardcover)
ISBN 978-1-250-79408-6 (ebook)

First Edition: 2023

10 9 8 7 6 5 4 3 2 1

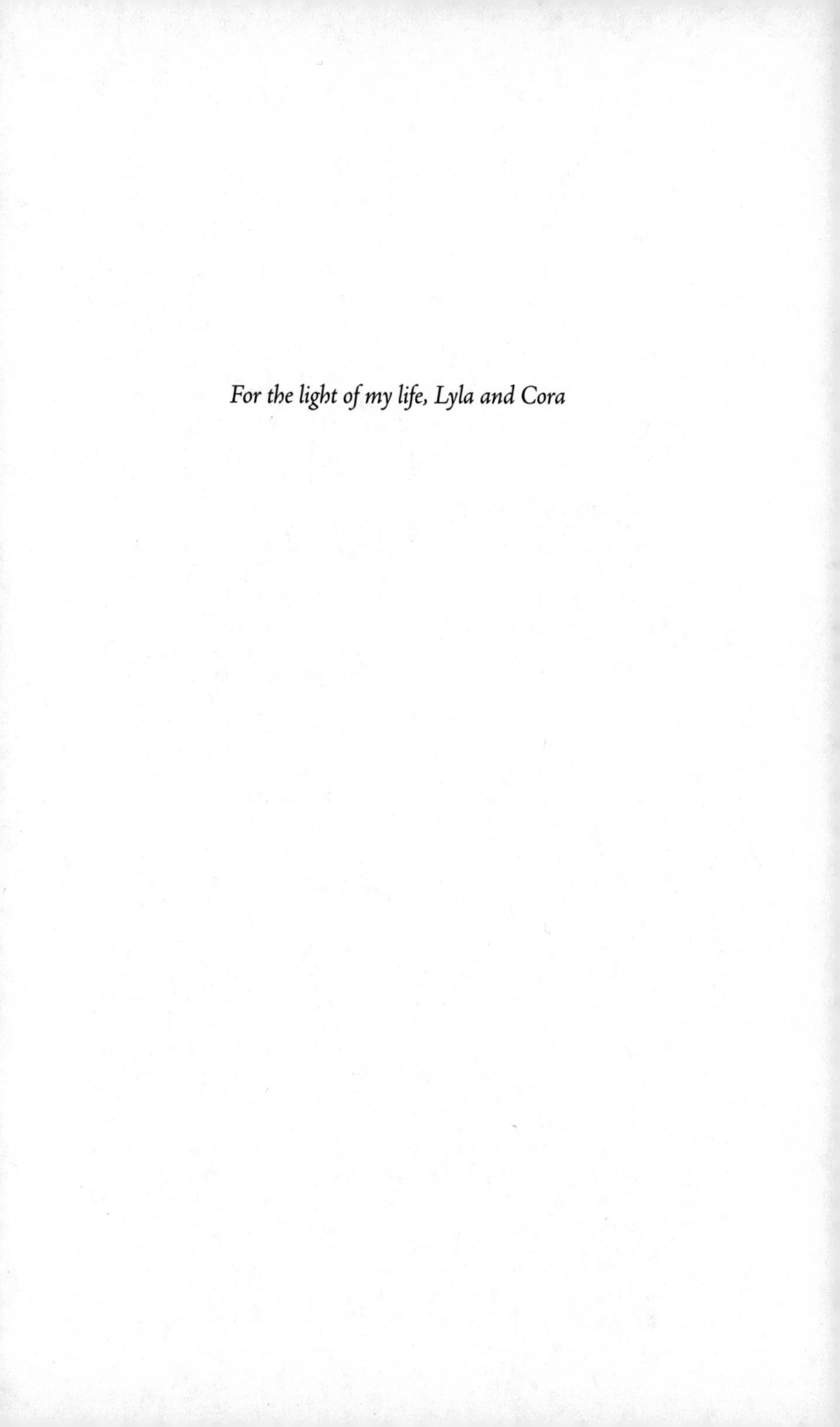

For the light of my life, Lyla and Cora

One

Every day, Dante's body betrayed him.

So he punished it.

Sweat stung his eyes, blurring the ruddy-faced dockworker across from him and the crowd boxing them into the narrow alley.

Dante beckoned with a flick of his fingers, and his opponent raised two meaty fists.

The guy's opening swing was hesitant. Weak. Not worth dodging.

No one hit as hard as they used to.

A quick jab, a few more insults, and the brawler responded with more energy.

Finally.

Jab. Parry. Land a hit. Dodge. Swing again.

Dante ducked a blow to his face, allowed one to his ribs. Took a few, landed more. He could have knocked the guy flat in minutes, but then it would've been over. No fun in that.

"Referee's here!" The cook swung ten-year-old Addie onto his shoulders for a better view, but she didn't have much to do. The other guy bowed out a few minutes later, waving off the crowd's friendly ribbing, and the dockers resumed their work, rolling barrels and hefting crates in better spirits for the brief distraction.

"The Wolf wins again!" Addie crowed.

Dante held out his hand, pretending to wince when she slapped his palm. Not much of a victory when your opponent refused to fight.

"The ship's getting closer, signor."

He squatted to look her in the eye. "I told you to call me Dante."

"And my uncle told me to respect my elders."

"*Elders?*" Dante grimaced. "Could you see anyone on the deck?"

"Like a lady in a fancy dress?" She fluttered her eyelashes. "Maybe, but extra information costs extra."

"So much for respecting your elders."

"Only suckers work for free."

"Fair enough." He made a show of counting out four shiny coins and handed them over.

Addie recounted, just to be sure, before answering. "It was still too far away to see anyone, but I sensed there *was* a lady, and she was pining."

"You sensed, huh?"

"Yup. And Signor Adrick said I'll get a whole cake if I tell the bakers next."

"A *whole* cake?" Dante feigned shock. "You better hustle."

The kid skipped away to inform Alessa's parents of her imminent arrival, leaving Dante alone in the late-morning chill.

He pulled up his shirt to check the damage: A few bruises. A shallow scrape. Nothing he couldn't hide. Some of the bruises might even have been healing a bit faster than usual. Maybe.

No one knew for sure if his powers were gone *forever.* People weren't supposed to come back from the dead, but he had. Maybe the rest of him could, too.

He shook out his arms, grimacing at a twinge in one shoulder. It had been easier to appreciate the burn of a good workout when it hadn't lasted so long.

Pain, he didn't mind. He could handle *pain.* Pain had been his only companion for years while he took dangerous work and brutal punishments to survive, relying on his healing powers to get him through it. It wasn't *pain* that bothered him. No, it was the constant reminder that ever since Alessa had brought him back from the dead, he was alive but not whole. *That* was the itch beneath his skin.

Towlines snagged in his chest, pulling in opposite directions. She'd be back soon, and he missed her with an alarmingly fierce ache, but he could feel the Cittadella walls closing in already, trapping him inside a labyrinth of memories—the scent of astringent, the bone-scraping sounds of suffering during the months the building had served as a makeshift hospital after Divorando—and people everywhere, watching him all the time.

At the docks, he could breathe. Sometimes even sleep. The memories and nightmarish visions sent by Dea still chased him, but they had a harder time catching up.

He pulled open the back door, crusted with decades worth of chipped paint, and stepped inside. He'd never expected to own anything, much less an entire building, but after a month of renovations, the Bottom of the Barrel no longer deserved its name. It wasn't fancy, but it suited him better than high walls and silk sheets, even if it did require constant repairs.

"You're still here?" Adrick's look of surprise shifted to something more thoughtful as Dante crossed the main room. Too observant by half, that kid.

"Obviously." Dante avoided his gaze, rolling up his sleeves as though it required his full attention.

"*Why* are you still here? You know she'll go straight to the Cittadella to find you."

"Yeah, I know." He ignored Adrick's pointed sigh and headed upstairs.

When Alessa had left for Altari, tasking her brother with babysitting him, Dante had been fiercely determined not to like the guy, but the Paladino twins shared a dog-with-a-bone determination to win people over. Nothing could stop them when they sniffed out a potential friend.

Not that he and Adrick were *friends,* exactly, but silence wasn't as comfortable as it used to be, and Adrick never let it last, filling quiet moments with jokes and chatter to avoid the things neither of them wanted to think about. After months of tending wounded soldiers in the aftermath of Divorando—and watching too many die—Adrick had a tighter set to his shoulders and a hint of darkness behind his eyes to match Dante's own.

So, no. He didn't mind Adrick hanging around. Most of the time.

In his rooms on the upper level, he eyed the package on his desk, debating for a minute before sliding it underneath the bed. She wouldn't want some ratty old book.

As he stood, a fat drop of water landed on his head. Another damn leak.

Alessa was used to luxury. He couldn't expect her to hang around a place like this. Especially if it was leaking.

He wrenched the window open and leaned out to peer toward the harbor. Above the roofline, tips of white sails cut the sky.

An hour. Maybe more. He had time.

A ladder was already propped against the building, and Dante made it to the roof a few minutes later. The first tile he tugged free was cracked, with signs of rot beneath, something he suspected might be true for most of the building. There was a metaphor about his life in there that he didn't want to think about.

A speck landed on his eyelashes, and he blinked to clear his vision, but it wasn't dust.

Tipping his head back, Dante watched the fluffy white flecks dance through the air. Alessa was back, and she'd brought winter with her.

He'd only seen snow once, ages ago. His father had dragged him out of bed, and they'd run through the flurries, catching snowflakes on their tongues.

He held out his hand, and a lone flake drifted onto his palm, melting immediately.

One touch of warmth and it died.

Alessa gripped the ship's railing, leaning forward like a carved mermaid. "Is that *snow?*"

"Looks like it," Kaleb drawled. "I hope you're a good swimmer, because I have no intention of delaying our arrival to rescue you."

Their "brief" diplomatic trip to Altari had turned into two months, and the longer time had stretched, the more her worries had grown about what she might find upon returning.

Kaleb squinted against the brisk wind ruffling his auburn

hair. "We should have dragged Saida along. My powers are clearly *best* for battle—congratulations on your excellent choice of main Fonte—but alas, electricity isn't as useful as wind for making ships move."

"Could you work on that? Make an electric-powered ship or something?"

"What am I, an engineer?" He rolled his visible eye. The other was covered by a silk patch. "I didn't sign up to be your personal inventor."

"Divorando's over. What use are you to me now?"

Kaleb gave her an indignant glare. "I point out your flaws to keep you humble, and I'm a stunning date at formal events."

"I have Dante for that." Six months ago she would have been mortified by the lovesick little sigh that slipped free, but her pride was a worthy sacrifice to annoy Kaleb.

"Dante could never pull off this ensemble." Kaleb claimed his colorful post-Divorando style was more befitting a savior, and they'd coordinated for the occasion, with her dress the same deep purple as his shirt and eye patch, rose underskirts perfectly matching the silk lining of his jacket.

"Dante would be irresistible in a burlap sack," Alessa said.

"Eh. Not my type."

She arched a skeptical eyebrow.

"Not because he's a *man*." Kaleb smoothed his hair. "That part's fine. Ideal, really."

"I thought so. You certainly never showed any interest in *me*."

"Who's arrogant now?" Kaleb said, jabbing her with his elbow. "You think everyone who likes girls is scheming to get under your skirts?"

"Hardly." Alessa sputtered as a lock of dark hair blew over her mouth, catching on her lip gloss. "People of all genders and romantic persuasions fled at the sight of me for nearly five years. I'm under no delusion that I'm irresistible." The wind was fast turning her carefully arranged curls into a tangled mess.

Still no sight of Dante waiting by the dock.

"Don't hurt your neck. He'll be there." Kaleb adjusted his cuffs. "The whole city's waiting to welcome us home."

She worried her lip. "He might not be up to it yet." Her hope that he was right, that Dante was fully recovered, physically, mentally, emotionally, was sharp enough to draw blood.

"It's been two months. He's probably hearty and hale and back to stabbing people." Kaleb's sarcasm didn't fully disguise his doubt.

She wasn't the only one who'd struggled with guilt over leaving Dante while he was still . . . not himself. Even as his physical injuries had healed, he'd grown more brooding, obsessed with finding the other ghiotte to prepare for battle with a mysterious threat he insisted the gods were sending, until his fears had begun to feel just as real to her. But being away from his haunted eyes had cleared her own.

Saverio's pattern never deviated: once a generation, the goddess Dea crowned a new Finestra with the power to magnify other people's gifts, and five years later Crollo sent the scarabei attack of Divorando, which the Finestra and their chosen Fonte—or in Alessa's case, more than one Fonti—were tasked to defeat. Then, after a respite of years or even decades—depending on how quickly the gods got bored—the Finestra's power transferred to a new chosen one and the cycle began anew. And *when* that day came, Alessa and Kaleb would guide the next Duo Divino, just as Renata and Tomo had done for them.

Dante's paranoia was understandable after a brush with death, but that didn't mean it was *true*. He'd get past it. She'd help him.

"Why are we slowing down?" Alessa nearly wailed.

"Probably to avoid crashing into the docks and causing catastrophic loss of life and property. Or to vex you. Hard to say for certain."

"First thing you'll do?" Alessa asked. Any distraction to keep the worry at bay.

"Eat something that's not seafood. I never want to smell another lutefisk in my life. You?" Kaleb said. "Wait, don't answer that. Just promise you'll take it somewhere private. Nothing ruins my appetite faster than displays of public affection."

Her laugh came out a bit hysterical. "I don't even know if I can touch him."

"Where there's a will, or enough pent up—ahem—*energy*, there's a way."

Her stomach flipped with equal parts excitement and anxiety. The unpredictable storm of her powers had retreated since Divorando, and she didn't even wear gloves half the time anymore, but her magic had caused too much pain and death in the past to trust it.

A hug? A hug would be safe enough. Probably. Even though she wanted so much more.

"*Please* tell me you aren't fantasizing right now," Kaleb said. "Do you need a minute alone?"

"I hope I live long enough to see you *destroyed* by love."

Kaleb scoffed. "Better eat your vegetables."

At last, the ship neared the dock and sailors scurried around, tossing ropes, lowering gangplanks, and doing whatever else sailors had to do to bring a ship home.

Their counterparts from Tanp, the farthest sanctuary island, were poised on the deck of their own ship, waiting to disembark. Both tall and slender with glossy black hair and amber skin, Ciro Angeles and Diwata Kapule had followed them to Saverio after the two pairs met on Altari, where they'd bonded over shared awkwardness as they attempted to uphold the post-Divorando tradition of touring, despite the fact that Altari had no Duo.

The Altarian saviors had tragically perished prior to Divorando, leaving the population to seek refuge on Saverio. Thanks to Alessa's protection—and her team of Fonti—the Altarians had returned to rebuild their decimated home, but instead of balls and banquets, the ceremonial visit from the other two islands' Duos had involved distributing donations and surveying the wreckage. Now they were back on Saverio, and it was time to celebrate.

Alessa gathered her skirts as the captain waved them over to disembark. The gangway swayed with every step, sending her stomach swooping, and the captain steadied her with a painfully tight grip on her arm. Alessa flinched but didn't pull away. She *could* touch people now without making them scream in agony, as long as she stayed calm and focused, but people had lost their fear of her faster than she had.

"Thank—" Her words caught in her throat as she met the captain's eyes. No one had ever looked at her like *that*—cold, blank, and vacant. Not even when half the city thought her a monster.

Strange, almost-whispers skirted the margins of her mind as the captain's gaze sharpened. Consuming darkness. A void with no end. A ravenous craving to *destroy*—

The captain blinked and her eyes cleared. "Careful there."

Dazed, Alessa pulled free.

"Another headache?" Kaleb said as she joined him on the dock.

Alessa swiped at the sweat dewing her forehead. "Just sea legs."

She'd had too much time to think on the journey. Too many nights dwelling on her past, the faces of her first three Fonti when she'd stolen their final sparks of life. Because of her, Emer, Ilsi, and Hugo went to their graves missing a piece of their souls. Headaches were a small price to pay for what she'd done. She was fortunate the gods hadn't punished her with worse.

"Shall we?" Kaleb said, extending his arm.

Alessa straightened her shoulders, pushing away the haunting moment with the captain. A cheer erupted as they waved to the crowd, and she basked in the adoration. *This* was right. *This* was what she'd been promised. Beloved. Victorious. Celebrated. Her reign was finished, and her time on Finestra's Peak was over.

No more demons. No more wars.

It was time to begin the rest of her life.

Happily.

Ever.

After.

Two

After a few minutes of craning her neck, Alessa was forced to accept that Dante wasn't waiting for her in the crowd. Or lurking behind it, which would have been more his style.

Diwata clutched Ciro's arm as they made their way across the dock, looking overwhelmed by the reception waiting for them.

"What a beautiful island," Ciro said. "That must be the peak where you battled—with *multiple* partners! Fascinating. Will we meet them all at tomorrow's gala? Even the—pardon, I forget what you call them here."

"Ghiotte." Alessa's smile took on a hard edge.

Diwata perked up. "It's still here?"

"*He*," Kaleb said firmly.

The roar of the crowd lining the road made it difficult to converse during their procession through the city, but Alessa pointed out key landmarks and interjected bits of Saverian history, to Ciro's delight.

Gregarious and charming, if a bit stuffy, he was the type of person who seemed genuinely interested in what everyone had to say, and she appreciated it as one prone to nervous chatter. And Kaleb got along well enough with meek Diwata. He made no effort at small talk, so she wasn't obligated to try.

After presenting them at Saverio's finest inn, Alessa set a bruising pace the rest of the way to the Cittadella, but Dante wasn't waiting for her at the gates, either.

Obligations, however, were. Renata and Tomo, the previous Finestra and Fonte, swooped in immediately.

"The conquering heroes!" Tomo called, glowing with health and a tan.

"At last," Renata said. "We were starting to worry you'd miss your own celebration and we'd all have to drown our sorrows in the prosecco fountain."

"Is Dante here?" Alessa asked.

Tomo frowned. "I haven't seen him since we arrived."

Alessa's feet twitched to search for him, but the caterer had questions, and apparently it was crucially important that the Duo Divino selected the right napkins.

Alessa nearly hugged the guard who interrupted to inform them that a light repast was laid out in the library and "the young gentleman" was waiting.

"Oh, go on," Renata said with an affectionate sigh. "We'll handle the rest."

Alessa wasn't proud of how fast she left, but she wasn't too dignified to speed walk, either.

"You are *not* leaving me to choose candelabra when there's food upstairs," Kaleb muttered, hot on her heels. "Slow down. Desperation's not a good look."

They jostled to get in front of each other, but Kaleb didn't have skirts slowing him down and he reached the fourth floor first, lunging to hold the library door shut. "I'm helping you, here. Take a beat so you don't scare the poor guy away."

Alessa glared. "Open the door."

"Just don't pounce, for Dea's sake." Kaleb pushed the door open, and his expression shifted from haughty to aggravated. "Why are *you* here?"

"You're not Dante," Alessa blurted out.

"Wonderful to see you too, sister." Adrick's lanky form unfolded from an armchair.

"Sorry. It *is* good to see you," Alessa said. "If unexpected."

Kaleb swept past to glare at the charcuterie. Prior to their departure, he had determinedly ignored Adrick whenever her brother visited the Cittadella, harping on how Adrick had exposed Dante and tried to poison Alessa. But she suspected the long night Kaleb spent in a cold subterranean tomb after taking Dante's place was as much to blame.

Adrick shook his blond curls back. "Mama and Papa are up to their necks in lemon zest making desserts for your reception, but they send their love."

"And Dante? Where is he? *How* is he?"

Adrick gestured at the spread on the table. "Prosciutto?"

"Adrick," Alessa warned.

"Breathe. He's . . . fine. Physically."

Alessa squinted at her brother. "But not mentally?"

"Don't put words in my mouth. He's been through a lot. Just go easy on him, okay?"

"I will. When I *see him*. Which I cannot do if I don't know where he *is*."

"*Where is Dante?* See, that's a question that raises more questions."

"I may have to kill you, after all."

"At least let me eat before you commit fratricide. I'm famished."

Kaleb cracked his knuckles. "Want me to hit him? I can hit him."

"No," Alessa snapped. "Adrick, *where* is Dante?"

When Dante sat back on his haunches to inspect his handiwork he realized with a start that the sun was hanging low over the city. Time had slipped away from him.

He hurried to pack his tools, but movement below caught his eye—a lithe figure running down the street toward him. His heart made a strange little thump.

Grabbing the edge of the roof, he swung down, using the windowsill and signpost to slow his descent, and landed before Alessa.

"Dea above!" She skidded to a halt, clutching her chest. "Can you *try* not to kill yourself the moment I return?"

He quirked a smile. "I always *try*, but death seems determined to find me."

Alessa laughed, still breathless—from the shock, the run, or nerves, he couldn't tell. Her nose was pink from the chill, freckles dancing across the bridge. Tiny, barely noticeable, but new. Everything else about her face was exactly as he remembered, yet somehow more perfect.

Her gaze darted from him to the sign, back at him, then to the newly painted siding, flighty as a bird searching for a safe perch. Nervous, then. He opened his arms, and she took a half step forward, hesitated. Stopped.

"Seriously?" He kept his tone light, with effort. She bit her lip with a flash of white teeth, the flush deepening in her cheeks.

So focused on her, Dante didn't see Kaleb hurtling closer until he got slammed with something between a tackle and a hug.

"Sorry!" Kaleb thumped his back, laughing. "Still working on depth perception. Feeling solid, man. And a business owner? Didn't see that coming."

"I tried to slow him down." Adrick made an apologetic face and shoved Kaleb toward the door. "Let's give these two a minute, eh?" Kaleb took the door handle with two fingers, and Adrick jabbed him in the back. "For the love of Dea's left tit, commoner dirt won't kill you."

Their voices faded as the door slammed behind them.

"So . . ." Alessa twisted her hands—her *bare* hands, he noted with surprise. "How—how are you?"

A loaded question. "Good. Better."

"Any signs of . . ." She waved at his body as though that was supposed to make sense. Which it kind of did.

"Nope." His smile faltered. "Still just a regular human."

"Oh." She gnawed her lip. "But you did all of the exercises the doctors advised?"

"Yep."

"Are you still taking Adrick's tinctures?" she asked.

Dante's eyes glassed over. "*No*. Because I'm better."

"Except . . ."

Dante blew out a breath. "Except for that."

"Well, this is going *great*," Alessa said with a nervous smile. "Not awkward at all."

He snorted a laugh. "Then stop fussing, will you? I did everything I was supposed to. Combed my hair and brushed my teeth every day, too. You want to check that I buttoned my pants correctly?"

Alessa raised her chin. "Ladies do not investigate a man's pants in the middle of the street."

"That's a damn shame." He held out his arms. "Look, I'm fine. I'm in the best shape of my life."

"Hmm, yes, I can see that." She ran a light hand down his chest with an approving sound that stirred something low in his belly. "I can't tell if you're actually bigger or if I just forgot how large you are."

"I've been lifting crates, running every day." Bemused, he watched her squeeze one bicep. "Find one you like?"

"Hmm?"

"Looks like you're choosing a piece of fruit."

She squeezed his other bicep. "Oh, I could never choose. I love them both."

"If you can grope me on the street, you can hug me."

Alessa squeaked as he hauled her off her feet, but her grip tightened around his neck after a beat. A knot unraveled in his chest at the scent of salt and cold and *her.*

The fur ruff of her cloak tickled his face as she leaned back to look at him, and the honeyed ring around her irises caught him like a moth to a flame. He didn't even realize he was leaning in to kiss her until she ducked her head.

Right. He lowered her to the ground, swallowing heat in his throat.

"You want the tour?" He nodded toward the building, shoving his hands in his pockets so he wouldn't reach for her again.

Fine, so she'd panicked.

Dante wasn't the wounded warrior she'd left behind *or* the

nearly invincible bodyguard. He'd changed yet again, and she needed a moment to catch up.

"I can't believe you bought a bar," she said as they stepped inside.

Dante shrugged. "The Consiglio kept throwing money at me. Had to do something with it."

"Expensive clothes, presents for me?" Surely he could have come up with something simpler to spend his government stipend on.

He tapped his temple. "Right. Next time I'll remember that."

It was early for a dinner crowd, but the room buzzed with boisterous conversation and unchecked laughter. New floorboards covered what had previously been a blood-spattered dirt floor, and the fighting cage was gone, replaced by sturdy tables and mismatched chairs.

"We got tables," he said gruffly.

She arched a brow. "Fancy." He was *nervous,* she realized with delight. He cared about her opinion of his project.

"Nothing's watered down anymore." Dante patted the bar. The surface was still scarred with burn marks that would never get sanded off entirely, but it gleamed with finishing oil, and the shelves behind it were lined with bottles of every shape and color. "Hired security, too." Dante nodded at a burly man standing watch. "Believe it or not, there was a kitchen buried in there. Took a week to dig out all the trash."

"It's wonderful." And it was. Dante hadn't been wasting away, gripped by paranoia. This was good. Very good.

"Come on, I'll show you upstairs."

At the end of the wood-paneled corridor past the kitchen

and storeroom, a young woman skipped down the stairs. "Hey, boss."

"I'm your landlord, not your boss," Dante said.

"Close enough." She handed him a small coin purse. "Looking a little tight out there earlier. If your shoulder's still bugging you, my door's always open. One hour with me and you'll feel like a new man."

Alessa coughed.

Dante tucked the bag into his pocket. "Katya, this is the Fines—"

"Alessa," she interrupted. Too late. The girl was already ducking a hasty curtsy. "And you are?"

"Katya, Saverio's finest in massage therapy and bodywork."

Alessa's eyebrows rose. "The girl with the magic hands?"

"You've heard of me?" A smile dimpled her cheeks. "Apologies for not recognizing you. I know Dante used to work for you, but I never expected to see you here."

Alessa's smile wavered. "I had to see his new project."

"That's so nice." She slid a glance at Dante. "I have to run, but it was an honor to meet you."

Upstairs, Dante unlocked one of the two doors and motioned for Alessa to go first. "Not much to look at."

True, the room was small and minimally furnished with battered furniture, but it was cozy, smelling faintly of whiskey and leather. The shelves were full of books, with more stacked beside the cracked leather armchair, and a faded quilt was neatly folded on the narrow cot, with faint creases visible on the pillowcase.

"You moved out of the Cittadella?" she asked.

"I didn't *move out*. It's just easier to stay here than trek back every night." Dante dropped the coin purse onto the desk. "Besides, you weren't there."

She resisted the temptation to ask if it would have mattered if she was. "Are Katya's rooms just for her practice?"

Dante frowned at the change in topic. "She lives there, too. Does good business and I get a cut."

Alessa peered around the room. "Do you use her services often?"

Dante leaned against the desk, arms crossed. "What *exactly* do you think Katya's profession is?"

Alessa raised her chin. "Massage and . . . bodywork?"

"You don't think . . ." He barked a laugh. "You did! You actually thought I went into business with a courtesan, slept with her, *and* casually mentioned it to you!"

Well, *now* Alessa felt ridiculous. "She did seem *very* surprised to see us together."

"Because I don't talk about my personal life." He was still laughing. "You've barely been back one hour and you've already felt me up on the street and accused me of running a brothel. Pace yourself."

She huffed. "In that same hour, I watched you jump off a roof and found out you bought a bar. Pace *your*self."

With a grin, he shrugged out of his moss-soiled shirt and tossed it in a basket.

Alessa gasped at the mosaic of bruises and cuts marring his beautiful torso. "What *happened?*"

Dante froze. "Crates fall, guys like to spar. It's no big deal."

She exhaled through her nose. *Deep, calming breaths.* Fine, so he'd been treating his body like a punching bag. She'd steer him toward less destructive hobbies going forward.

She strolled toward the desk to be *casually* nosy, but the top book in the stack ruined that plan. "*A Treatise on Hunting Ghiotte*? What *is* this?"

Dante turned around, buttoning his new, clean shirt. "Nasty, huh? There are clues in there, though, I know it. For one, it says to separate ghiotte, because they fight better and heal faster in groups. Maybe once I find the others, my powers will come back."

Her stomach sank. "You're still having nightmares?"

His jaw tensed. "They aren't *nightmares*. They're visions. *Warnings*."

"Sorry. Of course." Yet another topic best avoided. Her gaze landed on a flash of color beneath his bed. A paper-wrapped package, tied with ribbon. "Is that for me?"

Dante glanced over, then away. "Uh, yeah. It's nothing special. Found it in a pawnshop."

She unwrapped it to reveal a shabby little book, worn by countless hands. "A primer in the old language? That's so thoughtful."

Dante shrugged. "You wanted to learn."

"I love it." She wanted to gush more, but expressions of gratitude always made him squirm. In the coming days, she'd get more lavish gifts, but none would be as precious as her growing collection of old books from Dante. "I was starting to worry I'd miss my own Name Day Celebration," she said, flipping through the primer.

"When's that again?" Dante glanced over, eyes twinkling.

"Tomorrow. And you have to be there. We have matching ensembles."

"Is that supposed to *convince* me?"

"It's my big day!"

"You have a *lot* of big days." He counted on his fingers. "Weddings, battles, ceremonies—"

She hopped up to sit on the desk with a loud *humph* that made him laugh. "Please tell me you let the tailor fit you before you fled the Cittadella."

"Afraid I'll show up stark naked?"

"Even *better,*" she said with a cheeky smile. "Clothed or not, you *will* be my escort, won't you?"

"Si, luce mia. I will escort you to the ball." The teasing glint in his eyes turned dark as he prowled toward her, his voice going soft and low. "And now I'm going to kiss you."

She swallowed, hypnotized by the wolfish curl of his lips as he pulled her flush against him, his body firm everywhere hers was soft. The scent of soap and whiskey and something indefinably *Dante* flooded her senses, and the moment his lips found hers, every day they'd spent apart evaporated.

Oh, yes. This is what she wanted. This is what she *needed.* She threaded her hands through his hair to pull him closer. Hours spent lost in daydreams, and not one had come close.

Dante tensed, his frame going rigid. Panicked, she shoved him, and he stumbled back.

"I'm sorry!" she cried.

Breath hissed through his teeth. "I'm fine." Clearly untrue.

"I've been so much better at controlling my power, I swear, but it's always harder when I'm tired." She wrung her hands. "I'm so sorry."

"Stop apologizing." Dante didn't quite meet her gaze as he fastened the last button on his shirt. "I have to get downstairs."

Alessa toed the floor. "I was hoping you'd walk me back to the Cittadella."

"Yeah. I will." He rolled up one sleeve. "As soon as I can

leave without everything falling apart. You can rest up here if you want, or come on down, and I'll make you a drink."

She was buzzing with energy and had no interest in napping, but she lingered to poke around his room for a little bit before following him and claiming the barstool beside Kaleb. The last time she'd sat there, Dante had been an intimidating stranger fresh off a fight, and she'd been working up the courage to ask for help.

Dante didn't look up as she rested her gloved hands on the bar, but his lips twitched into a smile. "Careful. Someone might recognize you."

He *did* remember. She peeked up at him through her lashes. "I'm not worried. I have a very good bodyguard."

"Can't be that good if he let you walk here without protection."

"Excuse me," Kaleb said. "I am a Fonte. Besides, no one's trying to kill her anymore. Not even her family."

Adrick slipped behind Dante with a stack of drinking glasses. "She's stuck with you. That's punishment enough."

Kaleb ignored the dig. "Pour me a glass of the most expensive liquor you have."

"You know I won't let you pay," Dante said, pulling bottles from the top shelf.

"Then make it a double." Kaleb spread out a napkin like a tablecloth. "Finally back on Saverio, and we're spending our first evening in the docks. How the mighty have fallen."

Adrick slammed down a water glass, splashing Kaleb's lap.

Alessa tossed him a napkin. "The last time I sat here, a very grumpy stranger told me he didn't care if I lived or died."

"I was a bit of an ass, wasn't I?" Dante rested his elbows on the bar. "And yet here you are. What can I get you?"

"Surprise me."

Dante smiled like he'd been hoping for that response. He mixed limoncello, prosecco, and a splash of syrup from a bottle with a dried hot pepper floating in it, strained it into a glass rimmed with a mixture of sugar and sea salt, garnished with a lemon slice, and slid it toward her.

She took a sip and paused to savor the bubbly combination of sweet and tart, followed by the tang of salt and a lingering hint of spice. Her eyebrows arched in delight. "What is this called?"

"Guess."

"*Please* tell me it's called the Luce Mia."

He winked, but she barely had time to bask in the warm fuzzy feeling before she was nearly knocked off her stool.

"Hey!" Dante shouted. "Watch where you're going."

"It's okay," Alessa said. "I'm fine." She turned to look at the man who had stumbled into her. His bloodshot eyes were too close, and she could *feel* his anger like it was her own, as though a miasma of palpable hatred flowed off him and into her.

The man's bleary gaze sharpened into something cruel. "She was in my way."

Dante vaulted over the bar. Catching the man's fist as he took a swing, Dante spun him around, yanking his arm up and back. The man's buddy pushed over a table, scattering playing cards across the floor, and smashed a beer bottle against the edge. Brandishing the jagged neck like a knife, he came running to join the fray.

Dante threw his captive to the side, swiped the makeshift weapon out of the other man's hand and turned it back on him as the security guard finally reached them.

"And the entertainment is free!" Adrick said.

Alessa swallowed the sour taste of fear as Dante and the guard strong-armed the brawlers out the door. Her gift was meant to absorb a Fonte's powers, and she sometimes picked up a taste of their emotions when she touched them to do so, but that required skin contact, and she hadn't touched that man. Impossible. She shook herself. She must be more tired than she realized.

She bent to pick up a sticky playing card from her feet and flicked it onto the counter. A Crollo, god of chaos. Fitting.

Dante returned, dusting his hands. "You okay?"

"*I* am fine. Why hire security if you're going to jump in anyway?"

Dante scowled. "I won't ask my employees to do anything I won't do myself."

"His friend almost slit your throat!"

"I can handle myself in a fight," Dante grumbled, pulling his beer-soaked shirt away from his skin.

"But you don't *have* to. Most people only get one chance at life. You've already gotten two. Don't tempt fate."

Three

Placing a card on the scarred wood tabletop, she heaved a weary sigh. "You still insist people are inherently selfish, after all this time? Your cynicism is more durable than the heavens. You saw the sacrifice—"

Her opponent scoffed. "Dying to save someone you love isn't sacrifice. It's self-preservation."

"That's absurd. It's an act of love." She shuffled her cards. With every piece of evidence provided, he dug his heels in further. Maddening.

"Love and selflessness are not the same. Your evidence simply hasn't changed my mind."

"One more wager, then." She placed a pair of hearts on the table. "Same players."

He chuckled. "And if you lose?"

"I won't," she said with dignity. "You set your terms; I'll set mine."

A slow smile spread across his face. "Are you sure? No amount of pleading will get you out of this one, my dear."

"Absolutely." She fanned her cards out. "It's time to settle this once and for all."

He grinned, and his cards burst into flames.

• • •

The previous day's cold snap withered as Dante stopped to catch his breath at a rocky outcropping on the beach. Hands on hips, he savored the tang of brine and citrus, the tingle of ocean spray on his bare chest.

Lying next to Alessa had been an exquisite kind of torment, with every soft sigh and rustle of sheets a promise denied. He'd lain awake for hours, watching her sleep, full of regret for every night he'd insisted on keeping his distance. When he *had* finally dozed off, another damned vision—*not* nightmare—snatched him right back from the brink of sleep.

An hour of running wasn't enough to escape the specter of choking ash, streets running with blood, hordes of leering eyes, and the crackle of scorched flesh, but at least he got to leave the city behind.

No walls, no expectations, no curious looks from strangers. Nothing but the air in his lungs, the rocky beach beneath his feet, and the sea beyond.

Somewhere on the other side, his people were waiting to be found, his best hope for regaining his powers and warding off Crollo's threat.

Unease stirred in his gut. *Were* the ghiotte still his people now that he'd lost his powers?

It stung how Alessa skittered away from the topic, as though speaking it aloud was what would *make* it true. After staying by his side for months while he recovered, never questioning his visions or the mission Dea had given him, he was finally fit and ready to find them, but *now* she had doubts? Whether she believed it or not, Crollo was coming, and Dante would be there to greet him.

But first, he had a part to play.

Alessa's Name Day Celebrations were a formality—an archaic one at that—but they marked the end of her servitude, when she'd finally reclaim her name, or a new one of her choice, and no longer have to exist as an idol set apart from the rest of society, addressed only by her title.

It was important to her.

So he'd endure an evening of wearing the stiff clothes, mingling with pompous strangers, and even—he gritted his teeth—being *nice* to Saverio's elite.

Nice might be a stretch. Civil would have to do.

With a reluctant sigh, he turned back toward the city. Everything would be open by now, and he had something to finish before returning to the Cittadella.

It was a big day for Alessa. People gave gifts for that sort of thing, didn't they?

An hour after Kamaria and Saida arrived to help Alessa and Kaleb prepare for the festivities, the mood in the Fonte suite was deteriorating rapidly.

"Love is terrible. *Boys* are terrible." Saida made an exquisite portrait of heartbreak, reclining on the chaise longue, her curves swathed in cobalt silk. Even her black curls draped dramatically over one shoulder.

"Valid," Kaleb said, stuffing an entire samosa in his mouth.

Apparently, Saida had embarked on a brief but tumultuous relationship while they were away, and Kaleb's attempts to find a date for the after-party had not gone well.

"I am *likable*," Saida said stubbornly, bracelets glittering as she dabbed at her kohl-lined eyes. "Even *Kaleb* likes me!"

Kaleb nodded, looking slightly alarmed.

"You're the most likable person I know," Alessa said. She

pulled her robe tight and began gathering crumb-covered plates and hiding half-empty bottles, careful not to muss her pile of curls as she tidied.

Saida glared at the uneaten samosa in her palm. "I wish I liked girls instead."

"Bad news, cupcake." Kamaria patted her head. "Girls are just as bad. Ask me how I know."

"Not you too," Alessa said. "Is heartbreak contagious?"

Kamaria smirked. "Gods, no. I'm young, famous, and I helped save the world. You couldn't pay me to get tied down right now. No offense." She flicked a hand between Alessa and Kaleb. "At least your marriage isn't a *real* one."

"Thank Dea for that," Alessa said, patting a stray curl back into place.

"*What?*" Kaleb clutched his chest in mock outrage. "You mean to tell me this gods-sanctioned marriage of convenience hasn't evolved into a *love match*? You aren't soaking your pillows with tears every night over my callous indifference? Here I thought Dante was your consolation prize."

Alessa waved a bottle at him. "Don't even joke about that. You know how he is."

"I *do*." Kaleb plucked the samosa from Saida's hand. "Dante has more baggage than anyone I know, and I collect luggage."

Kamaria took a swig from a wine bottle, unfazed by the angst all around. Her black hair was newly cut, shaved on the sides with tight curls on top, and her sleeveless black tunic showed off her tall frame and lean, muscular arms. She'd have no trouble finding dance partners.

"I saw our portraits downstairs, and yours is *stunning*, Saida," Kamaria said. "Just pose next to that all night and you'll be the belle of the ball."

Alessa had bucked the trend of having the Duo painted together and requested to have individual portraits of herself, Kaleb, Dante, and the other Fonti on display instead. After all, Kamaria, Saida, Josef, and Nina had also been on Finestra's peak, lending their powers to Alessa during Divorando, and a team effort deserved team recognition.

"Did you see mine?" Kaleb struck a pose to match his portrait. "I look like a pirate king."

"I don't want to dance with anyone," Saida groused. "Love is evil."

"It's not *evil.*" Alessa snatched the last cream puff from the tray before it vanished into Kaleb's insatiable maw. "You just need to find the right person."

"Ha!" Saida chucked a pillow at her. "Easy for you to say. You found your true love at eighteen."

Alessa's cough sent a puff of powdered sugar into the air. "And he *died.*"

"Yeah, but he's fine *now,*" Kamaria said. "All's well that ends well."

"I can barely touch him!"

"That part stinks." Saida nodded sagely. "I'll give you that. But you still lose, even if you have to sleep with a pillow wall between you."

Kamaria shrieked, pointing at Alessa's face. "Do you *really*? Sorry, I shouldn't laugh. It's not funny."

"Yes, it is," Kaleb said. "Where is he, anyway?"

"I saw him running stairs earlier," Kamaria said. "Seems he has some *energy* to burn off, if you know what I mean."

Shirt untucked, hair still wet with sweat, Dante strode through the Cittadella gates and stopped abruptly. Tomo,

Renata, Nina, Josef, and two finely dressed strangers gaped at him.

"And there he is now." Renata's smile was strained. "Alessa's consort. Dante, this is Ciro and Diwata, the saviors from Tanp."

"Ciao," Dante mumbled.

Nina gave a small wave and Josef bowed, but the visitors stared like he was a rat on a wedding cake.

"Alessa and the others are upstairs getting ready," Tomo said. "We won't keep you."

Dante jerked a nod. Muttering obscenities under his breath, he took the steps two at a time.

No one cared if he was dusty or sweaty at the docks. Hell, he'd stand out *more* if he showed up there looking like some fancy prick.

Not like it mattered what he wore. No change of attire would have made a difference in their reactions. People noticed when someone didn't belong.

At the top, he veered toward the sound of laughter. The interior of the Fonte suite looked like a storm had blown in the contents of a *modiste,* a bakery, and a wine cellar. Kaleb, Kamaria, and Saida lounged amid strewn clothing, nearly empty trays of sweets, and too many uncorked wine bottles for so few people.

In the middle of the chaos, Alessa stifled a horrified laugh. "Can we *please* not discuss Dante's sex life?"

"Excuse me?" Dante stopped in the doorway, eyebrows arched.

"We're competing for the title of most tragic love story," Kamaria announced, entirely nonplussed to see him there. "Sorry to be the bearer of bad news, but you didn't even make runner-up."

Dante blinked. "*I died.*"

Alessa threw her hands up. "That's what *I* said!"

"Briefly," Saida said, glaring at the last sticky bun. "It doesn't count."

Dante shook his head. "Tough crowd."

Kamaria made an unsympathetic face. "And no bonus points for forced celibacy, either. Saida got dumped, Kaleb got shot down—again—and I have three, count them, *three* girls mad at me right now. I don't even know why."

"Probably because there are three of them," Dante said dryly.

Alessa picked up a large, shiny book and sashayed toward the door. "Excuse us. My consort and I must go pine from afar while getting ready. We'll see you all after the ceremony."

Dante unlocked Alessa's suite and scanned for threats before letting her in. "What's that?" he asked, nodding at the book as he kicked off his boots.

"Isn't it beautiful?" She tilted it so the light slid over the gilded lettering. "It's an ancient book of Saverian poems that's been on Tanp since the first Divorando. Their saviors returned it as a gift."

He grunted. "Saw them on my way in. Made a great first impression."

"Sorry," she said with a wince. "I meant to warn you, but you were gone when I woke up."

Alessa placed the book on her end table beside the primer he'd given her, which looked even shabbier in comparison.

Dante patted the weight in his pocket. He'd give it to her later, when she wasn't drowning in gifts from other people.

Leaving her arranging their outfits on the bed, he went to the bathing room, stripping off his clothes and tossing them into the laundry bin. He turned on the water and stepped in before it warmed up. Tipping his head back, he let the water course down his face.

Consort. As a bodyguard, he'd known his role. His job. Now, somehow, he'd become an *accessory.*

Alessa was still debating whether to risk mussing her hair by pulling her gown over her head or wrinkling it by stepping in when Dante cracked the door, releasing a wave of steam. Towel around his hips and razor in hand, he wiped the mirror, eying her reflection as she shed her robe.

She took her time gathering the voluminous folds of fabric so he got a good look. "You're going to cut yourself if you don't pay attention."

"No, I won't." His flinch said otherwise. He might not be able to touch her, but at least she knew he wanted to.

It was probably horrible to hope the next Divorando would come sooner so she could relinquish her powers to the next Finestra.

Wobbling, she lifted one foot—the shoes might have been overly ambitious—and stepped into the puddled fabric, sliding it up her body.

Yes, it was *definitely* immoral to wish for an invasion of demons for the chance to kiss a boy. She'd just have to focus on getting her powers in hand before they both combusted.

The neckline plunged almost to her navel, held together with sheer fabric that also covered her back and arms. Dotted with tiny black crystals, it made her skin appear to glitter with midnight stars. A delicate tiara studded with the same black gems waited for her at the temple—fragments of a scarabeo's carapace, smashed into tiny fragments during Divorando, when she'd frozen it using Josef's gift.

Slayer of demons, she wore the spoils of victory on her skin.

"Help me with my buttons?" she said, clutching the unfastened bodice to her chest.

Dante's breath feathered her neck as he fastened the buttons at quarter speed, sending a pulse of longing through her. When the last button found its loop, he bent to kiss the nape of her neck and their eyes met in the reflection for a long, breathless moment. Then she pulled free, clinging to her last shred of self-control.

"Stunning, don't you think?" She rocked from side to side, making her skirt swish like a bell so the tiny crystals, sewn into glittering swirls representing gusts of wind, dancing flames, crackles of lightning, and cresting waves, twinkled with every movement.

Dante grunted assent.

Fashion was as unfair as life, so he was dressed and ready in a fraction of the time, wickedly handsome in a suit of midnight blue so dark it was almost black, with glossy new holsters for his daggers, his damp hair combed back to highlight the sharp lines of his face.

He glowered at his reflection. "I look like a scarabeo."

"You *look* delicious."

He arched a brow. "Hungry?"

"Famished. Alas, duty calls." Taking his arm, she grinned so brightly he smiled back despite himself. *Much* better. "Come on gorgeous, let's dazzle them."

Kaleb was fiddling with his jeweled eye patch in the hall. "Damn thing keeps slipping." Resplendent in winter white with gold accents, the scarabei crystals glittering on his eye patch and lapels subtly tied their ensembles together.

Dante's grip made up for Alessa's precarious heels, and safely on flat ground again in the courtyard, Alessa found herself face-to-face with . . . herself. Poised. Radiant. Brave. It was *her,* but more. Clad in scarlet with a mysterious smile as she looked at something—*someone*—in the gardens behind the artist.

Dante examined Alessa's portrait with the ghost of a smile.

"I still have the Mastra's card if you need another hobby," she said with a laugh.

"Look at *us.*" Kaleb thumped Alessa's back, sending her stumbling in her heels. "Damn fine-looking saviors."

"For goodness sake, Kaleb, I'm not a horse." Steadied by Dante's arm, Alessa regained her balance.

If she looked like a goddess, Dante's portrait must be spectacular. Wherever it was. "Didn't you sit for your portrait?"

"Ah." Dante scratched his neck. "About that . . ."

"I wanted to have all of my Fonti on display at the reception!"

Dante scowled. "And I'm not a Fonte."

"Your powers defeated the scarabei. That's the *definition* of a Fonte." She sulked. "I paid the Mastra for a miniature, too."

"You don't need a portrait," he said. "You have the real thing."

"You should get seated before the good pews fill up," Kaleb interjected, probably trying to save Dante from a lecture.

Alessa took Dante's arm. "He's escorting me in."

"I thought *I* was." Kaleb followed them out of the courtyard, his whine echoing through the arched tunnel. "I can't go alone to my own Name Day Ceremony. I'll look pathetic!"

Adrick stuck his head through as they neared the gate. "They're ready for you."

"You!" Kaleb pointed. "Adrick."

"Yes," Adrick said. "I *am* Adrick. Very good. And you are Kaleb, in case you've forgotten that, too."

"I *mean*, you can do it."

"Do what?" Adrick asked, only half paying attention as he fist-bumped the guards on either side.

"Be my escort. You're good-looking enough when you aren't talking."

"You want me to be your arm candy?" Adrick smirked. "And here I thought you didn't like me."

"I don't," Kaleb said. "I *really* don't. But beggars can't be choosers, and people will credit me for being nice by including Alessa's brother."

"No one who's *ever* met you will assume you're being nice," Adrick scoffed. "But as long as I get to sit at the head table and drink the expensive wine, I'd be honored."

Kaleb bared his teeth. "Just keep your mouth shut."

Adrick clucked his tongue. "Not my strength."

Four

Hypnotized by the dust motes swirling around the candles, Alessa struggled to focus on the Padre's words.

The last time she'd knelt on the cold, unforgiving stone of the altar, she'd been draped over Dante's body, his chest still, heart silent. Her breath quickened and blackness encroached on her vision. *No.* Not now.

Ghosts didn't have shadows. He was there. Still watching over her, though she didn't need protection anymore. The crushing grief was her past, not present.

She lifted her head, and Padre Calabrese lowered the glittering tiara to rest atop her curls. The Duo Divino were permitted to choose their own names after Divorando, but she and Kaleb had both opted to keep theirs, with new additions. Kaleb had added a surname, and she'd claimed a tribute.

Kaleb held his arm at the ready to support her like they'd practiced, so she wouldn't kick off the festivities by falling off the altar. There were probably a few who would enjoy the spectacle, but she wasn't one of them.

"Rise, the faithful and powerful, Kaleb Toporovsky Dunamis," Padre Calabrese intoned. "Rise, the gods' beloved warrior of light, Alessandra Diletta Lucia Paladino."

Together, they turned to the packed temple, and Alessa's chest eased at the sight of Dante, alive and well.

You did it, his eyes said, and she knew his applause was for her alone.

For so long she'd felt like a failure, but she'd saved Saverio, made friends, reconciled with her family, *and* fallen in love. Tonight was her reward, and she would revel in every perfect moment.

Prosecco poured like rain, but there wasn't enough booze in the world to drown out the five-hundredth toast of the evening.

Dante could count on one hand the people who gave a shit about him, and they weren't the blowhards singing his praises now. Filthy hypocrites. Saverians might pretend to accept him, but plenty were silently holding on to centuries of hatred, waiting for any excuse to turn on him.

He tried to ignore the glances his way, the eyes searching for any sign of otherness, but the head table was practically on a damn stage.

At least the food was top-shelf. Tiny plates of olives, antipasti with prosciutto and crusty bread to dip in olive oil, a risotto so creamy he'd nearly groaned aloud. He might hate feeling like a caged pet in the Cittadella, but he'd never get tired of eating like one.

Alessa was still greeting guests, her every movement causing a swirl of activity as the crowd around her vied for spots around their star. She was the center of Saverio's universe, and he wasn't in the same solar system.

"It's good to see her happy again." Adrick took a sip from his crystal flute and wrinkled his nose. "Ugh. Warm."

It was. She was so damn happy to be embraced by society at last.

"I'll check if she needs anything," Adrick said. He and Dante had been taking turns bringing her appetizers ever since they realized she and Kaleb were unlikely to get a chance to sit for the meal.

Diwata eyed Dante from across the table, her gaze darting away when she accidentally met his. Hard to imagine such a mouse of a girl braving a battle with the scarabei. The closest she'd come to speaking all night was nodding as Nina chattered about her upcoming voyage.

"We couldn't miss tonight, of course," Nina was saying. "Even though it meant delaying our mission trip to the Continent because every passenger ship is booked this month."

Dante frowned. That could pose a problem.

"I can't wait to get out there and rough it with the common folk," Nina said. "I feel like we've been *called* to help them."

Josef looked a bit less enthused. "It will be very rewarding, I have no doubt."

The settlers on the Continent endured enough without Nina's religious fervor, but Dante kept that thought to himself.

Renata bustled over to inform the Fonti that it was time for their demonstration with the Duo, leaving Dante to listen while Ciro raved about the people, architecture, food—apparently all were *fascinating, spectacular, divine*—until Adrick returned.

Thank Dea, the trumpets blared shortly after and saved them.

Saida, Kamaria, Josef, and Nina had arranged themselves in a circle around Alessa and Kaleb on the dance floor. At the first touch of Alessa's hands, a burst of swirling snow and flickers of flame blossomed around them, and the crowd oohed.

It was difficult for Dante to enjoy the spectacle.

It grated on him—that every time Alessa used a Fonte's powers, a part of them got to live within her for a moment and he couldn't. Not anymore. He had nothing left to give.

"Isn't it beautiful?" Diwata's voice was barely over a whisper.

"Uh, sure. Beautiful," Dante said, caught off guard. She *could* speak.

"I forgot you can't see it," she said, looking alarmed by her own daring.

"Scuzi?"

"Auras. A person's energy, if you will." Chin ducked, she spoke to her hands more than him. "That's all we are. Energy in different forms. You're light blue, like the sea at daybreak. It's quite lovely."

"Ah . . . right." This was one of the oddest conversations he'd ever had, and he'd conversed with a goddess during his brief trip to the afterlife. "I'm sure yours is nice, too."

"Oh, yes, it's *glorious.*" Diwata's expression turned beatific as she watched the next burst of magic. "The Finestra's is golden, and Signor Kaleb's a pale green. The tall girl is bright red." Kamaria. Fire. Made sense. "And when they share their powers, it's like a dance, with each of their lights moving to fill the empty spaces left behind."

As a Fonte, Diwata should have understood how it worked, but maybe the mentors on Tanp had never broken it down for her.

She was half right. By touching someone, a Finestra's

powers absorbed and magnified a bit of their energy. When it worked as intended, Alessa's gift fanned their sparks into a blaze. But if she took too much or tried to take from someone who didn't have any power . . . it hurt like a bitch.

"Alessa talks about her powers *taking*," Dante said. "You don't see it that way?"

She'd told him about it often, how it stung even though she'd understood why no one wanted to become her Fonte and "share" their gifts with her when all she did was take.

"Perhaps mortals aren't meant to understand the gods' gifts," Ciro said.

Well, *that* was helpful. "Do the colors blur together?" Dante asked Diwata.

Her laughter tinkled like wind chimes. "Oh, no, an individual's energy remains distinct, even when they trade their light. It's only upon death that it returns to the universe."

"I died once." He didn't know why he said it, but she didn't seem surprised.

"Could you feel your energy dispersing?" Diwata asked. "Did it hurt?"

"Not sure if it was energy dispersing or nerve damage, but yeah, it hurt."

"Telling horror stories at a party?" Ciro asked.

Diwata smiled sweetly. "I prefer romantic tales with happy endings."

"Of course you do." Ciro's smile was fond, if patronizing. "Personally, I've always thought the distinction between a happy ending and a tragic one is in the eye of the beholder."

The demonstration came to a close, and Ciro leapt to his feet. "*Bravissimo! Bravissima!*"

Everyone sat back in their seats while the servers passed

out cake, but Dante didn't get a moment to enjoy the silence before Ciro was at it again.

"So, the demon guardian himself, eh?" Ciro chuckled nervously at Dante's glare. "People seem divided on whether you switched loyalties or if there's been a misunderstanding about your kind. Do you have an opinion?"

Dante took the last slug of his drink. "Many."

"I'd love to hear them."

"No, thanks."

Ciro cleared his throat. "My apologies. I was rude at our first meeting, and now I'm making it worse. I'm simply curious. You see, my own island has a similar lore, and if we are wrong—if *I* have been wrong—I'd like to correct the record."

Dante tapped his fingers on his glass. "I'd need another drink."

"Of course." Ciro waved down a server who had been ignoring Dante a moment earlier.

They already knew about Divorando, but he gave a truncated version of Dea's mission for him to find the ghiotte and stop whatever Crollo was planning.

Ciro let out a whoosh of breath. "Have you seen any other warnings? Or has anyone else experienced something similar?"

"Coming back from the dead?" Dante asked. "No. Just me."

"I meant, has anyone else, the Finestra or a Fonte, experienced any, eh, ominous signs?"

Dante pinned him with a look. "Have *you*?"

Ciro's nostrils flared. "Of course not. Forgive me, but it all sounds a bit far-fetched."

"More so than the gods sending an apocalypse every few decades?" Dante said.

Ciro gave a cool smile. "We've known about those for

centuries. It's a bit different to rely entirely on someone claiming to hear the voice of Dea."

"If Dante says Crollo is sending another attack, then he is," Adrick said, casually twirling his fork between his fingers. "And if we need to find the ghiotte to stop it, we will."

At least *someone* believed him.

"Forgive me," Ciro said to Dante. "I can't help being skeptical by nature, and, after all, you *are* just one . . . person."

Dante picked up his plate and left without a word. *Civil* would be easier at a distance.

Five

Alessa took her final bow, and the ceremony master invited guests to the dance floor as the orchestra struck up a lively tune.

"Do you have your eye on anyone tonight?" she asked Kaleb. They still had a few tables to greet before they were free.

"Hardly." Kaleb tugged at his collar. "I plan to befriend the bartender and be antisocial the rest of the evening."

"Absolutely not. You're the star of the evening. I'll find you a companion if you tell me what you're looking for."

"Precisely why I won't. I don't need a matchmaker, and if I did, it wouldn't be you."

Alessa gave him a haughty glare. "How rude. I'd be an excellent matchmaker."

"You've been locked in a tower since puberty. I doubt you have the most comprehensive knowledge of single men on Saverio." Kaleb paused to nod politely at a trio of giggling matrons.

"What about Chasten Rutledge?" Alessa asked.

"I hate beards," Kaleb said. "Stop wasting your time. I'm not the relationship type."

She would've let it go—was about to—but for the look that flashed across his face. "What makes you say that?"

"Oh, come on. You know I'm a total prick. Who wants to tie themselves to that?"

Alessa pursed her lips. "Have you tried being *less* of a prick?"

He gave her a haughty look. "Why? So some poor sucker can fall for me and be disillusioned when I stop trying so hard? Better to start as a prick than revert to one later."

"Ah. Setting low expectations so you can't disappoint people. A classic. Despite your best efforts, Kaleb, *I* like you, and as someone who used to daydream about electrocuting you with your own powers, that's something I never, and I mean *never*, expected to say."

He smirked. "I'll have to try harder, then."

"Maybe if you showed a little *less* of your personality up front, I could set you up with someone lovely. Give me *one* clue about what you look for in a beau."

"*Beau?*" Kaleb arched a brow.

"Paramour? Inamorato? Lover?"

Kaleb made a convincing gagging noise.

"Give me something to go on," Alessa pressed. "I'm not your type for obvious reasons, and you said Dante's not your type, because . . ."

"He's too prickly."

"Prickly? You're one of the prickliest people I know."

"Exactly. The role is taken."

"Do you find him *physically* attractive, though?"

"Gah! How weird do you want to make this?! *No.*"

"I'll keep asking until I wear you down," Alessa said.

"Ugh, fine. I prefer . . . softer. Not too muscular, long eyelashes, that whole thing."

"Pretty boys."

Kaleb grimaced. "Don't say it like *that.*"

Alessa tipped her head toward a nearby table. "Alejandro Gonzales? Newly single and *very* pretty."

"Been there." Kaleb smirked. "Done that."

They both snickered.

"I'll think of someone," Alessa said. "It's become my life's mission."

"I thought your mission was to save the world."

She patted his arm. "I can multitask."

"Oh, gods, hide me." Kaleb ducked behind Alessa, a hopeless effort since he was considerably taller than she was. Walking toward them was a tall, auburn-haired woman flanked by a silver-bearded man and dark-haired younger man.

"Aren't those your parents?" Alessa asked.

"And my brother. He's a saint. You'll love him. *Everyone* loves him."

Alessa's eyes widened. "You have a brother?"

"Unfortunately." With no feasible escape route, Kaleb planted his feet and faced his family. "Mother. Father. You've met the Finestra. Alessa, this is my brother, Dottore Toporovsky."

"Please, call me Everett." A darker-haired version of his sibling, Kaleb's brother had a wide-eyed sincerity in his eyes that would never have fit on Kaleb.

"I hope Kaleb has been serving his duties respectfully." Kaleb's mother curtsied, shooting Kaleb a pointed look. "As we raised him to."

"Kaleb is a wonderful Fonte," Alessa said. "He impressed everyone on Altari with his diplomacy."

Kaleb's father got a pinched look to his face.

"You'll have to forgive my parents their shock," Kaleb drawled. "They aren't used to thinking much of me."

Ah. If anyone could charm their way through an awkward conversation, it was Alessa's silver-tongued sibling. She signed a quick plea in the guise of fixing her hair, and Adrick changed course to head their way. Their father was fluent in Sign Language from growing up with a Deaf parent and had signed to them from birth, but their mother never progressed past a basic proficiency, so they often used the skill to escape tricky situations.

"This is *my* brother," she said brightly as he joined them.

"A pleasure, as always." Adrick nodded to Kaleb's parents.

"Ah, the baker's boy," said Kaleb's father.

"That's me," Adrick said. "Son of bakers, brother to the divine." The subtle edge to his smile was one only a sister could read. They'd made strides in repairing their relationship now that he'd admitted his envy, but Alessa knew it rankled him when people said that sort of thing.

"This is *our* older son." Signora Toporovsky beamed proudly. "Everett is a—"

"Doctor," Kaleb muttered under his breath.

"How wonderful," Adrick said. No one else seemed to notice the hint of facetiousness. "I'm an apprentice apothecary myself, but . . . maybe someday." He shrugged, all modesty.

Kaleb's father nodded with approval. "A noble calling. Your studies will serve you well."

"I'm surprised we haven't met before," Adrick said to Everett. "I thought I knew everyone in the city."

"I recently returned from the Continent. Haven't been back to Saverio in years."

"You didn't return for Divorando?" Alessa asked. Even the settlers sought shelter in the Fortezza beneath the Cittadella for their own safety.

Everett chuckled sheepishly. "Waited a bit too long, I'm afraid. The last ship was nearly full, you see, and a woman arrived at the last moment with her baby. I couldn't have left them to stay behind."

Kaleb cut in. "So he holed up in a cave for weeks, surviving off jerky and dried fruit, and Dea was so impressed that she spared his life. A bona fide martyr for the ages."

"Everett takes after me," said Kaleb's father, as though Kaleb had never spoken. "I'm retired, but I was a doctor in my day. I delivered over a hundred babies and saved more than a few. I've always said there is no greater calling than saving lives."

Alessa patted Kaleb's arm. "Then you must be so proud of Kaleb for saving so many during Divorando."

"Yes. Of course," said Kaleb's father. "Once he finally committed to a job, he did it. For one day. Not *quite* the same as a lifetime dedicated to healing the sick and wounded, but we all have different callings, I suppose."

"Now, dear," Kaleb's mother scolded. "Kaleb used the gifts Dea gave him. What more can we ask?"

"The Finestra and I should really be going." Impressive that Kaleb could talk with his jaw clenched that tight. "So many people want to speak with us, you know. Very important people."

"What was all that about?" Alessa asked as Kaleb practically dragged her away, leaving Adrick to orchestrate the small talk on his own. "I didn't even know you had a brother."

"What's to know? He'll give you the shirt off his back, the

food off his plate, and if you're looking for a fight, he'll offer his face for you to punch. Who wouldn't love having a brother like that?"

Alessa wrinkled her nose. "Adrick has caused me plenty of grief, but at least he didn't have the nerve to be perfect." Spotting familiar silver curls, she waved to get their attention. "Your turn to meet *my* family."

Now she could finally introduce Dante to her grandparents. If she could figure out where he'd disappeared to.

Dante wasn't *hiding*, merely staying out of sight.

If that meant lurking around the margins of the party, well, a man had to do what a man had to do. Besides, it gave him a better vantage point to monitor anyone near Alessa.

Voices grew louder, laughter more boisterous, and most older guests began saying their farewells, leaving the afterparty to the younger folk.

Dante leaned against a pillar to keep watch as Alessa signed with an elderly couple he could only assume were her grandparents. Their conversation was interrupted every few minutes by guests, but Alessa didn't miss a beat, switching between Sign Language and the spoken word to greet everyone with enthusiasm.

A few curls had slipped free from her elaborate hairdo, and her cheeks were flushed, her eyes bright. Radiant with joy, she was a stark contrast to the miserable recluse he'd met when she was shunned and feared by the same people fawning over her now.

Glittering like a diamond among gemstones, she dazzled everyone. Even him. After a life in the shadows, he wasn't so comfortable in the light.

Kamaria strode over and yanked Dante's plate out of his hand. "Ask her to dance."

"I'm eating."

"Stop eating. Go dance."

"No." One hand freed by Kamaria's cake theft, he picked up his drink.

"Come on. It's like fighting, but with less blood. See, you put your hands—"

"I know *how* to dance. I choose not to."

"If you aren't going to ask her, then I will." Kamaria held up her own glass. "Hold this for me?"

Dante glared but made no move to take it.

"I should warn you, I'm a fantastic dancer," Kamaria said. "I've been told it makes me irresistible. Oh, look who *isn't* afraid to dance."

Alessa smiled as Ciro approached her. The orchestra was between songs, and Dante could make out their conversation even from afar. "I hope you wore comfortable shoes," Alessa joked. "Half the island is hoping you'll ask for a dance."

Ciro bowed and dropped a kiss on the back of her hand. "Dare I hope you're one of them? I'd love to see what magic we could create together."

If the Cittadella didn't have such thick crystal glasses, Dante's might have shattered.

Alessa didn't shy away from touching anyone *gifted,* only mere mortals. Like him.

Alessa turned away from Ciro at the end of their spin around the dance floor and nearly ran into Dante's chest.

"I was told to dance with you," he grumbled.

She arched a brow. "And how could I resist such an enthusiastic invitation?"

His hands slid down her waist, tracing her hip bones, as the orchestra began a languid, romantic melody.

The first turn in his arms took her breath away. "I thought you couldn't dance."

"*Don't*. Not *can't*. Why does no one get this distinction?"

"A man of many talents. Whatever will you reveal next?" Her body fizzed like bubbles in a glass of prosecco, sparkling with joy to twirl across a starlit dance floor with the man of her dreams.

"There's a lot you don't know about me." Dante's thumb caressed the sliver of bare skin between her sleeve and glove. "Vorrei che fossimo soli."

"Starting with half the things you say." She couldn't help going all melty when he spoke to her in the old language, but for all she knew, he could be telling her that his shoes were too tight. "Would it kill you to say something sweet I actually understand?"

He considered. "Probably."

"You wait. I'll learn the old language *and* all your secrets."

Now he raised an eyebrow. "And how do you plan to do that?"

"I have my ways." Somehow, he managed to steer them perfectly while studying the triangle of bare skin below her collarbone. She arched her back. "You like my dress?"

His affirmative grunt seemed a promising start to her interrogation.

"Gabriele Dante Lucente," she said. "Age, twenty. Male—*very*. Languages spoken, common and ancient. Son of Emma and . . ."

Dante arched an eyebrow. "Ludovico. What are you doing?"

"Cataloging everything I know about you so far. Research projects always start with the information at hand. Height: um . . . tall? Weight: heavy, mostly muscle." She kept going despite Dante's snort of laughter. "Hair: dark brown, almost curly. Eye color: same, but with a sprinkle of gold."

"Do I get to play?" he asked. "Alessandra Diletta *Lucia* Paladino, age eighteen—

She cut in. "Almost nineteen."

"Almost nineteen. Size: short but not *super* short. Speaks: fast. Hair: brown and wavy-ish. Eyes: . . . um . . ."

She squeezed her eyes shut, trusting he'd guide her through the steps. "I swear, if you don't know my eye color by now—"

Dante's laugh rumbled through her. "I *know* what color they are, I just don't know what to call greenish brown with gold."

"*Hazel!* Because greenish brown sounds revolting." She cracked one eye.

"Don't worry, mia amata. Your eyes are *not* revolting."

"Careful or I'll get impossibly arrogant with that kind of praise."

"You know me, great at compliments," Dante said. "Che begli occhi."

"Too bad for you, I understand that one," Alessa said with a laugh, cut off as Dante spun her off the dance floor, twirling her out of sight from the rest of the party.

Caging her with his hands against a pillar, he said, "I wore your fancy clothes, put up with fancy people, and I even danced. Do I get a reward?"

She chewed her lip. "I'm not sure we should . . ."

"We *definitely* should." He traced her jawline, caressed her lower lip with his thumb. "See? No problem."

Bad idea. Dangerous idea. But, of course, Dante never shied from danger.

She was buzzing from exhilaration but not anxious or out of control. Maybe she *could* do this. After all, she'd come so far, mastering her gift when it used to master her.

At her tiny nod, his calloused hands cupped her face ever so gently.

He started slowly. A brush of his lips that left her aching for more. A nibble, a tease. With every touch, her confidence grew. She could do this. She *was* doing this.

The world fell away, and nothing existed but his hair between her fingers, the languid slide of his lips against hers, the beguiling heat that pooled in her belly and turned her legs all wobbly so she had to clutch him to stay upright.

He tensed. Just a fraction, but there was a new tension in his posture. A . . . determination . . . to his movements. As though he was steeling himself to kiss her.

The realization was like having a bucket of ice water poured over her head.

She broke the kiss and opened her eyes. Dante stared at a point past her ear, jaw set, the fire in his eyes gone, where there had been a smolder before.

She wouldn't cry. She would *not* cry. "It's my fault."

"I'm the one who changed, not you." He ground out the words.

"We'll figure it out. We will. I'm fine with everyone else."

Dante tried for a smile. "Only me, huh?"

"It's not that it's *you*, it's what I *do* with you. It's like . . ." She grasped for a way to explain. "My power *wants*. And when *I* want to be close to you, those threads of wanting get tangled up and my power doesn't know the difference. I need to figure out how to separate them."

"Practice," Dante said, twirling a curl of her hair around his finger. "Lots of practice."

"Exactly." It wasn't just the prosecco making her senses tingle. Something plucked at her nerves. Something . . . wrong. "Wait."

"What is it?" Dante's voice sounded distant.

Her vision went dark around the margins, the piazza disappearing, replaced by another scene: *A spatter of blood across white stone. A craving to wound, slash, hurt.*

She jolted at the cold touch of metal. Dante's hand, warm and firm, closed over hers, moving it off the hilt of his dagger.

"What is it?" he asked again, serious now.

"Someone's coming," she whispered.

"Oh, *eventually.*" Kaleb's drawl echoed against the marble. "As long as you decided against killing your sister *eventually*. Do you want a medal? An official title? Saverio's Best Brother . . . *eventually.*"

Dante's posture eased. "It's Kaleb and Adrick."

"No, that's not it." Alessa cocked her head, trying to catch the sound again.

"She's forgiven me, so why do you care?" came Adrick's retort.

"She's the Finestra! And you're her *brother*! Who tried to *kill* her! Sorry I don't find you as delightful as the rest of Saverio."

The orchestra finished its song, and the crowd burst into applause, but Dante's gaze didn't waver from Alessa's face.

It was gone, or more likely, had never been there at all. It was nothing. It *had* to be nothing. She smiled brighter. She wouldn't slip again. "Never mind. I've had bad experiences here, that's all. A memory caught me off guard."

A voice, but not quite words. Almost a hiss.

She went cold, like an icy hand gripped the back of her neck, and the clamoring in her mind grew painfully loud.

Her hands clenched in Dante's shirt. "Look out!"

A figure stepped out of the shadows.

Six

Dante whirled but stopped, knives half drawn, at the sight of Diwata. He scanned the area, but there was no one behind her. He was about to ask Alessa what had alarmed her, when Diwata bared her teeth and leapt, slender fingers curled into claws.

He caught her wrists, holding her off as she hissed and spit. Behind her eyes there was nothing. No emotion. No thought. No person. Only mindless rage.

"Hey!" Dante shouted in her face. "Snap out of it!"

He'd snap her like a twig if he wasn't careful. She was barely more than a girl, her bones thin and delicate, but somehow gripped with a ferocious strength.

Alessa yanked off her gloves, circling behind Diwata.

"*No*, I've got it!" Dante said.

Flames flickered between Diwata's hands, tendrils of fire snaking their way toward his. Her magic might not hurt Alessa, but her inhuman fury could.

Alessa wrapped an arm around Diwata's shoulders, yanking her back, but Dante held firm as Alessa closed her eyes in concentration.

Diwata went limp and Dante lowered her frail body to the ground. He checked her wrist. Found a pulse: slow but present.

Diwata's eyelashes fluttered open, and the rasping hiss that emerged from her mouth wasn't hers.

"What's white turns red then black
To summon the attack
As dark hides light and day turns night
And halos fall upon the banished
Dea's gifts divided, must be united
In order to turn the tide
Choose to fight or choose to die
Lest what is loved be vanished."

Her eyes cleared and she shrieked, slapping at Dante's hands.

"Easy, girl." He rocked back on his heels as footsteps pounded closer. "*You* attacked *us*."

Ciro careened around the corner. "What in the gods' names have you done?"

Dante reined in a surge of anger as Ciro crouched beside Diwata, whispering reassurance. He *had* been on the floor holding the guy's distraught partner in the middle of a gala.

Dante stood, fixing his jacket, as Tomo and Renata hurried into sight and stopped short, taking stock of the bizarre tableau: Alessa, pale and disheveled, standing over two visiting dignitaries on the ground, one sobbing.

"She had some kind of fit and attacked us," Alessa said. "Something's wrong with her."

Diwata wailed louder, her tears a better defense than any words.

Tomo choked on air. "Nonsense. We're all friends here. I'm certain the poor dear didn't mean to *attack* anyone. She must have had some sort of a seizure."

"It wasn't a seizure," Dante said. "She was possessed."

"Don't be silly," Tomo said, his smile rigid. "We'll summon the doctor, but I'm sure she'll be fine after some rest."

"She was talking about an attack," Dante said.

"Tomo, dear, help them inside." Renata turned to Dante and Alessa. "There is *no attack* coming. Your war is over. There's nothing more to fear, no more battles to fight. Go back to the party and show Saverio that everything is fine."

Alessa dropped her gaze. "Yes, Renata."

Unbelievable. "You've got to be kidding me," Dante muttered.

Renata pinned him with a weighted look. "We shall return to our duties as hosts and stamp out any rumors before they can spread, and you two will *dance.*"

At least dancing meant he could get Alessa away from them. Her face was blank as he took her hand. Tomo and Renata had drilled Alessa on the need to always put duty first, and a few curt words from them took all the fight out of her.

No one seemed to have noticed the incident. The dancing was in full swing, the bar surrounded, and most dark corners were occupied by couples.

As he pulled Alessa into his arms, Dante realized with grim satisfaction that he finally had proof: the threat from Crollo was undeniable now.

It wasn't exactly the gift he'd had in mind.

Alessa could still feel it. The wrongness she'd pulled from Diwata during their brief touch. Her arms and legs were stiff, but Dante's grip was sure as he led her through the steps with the precision of a military exercise.

"Breathe. One step at a time," Dante said. The barely leashed emotion in his voice made it clear he wasn't returning to the dance floor because he was following orders for once. He was getting it over with, and she wasn't ready to discuss what had happened. She needed to be alone, to pick apart the threads tangling in her mind without a thousand eyes on her. Without *his*.

"Look at me," Dante said quietly.

No. She couldn't do that. He would see too much.

One step at a time. One thought at a time.

"Alessa . . ."

She drew on years of training to smooth her expression before looking up. "Mm-hmm?"

Dante focused so intently she knew he saw right through it. "How did you know someone was coming?"

She gave a tiny half shrug. "I heard something."

"No. You *knew* someone wanted to hurt us. Why are you lying to me?" The snap in his voice made her flinch.

The final notes of the song shivered in the air, but Dante didn't let go.

"I had a bad feeling, and something bad happened. That's all." Pulling free, she wiped her forehead. "I need to visit the powder room."

"I'll walk you there."

"No need. Kamaria's heading that way."

She didn't wait to see if he would follow. She couldn't outrun him, but she needed to escape. To *breathe*.

The walls of the courtyard, sturdy enough to endure countless attacks, weren't strong enough to hold her up. Sliding down, she wrapped her arms around herself. Ice threaded her ribs, tightening around her lungs, a cold both foreign and unwelcome inside a body of warm flesh and blood.

"Get out of my head. Leave me alone." She covered her face, but it couldn't block out the memory of Diwata's eyes, so like the captain's.

It was all wrong. Everything was wrong. She had done her duty. She'd saved Saverio. Saved Dante. Renata said it herself—their war was over. *It had to be over.*

But a thrill of recognition had shot through her when she'd touched Diwata. The strange echo in the girl's mind was one Alessa knew, and the jolt of like-meeting-like left no doubt.

A seed had been planted inside her when she'd touched a dying scarabeo during Divorando and harnessed its power of collective mind control to rally her army. Now, when she'd finally—almost—mastered one deadly power, another was taking root.

She didn't move at the sound of Dante's footsteps. He'd find her. He always did. Always protected her. But the threat hadn't been coming for her. Not this time. This time it had been coming for him.

Seven

Dante regretted giving Alessa a head start when he spotted her huddled in the corner of the courtyard, glittering like a lost jewel. He crouched, pulling her to him as gently as cupping a butterfly between his hands. "Ah, poveretta. You finally believe me?"

"It's not fair," she whispered. The hollow defeat behind her eyes was a hundred times worse than tears.

"No, it's not." He'd wanted an excuse to leave the gala, and now that he had one, he felt like a thief. "Do you want to go back? We don't have to talk about this now."

Alessa braced herself on the wall to stand. "The end of the world is coming *again*. Why waste time dancing?"

She didn't look capable of performing nonchalance for the masses, anyway. She needed a tall glass of water and some sleep. He could give her that and get her somewhere safe.

He helped her back to her suite and settled her in an armchair with water and a baguette, which she ignored, and sat on the couch across from her, elbows propped on his knees, to watch her stare at nothing.

An hour ago, she'd been sparkling with energy and joy, and

now . . . he'd never seen her sit still for so long. Guilt turned his stomach. He could have let her brush off Diwata's attack and pretend everything was fine for a few more hours, but instead he'd made her face it.

Alessa let out a guttural cry and threw her drink to the floor, shattering it in an explosion of water and glass shards.

With a curse, Dante leapt to his feet.

"I can't do it again," she cried, collapsing in on herself. "I can't, I can't, I can't. I *won't* do it again!"

Scooping her up, he shook the glass from her skirts and carried her to the bathing room, where she'd be safe from the rest.

He sat on the edge of the tub, cradling her in his lap as she cried and argued—with the gods, with him, with herself—it didn't matter. They all had the same answer.

When she was all cried out, he brushed strands of hair from her wet cheeks.

"Don't," she whimpered. "I'll hurt you."

"You're too weak to hurt a kitten right now."

"Perfect. I'm finally too weak to hurt you, and too much of a mess to take advantage of it." She swiped at her eyes, smearing makeup everywhere. "Stop looking at me, or you'll never even *want* to touch me again."

"Impossible." He kissed her forehead, lingering for a long moment despite her weak objection. She *was* a mess. His mess. He couldn't fight a smile. "Did you eat anything at the party or was your dinner three courses of prosecco?"

She stuck her lower lip out in mulish nondenial.

"I'll take that as a no."

"I'm not hungry."

"Then let's get you out of this sparkly straightjacket and

into bed. Crollo won't strike again tonight." As the grief and anger drained out of her, a crash was sure to follow, so instead of running a bath, he turned on the tap and wet a small towel.

She let him unbutton her dress and maneuver her arms out of the gossamer sleeves dotted with pinpricks of blood. He tried not to notice every curve revealed as she gripped his arm to step out of the skirts.

Not the time, he reminded the parts of him incorrectly reading the situation.

She sagged against the wall and let him run the wet cloth over her.

"What did I do wrong?" she whimpered. "Why did they change the rules for me?"

"Ah, luce mia. Don't take it personally."

Her eyes ringed with makeup, skin freckled with blood, she was the most beautiful broken thing he'd ever seen. He would've made glue from his bones to fix her world if he could.

The aftermath of her meltdown left her shaking, so when he'd finished and helped her into a nightgown, he carried her to bed and tucked the blankets around her.

"You already died once." Her eyes fluttered closed. "Why can't they leave you alone?"

There was a knock on the door. "I'll get it," he said. "Go to sleep."

It was Kaleb, looking sheepish. "They gave my room to Ciro and Diwata, and I can't deal with my family tonight."

Dante pointed to the couch, but Kaleb kept talking. Hopefully Alessa would sleep through it. She was terrible at falling asleep, but when she didn't toss and turn all night, she slept like the dead.

Kaleb only knew that Diwata was "ill," and he clearly wasn't concerned. "Look at me, I'm Adrick Paladino, so charming no one cares I tried to kill my sister. He's not even *that* good-looking, he just has this *thing* that makes people like him."

"Uh-huh." Not much to say to that. Dante dropped a pillow and blanket on the couch.

"Not us." Kaleb thumped his chest. "We're real, you know? Not *charming*."

Dante gave Kaleb a droll look. "You don't think I'm charming?"

Kaleb snorted. "Look at us. Practically friends. And we rarely try to kill each other anymore."

"Amazing we made it this far without someone getting hurt."

"*Me*. You know it would be me."

"Correct." Grabbing Kaleb by the shoulders, Dante shoved him to sitting. "No more talking. No more walking. Shut up and sleep it off."

Kaleb smiled up at him. "You're a good man, Dante Gabriele."

"You've got the order wrong."

"That's cause I'm a bad friend." Kaleb frowned. "Don't know how to be anything else."

"You aren't a bad friend. You're just a drunk pain in the ass. Go to sleep before I suffocate you with a pillow."

Kaleb swung one leg onto the couch, widening his eyes in the way of drunk sots trying to stop the world from spinning.

With a sigh, Dante yanked off Kaleb's shoes and turned off the light, leaving his second charge of the night to return to the first.

Alessa was blessedly unconscious, and he indulged in the rare luxury of sliding in behind her with no pillows between them. Nuzzling the nape of her neck, he drank in the heady scent of her. Out cold, she'd never know how long he lay awake into the night, thrumming with fierce tenderness.

Why can't they leave you alone?

She loved him, more than he'd ever loved himself, and he didn't deserve her, and someday she'd realize that.

Eight

Dante was waiting with a steaming carafe and a tin of biscotti when Alessa stumbled out of bed in the morning. He hid a smile as she dropped into the chair across from him with a *humph* and a glare for Kaleb snoring on the couch. Even grumpy, she looked adorable with her hair mussed, eyes smoky with remnants of makeup, her full lower lip pouting.

Dante cleared his throat. *Focus. Mission. Ghiotte. Heavenly war.*

"Wait." Alessa made grabby hand motions at the espresso.

He filled two minuscule espresso cups and let her take a sip before he spoke. "I ran into Tomo downstairs. Ciro and Diwata have asked for privacy until they leave in a few days, so you're off the hook with hostess duties."

"One less thing to worry about," Alessa said with a sigh. "Where do we start?"

"First, we figure out what that message meant."

Alessa picked up a biscotto, examined it, then put it back, repeating the process a few more times until she found the one she wanted. "We'd still have no idea where to look for the ghiotte. It's a big continent."

"You're starting to sound like me." Dante nudged her cup closer. "Here, liquid optimism. Chug, chug."

Alessa knocked it back and beckoned for another.

"Atta girl." He spun his saucer with one finger, watching her nibble the end of her biscotto. He didn't realize he'd lost the thread until she met his gaze with a confused frown. Right. Mission. "Every map in the library is completely shaded in—no mountains, rivers, nothing but the outline of the shores, so we don't have a lot to go on, but if they've managed to find each other for centuries, they can't be too far from the settlements."

Alessa reached for her almost empty cup with shaky fingers, frowned, and pushed it away. "You can have the rest."

He held the rim, still warm from her lips, to his for a moment before finishing it.

"My grandfather collects old maps," Alessa said. "I doubt any are marked *Ghiotte live here,* but we can look tonight."

Dante's mind went blank. "Tonight?"

"They invited us and Adrick to visit. I told you."

"No you didn't."

She frowned. "I thought I did."

"I would have remembered." Dante tugged at his collar.

"Huh. Well, I *thought* about telling you, so it feels like I did. Ciro's ship won't depart for a few days anyway, so we might as well. They don't live far from the city. Wouldn't it be nice to get away?"

Away, sure. Away from the Cittadella, the parties, the servants, and people. *Alone* away. Not *meet-the-family* away.

"We really don't have time to waste. . . ." He trailed off as Alessa's lips tightened like she was trying not to cry. The Cittadella had spent five years browbeating her into stifling her own needs for the "greater good." He'd tear it apart brick by brick before he did the same.

"Yeah, sure, we can go," he said with a stifled sigh.

Kaleb sat up on the couch. "Where are you going?"

"My grandparents' house in the country," Alessa replied.

"Oh." Kaleb deflated. "Have fun."

"You should come," Dante said, a little too quickly.

"Nah." Kaleb scratched his head with a yawn. "You don't need a third wheel."

"We don't mind. Really." Dante strode over and clapped him on the shoulder. "Join us."

"Dante," Alessa said slowly. "Are you *afraid* of meeting my grandparents?"

He scoffed. "No."

"Please do come, Kaleb." She picked up Kaleb's discarded pants from the floor and tossed them at him. "Save Dante from my grandmother's undivided attention."

Kaleb glanced at Dante and cackled at whatever he saw in his expression.

"Shut up," Dante muttered. Grandparents? Shit. He'd rather fight Crollo alone.

Eyes fixed on the road, Dante nodded absently while Alessa reminisced about her childhood visits to the countryside.

He recognized it now, the determined lightness in her voice as she fought to keep afloat despite the fear lurking beneath.

She was wearing gloves again, too. Her hands flew as she signed something to Adrick that made him crow with laughter.

"Not fair," said Kaleb. "Dante and I can't sign, and for all I know, you're insulting me."

Adrick grinned. "Always a safe assumption."

"Does everyone in your family know how to sign?" Dante asked Alessa.

She nodded. "My mother isn't as strong as the rest of us, but Nonno was born Deaf, so my father grew up with it. When Adrick and I were born, Papa signed to us all the time."

Adrick cast Alessa a sidelong glance. "Remember when you got caught teaching our whole class the signs for certain—*ahem*—positions? Your first disciplinary note. I was so proud."

"*First* disciplinary note?" Dante said. "What else did you get up to?"

Alessa wagged a finger at her brother. "Nothing *terrible*. Usually daydreaming or forgetting my homework."

They rounded a curve in the road and a village came into view, red roofs baking in the sun. A quiver of revulsion ran down Dante's spine. He hadn't realized how close Alessa's grandparents lived to the nearest town. Or which one it was.

"How did the teachers know what you were signing?" Kaleb asked.

Alessa flushed. "*Well,* some signs aren't too difficult to figure out."

Adrick and Kaleb laughed, but Dante couldn't.

Steady. The ground beneath his feet was packed dirt. Not ash.

The crisp air smelled of grass and lemons, not soot.

But it looked the same as it had five years ago. And his heart pounded like he was running down the main street again.

Talia's house had been his lodestone during three years of captivity, the one sanctuary left. No matter how sharp the words or heavy the blows as the *holy* man tried to beat the sin out of him, Dante clung to one thought: That Talia, Uncle Matteo, and Aunt Giulia were out there somewhere, and they loved him. They would come for him.

But no one had. And so, left with only bitterness, he'd clung to that instead, and saved himself.

When he escaped, he'd headed for the only other home he'd known, hungry for targets who would let him rail at them but hold out their arms and embrace him anyway. He'd worked up a righteous fury by the time he crested the hill above the scarred earth where their house should have stood. Then the last sliver of hope abandoned him, too, until a familiar face appeared inside the tailor's shop, and he thought he was safe at last. . . .

"Sorry, what?" he said, realizing too late Alessa had stopped speaking.

"I said we're almost there." Her breathless relief made it sound as though she was running away, too.

Alessa's first glimpse of the picturesque villa overlooking the ocean, framed by rolling hills and lemon orchards, hit like a hunger pang.

"Come in, come in!" Nonna hugged her grandchildren before looking Dante up and down. Turning her head away, she spoke to Alessa in a stage whisper. "He *is* even more handsome up close. Could use some padding, though. No one wants to snuggle a rock."

Alessa's cheeks heated. "Nonna, he can *hear* you."

"Bah!" She waved it off. "Come in. I'm making pasta and I need an assistant."

"*I* will help you," Alessa said.

Dante nudged her with his elbow. "Aw, cara mia, you don't trust me to make pasta?"

"I don't trust *Nonna* not to embarrass me if she gets you alone."

The counters were dusted with flour, and Nonno was stirring an enormous pot of his special sauce. Alessa dropped her bag by the door, flapping a hand in his peripheral vision until he turned with a crinkly eyed smile and she could sign introductions, remembering to speak aloud so Dante and Kaleb would understand.

Nonna *tsked* at Dante to put on an apron and set him to work whisking flour and salt, scolding until he figured out the precise rhythm she expected. Alessa caught his eye and pinched back a smile at his grimace of faux alarm.

Adrick darted back and forth, fetching eggs and setting the table, and Kaleb looked marginally more relaxed once he had a wine goblet to keep his hands occupied.

In her favorite place, with her favorite people, Alessa's heart felt full enough to burst. As long as she kept moving, kept talking and signing, the fear couldn't catch up. But it tried.

Nonna sent her to the sink with some dishes needing washing, and the conversation lulled. It should have been peaceful, but her chest tightened. Fighting to breathe normally, she scrubbed the bowl.

It was starting all over again.

She could lose him. She could lose them all. Her friends. Her family. They'd survived one match with the gods, but with every flip of the coin, the odds got worse.

Her life suddenly felt like a house made of straw, with a gale bearing down on her.

Nonna frowned out the window. "Patatina, take that handsome boy and catch the little monster for me. No matter how high we build the fence, he always gets out, and my old bones can't take another chase today."

The "monster" was a very small, fat pony, but worthy of its reputation, as Dante learned for himself when he reached for Figuro's bridle and the animal bolted, yanking it out of his hands.

"Che cazzo fai?!" Dante cursed, jogging after it.

Despite its short legs and round belly, the ancient pony was faster than he looked, and Alessa was wheezing with laughter by the time they herded Figuro into his pen.

Dante dusted his pants, glowering. "Entertained?"

"Very," she said. Outlined against the setting sun, for one moment he appeared nothing more than a black silhouette, and her laughter stuck in her throat.

"You okay?" As he walked toward her, the light shifted and she could see the concerned crease between his eyebrows.

"Of course." Smiling shouldn't take so much effort. "Come, let's visit the lemon trees. You always say they smell like home."

Dante's eyes softened as he looked down at her. "I said *you* smell like home."

"*Because* of the lemons," she said with a cheeky grin.

She'd imagined being there with him a hundred times, but as they strolled past trees dripping with plump yellow fruit below a sky of pink and gold, she wanted to weep.

Instead, she removed one glove and plucked a fat lemon from a low-hanging branch, scratching at the rind with her thumbnail to release the scent.

"When life gives you lemons . . ." She trailed off, lifting it to her nose.

Dante finished for her. "Throw them at Crollo."

"I was going to say make limoncello. Crollo doesn't deserve them."

Dante picked his own. "I used to eat them by the slice."

"With sugar?"

"Nope. Straight up. The more tart, the better."

"Figures. I *am* the sweet one in this relationship."

"So you keep telling me." Dante looked down at her.

She ducked her head before he got any ideas. When he'd kissed her at the gala, she'd been blissfully happy and relaxed and she'd still hurt him. Now she was a bundle of nerves. The next time might stop his heart.

Everything was so fragile. Their future. Their lives.

"Have you ever felt so happy it scares you?" She tried to poke through the rind with one of her fingernails, but she'd gnawed them to nothing after Diwata's attack. "As though you have to hold your breath or it will all blow away?"

The simple frustration of being unable to taste the fruit threatened to loose the flood of tears she'd been running from. She might never get another day like this. She was *not* going to waste a moment crying.

"All the time." Dante took the lemon from her hand, lopped it in half with his dagger, and handed one half back to her.

Juice dripped from Alessa's palm as if it cried for her.

Dante assumed Alessa chattered in Sign Language the same way she did aloud, because her hands flew at twice the speed of anyone else during dinner, with some impressive juggling of utensils and a few near misses before he moved her wine glass to a safer location.

She and Adrick attempted to interject spoken translations for Kaleb and Dante, but Alessa kept getting caught up in flurries of conversation, so they spent much of the meal only half following what was being said. It didn't matter. The glow of affection between them spoke for itself. The whole scene felt like something from a children's book: the kindly, gray-haired patriarch, the cozy building decorated with home-made artwork and knickknacks, faded floorboards worn by generations of family. It ached within him, like prodding a loose tooth.

When everyone was stuffed with pasta, breaded chicken, and at least three kinds of cheese, the women shooed the men out of the kitchen so they could wash dishes, though Dante suspected it was less about gender roles and more about stealing some time alone.

Dante correctly interpreted the old man's gestures as a command to stoke the fire in the hearth, and Alessa's grandfather supervised from a leather armchair, a twinkle in his eye despite his scowl. Dante had spent enough time trying to intimidate anyone who might harm Alessa to begrudge him that.

The stack of maps Adrick unearthed were an improvement on those at the Cittadella, and Dante spread them across the table while Adrick and Kaleb struck up a combative game of chess. But, as Alessa had joked, it wasn't as though any of the maps were marked with a ghiotte hideout.

Soon the fire was crackling, the old man was dozing, and Dante sat back to watch Alessa from across the room.

Even though they were both hearing, she and her grandmother were still signing to each other. Habit, he supposed. The old woman glanced his way and signed something that made Alessa go pink. *Or* they were talking about him.

He was good with languages, always had an ear for them,

but this was different. This was a language of hands—he was good with those. And facial expressions—less so.

Alessa stopped midsign and stalked over to him. "Don't even *think* about learning to sign as fast as you learn everything else. This is the first time in *ages* I've felt superior, and I want to savor it."

Dante leaned closer. "You'd prefer me unable to communicate just to know something I don't?"

She perched on the arm of his chair. "It's only fair. You keep using a language *I* don't know."

They all jumped at a loud snore from her grandfather.

Nonna bustled toward her husband, wiping her hands on her apron. "Foolish man always complains about a crick in his neck, but he keeps doing this." Her expression was scolding but her hands gentle as she roused him and signed something that made the old man grumble but get to his feet and shuffle off.

Tutting, she returned to wiping the counters.

Adrick yawned. "I'm done for. Too much fun last night. Who's sleeping where?"

"You two can take the guest bed," Alessa said. "We'll be fine out here."

Kaleb balked. "I'm not sharing a bed with him."

"Help yourself to the barn then." Alessa moved to sit across from Dante. "Found anything yet?"

He grunted a negative. "I don't even know what to look for."

"What did Diwata say again?" Alessa stared into space. "What's white turns red then black . . ."

"Here." Dante tossed her a pocket journal, but it hit the floor. His mistake.

Alessa picked it up and read aloud. "What's white turns red then black, to summon the attack, as dark hides light, and day turns night, halos . . ."

"Are you talking about the eclipse?" Nonna paused halfway through taking off her apron.

"Which eclipse?" Alessa asked.

The old woman shrugged. "Whichever one is next. I assumed that's what you were talking about: a full moon is white, a new moon is black, a blood moon is red, and day turns to night during a solar eclipse. Do you remember the partial eclipse we had when you were little? Your mother kept fussing that you'd go blind, until Nonno showed you how to poke holes in paper to make the little semicircles on the ground."

"I do remember," Alessa said. "The trees made crescent-shaped shadows."

"Do you know when the next one will be?" Dante asked.

"Here?" Nonna said. "Not off the top of my head, but I can get my charts."

"She loves astrology," Alessa said as her grandmother bustled off to another room.

"Astrology and astronomy aren't the same thing," Dante said.

Alessa gave him a withering glare. "I'm aware, but both involve stars, and I don't know any astronomers. Do you?"

Nonna returned with a box full of star charts and calendars, visibly disappointed when Dante declined her offer to dissect his personality based on his birth date. The first few charts weren't especially helpful, but he *was* informed that his zodiac sign was compatible with Alessa's. The women seemed a bit too relieved.

"What would you have done if it wasn't?" he asked Alessa.

She patted his knee. "Let's be glad we don't have to find out."

Nonna shook her head. "No full eclipses for at least the next seven months."

Dante frowned. It made no sense for Crollo to send such a dire warning so far ahead of time. They were missing something.

Nonna excused herself for bed, but Dante kept looking. The fire burned low as he rifled through map after map, until Alessa fell asleep on the other end of the couch, and there was nothing left but embers.

He caught the quilt that was sliding off and tucked it around her before sitting back with a sigh. Diwata's warning had to mean *something.* If it wasn't a clue about the timing, then maybe it referred to landmarks. Dropping his head back, he closed his eyes.

White, red, black . . .

Dante jerked upright at Alessa's scream.

"Don't leave me alone!" She scrabbled for something in the dark. Him, maybe, because she stopped searching at his touch.

"I'm here," he said, grateful she was too tired to realize her bare hands were clutching him as he wrapped her in his arms. "What is it?"

"A dream." She shook so hard he had to clench his teeth. "You. After . . . I'm sorry."

Oh. That. He never knew how to soothe her when she dreamed about his own death. It had happened a few times in the months after, and she'd been wracked with guilt each time, as though he might have forgotten that he'd died if she didn't remind him.

Her fingers plucked at the quilt with frantic movements

that slowed as he murmured to her in the old language, nonsense phrases that barely made sense strung together. She always calmed faster when she didn't understand what he said and couldn't overthink every word.

"I don't want to fight another war," she murmured sleepily.

His heart twisted again. "I'll fight it for you. Stay here, where it's safe, and I'll go. It's my mission, not yours."

She patted his chest. "Nice try. I'm not letting you do this alone."

Satisfaction warred with frustration. He wanted her far from danger, but he didn't trust anyone else to keep her safe.

They both looked up at a flash of light. Nonna peeked around the corner, lantern in hand. "Oh, good, you're up."

"I'm sorry," Alessa said weakly. "Did we wake you?"

"No, I thought of something." She shuffled over and found one of the star charts they'd put aside earlier. "I was thinking of Saverio, and we'll be too far west, but there *will* be an eclipse for part of the Continent soon. There aren't any folk there to see it, but if there were, they'd get to see a blood moon and a solar eclipse. See?"

Dante leaned in. On the far side of the peninsula, there would be a blood moon in two weeks, then . . . there it was—a full solar eclipse, midmorning.

Dante squeezed Alessa's hand.

A year ago he would have let the world burn. Now he had a month to save it. For her.

Nine

DAYS UNTIL THE ECLIPSE: 28

Alessa told Adrick and Kaleb about the eclipse and Diwata's foretelling of doom over breakfast.

"When do we leave?" Adrick asked, kicking back in his chair.

Kaleb scoffed. "Didn't hear them invite you, Paladino."

"If my sister's going on a quest to find mythical warriors—no offense, Dante—and stop an attack from the gods *again,* I'm going to protect her."

"But then *I* have to go to protect her from *you,*" Kaleb groaned. "How are we even supposed to go on a quest if we don't know where we're going?"

Alessa laid a hand on Dante's knee. "Your parents never said *anything* about where the exiled ghiotte might have gone?"

Dante shook his head. "If they did, I didn't catch it."

"They didn't give you a map at birth?" Adrick waggled his eyebrows at his sister. "Tattoo it on your ass or something?"

Alessa went wide-eyed. "You think *I* would know whether Dante has intimate tattoos?"

"I know someone we can ask," Dante said without looking up from the table. "My aunt used to work in the village near here."

"Is she a ghiotte too?" Adrick asked.

"No," Dante bit off. "But she might remember something."

"Your aunt?" Alessa repeated. "The one who—"

"Yeah." Dante cut her off. He rarely spoke about his parents, or life before they died when he was twelve, so Alessa didn't know much about the other ghiotte family he'd grown up with, but she knew *that woman* had turned her back on an orphan newly escaped after three years in captivity, abused for simply being a ghiotte.

That's all Alessa needed to know.

Perhaps she should have felt more sympathy for the only other person on Saverio who had loved—and lost—a ghiotte partner, but she couldn't.

Losing a daughter and husband was a tragedy.

Abandoning Dante was unforgivable.

Dante's mouth went dry as they stopped in front of the shabby dressmaker's shop. "You don't have to come in."

Alessa took his hand. He meant to let go, to tell her to wait outside, but his fingers curled around hers instead, and he opened the door before he could change his mind. His breath caught at the sight of the middle-aged woman with sleek black hair and handsome features draping fabric over a dress form inside.

"Can I help you?" She looked up and her face blanched. "*Ludo*—Gabriele?"

She cast a nervous glance at the door. Being married to a ghiotte might have been deemed less sinful than being one, but clearly she hadn't forgotten how close she'd come to the pyre.

"Tita," he said coolly. "We won't trouble you. I just need to know if Matteo or my parents ever spoke about where the banished might have gone."

Her gaze went from shocked to wary. "Saverio celebrates you now. Surely you aren't fleeing?"

"No," he said. "But we need to find them."

She picked up a pair of shears with trembling hands. "Sometimes when you children were especially noisy, they'd joke about fleeing to where there were no roads, but it was only teasing."

Dante frowned. "I always assumed that meant the Continent."

She nodded sharply. "Yes. Matteo would say he was going outside to build a boat."

"But he never—"

She cut him off. "I'm sorry, that's all I know."

"Grazie." Dante turned to leave.

Alessa didn't. "If you think of anything else, you can send a letter to the Cittadella. This is your chance to *help*."

Her pointed tone drew a guilty flush from the older woman, who couldn't seem to look at Dante. "I hope you do find them. And I *am* sorry. For everything."

"Andiamo," Dante said softly, holding the door open. "Let's go."

He'd asked his question. It was done. That part of his life was dead and buried, and he'd never visit the grave again.

Adrick and Kaleb waited outside with curious looks, but Alessa shook her head, silencing their inevitable questions. She couldn't wrap her mind around the fact that such important people from Dante's childhood had lived so close to her grandparents' farm that she might have seen them at the market, or built sandcastles beside their daughter, Dante's childhood playmate.

Dante still hadn't said a word when they settled on a grassy knoll overlooking a pond for their picnic lunch of baguettes, olives, and cheese, so Alessa filled Adrick and Kaleb in on what little they'd learned.

"Boats? That's not much to go on," Kaleb said, dusting crumbs from his shirt. "Obviously you have to take a boat to get to the Continent."

"Ship." Dante picked up a smooth rock. "You take a ship to the Continent, not a boat."

"Same thing," Kaleb said.

"No, it's not." Dante walked toward the water's edge, tossing the rock into the air and catching it. "Matteo was a sailor and he always corrected people that they were called *ships,* not *boats*. I never thought about that until now."

"So we need to find a place with boats, not ships," Alessa said. "A town near a river, or a lake, maybe."

"That narrows it down," Kaleb grumbled.

"It's a start." Dante sent a stone skipping across the water.

Kaleb and Alessa lounged in the weak sunlight as Adrick and Dante's hunt for perfect skipping stones took them to the far side of the pond. Dante cocked his arm to send a stone skipping across the water, and stood, fist clenched around another, staring at the ripples left in its wake.

"Do you think he's okay?" Alessa asked, propped on her elbows to watch.

"No." Kaleb tossed a rock and it plonked into the pond with a splash. "What? You asked."

"You're supposed to say something *reassuring.*"

Kaleb flopped to his back, sunlight glinting off the red-gold highlights in his hair. "Nothing like digging up some family trauma to kick off a quest."

"Speaking of . . . your parents—"

"Nope." Kaleb threw an arm over his face and pretended to fall asleep.

Alessa sat up as she caught the tail end of what Adrick was saying as he and Dante returned.

"—asked around, and Nina's right, so that might be a problem."

"*What* might be a problem?" she asked.

"All the passenger ships are booked up," Adrick said. "We have no way to get to the Continent."

"We can use the official vessel," Alessa said.

Kaleb stirred with a fake yawn to match his fake nap. "Those are only for diplomacy and official military operations."

"We're launching a diplomatic mission to find the ghiotte and combine our armies," Alessa said. "What could be more official than that?" She'd prefer to hide in a cave and pretend none of this was happening, but fate offered no escape. "I'll tell Renata to submit the request as soon as we get back."

Adrick looked impressed. "You can do that?"

"I'm the Finestra. They can't say no to me."

"Absolutely not." Renata seemed to have forgotten she was holding a knife poised over her plate.

Dante did his best to blend into the shadows by the door. Maybe he shouldn't have let Alessa rush right into the dining hall.

"But we have to find them," Alessa repeated.

Renata put down the knife. "The Consiglio isn't going to panic Saverio because traumatized adolescents have decided an unprecedented attack is imminent. Tomo, tell her."

"It's completely normal to feel unmoored after Divorando," Tomo said, gentle and placating. "You spent five years preparing for battle, and with that over, one can feel bereft of purpose. You simply need a new focus. A hobby, perhaps. You could start a philanthropy."

A muscle ticked in Alessa's jaw. "Are you forbidding us to leave Saverio?"

Renata made an offended noise. "Of course not. If you'd like to visit the Continent on your own, go right ahead."

Pushing off the table, Alessa stood. "Fine. We'll make our *own* arrangements."

Tomo smiled. "Travel is good for the soul. Have a lovely time, dear."

"Safe journeys," Renata said. "Do say hello to the ghiotte for us if you find them."

Dante held the door open for Alessa to storm out.

"We have nothing," Alessa ranted, waving her hands in angry swirls as she climbed the stairs. "No ships, no soldiers, no supplies, no maps, no timeline, no clue what's coming."

"We'll figure it out." Dante was almost relieved. It was his mission, not Saverio's. They didn't need a first-class vessel loaded with supplies, horses, or soldiers for backup. Bureaucracy and rules would only slow them down. They'd do it on their own.

As they reached the top floor, Ciro emerged from the Fonte suite. "There you are. I was hoping to catch you before we departed."

Alessa hurried over to him. "How's Diwata?"

Ciro scrubbed his face. "Traumatized, but she'll recover. Your doctors insisted she rest, but she hasn't had another episode, so we plan to leave this afternoon." He looked at Dante. "I owe you an apology. I shouldn't have dismissed your quest to find the, um, others. If there's anything I can do to assist, please—"

"Does your ship have extra passenger cabins?" Dante interrupted.

Ciro stuttered. "It does. Yes. Why do you ask?"

"Could you make a detour?" Dante ignored Alessa's attempt to make eye contact. He wasn't about to let their first lucky break get away.

They needed a ship. Ciro had one.

Ten

Alessa's stomach flipped in time with every clang of boots on the gangway in a silent chant of *Not. Again. Not. Again.*

Ciro and Diwata's vessel was larger and more elegant than any of Saverio's, but it was still a floating death trap.

She eyed the smudged horizon warily. If the crew felt it was safe enough to depart, it must be. Then again, hundreds of ships had sunk throughout history after crews made similar decisions. Thanks to the Cittadella's logs of maritime deaths and injuries, she knew of a dozen ways to lose a limb or perish at sea.

"I've never been on a ship," Dante said, craning his neck to look at the sails.

Like it was a treat.

He had some nerve being so ridiculously *attractive* as they sailed to their doom. How was she supposed to plan her survival strategy if she had to clutch the railings to resist brushing a curl off his forehead?

"I swear," Alessa muttered, "if the gods put me through all this and then give the next Finestra a normal run of things, I'm going to take it *very* personally."

"Maybe there are no more," Dante said, watching a sailor clamber up the riggings. "Maybe you're the last Finestra."

"No. I refuse. A Finestra's power only goes away when it moves to the next, like a relay race. If I get left holding the baton . . ." Alessa glared at the sky. "When this is over, you'd better give him back his powers or take mine away, you hear me?"

"Threatening the gods?" Dante said. "I may have been a bad influence on you."

"Oh, no doubt." She aimed a silent half apology to Dea. Probably best not to sound ungrateful when the gods could send any number of horrors—sudden squalls, massive fish with teeth like swords, squids with tentacles as long as a city street. . . .

Alessa jumped as something brushed her leg.

Not tentacles. Just a cat.

"Hello, gorgeous." Crouching, she clicked her tongue in her best feline-attracting noise, but the fluffy gray beauty sauntered away, snaking its enormous tail through the air.

Dante jogged off to help a sailor with an unwieldy piece of luggage, and the cat trotted after him, because of course it did. Why choose a person who openly desires your affection when you can chase someone who doesn't? She furrowed her brow. She might be insulting herself as much as the feline population.

Adrick stepped aboard, hefting a bag over his shoulder, and strolled over to the crew member overseeing the transfer of luggage to the ship. "You seem like a brave guy. Ever explore beyond the settlements?"

"What's he up to?" Kaleb asked.

She shushed him. "Pretend we're talking."

"We *are* talking." Kaleb made an exasperated noise as Adrick poured on the flattery.

Alessa elbowed him. "A little charm goes a long way."

"Charm is just lying in a prettier package."

The joke begged to be made. *Begged.* Alessa clamped down on her lower lip.

"What?" Kaleb drawled. "You're going to hurt yourself. Just say it."

She choked on a laugh. "I hadn't realized you thought Adrick's package was so pretty."

Kaleb rubbed his temples. "I cannot *believe* Dea saw godliness in you."

Dante rejoined them, examining a scrape on his hand.

"How did you injure yourself already?" Alessa asked. "You're a *passenger.*"

"It's nothing." He slid the map case from her sweaty grasp as Ciro emerged from the helm, arms wide in welcome.

"Off we sail, bound for adventure," Ciro proclaimed. "My deepest regrets we cannot offer more luxurious hospitality, but I'm afraid we only have three passenger cabins—one with a cot and hammock, two with bunk beds—so alas, you will have to share."

"Fine with me." Kamaria tossed an arm around Saida's shoulders. "Sleepover time."

Behind Ciro, Diwata waved. Her wan smile made Alessa's skin crawl. It wasn't her fault, but it was difficult to forget how she'd attacked them. The cabins better have sturdy locks.

Kaleb glanced around, his jaw dropping open as Dante picked up Alessa's bag. "I have to share a room with Adrick *again?* He's *your* brother. You stay with him."

Alessa wrinkled her nose. "Hmm . . . Bunk with Dante, or my brother? I'll stick with Dante, thanks."

"Come on, roomie." Adrick hefted his bag with a smirk. "Top or bottom?"

Kaleb's face took on an unhealthy shade of red.

Inside their assigned cabin, Dante rapped a knuckle on the wall paneling, trying to gauge what kind of wood it was made of.

Alessa seemed glued in place outside the door. "I *hate* sailing. *Hate*."

Dante eyed the hammock hanging in one corner. "I could distract you."

She held her breath and stepped inside. "Please do. By telling me more about your life before we met while I unpack."

Eh, it had been worth a shot. He hoisted himself into the hammock. "What do you want to know?"

"Everything." She unlatched her trunk and began withdrawing items. "For one, how'd you learn to kiss so well? *That's* not a skill one can learn from a book. Believe me, I tried."

"There's no story. Met a few girls as I went from town to town, messed around in some haylofts. The usual."

"Leaving a trail of broken hearts across Saverio?"

"Doubtful. Never stuck around long enough for anyone to get attached."

"You'd be surprised how quickly girls can develop a soul-destroying crush when someone looks"—she waved a hand at him, brow creasing—"how you insist on looking."

He cracked a smile. That reaction might have been the first endearing thing he'd noticed about her. Justifiably hostile toward him at first, she'd still tripped over her words whenever he came near, and she'd always looked so damn *indignant* about it. For a while, he'd convinced himself he was only getting close *to* fluster her. That didn't last.

Alessa shook out a dress. "So, you spent years learning to fight and kiss. A broad course of study."

He stretched to grab the hammock's chain, pretending not to notice her gaze following the movement. She actually thought she was subtle. "Not that different, really."

"I'm listening."

A slow smile spread across his face. "Pay attention, note reactions, learn to anticipate their moves. Pretty straightforward if you're observant."

Alessa blinked again. "I must be terrible."

"Enthusiasm goes far."

"Oh, *no*." Alessa raised a hand to her mouth. "What if I'm stealing *your* kissing skills when I'm kissing you, and I'm actually terrible at it, and we'll only find out when my power goes away?"

She looked so alarmed he couldn't laugh, but his sides ached from holding it in.

"It's not funny!" She swatted in his direction. "What if I'm the worst kisser ever and you're stuck with me?"

"We'd practice day and night until you sorted it out. A sacrifice I'm more than willing to make."

She frowned. "You promise?"

"Do I promise not to leave you if *your* kissing skills turn out to be *my* kissing skills? Yes. I promise."

She pursed her lips. "What was the worst kiss you ever had?"

He scratched his chin. "It's not polite to kiss and tell."

"At least tell me how I rank?"

"Hmmm." He pretended to mull it over. "Top five?"

Her mouth fell into an indignant little O. "You're terrible!"

"Pity the girls who came before you, luce mia," he said with a laugh. "They never stood a chance."

"I hope they were so lackluster you forget they ever happened."

"Oh, *that's* nice."

"Am I supposed to want competition from your past affairs?"

Dante shook his head. "You make it sound much more exciting than I remember."

"Good. Stop remembering. Actually, don't. I have more questions."

"Dea help me."

"She already did. Who was your *first* kiss? I might as well live vicariously through your memories."

"Not sure it's worth reliving in my *own* memory, much less vicariously." He crossed his arms. "You first."

A slight shrug. "When I was thirteen I convinced my neighbor, Maria Bocelli, that we should practice so we'd know what we were doing when we finally got an opportunity. But looking back, she was the prettiest girl I'd ever seen, and I spent more time anticipating the practice than anything that might come after, so I may have been more clever than I realized at the time. It was awful. I went too fast and our teeth knocked together and her eyes got watery and I ran away crying."

Dante cringed. "Oof. Did you try again?"

"I was *going* to, but I didn't want to mess up again, and the boy next door had a huge crush on me—"

"Please don't tell me you seduced some poor boy into being a test subject." It was too easy to imagine awkward preteen Alessa strategizing to kiss half the neighborhood for research purposes.

"Of course not. I asked—*nicely*—if he wanted to practice kissing, and he eagerly agreed, but Adrick overheard and teased him so horribly he never showed up. Anyway, I was too embarrassed to apologize in person, but I did write Maria a letter."

"An 'I'm sorry your first kiss was terrible' letter?"

"Basically."

"And? Did she confess her undying love?"

"I'll never know. I got my powers before I heard back. Your turn."

Dante sucked in a breath. "I was . . . precocious."

"Of course you were. How old?"

"Eight? Nine, maybe? We were visiting my aunt and uncle, and the adults always stayed up late, telling the same boring stories, so Talia and I went to the woods—"

"Your first kiss was your *cousin*?" Alessa made a face.

"Not my *real* cousin. We weren't blood-related, just the kind of family friends you don't call Signor or Signora. Anyway, Talia dared me to beat her to the top of this tree. She fought dirty—almost knocked me off—but we reached the top at the same time, and . . . I kissed her."

"In a tree. Just like the nursery rhyme."

"I was quite pleased with myself, but she seemed underwhelmed."

"Her loss, my gain." Alessa's voice turned serious. "Then they were killed, too, and you wandered around Saverio for years, all alone."

"Kissing and fighting and doing odd jobs." He forced a half smile. "Don't waste your tears on me."

With a sniff, Alessa turned back to her luggage. Riffling through the contents, her movements grew frantic.

"What are you looking for?" he asked with a yawn. She made detailed lists before any expedition, but she always forgot something, and he'd gotten in the habit of checking both of their bags, so he knew they had the essentials.

Pushing her hair back, she dug through the contents faster. "I know I had it."

"Hey," he said, rolling out of the hammock. "Whatever it is, it's okay."

She fluttered her hands by her side as he crossed the cabin. "The maps," she said, her voice thick. "I had them when we boarded. I don't know how—"

"I took them," he said quietly. "Remember?"

She whirled. "You did? You did! On the deck. You took them. Oh, thank goodness." She exhaled shakily. "I thought I'd ruined everything."

"Even if you *had* lost them, you wouldn't have ruined everything," he assured her. "We can handle much worse than a little forgetfulness, I promise."

Her lip quivered as she smiled. "Thank you."

Before meeting her, he'd never had to worry about letting anyone down, and if her anxiety about doing so was any indication, that was a blessing. She always got so worked up, as though he'd stop caring about her for some silly mistake.

At a distant roll of thunder, Alessa squeezed her eyes shut. "Do you think this is a sign Dea doesn't want us to do this?"

"Or that we're on the right track, and Crollo's trying to slow us down."

The clouds rumbled in response.

Diwata didn't say a word during the evening meal in the state room, but Ciro presided over the table like it had been his idea to invite them on an adventure all along. Saida, Adrick, and Kamaria kept the conversation going, while Kaleb poked sadly at the fish dinner, and Alessa plotted her escape. With her stomach roiling like the storm-tossed sea, if she didn't get above deck soon, she'd be doomed.

"No couple teams," Saida said, turning a scolding eye on Dante, who didn't seem to be paying attention. "Couples are too good at guessing games."

"*Scuzi?*" Dante asked.

"Charades," Kamaria said. "Saida wants us to entertain her by making numpties of ourselves."

Ciro clapped delightedly. "I do love games." He was, as her nonna would say, a bit of an odd duck.

"We could do boy-girl pairs," said Saida. "Kamaria and Ciro, Adrick and Alessa—"

"No way," Kaleb said. "They probably have some secret twin code. I'll be with Alessa."

Kamaria waved a spoon at him. "She said no couples."

Kaleb choked on air. "It's not that kind of marriage!"

"Well, I claim Dante," Saida said. "Kaleb's a sore loser."

Kaleb threw his hands up. "You think Dante will be a gracious loser? He doesn't lose at anything!"

Saida looked smug. "Then I won't have to worry about it."

Dante folded his napkin. "I'll pass. I'm going to look around the deck."

"Wait for me," Alessa said, steadying herself on the table. At least from up there, she'd be able to see the sky when they sank to a watery grave.

The situation above board wasn't reassuring. The wind had picked up, and the clouds looked distinctly foreboding. They hadn't even made it around Saverio's southern coast, and already the waves were noticeably choppier, the sails snapping as the wind picked up.

Alessa's dress whipped around her ankles as she hurried to the railing. "I'll stay here, holding on for dear life. Be careful. Ships are dangerous."

Shortly after Dante left to explore, Kaleb chased Adrick onto the deck, shouting, "*Pie* as in 'pirate!' How is that so difficult to figure out?"

"It looked like a quiche," Adrick said.

"Round and edible! Pie is the most *obvious* guess. I can't believe they stuck me with you *again*."

Adrick looked over his shoulder with a smirk crafted to annoy. "You're following me to tell me how much you don't want to be around me?"

"Alessa should have eaten you in the womb and saved us all!" Kaleb turned on his heel and stomped back down.

Adrick sauntered over to Alessa. "If it storms tonight, will you help me tie Kaleb to the mast? We can say it's for his own safety, but maybe we'll get lucky with a lightning strike." Adrick threw his arms above his head, face twisted in a ridiculous parody of electrocution.

"Be nice," Alessa scolded. "Besides, Kaleb controls electricity. He'd be fine."

She pulled an extra ribbon from her pocket and motioned for Adrick to turn around and duck so she could twist his curls into a low bun. "You look like a runaway sheep who missed shearing."

"You got the death touch; I got the hair." Adrick straightened with a wink. "Is that cat supposed to be there?"

A gust of cold wind snapped the sails as Alessa turned to see the cat practicing for a career in acrobatics on the far side of the deck. Dante followed her look of alarm to the netting above him and strode toward it. She shouted for him to stop, but the wind swept away her protest. With the ship listing from side to side like it had drunk the contents of every barrel in storage, it took her an eternity to make it across the deck.

Dante climbed down, cat under one arm and a satisfied look on his face that died the instant he saw hers.

"What were you thinking?" Alessa reached for the animal. "It's a *cat*. Cats land on their feet. You are not a cat. A fall from there could've killed you or thrown you overboard to drown!"

The cat squirmed, claws out, and Dante stepped back before putting it down where she couldn't reach. "You looked worried, so I got it."

Alessa calmed her voice, with effort. "Could you *try* to avoid life-threatening activities *please?*"

Dante didn't *quite* roll his eyes before walking away.

The door to Kamaria and Saida's cabin swung open at Alessa's knock.

Kamaria looked up from a sketch pad. "Trouble in paradise?"

Alessa flopped onto the bottom bunk. "I don't understand why Dante's acting like this. Ever since I got back from Altari, he's been jumping off roofs and into bar brawls, and now he's climbing the riggings as we sail into a storm. He doesn't have healing powers anymore, and he wasn't this reckless when he *did*."

Saida made a sympathetic face. "Maybe he feels he has to prove himself . . . or something."

"Not even death can stop a guy from being a dumbass on occasion," Kamaria said. "He got knocked down and he's Dante, so he can't just get back up; he has to climb higher than before. Literally."

Alessa grabbed a pillow, pressing it to her face for a short but satisfying scream. "I'm starting to think he's trying to die all over again."

"He's a certified mess," Kamaria said with a nod. "But he's worth it, right?" Alessa opened her mouth to defend him, but Kamaria waved it away. "I'm not saying he *isn't.* I'm saying, in the span of a few months, you two met, fell in love, he almost killed you, you fought a war where you *did* kill him, you brought him back from the dead, and now, after a long recovery, he's not the same as before. You've been through *a lot* and you're probably both horny as hell. Maybe go easy on each other?"

"I should bite my tongue and let him run face-first into danger?"

Kamaria closed her sketch pad. "Of course not. Just pick your battles. And if he doesn't care enough about your feelings to keep his ass safe, find someone who does."

"Is that an offer?" Alessa asked with a weak laugh.

Kamaria smirked. "Baby girl, you couldn't handle me."

"If I could master *that* look, I'd definitely have more romantic luck," Saida said. "Teach me how to smolder, Kamaria."

Kamaria wagged a scolding finger. "Don't you change a damn thing about yourself. You're a gem of a girl. Just walk into every room with your head high like you *know* what a gift you are, and boys will grovel at your feet."

"Aw," Saida sniffed. "You really do like me."

Kamaria slapped her knees and stood. "This is too much sincerity for me. I'm going to see if any lady sailors need help trimming their sails. Or whatever they do all day. Batten hatches? What's the best maritime euphemism for oceanic recreation?"

"Shivering timbers?" Alessa mused. "That doesn't work as

well for girls. Ooh, blow the man down! Nope, same problem. Poop deck is funny but not what you're looking for. All hands on deck . . . Maybe something about booty? Oh! Offer to plunder their treasure chests!"

Kamaria snapped her fingers and pointed at Alessa. "Knew I could count on you."

Saida looked a bit stunned. "I can't decide if this talent of yours is a gift or a curse."

Alessa groaned. "Both, obviously. Story of my life. Ugh, I *really* need this ship to stop rolling. Promise you'll make up a good tale about my heroic end so I don't go down in the history books as the Finestra who died from seasickness."

"You do look pretty green." Saida clucked sympathetically. "You're *sure* it's motion sickness?"

"Positive. It's been half a year since . . ." Alessa's cheeks flamed. "I'm sure. Boy problems and seasickness at the same time is just cruel."

Kamaria patted her head on the way to the door. "If you're going to vomit, please don't do it in our room."

Eleven

DAYS UNTIL THE ECLIPSE: 27

The following evening, the storm raged on, and Dante was certain the cabin was shrinking.

Hunched over her primer on the desk, Alessa looked up as a loud bang shook the walls, followed by muffled shouts from Adrick and Kaleb's cabin. "They're going to kill each other."

"Nah. Wound, maybe." That kind of animosity was bound to turn into *something*, but he wasn't going to be the one to tell her. Besides, he didn't want to think about Kaleb and Adrick. He wanted to tip her chin up and kiss her senseless, but when he brushed the back of her neck, she sat forward so fast he almost pulled her hair.

"Alessa, what are we *doing*?" he said with a groan. "How long are you going to keep dodging me?"

He'd never been one for words, but he used to be able to *show* her how he felt. Now he felt muzzled as the distance between them kept getting wider.

"I won't blame you if it's too hard to wait." Alessa knotted her hands in her lap.

"I'm not looking for a way *out*. I'm asking you to *try*."

"You have no idea what it's like to watch the person you care about most in the world die at your own hand," Alessa said with a sniffle.

He scoffed. "I *stabbed* you."

"That was different. We were still getting to know each other."

"We're *still* getting to know each other. And I know my own body. If I say I can take it, I can take it."

She coughed a disbelieving laugh. "Do you hear yourself? You sound like you're preparing for a wrestling match with a rabid animal, not romance."

"Fine." He cracked his neck. "I'm going to see if they could use a hand on deck."

"You don't know anything about sailing a ship. You'd just be in the way." Alessa's exasperated sigh tipped his temper over the edge.

"I won't be *in the way*." He'd learned a dozen trades, many more dangerous than sailing. Sure, he *had* been harder to injure then—he viciously crushed the thought—but even if he wasn't a ghiotte anymore, he wasn't helpless.

Alessa stood, clutching the primer. "Just stay here with me where it's safe."

"Why? You won't even come near me." Lightning cracked as he yanked the door open.

She jerked back. "That's not fair."

Maybe not, but when she acted like she was afraid of breaking him, it made him feel so damn *broken*. She didn't want him protecting her, didn't want him touching her. What the hell was he *supposed* to be doing?

He'd been hired to put his life on the line to protect her,

and she acted like he was made of glass. Like he should hide from anything dangerous.

Not a chance. Once in his life, he'd hid, and he would *never* make that mistake again.

Above board, the wind flung rain sideways, making the deck slick and treacherous, but the crew didn't turn down an extra hand, and Dante soon found a rhythm that required enough focus to crowd out the worst of the memories.

Months. He'd wasted *months* of his life in bed, trapped in a body that didn't feel like his own. The memory crawled under his skin. He was *alive,* dammit. He wasn't going to stop living now.

Rain stung like a cold whip as waves battered the ship. It was dangerous and exhilarating—exactly what he needed. And no place for Alessa.

"Hey!" Dante shouted, yanking on a knot to be sure it would hold. "What are you doing up here? It's not safe."

Fire flashed in Alessa's eyes.

Oh, shit. "I mean, it's not *un*safe. It's just—" Either Alessa could growl louder than he realized, or a roll of thunder drowned out whatever sound she had made. "You don't know anything about sailing, so you should get back to the cabin, that's all."

Alessa grabbed the closest riggings. "If it's safe enough for you, it's safe enough for me." Another wave crested the sides as she stepped on the lowest rung.

"Enough, all right? You've made your point." He grasped the ropes on either side of her, trapping her between the net and his body. "I get it."

"I doubt that."

A rough swell threw him off-balance, and he pulled the net

tight, pressing their bodies closer. "Please, go below before you hurt yourself."

"Only if you come with me."

He exhaled. "I can handle myself."

"Do you really not see your hypocrisy?"

Crack. Only his quick reflexes got them out of the way. Alessa froze in shock, making it easier for him to shield her before a chunk of the lightning-snapped mast shattered against the deck.

"Are you all right?" he shouted.

She nodded, white-faced. He wasn't so lucky. Hissing, he yanked a splinter the size of his dagger out of his arm. He wouldn't be much use to the crew while bleeding all over the deck. One hand pressed to his bicep, he ushered Alessa back to the cabins. As they passed Adrick and Kaleb's room, she shouted for her brother to get his medicine bag.

"I don't need—" Dante clamped his mouth shut at her glare.

Adrick arrived momentarily, medicine bag in hand. "Novice surgeon, at your service. Clean him up while I thread the needle, will you, sis?"

Dante intercepted the bottle Adrick tossed before it hit the floor.

"Sit," Alessa said, pointing to the chair.

All this fuss for a little cut . . . Grumbling, Dante did as he was told while she doused a cloth. Whatever it was soaked with stung like the fires of hell when she pressed it to his arm. He would know.

Adrick nudged her hand aside. "This is going to hurt. Look away."

Dante wasn't afraid of a little—"The *hell*?! What'd I do to you?"

"Oh, suck it up. I'll be quick."

He was, thank Dea. A few minutes later, Adrick stepped back to admire his handiwork. "Salve's on the table. Cover it with a clean bandage and keep it dry."

Alessa told Dante to prop his forearm on the armrest as she cut the excess bandage free. The remaining bundle slipped from her grasp and rolled across the floor.

Dante stood to chase it down.

"Sit," she snapped.

He sat. "I can tell you're mad."

She stomped after the bandage. "Furious."

"You don't expect me to wrap myself in wool and sit in a rocking chair the rest of my life, do you?"

Every line of her body looked brittle. "I expect you to *try* to stay alive."

If she hadn't been on deck, he wouldn't have been beneath the mast at all, but that seemed like a losing argument. "I'm sorry I scared you."

"Are you?" Her eyes glittered with tears. "Because you keep doing it."

He half stood, wincing.

"Sit *down*," she snapped.

"Then come here." He kept his voice low and gentle. "I can't watch you cry and do nothing about it."

She pressed her lips together until they stopped trembling before speaking again. "Keeping you safe is like babysitting a toddler with a death wish."

He tugged her into his lap. "Then stop *babysitting*. I'm not a child. You asked me not to do anything reckless, and I didn't. That was a freak accident."

"I've already watched you die once. I don't want to do it again."

"That's a *little* dramatic—" He caught himself at her glare. "Okay, cara, I'll stay off the riggings if it makes you feel better." He took the chance and kissed her, quick and soft.

"And all other dangerous—"

He cut her off with another kiss, nodding against her mouth. Her lips softened, parting. She wanted this, too.

The base of his neck began to tingle but he ignored it, deepening the kiss until she let out a breathy sigh. The tingle became a crackle, a burn. His hand twitched. He refused to let it win. Not now. Not when he finally—

Alessa pulled away, horrified. "I'm hurting you again, aren't I?"

"It's nothing."

She scrambled to her feet. "That's what I mean! The bar fights, the riggings. If you want to prove you know your limits, stop pushing them!" Her lip trembled. "I don't even know if you want to kiss me or if it's just another challenge to prove how tough you are."

He jerked back. "You think I'm using you for thrills?"

"I don't *know* what you're doing."

"*Merda,* Alessa, what does a guy have to do to get a break?" He raked a hand through his hair. "For Dea's sake, I *died.*"

She closed her eyes for a long moment. "I know."

She didn't, though. She *couldn't.*

"I. *Died.*"

"I know!" The tears in her eyes seemed to freeze. "I *know* you did, because *I* had to live through it!"

She turned away, hugging herself like she'd fall apart if she let go, and the full weight of it hit him like a brick to the face.

He'd been too damn busy feeling bad for himself and mad at the world, and mad at her—there it was, yes, mad at *her*—to see it until that moment. Not mad because she'd taken the life he'd willingly offered, but because she'd given it back with a piece missing.

He was *mad* that he wasn't who he'd been and that she made him *want* to be close to someone, but now he couldn't. Mad that she'd softened the callus around his heart and he couldn't stop *feeling* all the damn time. And mad that she had the nerve to love him, because he could hurt her. He didn't deserve that kind of responsibility.

"I'm going to change now, and I don't want you to watch." Her voice was flat.

He hadn't even known a person could hold so many feelings at once, and he sure as hell had no idea how to explain them, so he stared at the ground, grateful she wasn't looking.

When the cot creaked, she was curled under the covers, facing the wall.

"Kissing shouldn't hurt." Her voice was choked with tears. "It shouldn't be a—a *challenge*. Or a test. Or whatever you're trying to prove."

He rubbed his temples. "That's *not* what I'm doing."

"Are you sure? Because it seems like you're daring the gods to finish what they started. And maybe I can't stop you, but I won't be the one to do it for them."

Twelve

DAYS UNTIL THE ECLIPSE: 26

Bedtime stories and hushed whispers painted the Continent as a wasteland where poor souls eked out a living between each Divorando by farming hearty crops and fending off violent outlaws who'd been banished from Saverio for their crimes. But while the tumble of buildings climbing the hills needed paint, and the sparse trees were missing some limbs, the settlement looked more like a tarnished version of Saverio than a hellscape.

Dante squinted through the sea spray at the shoreline, only half listening to Kaleb and Kamaria's conversation. Alessa hadn't opened her eyes that morning, feigning sleep until he left. She'd never done that before, and the glaring light of day left no place to hide from his guilt.

He didn't want her to worry, and he definitely didn't want her to cry. There was no way around it. He'd have to suck it up and apologize. Promise to be more *careful,* or whatever she wanted to hear. He took a vicious bite of hardtack.

Still. He shouldn't *have* to.

Ciro and Diwata, holding the cat, walked over to join them as Kaleb spoke through a mouthful of crumbs. "My brother said there's a dozen tiny towns—if you can call them that—inland from the main settlement, but it's a no-man's-land beyond those, and explorers go missing a lot."

"Who *doesn't* love places where people mysteriously vanish?" Saida's wide-eyed expression was slightly hysterical. "I'm *so* excited to set off into the unknown all alone."

"You won't be alone." Diwata raised the cat in front of her and stared into its golden eyes for an awkwardly long moment. "There. This furry goddess will protect you."

Ciro recovered from his confusion before the rest of them. "Diwata will remain with the ship during repairs. However, *I* am going to join you."

"No need," Dante said. "We've got things under control. And . . . a cat, apparently."

"I insist. My ship has failed you, and I offer myself as compensation. One more magical warrior in your party can only be a boon."

The others looked to Dante, and he shrugged. If the stuffy prick wanted to follow them around the Continent, so be it. He'd either keep up or they'd leave him behind.

Kamaria whistled. "Well, *hello there*, Finestra."

Dante looked up and forgot to exhale. Alessa had traded her usual skirts and dresses for skintight breeches, knee-high boots, and a flowing white blouse that clung to her with every gust of wind as she crossed the deck.

"Is it 'Dress Like Dante Day'? I must have missed the memo," Kamaria said. "Oh, wait, no I didn't."

It wasn't unusual for Kamaria, but Alessa never dressed that way, and Dante was *not* prepared for how the masculine attire accentuated her curves. The wind was either his new best friend or sworn enemy, depending on who else was seeing what he was.

Kamaria elbowed him with a conspiratorial chuckle.

"Mine," he said under his breath

She barked a laugh.

Alessa stumbled as the ship hit a wave, and he jumped to steady her. For a beat, he thought she wouldn't take his hand but she did. Her silk gloves were damp from the spray, her fingers rigid in his grip.

She let go of him for the railing when they reached it, and he handed her a piece of hardtack. Even pale from nausea, she was a sight to behold as she gazed at the shoreline, her profile outlined against the cloud-washed sky, sea spray dewing her skin. Her hair was twisted into a messy topknot, and curly wisps danced across the line of her neck.

Madre. He was captivated.

She wouldn't look at him. "The captain says we should reach shore within the hour."

"You're still mad," he said.

"A little." She shrugged one shoulder. "And I'm not kissing you again until I know you're doing it for the right reasons."

"Oh, yeah?" Maybe he should have been peeved, but he couldn't hide a smile. He wasn't some lapdog who'd roll over for a treat. "You think you can manipulate me?"

"I'm not *manipulating*. I'm telling you to your face that I won't be a part of your drive for self-destruction. If you kiss me, it should be because you *want* to, not because you're testing how far you can push your body. I need to trust that you'll be honest about admitting weakness in order to feel safe about trying to get close to each other, and right now, I don't.

When you promise you'll protect your life as carefully as you do mine, *then* I will practice kissing you again. Those are my terms. Take them or leave them."

He crossed his arms. "What if you kiss me first?"

She raised her chin. "I won't. I'm a master of self-control."

"You think you have more self-discipline than *I* do?"

Judging from her face, she absolutely did not, but she wouldn't admit it. "I survived five years without any physical contact. I've proven my endurance."

He leaned closer. "And yet, a few weeks in my presence, and you couldn't resist my charming personality."

"Ha! You spent half the time scowling."

"You made the first move."

"Revisionist history. It wasn't *my* hands that went wandering."

"We already decided that didn't count. You *definitely* kissed me first."

Alessa *humphed*. "Then it's your turn. Promise to be careful, and you can kiss me whenever you want. A win-win."

She wanted to challenge him? Fine. Game on.

Alessa hooked her thumbs in her belt loops as she stepped onto the dock, surreptitiously adjusting her breeches. They were a bit snug. Not necessarily in a *bad* way, if Kamaria's teasing was any indication, but a sign she hadn't fully thought through her adventure wardrobe.

Dante was already on the dock, scribbling additions to their supply list and looking impatient about the disembarking process, while Ciro took his farewells from Diwata.

"We're really letting the cat come?" Kaleb asked.

"I don't think anyone decides where cats go or don't go." Alessa bent to offer her hand and was finally deemed worthy of scratching behind one tufted ear. "What a sweet girl."

"Sweet?" Kaleb said. "That thing is a hellion."

"She's just feisty. We should name her something *fiery*. Like Fiore."

Dante glanced over. "That means flower."

Alessa frowned. "I still like it."

Dante hollered for everyone to move out, and she had to jog to catch up, which alerted her to yet another wardrobe issue. Devoting so much of her luggage space to trousers and blouses instead of dresses was practical enough, but undergarments might pose an issue, especially if they had to travel on horseback. Ribbons and lace were fine beneath structured gowns, but she'd have to rewear her training garb every day beneath her clothing—or clutch herself in an embarrassing manner—to avoid some uncomfortable bouncing.

"We'll need ropes, weaponry, canteens, blankets. . . ." Dante checked items off on his fingers as they strode through the harbor town. "Adrick, you're in charge of medical supplies. Saida, food that travels well. Alessa—"

"—can barely walk a straight line," she finished with a pointed smile. She was in no mood to be a martyr. "We all need a hot meal and a good night's sleep in real beds before we set off into the wilderness. The sailors say there's an inn near the edge of town. Ciro and I will book rooms and start asking if anyone knows where we might find what we're looking for."

"I'll join you," Kamaria said. "I'm great at charming information out of strangers."

Dante frowned. "Fine. We'll meet there at sundown."

Alessa peered into windows as they strolled the cobblestone roads bustling with people in homespun fabrics and practical footwear, hats shielding sun-burnished faces. Surely one of the shops would have what she needed. With her figure, Kamaria probably didn't need much support, but Saida might have suggestions. The thought gave Alessa a little thrill. Finally, she had friends she could ask such things.

The inn's front desk was empty, but the food smelled divine, so Alessa and Ciro found a table in the common room while Kamaria went to investigate the stables. Unlike the Continent itself, the settlers perfectly matched Alessa's expectations: rugged, tanned, and fit, they all looked like safe bets in a brawl.

Across the room, a young woman with flawless olive skin and glossy black hair hooted with laughter as a freckled young man with bright red hair slapped the table for emphasis, earning glares from nearby diners. Alessa was more interested in the girl's leather vest. Laced up the front, it bared most of her toned stomach and accentuated strong shoulders. It would be a leap from the Cittadella's expectations, but worn *over* a blouse. . . .

A burly man in an apron arrived to detail the inn's offerings. Ciro ordered a wide selection, then stared into nothingness for a while before blinking and seeming to find himself.

"No offense, Ciro," Alessa said. "But sometimes you look like you've just woken up, completely confused about how you got here."

Ciro's knee bounced, jiggling the table. "Sometimes I feel that way. Like I've been watching myself from a great distance, half asleep. Our healers say it's a trauma response, but I don't know. We lost so many people, and I grieve for them, but I don't *feel* traumatized. I suppose everyone processes differently, though. Have you ever had that feeling?"

Alessa looked down. "Not exactly. In other ways, though, Divorando left marks I'm only just beginning to understand."

A server arrived with their food, pulling napkin-wrapped flatware from his apron pocket. "Never seen you before," he said. "Which settlement you from?"

"We aren't from a settlement," Alessa said.

The man's eyes narrowed. "You don't look like fringe."

"*I* am from the island nation of Tanp, and the rest of our party is from Saverio," Ciro said coolly.

"Hadn't heard about a big drop-off." The man's expression grew stern. "Best you know up front, we don't ask a lot of questions here on the Continent, but keep your noses clean if you want to stick around. We take care of our own here. No trials or tattoos, either. Anyone crosses a line, they regret it. The fringe is wide open if you want that kind of life."

"Oh, we aren't *exiles,*" Alessa said. The vested girl cast her a dirty look, and Alessa lowered her voice. "We're not *judging* anyone who is. But we're here on . . . um . . . business."

The server looked leery. "What kind of business?"

"A treasure hunt of sorts. Have you ever heard of a city on the *other* side of the Continent, near a body of water—"

"Nope." The server took his tray and hastened away.

The girl in the vest and the redhead slung their packs over their shoulders to leave.

"Heard what you're looking for," the girl said to Alessa as she passed. "Why do you want to find the drowning city? People say no one lives there but ghosts."

Alessa's heart rate kicked up. *The drowning city.* "Do you know where it is?"

The girl laughed. "If I did, I wouldn't tell you. Fools who go looking for the drowning city never come back."

Thirteen

Dante walked the length of the settlement and back, but he had no luck hiring a guide. When the skies opened to drench him, he took the hint and turned his boots toward the inn. He wanted a cold drink, a hot bed, and—*That,* he couldn't have. Not unless Alessa had given up on bringing him to heel. She'd drawn the line in the sand, and she'd be the one to cross it, or his name wasn't Gabriele Dante Lucente.

Apologizing was one thing—he'd been ready to do that—but roll over and let her think she had more self-control? Not a chance. *She'd* kiss *him,* and *then* he'd say whatever it took to put the whole argument to rest.

Adrick and Kaleb were facing off across a game of cards in the dining room when he squelched inside.

Kaleb grimaced. "No luck finding a guide?"

"None." Dante dropped into a chair. "It's like they were warned against it. The second I opened my mouth to ask, everyone clammed up."

"Guess they don't like outsiders. Or money means less

here." Adrick mused, "Maybe we could barter or offer some kind of service?"

Kaleb snorted. "You're welcome to service people, but I have my pride."

"You wouldn't be worth enough anyway." Adrick slid a key across the table to Dante. "Room number three. Alessa went up a while ago."

Dante turned it over in his hands. If he stalled long enough, maybe she'd fall asleep and roll over to greet him with a kiss before she remembered she was mad at him. Voilà, game over.

He ordered a beer and nursed it in silence while Kaleb and Adrick sniped at each other.

"Are you going to sit there dripping on everything all night?" Kaleb asked.

Adrick took a swig of beer. "He's scared of my sister."

"No, I'm not."

"Sure, you are. And I don't blame you. She's fierce as a wet cat when she's mad. Hope you're prepared to grovel."

Dante shifted in his seat. "I don't grovel."

"Everybody says they'll never grovel, and before you know it, you're making a big speech about how much you *love* them and how you'll do *whatever* they want."

Dante glared at the younger man.

Adrick shrugged. "You could buy her a present. She's easily distracted by shiny things."

"I did get her something. You think that'll work?"

Adrick looked impressed. Shocked, even. "Depends how shiny it is."

Dante withdrew the package from his back pocket and set it on the table.

Kaleb unwrapped it and began to laugh. "Hey, it's the thought that counts."

Alessa tried to feign disinterest as Dante stepped inside their room, but his muscles flexed in a very distracting way as he peeled off his soaked shirt

"Are you trying to get pneumonia just to spite me?" she said, peering over her primer.

"It's not even cold out."

"You weren't supposed to get your bandage wet. Sit down so I can replace it." She wrapped his bicep with a fresh bandage, her nerves sparking with every graze of skin against skin. "There, it's healing nicely."

Their eyes met and she couldn't move. The room felt hot and heavy, and she ached to climb onto his lap, to hold his face between her hands and kiss him until she forgot how to breathe, to make a fortress of his arms that nothing could breach. And she wanted to shake him for worrying her and making her angry, because it was costing them precious moments from a dwindling supply.

He raised his hand toward her and broke the spell. She stepped back, looking away as she tucked the tail of the bandage roll in so it wouldn't unravel. If she caved first, he'd continue being reckless, and they had enough to fear without Dante acting as his own worst enemy.

"I got you something," he said gruffly. "I can't be with you every second, and I don't want you defenseless."

"I'm not *defenseless*. Just because I don't kill everyone I touch doesn't mean I can't."

"Sure, sure," he said, a little too placating. "But you should be armed at all times."

"Shall I strap a sword on my back? Slip a crossbow in my pocket?" She patted her overfull bag. "Not much room for weaponry."

He handed her a small package and watched her face as she unwrapped it—a leather sheath and a slim silver blade with carefully wrought filigree along the handle.

"Oh, it's beautiful," she breathed. From Dante, a sharp weapon meant more than any jewels or love letter could.

"It's light, smaller than mine. Should fit your hand better. Test the grip."

She flipped it like he'd taught her, catching it neatly. "Oh, yes. I like this very much."

"The strap should fit your leg. I had to estimate, but I think I got pretty close." His smile was smug but earned. He'd certainly had opportunities to measure her thighs with his hands.

Alessa pulled up her nightgown and extended her leg, but she needed two hands to fasten the strap, and the hem kept tumbling back down, blocking her view. She glanced up to find Dante watching her intently. Very intently.

"Give me a hand?" she asked.

Dante knelt before her. The metal hilt was cool, his hand hot behind it. Trapping his lip with his teeth, he took his time fastening the leather strap and checking the fit.

"What do you think?" She pointed her toe, hiding a smile. "Tight enough?"

Sitting back on his heels, Dante blew out a long breath.

"Are you all right?"

He just stared. "I need a minute."

Oh. She traced the leather band with a fingertip. "The addition of knives seems to have dramatically improved my appeal. Maybe I should get a matching set, one for each leg."

He rubbed his chin. "I might not survive. This is hard enough."

She opened her mouth.

"No." He raised a finger in warning. "Don't ruin this for me."

"Me?" Alessa touched her chest. "I was only going to ask how hard it is."

"You're ruining it." He cast a pleading look at the ceiling. "The most beautiful thing I've ever seen, and you are *ruining* it."

"I'm merely concerned for your well-being."

"Nope. Not doing this." Dante stood, gaze still fixed on her dagger-clad thigh. "Just let me have this."

"You look a bit dazed. Head rush? All the blood going elsewhere?"

He sucked his teeth. "And you look *so* innocent."

"Did I really ruin your fantasy?" she said, running a finger over her bare thigh as she sauntered toward him. The heat in his gaze said she hadn't ruined a thing. "I still think two would be better."

"Luce mia, I'll buy you as many weapons as you can strap to your body. A dozen. Two dozen. One for each thigh, ankle, hip . . ." Grazing her body, he paused at each place a clever fighter could conceal a weapon. "One here." A finger slipped over the valley between her breasts. "Another here, at the small of your back."

Her breath came faster. "How much time have you spent thinking about this?"

Dante closed his eyes for a long moment. "*So* much time."

"Makes you want to kiss me, doesn't it?"

Dante stepped back. "Makes me want a lot of things, but *I* have self-control."

Dammit. She'd been so sure she had him, too.

She whirled away with a huff. "Get out of those wet clothes before you come near the bed. I'm not sleeping on a damp mattress."

She took her time rummaging through her bag as Dante shed his shirt, then trousers . . .

Why wasn't he putting clothes on? Had he given up already? She shook out a nightgown as though she really, *really* cared about wrinkles.

She couldn't resist looking. His face blandly innocent, Dante stood an arm's length away wearing nothing but a smile.

"My eyes are up here," he said.

She jerked her gaze up. "You're doing this on purpose."

"Yup." He leaned in. "I'm testing your self-control. How long do you think you'll last?"

Heat climbed her neck. "As long as it takes."

Taking her hand, he brushed his lips against the inside of her wrist. "This doesn't count."

Her traitorous body disagreed. "Cheater."

The heat between them grew, but Dante didn't blink. Or reach for his clothing.

Two could play this game. "Shall I join you in this new lifestyle choice?" With a haughty glare, she tugged her nightgown down and let it fall to the floor. She left the knife strapped on.

Dante swallowed. Maintaining eye contact, she shimmied out of her undergarments. "So freeing. Thank you for choosing a holster that doesn't require clothing."

Dante's gaze, hot and heavy-lidded, traced over her at an

excruciatingly slow pace, and she fought the urge to cross her arms and legs as every nerve in her body lit up. There was a fire inside her. A furnace. The whole world was aflame. This was *not* going as she'd planned *at all.*

Dante leaned, a mere sway toward her, then caught himself, dragging a hand through his hair with a low "*Fuck.*"

Alessa turned to hide her triumphant smile and give him the best possible view as she bent—slowly—to retrieve her nightgown. "Shall we call round one a tie?"

"*No.*" Dante roughly pulled on his clothes, muttering in the old language. "Claim your victory. Round one is yours."

She wiggled into her nightgown. "If it makes you feel better, I would've pounced if I wasn't so annoyed at you."

Dante exhaled. "Nope. That does *not* make me feel better."

Alessa woke a few hours later feeling . . . off.

She shivered. Frowned. She wasn't cold. She was quite warm, actually, but her skin tingled with sensitivity like it did in the hour before a fever struck, and her head almost hurt, like holding a headache at arm's length.

Dante groaned from an armchair in front of the fire. *His* discomfort, not hers. That's what she'd sensed. Once again, someone else was in her head.

"What's wrong?" she said, throwing back the covers.

"I can't stop shivering." His eyes were glassy, his cheeks flushed.

"Do you need a blanket?"

"I have one. It's not working." The room was stuffy and warm, but his body shuddered.

"Let me check your arm." If his injury had become infected . . . A surge of fear propelled her out of bed. Dante began unwrapping it before she reached him, but the skin around the sutures was a healthy pink, with no streaks or discoloration.

They exhaled in unison, and Dante's breath turned into a cough. He blinked, startled. "I think my lungs are busted."

She hovered a hand over his forehead. "You're warm."

"Get Adrick. He'll know what poison could cause—"

"You haven't been *poisoned*. You're sick."

He looked deeply affronted. "I don't *get* sick."

"As a ghiotte, maybe not. But you do now." She gave him an apologetic smile.

Dante pulled away. "*Or* it could be *poison*."

Alessa inhaled through her nose, silently asking Dea to grant her patience. "Tell me your symptoms."

"My chest is heavy, my head feels fuzzy, and my skin hurts."

"Sounds like a cold."

He frowned. "I've seen you with a cold and you did *not* feel like this."

Alessa rolled her eyes, glared, then rolled them again for emphasis. "Oh, *no*, of *course* not. Your affliction must be much worse because you're a big strong man and I'm a delicate flower."

"I wasn't—" A coughing fit cut him off. "I don't have time to be sick."

"I admire your determination, but human bodies don't care what we have planned. Maybe next time you'll think before running around during a thunderstorm. It's probably not serious, but you have a slight fever."

Dante crossed his arms. "If I had a fever, I'd feel *hot*. I'm not hot, I'm *cold*."

Alessa sighed again. "Incorrect. When you have a *fever*—as

you do—your body temperature goes up, which makes everything else feel colder in comparison. If you'd ever *been* sick, you'd know that. You'll feel better after some rest."

"Or die in my sleep from the *poison*."

It took immense self-control not to roll her eyes again. "The stable master said we can't take the horses until the storm passes anyway, so get comfortable."

"I still think it's poison."

"And you're still wrong," she called over her shoulder. "I'll go ask for tea and see if they have a hot-water bottle."

"How will *that* help if I'm hot already?" he muttered.

He continued to grouse when she returned to mix up a hot toddy with lemon, spices, and a dash of whiskey.

He grumbled about how little whiskey there was, glared when she told him to drink it anyway, and if it was possible to swallow in an annoyed manner, he'd perfected it. The man endured grievous bodily injury without complaint, but *this* discomfort apparently wounded him on some deep moral level he could not tolerate.

"Why am I cold *and* sweaty?" he grumbled.

"I already explained this. I'll get you a new shirt." She crossed her arms as he pulled the blanket tighter. "Take *off* your clothes."

He gave her a droll look. "I don't like you saying that with *quite* that tone."

"Fine. Be sweaty, then."

Dante flung the blanket off to remove his shirt, his every movement—even the shivers—radiating grumpiness.

When he reached for a book, she swiped it from his hand. "No reading. You need rest."

Dante rolled over with a flounce of blankets. *Men*. Honestly.

An hour later, Dante stared at the ceiling, too miserable to sleep. Somehow, the sheets hurt his skin and he could feel the rain on the roof.

Alessa walked over, the line of her mouth softening as she looked down at him. "You look a little better. You'll probably be back to yourself by tomorrow."

She tucked the sheets around his chest, her gaze slipping away instead of lingering.

"The first time you saw me shirtless, you forgot how to talk," he muttered. "Now you can't even look at me?"

Why had he said that?

"Because I don't like seeing you sick or hurt. And even if I *did* temporarily find you less than irresistible, you're more to me than muscles, you know."

He laughed, soft and bitter. "I can't kiss you. Can't protect you. What use am I?"

"Don't be ridiculous. You're not my bodyguard anymore, and you're more than just a body, anyway. Although it's a damn fine one, and I'd appreciate you keeping it in one piece until I can get my money's worth." Alessa sat on the edge of the bed and rested the back of her hand against his forehead for a moment.

It *was* kind of nice, being taken care of, but even as he yearned to let go and lean into her tenderness, something wouldn't let him.

He'd never needed that kind of thing, even as a child. Ghiotte didn't get ill, and his youthful injuries had healed so fast his mother didn't have to tend to them. Then his parents had been gone and there'd been no one to worry about him as he bled on cold floors after fights, biting his tongue while his bones knit together, hiding like an animal so no one would sense a moment of vulnerability and go in for the kill.

If there was one thing the world had taught him, it was that baring your jugular was as good as asking someone to bite down.

Alessa studied his face. "I'm sorry I've been fussing so much, but I worry about you."

"Don't." He meant to sound firm, reassuring, but it came out snappish instead.

Instead of looking hurt, Alessa made a rude noise. "Oh, right, like I can just stop caring. Dante, please. I love you, and that means I will inevitably worry about you at times."

He scowled. "I hate this."

"Being sick isn't supposed to be fun."

"Not that. Being like *this*. Needing—" He clamped his mouth shut.

Alessa's mouth tightened. "Me? You hate needing me?"

"No. I mean . . ." *Yes*. But not the way she meant.

"You've taken care of me. Why is this any different?"

Because it sent him spiraling into the dark days after Divorando. Because it made his chest ache in a way he couldn't explain.

He stared at a knot in the ceiling. "Forget it."

She'd fallen in love with a guy who was strong and whole, who could protect her without hesitation. Not *this guy*. Whining, broken, pathetic. Heat smoldered in his throat. "You think I'm weak."

She brushed a sweaty curl from his forehead. "Taking care

of yourself isn't *weakness*, and avoiding danger doesn't make you a coward. Even if it did, I'd rather have you alive and cautious than brave and dead."

She smoothed the covers over his chest again, stopping to rest her hand over his heart. "I understand that you've lost something. Something integral to who you thought you were. And it's eating you up. But you're still *here*, and you don't have to be invincible."

His heart thumped too fast, too hard, as though every beat was an act of defiance. For a moment, he imagined her reaching through his ribs to cradle it in her hands, soothing its frenzy. Maybe it, too, couldn't forget the time it had stopped.

"I think maybe that's what love is," she said.

He frowned, confused at the change in subject. "What?"

"Letting yourself be vulnerable. It takes courage to love someone and to be loved, knowing there's a chance you could lose them, or cause them pain if they lost you. But it's worth the risk to love anyway."

The ache grew.

If only he could wrap her love around him like a blanket, to warm the coldest parts of his soul.

If only he could believe that love was enough to protect them both.

"That's the difference between us," he said, barely above a whisper. "You're afraid you *might* lose someone you love, and I don't know any other way it can end."

Fourteen

DAYS UNTIL THE ECLIPSE: 25

Dante woke to blazing sunlight and an empty room. His mouth was dry and his stomach hollow, but otherwise, he felt fine. Until he remembered the night before.

Che figura di merda. The things he'd said out loud... Someone should have warned him that fever humbled a man faster than a bottle of whiskey.

He found his team seated in wooden chairs in the yard behind the inn, studying their maps. Conversation stopped abruptly when Dante walked up, but they had the decency to not ask how he was feeling.

In the aftermath of rain, the landscape was more vivid, the greenery greener and the sky bluer. It would have been a great day to set off on a quest if they knew where to go.

Dante rested a hand on the back of Alessa's chair. "We can't just sit around here waiting for another clue. We'll have to visit the other settlements, see if they know anything about this city Alessa heard about. No one's seen the girl who mentioned it since then?"

Alessa shook her head. "Not since that first day, and no one else seems to know anything about it. The stablemaster gave us the rundown on the available horses, though. I can show you our options."

Her tenderness from the night before was gone, but the sharp edge of annoyance was, too. He'd already humiliated himself. Might as well accept defeat and—he grimaced—*apologize.*

"What are you wearing?" he asked as they walked toward the stables. She looked good—she looked good in everything—but the leather contraption over her blouse reminded him of a prison for her breasts. They couldn't be happy.

Alessa gave an indignant huff. "A vest. I think it makes me look tough."

"No, I mean, I *like* it. Just looks restrictive."

"It's *supportive.*" She did a little hop. "See? No bouncing."

"Some things shouldn't be caged," he grumbled. He'd have a much harder time getting through all that if she ever let him touch her again. "Let me get that."

Alessa flicked her braid over her shoulder and reached for the barn door. "I can do it."

"I *know* you can. I'm being chivalrous." He held the door open and followed her into the barn. The air inside was warm and sweet with leather and hay.

Alessa gestured at the row of animals whinnying softly in their stalls. "The black one is fast but known for biting; the gray is slower but reliable; and the one in the middle is easily spooked. Choose your mount."

Dante slid an arm around her waist.

"*Not* one of the options," she said.

Dante craned his neck to see over the nearest stall. "That one. Done."

She turned in his arms to face him. "Is this you admitting defeat?"

"Ay, luce mia. I'm waving the white flag."

"Is it *really* so hard to promise you'll try not to get hurt?"

"Yes, actually, but I'd slay a god to kiss you again, so I *guess* I can handle losing a bet."

She ducked his kiss with a smile. "We still need a strategy so I don't hurt you."

"You're overthinking it," he said. "We just need to get back on the horse."

"That's it!" Alessa said triumphantly. "It's like riding a horse."

His eyes narrowed. "Is this one of your dirty metaphors?"

Her laugh was warm against his neck. "*I* am not the horse. My *power* is the horse. When you first met me, the horse did whatever she wanted and trampled anyone who came too close. But we tamed her, and now she usually behaves as long as I keep a hand on the reins."

"Ah . . ." Dante cocked his head. "Where is this going?"

"I'm not good at kissing and riding a horse at the same time. I get distracted, the reins slip through my fingers, and she bolts every time. Until I train her better or you get worse at kissing, I'm not sure how to keep her in the stables, but we tamed her once and we can do it again."

He sucked in a breath. "That might be your best metaphor yet. Or worst. So if you're the rider and your power is the horse, what am I?"

She frowned in thought. "The cute farm boy who distracted me so I got thrown off?"

"And I got kicked?"

"Something like that."

He blew out a breath. "You need a better horse."

Back outside, Adrick and Kaleb were sweating around the firepit, attempting to light cigars while the innkeeper arranged extra wood into a neat pile.

"Want one?" Adrick asked.

"I don't put things in my mouth that smell like burnt feet," Dante said, settling into one of the wooden chairs.

"Ah, no, that's our fault," said the innkeeper, pointing to a plume of smoke on the horizon. "Boys nearly took out the whole town last time they tried to burn out the burrows. No one's offering to dig them up and see if it works, but it can't hurt."

Alessa shuddered. "I hadn't realized the scarabei burrowed so close to the settlements."

The man looked smug as he turned to leave. "You get accustomed to it."

Saida backed toward the inn after him. "Ciro, would you like to get tea with me? Inside?"

"Wait for me," said Kamaria. "I hate tea, but it smells better than roasted demons."

Alessa waved in front of her face as Kaleb blew out a plume of cigar smoke. "I can't decide which smells worse. Could you two move a bit farther away?"

Kaleb and Adrick walked off, puffing like chimneys, and she perched on the arm of Dante's chair. Her satchel slipped off her shoulder and thumped into his lap with too much force for his liking.

"What's in this thing?" He reached in and withdrew an ornate book.

Alessa snatched it back. "You're probably halfway fluent with another language already and I need to catch up. Why don't you read to me? Maybe I'll learn something by listening."

Dante squinted. "Isn't that usually how people learn languages?" He couldn't translate her signed response, but the vigorous hand motion *felt* rude. "Point taken. How about *you* read, and I'll help if you get stuck."

"You just want to laugh at my pronunciation."

"I won't laugh. Promise." A knot of tension and guilt unraveled in his chest at her teasing smile as she made a show of opening the book.

"Ti troverò." She paused, to wait for his critique, he assumed.

He kissed her hair instead. "I like hearing the old language in your mouth."

She read on, mispronouncing every other word in a sultry purr that stirred up a confusing mix of lust and righteous indignation, but she was warm and soft in his lap so he could forgive the grievous crimes being committed to his mother tongue.

"At least *try* to figure it out," he said when she finished and looked to him for clarity. "'Cuore' is 'heart.' You know that one."

"Water . . . looking for something." She shook her head. "That's all I've got."

"Relatable. Hand it over. Here:

My heart is broken, but my body whole,
I will find you where the tempests rage and the roads are
paved with water,
Where bridges never crumble and bodies never break,
And my heart, at last, shall mend to match.

Alessa turned a page and skimmed the next translation. "It seems to be a theme."

Dante peered over her shoulder. Loss, loneliness, searching for the unbroken, drowning streets.

Alessa sat up, drawing a wince from Dante as she leaned forward to shuffle through the abandoned stack of maps until she found one depicting islands off a sliver of Continent. "Look. The coastline here matches this part on the far side of the peninsula. It might be submerged now, but this region and the nearby islands once had networks of canals."

Canals. Dante inhaled. "Boats, not ships."

They knew where to find the ghiotte.

Fifteen

Dante would have continued riding through the night, but the horse pulling their luggage looked ready to keel over by the time evening fell, so when he spotted a river ahead, he called out for them to set up camp for the night and dismounted. He gripped Alessa's waist as she swung a leg over her mount with a grunt of pain, and he eased her the rest of the way down. She leaned back into him with a soft sigh of contentment, and despite saving her life more than once, he wasn't sure he'd ever felt like more of a hero.

"My bottom hurts," she said.

"Wish I could help," Dante said with a wry smile. "But I'm pretty sure we'd offend the rest of the group if I massaged that right now."

As they set up camp, Kaleb walked to the edge of the field to kick dirt over a hollow depression in the ground. "Doesn't it creep anyone else out? Scarabei are *right* there."

"It does, yes." Saida's smile was strained. "Thank you *so much* for reminding us."

Kamaria gathered sticks while Kaleb fired a bolt of lightning with a crackling noise from his mouth, like a kid playing pretend on the playground.

"Jolting hibernating scarabei with electricity?" Kamaria said. "*That* can't end badly."

"We're standing on our sworn enemies!" Kaleb shouted. "The sleeping demons who crave our flesh! The infantile insects who will rise to devour humanity! We should stab them or set them on fire or *something*!"

Kamaria kicked a clod of dirt at him. "Crollo wouldn't make it *that* easy. Even if you wiped out an entire field of them, it would barely make a dent for the next Divorando."

"Anyone care for a game of cards?" Adrick pulled a deck from his shirt pocket. "We can entertain ourselves while Kaleb gets eaten by prematurely roused scarabei."

"Ha!" Kaleb barked. "They can't kill me. I've already survived one Armageddon."

"Like a cockroach," Adrick said cheerfully.

Ciro returned, carrying his horse's tack. The cat trotted out from the shadows to rub Dante's leg but was quickly distracted by a cricket. Cats were enigmatic by nature, but this one seemed oddly hell-bent on keeping up with them when it could be chasing mice in a cozy barn somewhere instead.

Kamaria snapped her fingers, and blue flames blossomed within the hastily arranged circle of stones. "Hey, Dante, I'm feeling a bit underprepared for bloodthirsty marauders and hidden cities of gods-blessed warriors. Can you give us a ghiotte crash course or something?"

Dante didn't look up from unloading bedrolls. "I only knew mine and one other family."

"Literally any information would help," said Kamaria.

"We're all expecting an indeterminate number of *yous,* and that's a little intimidating."

"Don't expect a warm welcome. We've been hunted for centuries, warned that trusting anyone with our secret can put us all in danger."

"They'll welcome *you,* though, right?" Saida said.

"Every ghiotte I knew is dead, and I have no way to prove I ever was one of them. I doubt they'll be too excited to meet me."

Alessa was watching his face, but he didn't meet her eye. She kept knocking down the walls he'd built, and he needed them fortified now, not weakened.

"I'm trained in diplomacy," Ciro said. "I'd be honored to make our initial overtures."

Dante scowled. "Let me do the talking. We'll need your powers eventually but keep your identities quiet at first. Your lot were treated as heroes while we were painted as villains. There's bound to be bad blood."

"Aw, man," Kaleb grumbled. "I get all itchy when I don't use my powers every day."

"I thought that was just me," Saida said.

"At least you can let off a breeze without making anyone suspicious. People tend to notice if you start sparking."

Kamaria put the finishing touches on the campfire. "Then let's get our twitches out now. I had an idea I wanted to try, anyway."

Ciro sat on a large rock across from Dante as they left. "They all seem to work equally well together. It never occurred to me to try and use my powers with anyone but Diwata."

Dante poked at a pan of sausages. "Diwata said she could see people's auras or the color of their powers or something. Can you do that, too?"

Ciro brushed at a speck of dirt on his tunic. "Diwata is a pure soul and I adore her for it, but we don't always see the world the same way."

The cat's hunt for a cricket ended in a crunch and Ciro snatched his hand away as the animal found a new target. "Fickle creature, I admire your independence, but you cannot have my blood."

Kaleb furiously dusted himself off after Alessa and Saida's attempt to create a wind funnel and make him fly only knocked him over.

Stars blossomed in Alessa's vision, and she dropped Saida's hand abruptly.

One swallow. Another.

"Are you alright?" Saida asked.

She waved off Saida's concern, mumbling about water, and turned back toward the gleam of the campfire. The darkness gave her time to hide how she needed to blink rapidly to keep from fainting. But the night concealed the ground ahead of her, too.

Her foot caught on a stone, and she pitched forward, landing on her hands and knees.

The ground in front of her face was too dark. Too empty. She reached, grasping for the grass that should have been there but found empty air instead. Another burrow. She squinted into the darkness but couldn't make out a smooth curve at the bottom. The edges of the hole weren't sloped where the earth had settled above something, but crumbled. As though something had already clawed its way out.

Heart in her throat, she scrambled to her feet and walked faster toward the light.

Of course the scarabei had left behind empty burrows, too. Thousands had attacked Saverio during the last Divorando. They had to have come from somewhere.

Ciro stood motionless by the outskirts of their campsite, staring up at the night sky. At his heels, Fiore's eyes gleamed in the dark.

Alessa spoke quietly to avoid startling them. "Does it look very different where you're from?" Ciro's visible confusion had her second-guessing her astronomy coursework. "Doesn't the Southern Hemisphere have a different skyscape?"

"Ah, yes." He gave an embarrassed laugh. "Apologies. I struggle to focus these days."

Alessa smiled with more than a touch of irony. "I *always* struggle to focus."

"Our healers called it disassociation," Ciro said. "A protective detachment response to the trauma of war."

That *would* account for Ciro's lapses. It couldn't, however, explain how she sensed people's thoughts and feelings.

She swallowed. "You and Diwata didn't touch a scarabeo during Divorando, by any chance, did you?"

Ciro's lip curled. "Gods, no. Did *you*?"

"We were losing." Her hands fluttered at her side. "Dante was hurt and our troops were in disarray. I . . . I took a chance and used its power."

"What happened?"

"For a moment I was in everyone's mind at once, seeing the battle from every direction. I could make the entire army function as a collective by willing it to do so." She grimaced. "That may have been a mistake."

Ciro composed himself. "Well, I didn't go near any of them,

and I'm still a bit of a mess, so I'd say we're both just dealing with run-of-the-mill postwar trauma."

They both laughed, with effort.

Dante was arranging two bedrolls apart from the rest, on the other side of a copse of trees, and he stood when she neared. "You okay? You look pale."

"I'm a bit parched. Could you—"

He was already handing her his canteen, eying her as though she might keel over, which was fair enough. "Finish it and come lie down."

After overseeing her as she got into her own bedroll, he lay beside her, propped on one elbow to watch her face. He was stubborn as a mule about looking out for himself, but he hovered like a broody hen if she showed the slightest sign of discomfort.

They snuggled up together, as close as they could get in separate bedrolls.

Serenaded by his breathing as he slipped into sleep, she gazed up at the stars. It was so lovely to lay beneath the open sky with him that she didn't want to miss it by sleeping, and her eyelids grew heavy long before she let them close.

She was roused by darkness seared with fiery monstrosities and smoke as thick as water. A dream. But she was awake.

Dante twitched beside her.

Not *her* dream or her vision. *His.*

The spike of fear was all hers.

A faint hissing coalesced into a garbled whisper she felt she should understand but couldn't. Thoughts? Dante's thoughts? No. He could never sound that sinister. Not to her.

The scarebei? Impossible. Every grown scarabeo was dead, defeated by her hand or her army during Divorando. The only demons left were the undeveloped offspring slumbering below the dirt.

Dante mumbled something unintelligible. He'd been facing these visions for months, alone, while she'd brushed them off and dismissed his fears. She had no right to shut them out. Trembling, she let the spectacle play across her mind. Eyes—thousands of eyes, blank and unseeing—and a piazza flooded with blood. Trapped. Suffocating.

Dante sat up with a gasp, his outline a patch of darkness denser than the rest.

"I'm here," she whispered. His hand closed over hers, callouses rough against her bare skin. Holding her power in check, she held tight. He needed her. She wouldn't—*couldn't*—add pain to his fear. "It's all right. You're not alone."

Beyond the hills, the sky glowed with early dawn, but even the first glimpse of daylight couldn't banish the sense of something sinister watching. And waiting.

Sixteen

DAYS UNTIL THE ECLIPSE: 24

The sun rose over a wagon in shambles. Their supplies were torn apart and scattered across the field, rations ripped open and missing, leftover bits smashed into the dirt.

Wild animals. That was the collective verdict.

Alessa wasn't so sure. Exhaustion might've explained why she'd almost fainted the night before, but not Dante's visions playing inside her head.

Something was *wrong* with her. For all she knew, *she* might have sabotaged their supplies.

Adrick returned from a visit to the bushes and announced that their horses were gone. The ropes had been cut.

Still in his bedroll, Kaleb tried to stand and fell, flopping like a fish on land. "Who was on watch?"

Everyone jumped to defend their innocence, but Dante cut off the finger pointing. "Enough. It's done. Wild animals can't cut ropes, and if someone wants to slow us down, that means we're getting close."

While their party scavenged for scraps, Alessa crept across

the field toward the exhumed burrow. In the daylight, it was rather innocuous. A roughly circular ditch that could've been overturned days, weeks, or months ago.

She squatted to lay her hand on the dirt.

A whisper, the faintest hum of consciousness.

She snatched her hand back and hurried away.

Carrying their remaining supplies, they made their way on foot, considerably slower than before.

By midday, Alessa was aching, sweaty, and her feet throbbed. Which took the edge off her nerves, at least.

They pushed on through the afternoon, with Saida searching for every glimmer of optimism, Kamaria cracking jokes, and Ciro gazing at the scenery like they were on a sightseeing expedition. Dante never stopped scanning their surroundings, his thumbs brushing the hilts of his daggers.

He might not admit to being nervous about finding the ghiotte, but *she* was. One Dante was the perfect number. An entire city of people like him sounded extremely daunting.

"Ruins ahead," Dante called out. "We can stop there for the night."

Alessa blinked and he was standing in front of her, frowning with concern.

"I'm sorry, what did you say?" Alessa asked. She had no memory of him speaking. Or of crossing the last stretch of land. An hour had skipped right past.

"I didn't say anything," Dante said. "But you've been staring at nothing for longer than usual."

She laughed to cover up her confusion.

They reached the ruins at sunset. An entire crumbling city climbed the hillside, the outermost structures ready to collapse at a strong wind.

"Creepy," Kamaria whispered.

"My people believe spirits are content to walk among us as long as we intend them no harm," Ciro said in a cool voice.

"I would *like* to believe that," Saida said with a shiver.

"We're not here to mess with you," Kaleb said loudly.

Adrick took a big step away. "Kindly move away from the group before summoning vengeful spirits."

"I'm not scared of ghosts." Kaleb yelped as a furry projectile darted past his feet, and Saida burst out laughing.

Kamaria let go of the bedroll with their luggage on it. "Anyone have water?"

"We'll find some," Dante said.

"I gotta piss," Kaleb announced.

"Thanks for sharing," Adrick said. "Actually, wait; so do I."

The boys went down one alley while Saida and Kamaria began hunting for firewood, and Dante took Alessa with him to search for potable water.

The back of his hand brushed hers with every step as they made their way through the ancient city, chasing the last rays of sunlight.

The structures grew sturdier, more intact as they got farther in, and dusk softened the caved-in roofs enough to picture the city it had once been.

She could almost pretend she was just a regular girl strolling the cobblestones with a handsome boy at sunset, the playful easy flirtation they'd never had the fortune to experience. Perhaps, in a future without the constant specter of Divorando, couples could stay out late, fearing only a scolding from protective parents, not a return of the monsters.

"Do you think people would ever move back here?" she asked.

Dante glanced around. "If Crollo ever knocks it off, it could be a nice place to live."

The land was flatter than Saverio's, the ruins more sprawling than the city perched on those steep shores, but she could smell water nearby. It must have been a busy port at one point.

"My Nonna and I used to play pretend as innkeepers in the beforetimes," Alessa said with a smile. "A rustic establishment where everyone was welcome, and no one was ever lonely, and travelers told stories about faraway lands. Maybe that will be possible again someday."

She could picture the buildings restored, windowsills blooming with flowers, and cobbled streets ringing with voices. If the battle to come was the gods' last stand, she would fight for more than Saverio. She would fight for the chance to bring back that world, to rebuild at last.

Ahead, mist gathered on a river cutting through the city. They found a patch of grassy bank, and Alessa pulled off her boots to wade in, capping one canteen and tossing it to Dante before filling the next.

Water spritzed her back.

"Excuse me," she said, planting her hands on her hips. "We are not *bathing*."

His smile was unrepentant as he splashed her again.

She had no choice, really. Dante ducked, laughing, as the contents of her last canteen drenched his shirt.

She sloshed back to him, bare feet slipping on the stones, and reached out a hand that he eyed warily.

"I won't pull you in because I don't want you catching

another cold," she said, getting a good grip before taking another step. Although, the contours of his chest were outlined quite nicely by wet fabric. If she *were* to pull him in, the complete view might be worth it.

Dante arched a brow. "And *what* was that thought?"

She yanked her hand away. "Oh, gods, do you get a jolt every time? How am I supposed to maintain any air of mystery if you can tell when I'm mentally undressing you?"

Dante's eyes twinkled with mirth. "I could always tell."

She gasped. "*Liar.*"

"Even when you couldn't stand me, you got all pink every time I got close to you. Why do you think I did it so much?"

"Well, I'd *hoped* it was because you liked being near me."

Dante flashed a crooked smile. "I figured that out later."

Alessa mulled that over as she put her boots on. "If you knew all along, why did you keep insisting I didn't want you?"

"I knew you *wanted* me, I just didn't think you wanted *me*."

"Is this a riddle?" she said, looking up from lacing her boots. "Because I don't get it."

"You'd been alone for years. I was there. I didn't let it go to my head." He stepped close and his gaze dropped to her mouth. He, too, must have realized they were alone for the first time since he'd promised to be careful and she'd promised kisses in return.

Hands on the reins, she reminded herself. *Magical "horse" in the stable. Doors locked.*

He was patient, giving her time to categorize each sensation, so distinct from those she experienced while she was trying to use her powers: a brush of lips *instead of a firm hand grip;* the sweet build of warmth, *not the crackle of lightning or rush of wind.* Bit by bit, she untangled the threads of wanting.

"Mi manca il tuo tocco," she murmured.

Dante pulled back to look at her. "Impressive. You *almost* emphasized the right syllables."

She couldn't help a triumphant smile as he bent to kiss her again. "I've been practicing."

"With who?"

"Not *kissing*. Wait, you're distracting me." It was impossible to remember conjugations while he trailed kisses down her neck. "Ho una fantasia. La vuoi sentire?"

He nipped her ear. "I *absolutely* want to hear your fantasy. Or you could show me."

She reined in her power with a mental *Whoa there*. "We're *definitely* not ready for that, but I looked up some words, and I bet you can figure out the rest."

A few carefully chosen vocabulary words, and he dropped his head to her shoulder with a laughing groan. "Just let me *try*. If it kills me, it'll be worth it."

A scream rent the air.

Dante spun, shielding her. "Stay behind me."

Seventeen

Alessa's heart pounded in her ears as they wove through the narrow streets, canteens thumping against her side with every step.

Dante rounded a corner and stopped so abruptly she nearly slammed into his back. Raising a finger to warn her to be silent, he drew a dagger with his other hand.

Ciro and Saida stood in the dark intersection ahead, hands in the air, confronted by a knife-wielding woman. From their vantage point, the only detail Alessa could make out was a long dark braid.

"I should have slit your throats instead of freeing your horses," the girl said.

That voice. It was the girl from the pub, who had warned them not to seek the drowning city. And that meant—

Alessa jumped back as the red-haired boy, inexplicably bare-chested, leapt from the shadows and tackled Dante. They crashed to the ground in a tangle of fists and kicks.

Wrenching himself free, Dante sliced his opponent's chest.

The boy glanced down and laughed as the trickle of blood stopped almost immediately and the cut healed itself.

Ghiotte. The unspoken word echoed in the silence.

Kaleb barelled into the fray, but the redhead knocked him to the ground.

"Wait!" Dante said. "Listen—"

The girl growled and swung her knife.

Dante was bigger and stronger, but she was fast—wickedly fast—and *he* wasn't fighting to kill. His maneuvers were evasive, defensive, not meant to injure.

The girl had different plans.

Dante knocked her feet out from under her, but the girl was back up in a heartbeat, murderous intent in her every movement. As she stalked toward him, Dante did the one thing Alessa never expected.

He dropped his blades.

Everyone except the girl froze as they clattered to the stone.

Palms empty, Dante held his hands up. "Please. Hear me out."

This was what they had come for. These were the allies they needed, if anyone survived long enough to explain.

Alessa stifled a scream as the girl thrust her knife toward Dante's throat, stopping just before she broke the skin. With her blade pressed against his neck, they stared each other down.

The clouds parted, bathing the street with thin moonlight, and something flickered across the girl's expression. Doubt? Fear?

She lowered her knife and stumbled back.

"Gabe?"

• • •

Dante's world turned inside out.

Talia. She had the same straight hair, so black it was almost blue, in one braid instead of two, and the exact crescent-shaped freckle below her left eye—but he still wouldn't have recognized her if not for how she said his name, so rushed she almost dropped the final consonant. Always rushed. Always shouting at him to run faster, climb higher.

Dante blinked a few times, just in case he was imagining it all.

"I thought you were dead." She sounded angry, like he'd chosen to let her think so. "Everything was burned. Your house. Your—"

"A little help here?" Kaleb hollered.

"Call off your guy, will you?" Dante said. Kaleb might not resist the temptation to zap for much longer.

"Stand down!" Talia yelled. "He's one of us."

The redhead sucked his teeth. "Prove it."

Talia pointed her knife at him. "I say he is, so he *is*!"

That was the Talia he remembered. The girl who cackled as she jumped out of trees to tackle him and stuffed raw onions in his pillowcase. Whom his mother affectionately called "feral" but only because she didn't know how wild her own son could be.

"You've been alive, on Saverio all this time?" Talia asked.

It wasn't meant as a two-part question, so Dante only answered the easy half. "I moved around a lot."

Talia flicked a glance at his companions. "Who are *they*?"

"Allies," he said. "They know about us. No one's hunting ghiotte anymore."

Talia snorted derisively. "Bullshit. No way people changed their minds that fast."

"Maybe not. But the official word is we're not the bad guys anymore."

"Is that why you're here? An official envoy to tell us we're *forgiven*?" She sneered. "Apology not accepted. You can tell Saverio where to shove it."

"No. That's not why. We need your help. *I* need your help."

"You came a long way for some *help*."

"Yeah, well, it's important."

Talia crossed her arms. "Then talk. Fast."

"It's . . . kind of a long story."

Talia exchanged a look with her companion, some unspoken cue that sent him climbing up the nearest building to look over the rooftops.

"Fog's rolling out," he called down. "If you want to make it tonight, we need to go now."

Talia tapped her knife against her palm. "Fine. We'll take you, but it's not up to us if you get to stay."

While they hastily repacked, Talia looked down at the cat pawing her boots. "You brought a pet?"

Dante hefted his pack over one shoulder. "Uninvited guest."

Ciro chuckled under his breath.

Alessa and the others followed at a safe distance as Talia led them toward the shore, where the mist grew thick as soup. Dante took the chance to size her up, categorizing everything he could about the stranger he used to know.

She was taller now. Obviously. She wasn't a kid anymore. Still tiny, though, and ferocious.

Of all the changes, her wariness snagged on his memories the most. She moved like a wraith, every sense on alert. Her mother had always been the cautious one, insisting they keep their heads down to protect their secret, while Talia rebelled, taking risks and laughing off injuries no matter who was around. Dante had even scolded her about it once, told her she'd get them all killed. After drawing blood a thousand times, the moment he'd taken her mother's side was the first time he ever felt like he'd *hurt* her. The only time he'd ever seen her cry.

Talia's redheaded companion fell into step beside Dante. "You grew up with Talia, huh?"

"Yeah." If the guy wanted more answers, he'd need to ask more questions.

"Where've you been all this time, then? Decided you were better as the mortals' pet?"

Dante gave him a cool smile. "Bought my own leash and everything."

Red snorted. "Hey, I gotta ask *some* questions. I'm Blaise, by the way."

Dante eyed his hair. Easy enough.

"Leave him alone," Talia said.

"Just getting to know our new brother." Blaise let go of his oar and smacked Dante on the shoulder a bit too hard for affection.

"*Not* our brother. Not yet. So shut it."

"Ouch. Tough love for an old buddy."

"No. Tough love for *you*, so you don't spill everything you've ever heard."

"Just giving him a heads-up. Everyone *loves* fresh meat. He'll need to sleep in the—"

"Blaise!" Talia shot him a look of warning.

"Sorry."

"That one's ours." Talia pointed at two shadows in the reeds ahead. Boats. "Ghiotte only. We'll flash a signal if the rest of you can come over."

Blaise picked his teeth with a short dagger. "If an hour passes and you don't see the signal, I suggest you start running."

"What if we get lost?" Kaleb said. "It's too foggy to see anything."

"That's the point," Talia said. "No one can find us unless we want them to. If you can't figure out how to row your damn boat there, you don't deserve to make it."

"This hostility is a little much," said Ciro.

"Oh, I'm *so sorry*." Talia's voice dripped with sarcasm. "Did we *invite* you here? Are you our *guests?*"

Ciro had the sense to shut up.

Talia stepped into the closest boat. "No one sets foot on Perduta without an explicit invitation. Do *not* get out unless you get one. Gabe . . . Dante—*whatever*—you're with us."

Alessa shot Dante a panicked look.

"It's okay," he mouthed back. To the ghiotte, he spoke out loud. "Give me a minute?" Turning his back to them, he lowered his voice. "All of you, wait for the signal and *stay* in the boat. Don't do anything that might provoke them."

The others nodded, but no one looked happy about it.

Alessa whispered, "Be careful."

Dante jerked a nod, the most he could risk. If someone he *knew* was this hostile, he could only imagine how the rest of the ghiotte would treat outsiders. Alessa would be safer if he kept their focus on *him*. He'd go first and figure out what they were getting themselves into.

Talia perched in the front of the boat like a queen while the boys rowed. Stroke by stroke, Dante brought his breathing in line with the push and pull of the paddles.

Talia polished her knife on her jacket, her eyes fixed on his face. "What *have* you been doing all this time?"

Dante's jaw worked. He'd been prepared to knock on the door of a walled fortress with a carefully worded "take us to your leader" speech, a redacted version of events for suspicious strangers. Not this. Not rehashing the last few years of his life for a living ghost from his past.

"Got stuck with a guy who was determined to *reform* me for a few years," he said. "Odd jobs and paid fights after that. Worked as a guard at the Cittadella for a while."

Talia's head snapped up. "*You* protected the *blessed?* Why?"

"It was a job," he said, trying not to sound defensive. "And I thought I might find clues in their library about where the banished had gone."

Talia's shoulders relaxed a fraction. "Is that how you found us?"

"Not exactly. What about you? Your mother said you were dead."

Talia's mouth tightened. "I bet she did. After what happened to your family, we figured we'd be next, so Papa and I planned our escape. *She* decided we weren't worth leaving Saverio for, so she stayed behind."

Dante flinched. "I'm sorry."

Talia glared. "Don't be. We're better off without her. The only people we can trust are our *own*."

She might not count him as one of those if she knew the truth, but he'd deal with that later. One move at a time.

"What happens when we get there?" he asked.

"You'll plead your case to our leaders."

"Elected?" They could be anything, from rich elites to religious pontiffs. He didn't have a great history with either.

"Hardly," said Talia. "We hold quarterly competitions, and the champions become head council."

Fighters. At least he knew that type.

"If the council decides you can stay, you're in. If not, you'll leave. Fast. Either way, they probably won't kill *you*."

"And my friends?"

"Convincing anyone to trust *them* is your job."

Ahead, a tall bridge framed an arch of dense fog, like a portal to another world. Beyond it, the silhouettes of buildings took shape through swirls of mist.

The hull of their boat nudged the stone edge of a large piazza.

"Good luck," Blaise said ominously as they stepped out.

The buildings were dark and empty, but the air hung heavy with silent observation from points unseen as they crossed the expanse toward the massive building at one end. The enormous torches within were as tall as a man, but the sheer enormity of the building made them as effective as matches flickering at the bottom of a dry well.

Figures were scattered throughout the crooked pews on either side of the wide aisle, more in the dark margins beyond and the balconies above. For years, Dante's captor had taunted him, saying that he was the last ghiotte. In the smoldering ruins of Talia's home, he'd believed it.

Now, something like grief wrapped in exultation stole his breath.

His people. At last.

Eighteen

Alessa stared after the boat as it vanished into the dark leaving only a broken strip of moonlight on the water.

Dante never trusted anyone, yet he seemed to think he could trust this girl he hadn't seen in years. Talia had been the one who said people who searched for the drowning city never returned, and she'd cut their horses loose as a warning not to follow. What had sounded like an ominous tall tale at the inn now seemed more like a threat. What if Dante had finally found a piece of his past, only to be betrayed again?

"Are we *sure* we need the ghiotte?" Saida asked. "We've done fine without them so far."

"Too late now. They have Dante." Kamaria eyed the boat. "Odds this is a trap?"

"Fifty-fifty?" Saida tapped her lip. "No, I'll go with forty-nine to fifty-one. I'm not giving up my title as the group optimist, thank you very much."

Alessa patted Saida's arm absently, as though by reassuring her, she could quell her own rising panic. If the signal didn't come, she wasn't going to run. Not without Dante. They came looking for battle partners, but she'd fight them all before leaving without him.

They rubbed their arms against the chill as the hour crept by.

"Anyone else see that?" Ciro pointed at a tiny flicker of light in the distance.

"Here goes nothing." Kamaria got in the boat with more grace than Kaleb, who grunted and scrambled, causing the boat to tip side to side.

Adrick and Kaleb picked up the oars, but Kaleb's paddles barely skimmed the surface and the boat began to drift in a lazy arc.

"Pull, don't push." Adrick leaned over to fix Kaleb's grip. "Like this."

"Hope everyone likes fish," Kamaria said. "Because we're going to be in this boat for the rest of our lives."

Alessa peered into the murky darkness. Like a mirage, a ghostly city began to emerge. The drip of water and splash of paddles was punctuated by the scurry of rodents.

Their route took them down a wide canal before veering into a smaller one off to the side. The single point of light felt less like a lighthouse and more like a lure, but they had no choice but to follow it into a maze of canals.

"Real fixer-upper," Kaleb grouched. "I was hoping the 'drowning' part was poetic license."

"Are my feet supposed to be this wet?" Kamaria asked in a hoarse whisper.

Saida blanched. "We're taking on water."

Alessa stifled a shriek as a furry blur ran over her feet and the cat leapt to shore.

"Does that count as *us* stepping foot on the island?" Kamaria asked. "Because that doesn't seem fair."

Kaleb stood, making the boat rock. "I'm not sitting here and waiting to drown."

"Sit down," Alessa said. "They told us to stay in the boat."

"Then they shouldn't have given us one with a hole in it," Kaleb retorted. "If they want me dead, they can kill me on land."

Kamaria flicked water at him from the end of her oar. "We still have our powers, thickhead. We're not defenseless."

"I am," Adrick said with cheerful resignation. "Put up a good fight, will you? I'll stay out of the way."

The narrow canal didn't look very deep, but unless they wanted to sacrifice their luggage and tread water, they had no choice.

"Fine, we'll get out," Alessa said. "Everyone stay close and no sudden moves."

Saida frantically shushed everyone as they grunted and whisper-shouted in a chaotic scramble of tossing bags and hauling each other out of the rapidly sinking rowboat.

Buildings loomed over them on all sides, broken windows leering like sightless eyes at their pathetic huddle as the canal swallowed the little boat, leaving only ripples to lap against the sides of the canal.

Adrick's throat bobbed. "Mood lighting's perfect for a deadly ambush. Maybe it wasn't the best idea to hand over Dante and our weaponry."

Alessa's new power had warned her about Diwata's attack, but she had no way to direct it and only sensed her friends' fear. Not very useful, this cursed gift that only told her what she already knew.

"Shall we break into teams?" Ciro deadpanned. "Split up or

stick together? What is the standard approach when it comes to facing an invisible army?"

"We've already broken one rule," Saida whispered. "I say we wait."

"They don't know our boat sank," Adrick said. "They're probably wondering what's taking us so long. We'll have to continue on foot."

He took a step forward, a light flashed, and a flaming arrow burst at his feet.

For the first time in his life, Dante wasn't feeling too confident about his odds.

"Looks like it's Nova's turn as chair," Talia said from the side of her mouth. "Could be worse. Don't let her get a rise out of you. Be respectful. And don't look Leo in the eye. He'll take anything as a challenge."

Eyes followed them as they strode down the aisle, but Dante kept his focus on the two ghiotte waiting at the end.

At the foot of the altar, Talia took a knee. "I present Gabriele Dante Lucente. Both of his parents were ghiotte. We grew up together."

The woman—Nova—had midnight black hair, chin length on one side, shaved on the other, with deep brown skin, and the most commanding presence he had ever seen. Leo, on the other hand, appeared to be in his mid-twenties, with noble features, tanned skin, and a mane of dark blond hair. He looked like trouble.

"You came alone?" Nova asked Dante.

Somehow he suspected she already knew he hadn't. "Six others. Not ghiotte."

"And what brings you here, Signor Lucente?

"I come on a mission. *Our* mission, given to us by Dea."

Leo rested his hands on his knees. "Saverians finally figured that out, eh?"

Dante met his gaze. "I did."

"And after all these centuries, Dea sent *you* as her messenger to ask if we'll return as Saverio's little army for the next Divorando?" Leo's derisive laugh was echoed by others. "No. Saverians are on their own, and I hope they suffer for it."

"Not Divorando," Dante said. "Something worse. At the end of this month, Crollo is sending an attack. Here. Something only ghiotte can defeat."

"And *how* do you know this?" Nova said.

"You want the short version or the long one?"

She steepled her hands. "The *true* version."

A door creaked open somewhere in the cathedral as Dante chose his words carefully. Not lies, but omissions. The ghiotte were even less receptive to outsiders than he'd expected, and he needed to watch his step. They didn't know who was in his party yet, and he'd keep it that way for now. Saverio's elite had chased them for centuries. The last thing he wanted was for them to suspect that Alessa was the current pinnacle of Saverian society.

He kept it vague. Avoided names and pronouns. Told them he'd taken a position as the Finestra's bodyguard, and when he'd accidentally stabbed the savior—he didn't love how they smirked at that—they discovered the Finestra's gift could absorb his ghiotte powers, too.

The ghiotte sat up straighter when he got to Divorando.

It turned his stomach to remember those terrible moments when he knew Alessa was going to die, when he realized he could save her. That he had to.

The memory still felt like ripping his heart down the middle, yet he spoke of it as though he'd made a dispassionate decision.

Dea's warriors wanted a story about war, not love.

"The army was on the verge of being overcome. We would've been doomed without the Finestra, so I took a chance," he said. "The Finestra's power magnified mine into something that could protect more than just one person, but I . . . almost died, and while I was . . . unconscious, I saw Dea. She warned me Crollo was going to send another, bigger attack, and I needed to find you to stop it." He finished awkwardly. "So that's why I'm here."

The echo of unspoken words rang in the silence:

I died. I came back. But I'm not one of you anymore.

There was an interminable wait before Nova spoke. "We of all people know how powerful Dea is and why she gave us our gifts. But we can defend ourselves."

"I know. You're the only ones who can. That's why I need your help."

Leo scoffed. "We help our own."

Dante's hand curled into a fist. "I saw blood running through your canals. A piazza flooded with it. We fight together or we'll die alone."

Nova rolled her fingers across the arm of her chair. "A compelling story, but we aren't a monarchy, boy. We can allow you to stay on probation, but the council won't order anyone to join your fight. If you want soldiers, you'll have to convince them."

"Understood."

"And we don't allow non-ghiotte without a sponsor to accept the consequences should they betray us, so your companions must leave."

"I'll take any punishment they might earn," Dante said.

"Probationary members don't get that privilege. Talia, will you stand for them, too?"

"No," Talia said flatly. "Him and only him."

Dante froze as a man stepped forward. Short beard, dark hair—longer than it used to be—and the same soft eyes. Talia's father. "I'll stand for his companions."

Dante jerked his gaze away from the man he'd once called "Uncle."

"And if they betray us?" Nova asked Matteo.

"I'll accept any punishment the council decrees."

Nova's eyes flashed in the torchlight. "Even death?"

Kamaria snuffed the arrow's blaze with her powers before Adrick became a human torch.

"All right, then." Adrick swatted a smoldering ember from his boots. "We'll wait here."

"You okay?" Kaleb muttered.

Kamaria snuck a hand behind her back, cupping a tiny orb of fire. The wind picked up, then died abruptly as Saida stifled it. Alessa had never felt more envious of their powers, but they *weren't supposed to reveal them.*

Before she could hiss at them to cut it out, two forms appeared through the mist. Another sprang from behind a pillar. Others seemed to materialize where the moonlight bled into shadows, moving with feline grace and predatory movements. Human bodies with monstrous faces, leering grins with wickedly sharp teeth. Masks, Alessa realized with the tiniest relief.

"Sorry, we didn't dress for the occasion," said Kamaria cheerfully. "No one told us there would be a masquerade."

One of the half dozen strangers beckoned for them to follow. "Your quarters await."

"*Guest* quarters . . . or prison quarters?" Saida whispered.

"Don't think we have much choice either way," Kamaria muttered.

Alessa stepped up to lead their small group as they followed the macabre escort.

"If you decide against helping us, we get to leave, right?" Kamaria asked.

Her only answer was the slosh of water and soft bump of empty boats against stone walls.

The leader stopped in front of a U-shaped villa with a gated courtyard connected to the street by a short, narrow bridge. He unlocked the gate and pointed at the open door to the building and the hungry darkness within its crumbling walls.

"How charming," Ciro muttered.

Alessa nodded regally at their captors—*hosts*—and entered the courtyard. Saida followed, whispering a prayer under her breath.

The gates clanged loudly as the masked ghiotte locked them in. "Someone will return for you at dawn."

"What happens at dawn?" Saida whispered.

Kaleb dropped his bedroll with a sigh. "Probably our executions."

"Talia, Matteo. A *word*." Nova beckoned for them to step onto the altar, then bent her head toward Leo to discuss Dante's fate.

He thumbed the hilts of his daggers as it dragged on.

Before they could deliver a verdict, a boy jogged up the

aisle to whisper something that made Leo surge to his feet, murder in his eyes.

"Sit down, Leo," Nova snapped. "*I'm* the chair tonight. Talia, you *did* tell them our laws, did you not?"

Talia's nod in response could have cracked a nut beneath her chin.

Dante kept his expression blank. *Shit.* He'd told them to stay in the boat.

"It seems they don't listen." Nova addressed Matteo again. "You still stand for them?"

"I held this boy the day he was born. Knew his father since the day *I* was. If he says they're trustworthy, I trust them."

Nova sighed. "Fine. Probation. And make our rules extra clear next time."

Talia stormed down the steps and grabbed Dante's arm. "Get outside *right now* so I can yell at you."

He leveraged his greater mass to slow their pace down the aisle. He wasn't going to run away, no matter how angry she was.

They'd barely stepped outside before she whirled on him. "Fonti? You brought fucking *Fonti?* Che cazzo fai?! I put my name on the line for you!"

"Mi dispiace—"

She spit on the ground. "You're damn lucky Nova's angling after my dad, or your friends would be dead already. Now my *father* will pay for it if they screw up again!"

"Basta!" Dante had to shout to get through to her. "I'm sorry. It seemed like better strategy to plead our case before mentioning who they are."

"You could have told *me.*" Her voice cracked on the last word.

"I know. I should have. But you were *there,* out of nowhere, and you weren't dead, and I thought you might say no and leave, and . . . I couldn't."

Talia heaved a breath. "You are the world's biggest dick. I should beat your ass for this."

He held out his hands, subtly tensing in case she struck without warning. "I won't even fight back."

Talia coughed a laugh. "Where's the fun in that? I'll wait until you aren't expecting it."

He lowered his arms. "Something to look forward to, then."

"*Stronzo.*" Talia flicked a rude gesture in his direction as someone stepped outside behind her.

"Give the boy a break, Natalia." Matteo patted his daughter's stiff shoulders.

Sour anger crept up Dante's throat as he met his uncle's gaze.

"Hey, son." Matteo stared, before catching himself with a shake. "Mi scuze. It's like seeing a ghost."

"Yeah, it is." Dante's anger flared at the quaver in Matteo's voice. *He* wasn't the one who'd been left behind.

"Papa, can we do this later?" Talia said. "If you don't get back in there, Nova might change her mind."

"Sure. Right." Matteo looked grateful for the excuse to leave. "But you'll stay at our place tonight, and I won't hear a word otherwise."

Dante didn't have a chance to object as Matteo hurried back inside.

"Come on," Talia said softly. "It'll take him all night to talk Nova through her anger bender."

Dante breathed a little easier with every step away from the cathedral.

Talia's rage must have burned out, temporarily at least. He was grateful for her silence. For the dark. He focused on the chill of the rain misting his face, seeping through his clothing. Anything to hold on to control.

Talia fished a key from her pocket in front of a narrow, modest building overlooking a quiet canal. "I still can't believe you brought fucking *Fonti*."

Somehow, the interior of the house felt exactly like her old cottage on Saverio. It even smelled the same, of linen and sandalwood. The rush of memories made Dante's head spin.

"That key is for emergencies," Talia said. "Not so you can hide in the dark."

A flash of red in Dante's peripheral vision warned him before a heavy hand slapped his back.

"Best friend prerogative," Blaise said. "Congrats, man. Probation's better than dead."

Dante grunted a thanks, easing his knives back into their sheaths. "Where are my people?"

Blaise laughed. "They're being taken care of."

Dante's stomach clenched. "*Meaning?*"

Blaise shrugged. "They broke rule number one and stepped foot on our island without permission. They won't have the most comfortable night."

Dante pulled his knives out again. "If anyone hurts them—"

"Relax," Talia said. "We have rules here. Nova said they can stay, and we don't fight fragiles unless they attack first. They might have to sleep on a hard floor, but they'll survive. I suggest you make a good impression tomorrow if you want to keep it that way."

Dante relaxed. Slightly. "And who, exactly, do I need to impress?"

"Everyone." Blaise smiled darkly. "You were already going to get *so* many challenges, but they'll be lining up for a chance to put you in your place now."

Dante arched a brow. "Am I supposed to impress people, befriend them, or kick their asses?"

"What's the difference?" Laughing like he'd made the world's funniest joke, Blaise jogged out the door.

"Well, tonight was fun," Talia said, dropping her key in a bowl on the counter.

The years had been long, and Dante's list of questions were longer, but he didn't know where to start. As kids, they'd spent their days one-upping each other or plotting elaborate war games, not rehashing past trauma. They didn't have a guidebook for this.

The ornate but worn carpet muffled Talia's steps as she paced the little sitting room. "So what, exactly, *do* you think Crollo is going to send?"

"I don't know." Dante ran his hand over the familiar faded quilt covering the back of the couch. "It's always changing, like he wants to keep me guessing. The only thing that comes back every time is blood. Lots of it. What I'm still trying to work out is the *point*."

"Isn't *the point* to kill us all?" Talia asked.

"I don't think so. If Crollo wanted to, he could just do it. That's the story, right? Dea and Crollo disagreed about whether humanity deserved to exist, so they made a bet, and we've all been pawns in every round since. But all games end eventually, and now things have changed."

Talia stopped pacing. "Changed how?"

"The point of the Duo Divino is supposed to be reminding people to work together, right? Well, the current Finestra's power was too strong for one partner. There were five on Finestra's Peak this time. And now Dea says Crollo's sending something even worse. To *me,* that sounds like—"

"Double or nothing," Talia said.

"Exactly." Dante nodded. "Crollo's tired of the game, so he's raising the stakes. *I* think Dea wants me to finish her original play. Her blessing says she gave us three gifts, right? Fonti with powers, a Finestra to magnify them, and fighters with a source of healing. That's the ghiotte, but since people misunderstood and blamed us for stealing a fountain that never existed, everyone paid the price. The way I see it, Dea wants *me* to get the missing players on the board for the first time since this began. Then Crollo will send his worst, so we can win Dea's bet once and for all."

Talia eyed him. "And if we don't?"

He met her gaze. "Game over."

Nineteen

DAYS UNTIL THE ECLIPSE: 23

Dante felt guilty as sin when he woke with a start in Talia's guest room the next morning. He should have tossed and turned with worry, but familiarity had wrapped around him like a blanket and he'd slept like a rock.

He dressed quickly and threw the door open, nearly jumping out of his skin when he came face-to-face with Talia right outside.

She shoved an espresso into his hand. "First day of the rest of your life, and you slept past dawn?"

"You could have woken me," he said, knocking back the espresso as they thundered down the stairs.

"Hah. Last time I woke you up, you punched me in the stomach."

Dante chuckled. "You kicked me in the nuts for it, too."

"And I'd do it again. Hurry up."

"Where's my team?" he asked as they crossed a small bridge. "I need to know they're safe."

"They *are*. For Dea's sake, keep your shirt on. I don't remember you being so impatient." She kicked his foot. "Want my advice?"

His mouth twitched with the old urge to annoy her. "Not really."

She punched his shoulder. "Stubborn asshole."

"Learned from the best."

"Yeah, you did. Look, no one will give you a chance if they think you're taking orders from outsiders. If you're the one *giving* orders, that's different. One of us finally having the upper hand, you know? They're just your lackeys, or whatever." Talia studied him. "That *is* the deal, right?"

"Sure." He'd almost forgotten how bossy she was.

"Better be. You made everything harder by bringing outsiders, *especially* because they're blessed. You expect people to sign up for this bonkers mission of yours just because you're a ghiotte? Not likely. Loyalty has limits. No one knows anything else about you, and you're starting at a disadvantage. You've got ground to make up."

"Give it to me, then. What's the plan?"

"Step one: get the council's blessing. Done, but barely. The next part is harder."

"What's the next part?"

"Make a good first impression. Well, *second* impression. People need to see you with me before they see you with the riffraff you brought. Make it very clear that you're one of us."

Dante pretended to scratch his bicep, checking that the bandage beneath his sleeve was secure. The stitches were supposed to stay in for another few days, but he'd have to risk removing them sooner. It felt like a tattoo marking him as a fraud, an outsider. The kind of guy who'd lie to his oldest friend because he couldn't bear the thought of her knowing the truth about who he was. Or wasn't.

Talia trotted him through the places where ghiotte gathered, lived, played, and worked. People were wary, sizing him up, but Talia was clearly well-liked, and her endorsement appeared to carry weight.

"I'm never gonna keep all these names straight," Dante said after muddling through yet another introduction.

"Don't worry. I know everyone."

Dante hadn't even dreamed this many ghiotte still existed—definitely enough for an army—but whenever he tried to bring conversations around to his mission, Talia elbowed him hard enough to bruise.

"It's like you've never heard of strategy," she said. "Have you forgotten every war game we ever played?"

"This isn't kids playing soldiers on the beach, Talia. This is the real thing."

"Even more important then. If you start a recruitment drive right now, no one will show up and you'll look pathetic. People need to know who you are and that you deserve their respect first."

Alessa's day started with a bang.

"Get up!" Their red-haired captor stood in the doorway amid a cloud of dust from the door he'd slammed against the wall. "I'm Blaise, and you're on probation. Time to impress me."

She sat bolt upright, heart pounding. "Where's Dante?"

"Asking questions does *not* impress me. Pack your shit. It's time for a tour." Blaise tapped his foot as everyone scrambled out of their bedrolls, disheveled and half asleep. When they'd shoved themselves into clothes and grabbed portable food, they followed him outside, blinking in the sudden daylight.

"Everyone see *that?*" Blaise said, very loudly and extremely slowly. "*That* is a *canal.* It's like a *road,* but it's made of *water.* And if you fall in, we all point and laugh. *That* over there is called a *bridge.* If you're too scared to jump the canal, you can toddle over the bridge like little babies."

While Alessa peered down alleys, hoping for a sight of Dante, Adrick, Ciro, and Saida trailed behind Blaise, asking leading questions. It seemed most ghiotte lived on the island of Perduta itself, but some families had farms on the mainland, and there were a few small ghiotte villages there as well.

"Fascinating," Adrick said as Blaise expounded on their system of bartering.

"What a brownnoser," Kaleb said. "Sorry, Alessa, but I can't stand your brother."

Kamaria patted his shoulder. "Keep telling yourself that."

Blaise clapped. "Keep it moving. I don't have all day."

After an hour of random alleys and picturesque but not terribly exciting bridges, they hadn't encountered a single ghiotte other than Blaise, and Alessa was beginning to suspect the tour was to keep them away from anyone else. Her feet were throbbing by the time Blaise returned them to their dismal lodging.

Someone had dropped off supplies while they were out: buckets, rags, brooms, oilcloth tarps, hammers and nails, a few thin mattresses, a wobbly table, and rickety chairs, all heaped in one corner of the courtyard.

"Ah, the special touches that make a house a home," Ciro said, looking pained.

"Your welcome basket," Blaise said. "You want a nicer living situation, get to work."

Wrinkling his nose, Kaleb grabbed a broom, Kamaria filled her arms with rags, and Ciro peered into a bucket like he had never seen one before, while Blaise planted himself in the open gate to oversee their efforts—and presumably so his charges couldn't escape.

Only the cat seemed delighted with their new dwelling, chasing dust cyclones and mocking their captivity by slipping in and out through the bars of the gate.

"Do you think we could train her to pick the lock?" Kaleb asked. His answer was a disdainful tail flick.

To be fair, the house looked better in full sunlight. Crafted out of tawny stone, it must have been a beautiful home for a wealthy family once upon a time, and the building appeared sturdy despite its neglected state.

The main level had tall windows (boarded up with rotting wood), a large room (carpeted with dust), and a narrow kitchen (cluttered with refuse and broken tiles).

Kamaria crossed the courtyard, which opened to a bright blue sky. "I'm going to check out the upper level."

"I'll clear the dust." Saida crouched, hands out, directing the air to blow the worst of the dust out the door. Alessa took her hand to speed up the process, and Kaleb aimed his sparks so they could see better. Adrick picked up a broom, and Ciro began dabbing at the door handles with a damp rag.

Coughing and blinking dust from her eyes, Alessa struggled to see where she was going as she and Saida cleared one section after another.

Kamaria poked her head around the corner and declared that the roof was in dire shape, with no doors cordoning off the balconies with crumbled railings. "Better sleep down here again or someone might roll off and fall to their doom."

"Could you two go a little bit faster?" Kaleb said. "My scar's itching."

"You need light?" Kamaria asked. She took over at Kaleb's pained nod, and he slid down against one wall, pulling up his eye patch to rub at the scar where a scarabeo claw cost him an eye during Divorando. It looked considerably less gruesome than it had in the weeks after, but he often grimaced when movement tugged at the tight tissue.

"I have a salve that might help." Adrick walked over, rummaging through his pack of medicinal supplies, but Kaleb recoiled as he pulled out a jar.

Adrick planted his hands on his hips. "I'm a gods-damned medic. I can show you how to massage it to soften the scar tissue, or you can keep itching every time you irritate it with all your scowling. Your call."

Kaleb grumbled assent, and Adrick knelt, shaking his head in annoyance.

An odd buzzing, like the drone of distant conversation or a swarm of tiny bees, vibrated within Alessa's skull. She had the strangest feeling that if she chose, she could let the bees loose, but something warned her to be careful not to. They were *her* bees, and she wouldn't be able to catch them again.

She shook herself. Sleep deprivation or the crash following an intense day was making her ridiculous. If only Dante were there, with his steady strength.

Her stomach churned with worry. She didn't want to think of what could be keeping him away for so long.

• • •

"Pinned you again!" Talia crowed.

Dante sat up, brushing dust from his pants after another surprise tackle. "I *let* you win."

She offered him a hand. "Since when do you let anyone beat you at anything?"

"You told me to make a good impression."

"You think being a *loser* does that?"

"Have I mentioned I almost died a month ago?" He gestured for her to walk ahead.

"*Pssht.* We're ghiotte. Almost dead is nothing."

If she only knew.

Talia continued to insist his friends were safe, but "safe" could mean a lot of things, and Dante was itching to see for himself.

"Have I jumped through enough hoops to free the hostages yet?" he asked.

"I don't remember you being so impatient," Talia said with an eye roll.

"I need to know they're okay."

"Ugh. Since you clearly don't trust me, we'll bring them some food and you'll see that they're *fine*."

They didn't head back to Talia's place, thankfully, but to a building with rows of tables and a bustling kitchen on the other side of a counter loaded with food.

"Where do we pay?" he asked as they perused the selection of fresh bread, cheeses, and cured meats.

"We don't. This is the community kitchen."

"Everyone eats here?"

"Of course not. Most cook at home, but anyone who wants to, can. Perduta is a family. We're all expected to contribute our skills, and everyone gets what they need."

Ironic. Named and shunned for allegedly stealing Dea's mythical healing fountain, the ghiotte had built a more egalitarian society than Saverio could hope for.

"You're so twitchy," she said, clapping him on the back. "Relax."

"I've been watching my back for years. It happens."

Dante paid more attention to the buildings on either side of the canals as they left. Some shops and cafés looked like any on Saverio, but others had open doors and no visible employees. Talia caught him peering into one such shop, crammed with racks of clothing—in good shape but not brand new—and told him to help himself. "People donate things they don't want and pick up stuff they do. Waste not, want not."

They had packed light, and everyone in his group could use a supply of clean clothes. It was easy to grab items for the guys and Kamaria, since she preferred trousers and was almost his height and narrow-hipped enough that he could guess which would fit, but he'd never picked out women's clothing before.

Watching him examine a dress, Talia took pity on him. "That doesn't have split skirts, so it would be a pain to move in, and they aren't here to lounge." Rummaging through the racks, she pulled out skirts, blouses, and underthings. "These should fit the short one with the dimples—"

"Saida."

"Whatever. This dress may be too revealing for Saverian prudes, but it would probably fit the other one."

"Alessa."

Talia's eyes narrowed. "Why'd you say her name like that?"

"Like what?" He kept his fist behind his back so she wouldn't see the lacy scrap he'd snatched. Arms full, he followed her out and beyond the bustling center of Perduta to a residential area.

"What's your trade, by the way?" Talia asked as they passed a tiny park where a young man was shouting encouragement to a pack of shrieking children climbing trees. "I forgot to ask yesterday."

"Huh?" Dante said.

"You know, what *you'll* do to contribute to the community. You'll need to share it at your swearing-in."

"Back up. Swearing-in?"

Talia stopped short. "Oh, *cavolo*! I forgot. *I'm* your sponsor so *I'm* supposed to explain how it works. Newbies get probation until they make an official appeal to join the community. Voting is held on the last seventhday of the month, and anyone who shows up can participate, so the more friends you make, the better your odds. People can speak for or against you, everyone gives a thumbs-up or -down, then the council makes the final call. If they approve, you can claim a house and become a permanent resident. If not, you're allowed to come and go but not *live* here. And if you get too many thumbs-down or the council decides to overrule the majority, you're booted off the island for good."

Dante did some fast math in his head. "So, if I don't win over enough people or the council takes a disliking to me—"

"Too late."

"They'll kick me out days before Crollo attacks?"

"*Now* you're catching on."

"What's *your* trade?" he asked.

"I do supply runs. Hunting, gathering, buying or bartering with settlements for things we can't make ourselves."

"Can I pick that, too?"

She shrugged. "You *could*, but it's not the most compelling. What else can you do?"

Before becoming Alessa's bodyguard, he'd spent years leveraging his powers to win paid fights, but even if he *had* his ghiotte powers, that would be nothing special here, and while he'd tried his hand at other things, he'd never stuck around anywhere long enough for a true apprenticeship.

"I spent one summer working for a blacksmith. How's that?"

Talia raised her eyebrows. "That'll come in handy as we prep for a war."

The sounds of town faded as they trekked farther from the city center to a quieter part of town. Then another, quieter still, until the buildings on either side appeared abandoned. The house Talia had stashed them in was *really* out of the way.

Ahead, Blaise stood guard on a tiny bridge leading to a gated villa.

"If you need to give them a pep talk, make it quick," Talia said. "Papa's probably making lasagne in your honor, and I'm starving."

Dante rubbed his chin. "I'll stay with them tonight."

"*What?* Why?"

Dante shrugged one shoulder. "We're on a mission. I need to be a team player."

"By sleeping on the floor of some shitty house?" Talia rolled her eyes. "Is this because of Papa?"

"No." He met her gaze. "I told you, they're my team. If they're sleeping rough, so am I."

"If I'd known you were going to be so noble, I would've told Blaise to find a better house."

"*Are* there better houses?"

She thought. "Probably not. Anything in good condition will have been claimed already."

Dante's breath caught at the sight of Alessa sweeping

the courtyard, looking a little dusty but otherwise fine. He wouldn't have to kill anyone today.

As Blaise opened the gate, she looked up, tossed her broom aside, and bolted across the little bridge. She was already talking as she threw her arms around Dante's neck. "I was starting to think they'd killed you and we were next. Where did you go last night? What happened? What have you been doing?"

Dante pulled free with a surreptitious glance at Talia. "I'm fine. We thought it would be better if I met some people before the whole group complicated things."

Alessa fixed her expression, but not before he saw the flash of hurt. Guilt turned his stomach, but he'd explain once Talia was gone.

Alerted by the ruckus, the others emerged from the house. They had shadows under their eyes, but no signs of injury or abuse. His jaw unclenched a little more.

"What have you told them?" Talia asked Blaise.

"Not much. Just kept them out of the way."

"Good." Talia shoved a basket of food into Adrick's arms. "Let's get some things clear right now. Saverians worship you because they need you for protection. We don't. So keep your little magic tricks to yourself. Rumors are already flying, but no one needs to see that."

"Aw, that's rough," Adrick said. "If Kaleb can't electrocute people into talking to him, what options does he have?"

Kaleb sneered. "Says the only nonmagical person on the whole damn island."

"Cut it out," Dante said. "You heard her, no magic."

"We can't hide our powers forever," Kaleb grumbled. "We're going to need them to fight the 'big bad.'"

"First things first," Talia said. "Keep it to yourselves while

Dante makes his debut. Understood?" She looked at each of them, waiting for a nod or muttered response.

"Have no fear." Ciro swept a gallant bow, which Dante could have warned him would only aggravate her more. "I couldn't make a magical scene if I wanted to."

Talia gestured to Adrick. "I thought *he* was the only one without magic."

"Ah, yes, I do *have* magic," Ciro said with the gravitas of an elderly professor. "Yet I am but a mere magnifying lens."

"You have *got* to be kidding me," Talia said, pinching the bridge of her nose for a beat before glaring at Dante. "Did you bring *every* magical minion you could find?"

"Not *all* of them."

Talia muttered some choice words under her breath and wrenched open the gate. "Everyone get in." She pointedly let go before Dante reached it.

"*Yes?*" he asked.

"The chatty one looks at you like you're a piece of cake she wants to lick the frosting off."

"And?"

"*And* she'd better knock it off, or people might think you have a conflict of interest."

Complication. The word rolled around Alessa's head as Blaise made a show of slamming the gate and locking them in. Dante hadn't come for her all day because she was a *complication.*

Fine. She could be patient. Diplomatic. Whatever it took.

With the building blocking the last of the sunlight, the courtyard was grim. Kamaria made a small orb of fire, and Dante passed out the rest of the food and clothing, then sat on the crumbling stairs to fill them in on what he'd seen and learned while they were apart.

"A vengeful god sending an apocalyptic invasion isn't enough motivation for them?" Kamaria asked when he'd finished. "I thought that would be the easy part."

"They don't *have* to join us," Dante said. "This isn't their fight."

"It's a fight to save the world. It's everyone's fight," Saida said.

Dante made a frustrated noise. "You haven't lived their lives. You have no idea what it's like."

"To be hated and feared?" Alessa said. "I beg to differ."

Dante didn't take the bait. "This isn't an unpopularity contest. We need to *convince* them to work with us."

"If Talia's like family to you, why isn't she just telling them to join us?" Kaleb kicked a rock. One that was too big for kicking, judging from his grimace. "So much for loyalty."

"This *is* loyalty. She's telling it like it is."

"And if they decide they won't help us, what then?" Alessa asked. "We give up and go home?"

"Of course not. We'll do whatever it takes."

"Which is?" Kaleb asked.

"First, they need to believe I'm the boss of this operation." Dante met each of their gazes in turn, but despite some sullen looks, nobody objected. He landed on Alessa last, with a grimace. "And they can't know about *us*."

Saida made a sympathetic noise. Alessa bit her tongue. Briefly. As soon as the others drifted off to set up for sleep, she took Dante's hand and pointed at the stairs.

On the upper level, they found a balcony that looked

sturdy despite missing a chunk of railing, and sat, legs dangling over the side. Dante had been through an emotional wringer, caught between his past and present, and she could *feel* the pressure building inside him, but she'd wait.

She could be patient.

She swung her feet, tapping her heels against the exterior of the house.

Any minute now.

If only she knew how to whistle.

Any second.

"Seeing Talia and your uncle after all this time, finding your people . . . ," she ventured. "That's a lot." She wasn't *forcing* him to share, merely cracking the door open a smidge. An invitation.

"Yeah." His expression was unreadable.

She pictured herself shoving an invitation under a very tight doorjamb. "Are you okay?"

"I don't know." Dante picked up a shard of broken tile, idly rubbing it between his thumb and forefinger.

"Do you want to talk about it?"

A tiny smile tugged at the corner of his mouth. "Am I allowed to say no?"

"Yes, but you *shouldn't*. You can't bottle up your feelings forever."

"Oh, I bet I can." Dante tossed the tile into the canal below, the water rippling gold beneath the sunset. "It's like . . . I put them and my parents in the same box. Gone. But now Matteo and Talia are alive, so my parents should be, too. I mean, if two people can come back from the dead . . ." He blew out a gusty breath. "It's messing with me."

"Did you talk to your uncle?"

"Not really. I'm not even sure if I want to."

That didn't seem like the end of the conversation, but Dante clamped his mouth shut. Silence enveloped them as the last sliver of sun sank out of sight, and Perduta went silvery blue in the moonlight.

Dante had already had enough talk for one night, but Alessa was still watching him. *Very* intently.

He raised a brow. "Yes?"

"You're so scruffy," she said. "It makes you look quite dangerous."

"That bothers you?" he asked with a laugh.

"Not *now*." She shook her head vigorously. "I was just thinking I might not have had the courage to approach you in the Barrel that fateful day if you'd looked any more intimidating."

"Who'd have thought facial hair could change the course of all our lives?"

It wasn't his five o'clock shadow, but *something* was bothering her. The telltale scrunch of her nose always gave it away.

"So," she said, picking at her thumbnail. "You're our fearless leader, and I'm just one of the crew, huh?"

"Something like that." Dante leaned to bump her shoulder with his. "Aw, come on. Sneaking around? Forbidden fruit? Haven't you missed it a *little*?"

"I'd rather try a *normal* relationship, where we can touch each other *and* not have to keep it a secret. When do we get *that*?"

He swung an arm around her shoulders for a quick kiss on the cheek. "Soon. Just gotta cross 'build an army of super-soldiers' and 'win a battle with the gods' off our to-do list, then I'm all yours."

"Ugh. Why don't our to-do lists ever get *shorter?*"

The wind picked up, whipping Dante's hair into his eyes, and he caught Alessa hiding a shiver.

"Come on, let's get inside." He helped her to her feet, keeping one hand between her and the edge of the balcony. Downstairs, he fought a twinge of regret as he eyed the hard stone floor, a stark contrast to the soft bed and clean sheets he'd turned down again.

"Guess we're all sleeping in here tonight," Kaleb said with a dejected sigh.

Saida braced her hands on her hips. "Think of it like a slumber party. Cozy."

Such close quarters made Dante twitch.

He *could* escape. If he had to. But if he tried to sleep upstairs, Alessa would insist on coming with him, and with all the half-fallen walls, he didn't entirely trust her not to roll off the side of the building.

Gritting his teeth, he resigned himself to a night in the claustrophobic dark.

He'd twitch out of his skin if he got sandwiched between people in the main room, though, so whether it was prudent or not, they dragged two bedrolls into the narrow, dusty sliver of space that had once been a kitchen.

He probably wouldn't sleep at all, but at least he could roll over without bumping into anyone else. He couldn't even run off his excess energy or channel it into repairing the building without disturbing everyone.

Reluctantly, he got into his bedroll.

There was *one* other way to burn off nervous energy.

Tuning out the not-so-distant shufflings from the other room, he eased behind Alessa, and she wiggled her sweet little bottom against him, tempting enough that he would have wedged himself into her bedroll, lack of doors be damned, if he'd known he could follow through without dying.

So close but untouchable with two layers of clothing *and* two bedrolls between them, he regretted every moment of self-control that had kept them apart when he had been able to touch her. And because he was a glutton for punishment, he murmured exactly where he'd put his hands if he could, rewarded and undone by her quickened breath.

Her faint whimper was drowned out by a loud snore from the hallway.

Sti cazzi. He hoped the gods were enjoying his torment.

Twenty

DAYS UNTIL THE ECLIPSE: 22

Dante woke with a grunt and rolled over to find Talia glaring down at him, her foot wedged in his back.

Not how he'd meant for her to find him, but the house was crowded, with people crammed onto every available sheltered spot. He'd been asleep. Talia couldn't blame him for being a little too close to Alessa.

Ha. Of course she could.

"Staying there to be a team player, *huh?*" Talia called over her shoulder as Dante pulled the gate closed behind him. "You know, when we say 'Screw the blessed bastards,' it's not meant to be *literal.*"

Dante jogged to catch up. "No one's screwing anyone." *Technically.* "I slept on the floor within kicking distance of a half dozen people in a house with no roof, which you picked out for us. Sorry you don't like the spot I ended up in."

Talia threw a glare at the sky. "I *swear,* if you mess everything up by thinking with the wrong body parts—"

"*I'll* worry about my body parts, thanks."

"You'd better. No one will give you the time of day if they think you're involved with one of *them*." Talia clenched her hands into fists, then released them with effort. "You came here asking for help on a mission that sounds pretty nuts, and I've busted my ass to make sure everyone thinks *they* follow *your* orders, not that you're being led around by your—"

"*Enough*." His jaw ached from the words he bit back. "I get it."

She was right, and he hated it. If people suspected he was involved with the Finestra, they'd assume he was taking orders from the church, and no one would listen to a damn word he said.

"How good are you with knives?"

"Um. Decent." Dante thumbed the hilts of his daggers. "Why? We working through our shit by drawing blood?"

"Don't tempt me."

He stepped to the side, just in case.

"I still can't believe you brought Fonti and a *Finestra*." Talia made a rude sound.

A finestra, she said. *One*. Because Talia only knew about Ciro.

Dante steeled himself to broach the subject, but she cut him off before he could.

"Now that people know who you are, they need to *respect* you," Talia said as they headed toward what looked like an athletic-training area on one side of the piazza, cluttered with bins of weaponry: bows, arrows, spears, knives, and metallic throwing stars with wicked-looking edges. "On Perduta, that comes down to skills. You have them. Hit some targets and win a few wrestling matches, and you'll be gold."

"That's all it takes? People will follow me into battle for hitting some targets?"

"It's a start. No ghiotte can resist a challenge. Offer a good one *and* show you're a worthy leader, and they'll be lining up around the block. You were born for this." Oblivious to his discomfort, Talia skipped on ahead. "Follow my lead."

Leo and a pack of similarly muscular men loitered on wide, shallow steps near the targets, *not* watching Dante so intensely he could feel it on his skin.

"*Bull*shit!" Talia yelled—*toward* Dante, but not *to* him, since he hadn't said a word. "Bet you can't even hit the board."

Ah. Got it. Dante drew his knives, flipped one, and caught it. "Pick your distance."

Nonchalant, like she didn't notice the attention drawn their way, Talia sauntered a dozen paces from the targets. "I'll start easy. You're welcome."

Her dagger zinged through the air to stick, vibrating, a handspan from the bull's-eye.

"You've improved," Dante drawled. "Glad I won't have to pull your knife out of my hand. *Again.*"

Talia snorted. "You dared me."

"You were supposed to aim *between* my fingers." His blade struck the center. "Still better than you."

"I'm just warming up." Talia made a show of stretching before throwing her next.

Not bad. But he could do better. Showing off for a crowd wasn't his style, but skills meant respect, and he needed all the respect he could get. Eyes were on him, weighing and measuring his worth. People might not like who he'd come with, but as far as they knew, *he* was one of them. That was crucial.

"Che culo!" Talia shrieked as his knife knocked hers off its bull's-eye. "Brutto figlio di puttana bastardo!"

"*Wow,* your vocabulary skills have *expanded.*" He was laughing too hard to fend off her playful jabs. "Missed you, too."

She strode over to yank his blade out of the target. "Beginner's luck."

Dante caught sight of Leo from the corner of his eye and tamped down his smile. They were under surveillance.

"You still suck at archery?" Talia asked, grabbing two bows. "Because I feel the need to trounce you."

Dante caught the one she tossed at him. "You're in luck. Haven't had much practice recently."

"Time to fix that." She elbowed him out of the way. "Ladies first."

"Lady? Where?" Dante caught her fist. "Sheesh, channel that aggression into something healthy, will you?"

Talia's first arrow landed smack in the middle, and Dante let her run a victory lap before nocking his own arrow.

His first shot went wide, to Talia's intense amusement. She nailed another bull's-eye and did a backflip, landing lightly and flicking him off with her free hand.

"Lucky shot." Dante cracked his neck with a wince.

"Aw, what's the matter? Wishing you'd slept in a real bed instead of playing floor martyr with Miss Chatty and the sparkle squad?" Talia said with an arch look. "What *is* the little princess's power, anyway?"

Dante held up his arrow, eyeballing how straight it was.

"Well?" Talia said.

Shit. So much for dodging that reveal today.

Dante slid the arrow back. "Alessa's the Finestra," he mumbled, riffling through his quiver like he was hunting for the greatest arrow ever made.

"What?" Talia shook her head. "*Wait.* No. That Ciro guy said *he* was the Finestra."

At her shout, Leo's head swiveled in their direction.

"Ciro's from Tanp," Dante said quietly. "Alessa is Saverio's Finestra."

Talia gaped. "So . . . when you said you worked for the *Finestra,* you meant *her?*"

"Yeah." Dante drew out the word.

Heaving a labored breath, Talia raised her bow and aimed—not at him, thankfully—and nailed another bull's-eye.

"Let me get this straight." Her expression was grim as she nocked another arrow. "When you took a guard job and accidentally stabbed the Finestra and all of that—*none* of that story was about the weird guy who talks like an old man? It was all the perky little chatterbox?"

"Uh. Yes?" He hadn't meant to end with a question mark, but her tone demanded more than a simple answer.

Talia didn't let him take a turn before nocking another arrow. And another. When she finally ran out, she snatched his and burned through them, too.

Eventually, she collected herself. "Any *other* information you want to share?"

"Not really."

Talia wrenched his bow from his grip. "You *had* to march back into my life with Fonti, *two* Finestre, and a holy war on your calendar, didn't you?"

Dante followed her back toward the armory. "The old Talia would've loved a war with the gods, offered to fight blindfolded with one hand tied behind her back."

"Yeah, well, *this* Talia would have preferred a chance to catch up with her best friend after he disappeared for years."

"You'll have plenty of chances to kick my ass like in the old days after we fight off the apocalypse."

She turned so fast he almost tripped over her. "I'd better. Best friends are hard to find."

"Yeah, I know," he said quietly. "I didn't even try. Didn't have *any* friends until a few months ago."

Her face grew serious. "None?"

"Nope. Alessa was the first, then she dragged the rest of them along."

Talia glared. "You can't make me like them."

"Fine, don't. But they won't ask me to choose sides, and I hope you don't, either."

"Well, I can't *now*, not if precious Princess Finestra and her merry band of magical misfits wouldn't."

"Give them a chance. They'll grow on you."

"Doubt it."

As the afternoon wore on, they fell into a groove, and Talia's smile lost its guarded edge. Real, invigorated by a challenge. Dante had no room for distraction, but he couldn't help relaxing into their friendship like they'd only been separated days, not years.

When the skies opened up in the evening, Talia waved off invitations from passing friends and stayed with Dante on the empty piazza. Despite the rain, they shot arrows together for hours, content with silence, aside from the *thunk* of blades into targets and the whisper of rain.

After, Talia walked him back to the house to unlock the gate, and pretended to kick him in the rear as he walked through. "Make good choices!"

Like not get caught snuggling the Finestra again. Message received.

Dante stepped inside the house, shaking rain from his hair. With the refuse carted away, the floor scrubbed, and blankets tacked up over the windows, the house was much improved. But still crowded.

Alessa was seated by the hearth, staring at the dancing flames, while Kaleb and Adrick fought over a poker to stir the fire, and Kamaria snickered, making the flames leap whenever they got too close, then feigning surprise when they tried to catch her at it.

"How's the ghiotte recruitment drive going?" Kamaria abandoned her game as Dante maneuvered across the room.

"Haven't won everyone over yet, but ghiotte love a challenge, and Crollo is a good one," Dante said. "We will." Alessa looked up at the sound of his voice. She always did.

Kamaria didn't look very impressed. "I guess that's a start."

Dante sat behind Alessa, moving her hair over one shoulder so he could drop a kiss on the back of her neck. "Steps one and two, accomplished: We found them, and they're giving us a chance."

Alessa grimaced, rolling her shoulders, and Dante pressed his thumbs on either side of her neck. "What are you—ohhhh," she moaned as he worked his way down one vertebra at a time.

"Get a room," Adrick said with a laugh-tinged groan.

"When do we get to join this army?" Kaleb asked, yanking the poker from Adrick's hands.

"Soon. Once I—" As he reached her lower back, Alessa made a soft noise and Dante forgot what he was saying for a moment. "Once I get enough ghiotte on board, we'll bring you in."

Saida offered a thumbs-up, and Kaleb managed a sarcastic, "Yay."

The patter outside became a deluge, thudding against the windows, but neither the weather nor their grumbling could ruin Dante's mood. He felt almost peaceful—a strange thought, maybe, with an epic battle ahead, but he was finally where he needed to be with the people he needed to be with.

And Talia . . . was Talia. She was bruised and bitter—he knew what that was like—but she hadn't turned her back on him when he showed up with strangers. Even after catching him in a compromising position with Alessa that morning, Talia was still there. Still on his side. Taunting her with all the old insults, being mocked in return—it was as though a door had opened in the timeline of his life.

He'd forgotten what it was like to have someone who'd known him forever, who gave him shit but would forgive anything in the end. He'd forgotten what it was like to have a family.

A broken part of him had been glued back in place. A part he'd thought gone forever, that didn't fit the same anymore, but that didn't mean it *couldn't*. He just didn't know how to arrange the pieces yet.

For the first time in years, he could almost imagine a world where *he* fit, too.

Twenty-one

DAYS UNTIL THE ECLIPSE: 21

When Alessa woke at dawn, she found Dante already up and pacing the courtyard.

She wiped dried leaves from a bench in the corner of the courtyard beneath a gnarled lemon tree and perched on one end, patting the other side for him. He took up all the remaining space, forcing their bodies to press together from hip to shoulder. *Good bench.*

Dante stared at the locked gate as they ate their meager breakfast of stale pastries. "I've been surrounded by ghiotte for days, and I haven't seen any sign of my powers coming back."

Her heart squeezed in sympathy. "It's still early."

Dante might not recognize the feeling, but she knew the bitter grief when the powers that were supposed to be your strength betrayed you, setting you apart from the people you needed most.

"You know," she said, "I used to think you hated being a ghiotte."

He scoffed. "Me too."

"I recognized that feeling, because I spent so much of my life wishing I were different."

Dante finally looked at her. "Different how?"

"I thought things would be easier if I was like Adrick, who wasn't always forgetting things and letting people down. Or Renata, who knew how to be a brave and powerful hero. But I'm not. I'm different. My powers are different, too. And I finally accepted that I can't change who I am, but I can be kinder to myself and change how I *feel* about who I am."

She gave him a pointed look.

"It's not that simple," Dante said, his jaw set. "My powers were the one thing that tied me to my past. To this. To everyone here. It doesn't matter what I *feel*. It matters what I am. Or at least what they think I am."

She caught herself moving to rub her temples and clasped her hands. Dante had enough on his plate without worrying about her. He stood and began pacing the courtyard like a caged animal. No one liked being confined, but it was worse for him.

Damn Talia for putting him through it. Which reminded her . . . "Does Talia know about us?"

Dante frowned. "She might suspect it, but no, I haven't told her."

"Shouldn't you be able to tell *her*, at least?"

"Talia has a bigger chip on her shoulder than most. Her non-ghiotte mother bailed on them when things got rough. That leaves a mark." At the faint jangle of keys, he stepped away from the bench. "Give her a chance to get to know you first."

Talia might not the friendliest person, but she *was* Dante's oldest friend, so Alessa girded herself with what she hoped was a disarming smile and stood to greet her.

"Good morning, Talia. We haven't had much chance to speak yet, but any friend of Dante's is a friend of ours."

"Lucky me," Talia deadpanned.

Nice try, grumpy girl. It would take more than a few curt answers to scare her off.

Like Kamaria, Talia had the confidence of someone entirely unconcerned about whether anyone liked her or not, but while Kamaria's charm and humor softened it into charisma, Talia's stoicism sharpened it to a razor's edge.

Attempt number two. "Dante's told us so much about you." Alessa's smile felt more determined than friendly at this point, but it would have to do. "You two must have been quite the hellions growing up."

Talia flicked a glance at Dante. "Don't remember you being much of a talker."

Dante shrugged. "I said we climbed trees together."

Talia snorted a laugh. "More like battled our way to the top. Remember the time you broke your arm and cried like a baby?"

"Hey now," Dante said. "I never told anyone about your fear of bees."

Talia whacked him on the arm. "I was five! And you said they had magical venom!"

At Alessa's chuckle, Talia's smile met a sudden death.

"Is it really necessary to lock them in?" Dante asked as Talia brandished the keys.

"You expect me to trust them unsupervised?"

"*I'd* trust them with my life. You could meet me halfway here."

"Fine." Talia lobbed the keys over the gate. "If they burn down the city, that's on you."

Every good army needed weaponry, and Dante needed to prove his worth, so Talia took him to the forge where her friend Jesse loaded him down with tools and gloves and shoved him toward the fire to see what he could do. It was hot as blazes but satisfying how quickly the skills he'd learned years ago came back to him.

A blond girl around their age with fair skin and a pixie cut popped in a few minutes later and climbed onto the fence beside Talia to watch. *Kira,* Talia reminded him. Right. He'd met her the day before. Feet tapping, fingers flexing, she never seemed to hold still.

Jesse, a muscular guy with swarthy skin and long black hair tied back in a queue, wiped soot from his chin. "What kind of weaponry you think we'll need on hand when this thing goes down?"

Dante finished his swing, then held his hammer up while he thought. "Everything and anything, really."

Jesse frowned. "The armory isn't all that big, and it's full already. We have a decent artillery, but we've never had a full-scale war. You're going to need a place to store it all."

"Aren't there catacombs beneath the basilica?" Talia said. "Oh, wait, they're flooded. That won't work. We'll figure something out."

"The forge is gonna be running nonstop," Jesse said. "I hope we can keep up."

Dante raised a finger. "I know someone who's good with fire."

Talia made a face. "People are still getting over your disastrous arrival. It's too soon to let the glitter goons loose."

"When do *we* get to meet the newbies?" asked Kira.

"First things first," Talia said. "We'll integrate the twinkle turds once we've taken care of recruitment."

Jesse donned his mitts. "Any of the palace pets know how to fight?"

"They've all had training in the basics," Dante said. "I was only in the Cittadella for a month, though, so I could only do so much."

"They let a bodyguard train the blessed?" Kira asked.

"I was hired after the Finestra saw me fight, so yeah," Dante said. "When the Fonti showed up, they asked for tips."

"Let's see what they can do, then." Jesse waggled his eyebrows.

"No," said Talia.

Kira booed. "Aw, come on. I want to see how Saverio's most pampered hold their own in a fight."

Talia gave Dante a look that said, *See what I mean?* as Kira and Jesse traded bets on whether it would be a Fonte or Finestra who cried first. Despite the nonstop ribbing, the younger ghiotte who had grown up on Perduta didn't seem to have Talia's deeply held loathing for Saverians, but that didn't mean they respected them.

"You can't hide them forever," Kira said. "Rumors will get worse than reality if you wait too long."

"You suggest we throw them to the wolves?" Talia asked as Dante pulled a column of metal from the flames that would hopefully become a sword if he did his job right.

"I *suggest* you let them out of their cages at a time when people have better things to do than fight," Kira said with a pointed look.

Dante kept his mouth shut. There were already a thousand ways his mission could go wrong, and there'd be a thousand more when the two halves of his life collided.

It was one thing to gather tinder, another to light a match while standing atop the pyre.

Alessa picked up a heavy bucket of water and waddled across the main room, sloshing with every step. Bending to give Fiore a pat, her attention snagged. She could *feel* someone approaching.

Kamaria studied a piece of wood. "Anyone know how to make a bed frame? Or a roof?"

Kaleb dropped his hammer with a *thunk* at the knock Alessa knew would happen before it did.

A handsome older man with dark hair and laugh lines around his eyes stood outside.

"Ciao, I'm Matteo." He gestured at a cart piled with wood, tools, and textiles. "Thought you might need help fixing up the place."

Dante would have feelings about this.

"Heck, yeah, we could," Kaleb said. "You know how to fix a roof?"

Matteo grinned. "My specialty."

Unlike his daughter, Matteo studied them with interest, not wariness, as they introduced themselves. The others unloaded supplies, and Alessa took Matteo upstairs to point out the worst portions of the roof.

"You the girl my daughter's been ranting about?" he asked as he set up his ladder.

Alessa flushed. "Probably."

"Sorry about that." Matteo laughed. "Talia can be intense, but her heart's in the right place. Long as you don't cross him, you won't cross her. She'll warm up."

"I have no intention of crossing anyone." Alessa didn't know what Talia suspected about her relationship with Dante, but that seemed vague enough.

Matteo asked her to pass him a hammer, so Alessa stayed to play assistant, handing him items and offering a set of eyes from below. She was proud of herself for holding back a million questions, especially when Matteo caved first.

"Has he told you much about his past?" He paused to wipe sweat from his brow.

"Some. Dante's not much of a talker, but I know about his parents and the basics of what happened after."

Matteo's smile was tight. "You know more than I do, then. I won't pry. He'll talk to me when he's ready."

"I admire your restraint. I'm not sure how long I'll resist asking for embarrassing childhood stories."

Matteo laughed, releasing some of the sad tension. "I should probably get back on his good side before I start telling tales. I have a lot to apologize for."

Her face must have said it all, because the lines deepened on Matteo's face.

Knowing what she did now, she felt even more justified in resenting Matteo's wife, but a sick pit hollowed her stomach to think of how he must feel, learning he'd left someone he loved for dead.

It wasn't her place to say so, though, nor her apology to accept.

Matteo's gaze slid past Alessa, and his expression tightened as a gravelly voice spoke far too close to her ear.

"You don't have to *tend* to them, Matteo." A golden-maned man prowled into the room, blue eyes scanning the bare walls and stone floor before landing on Alessa. "I heard we had Saverian royalty on our island and came to pay my respects."

He extended a hand, palm up, and Alessa placed hers in it, even though she wasn't wearing gloves. He smiled, and she was almost surprised he didn't reveal sharp teeth. "Leonardo Piero Rossi of the Perduta Rossis, last in a long line of Perduta's founding family. You may call me Leo."

She could sense Matteo's silent presence behind her as Leo raised her hand to his lips. This was a test. Of what, she didn't know, but she had to pass it on her own.

She made a gut decision. "Alessandra Diletta Lucia Paladino, of the Saverio Paladinos, last in a long line of bakers and lemon farmers."

Leo's white teeth flashed with his laugh. "Well done, principessa. We don't bow to your kind here, and you're wise to know it."

"There's much less bowing in the Cittadella than one might think. And I expect none, there or here. I merely served my duty to protect my home and my people as you would."

"That's why you're here, no? That's what your ghiotte claims."

Speaking before thinking had often come back to bite her in the past, but this man was too perceptive to lie to, and something told her he'd prefer plain speaking than evasiveness, so she followed her instincts again.

"Despite years of mistreatment, one of yours proved better and more honorable than any of us. Dante saved thousands of lives, including my own. He would have come here alone, but we insisted on accompanying him, to repay our debt by helping protect *his* people."

"Mmm. If the gods are truly sending an attack to Perduta, why send the only warning to someone who wasn't even here?"

Ah. She'd been haunted by this thought enough to recognize it: *Why had the gods chosen this person and not someone else?*

She let self-deprecation color her smile. "I, of all people, have never understood why the gods choose who they do, but they made a better choice picking Dante than in choosing me. I hope you can forgive him for our clumsy mistakes. His intentions are nothing but noble."

Leo studied her for so long Alessa had to concentrate on not fidgeting.

"We'll see," he said at last. Pausing on his way out, he looked down at a tumble of stones that had fallen from the roof. "Tell your friends to tread carefully, *principessa*. It's a dangerous place for those who don't watch their step."

Twenty-two

"There's a party tonight," Blaise announced, throwing open the door.

Alessa pushed sweaty hair off her forehead. She'd never felt *less* suitable for a party.

"A welcome party?" Saida looked up from dusting with a hopeful smile.

"No. But people will *probably* be having too much fun to get violent, so we're letting you come." Blaise rubbed his hands together in anticipation. "Every seventhday there's a gathering for all of Perduta, and you arrived just in time. *However,* as the saying goes, 'cleanliness is next to godliness,' and you smell like hell. Grab your party clothes and let's go."

Blaise went back into tour-guide mode after ushering them into the forum of a large, columned building that smelled of brine. "On this wall, you'll see a fresco painted, uh, a long time ago."

"Do we really need the history lesson?" Kaleb asked.

Blaise kept going as though he hadn't heard. "On the floor, a mosaic by an artist I'm sure was famous for lots of stuff, but here on Perduta, we primarily admire their use of glass tiles to create genitalia with too many sharp corners. Nothing but the best for Dea's favorites. And entering to your left, the lovely Talia and her second-best friend."

Talia made a motion like pinching his lips closed, and Blaise shuffled backward to give her the floor.

Dante was carrying a parcel of clothes, and Talia had changed from her usual style of casually terrifying battle goddess to a sheer dark blue tunic and fawn-colored leggings that showed off her leg muscles. She'd also added shimmery blue color to her eyelids and let her hair down, which should have softened her appearance but somehow made her even more intimidating.

"It's really nice of you to invite us to your party," said Saida.

"I didn't," Talia said with a sneer. "And it's not my party. But I keep hearing that I can't keep you locked up forever."

What Talia lacked in charm she made up for with efficiency. "Changing rooms are at both ends of the hall. Entrances to the baths through them. The original builders intended one for girls and one for guys, but nobody cares which one you choose as long as you don't act like a creep. *Creeps* have to bathe in the canal. Creeps who try anything get to take a long nap at the bottom of the bay."

She headed in one direction while Blaise went the other, and the group split up.

"Are there any private bathing rooms?" Alessa dared to ask.

Talia gave her a sharp look. "Not for you. In fact, assume *nothing* is for you unless I say so. If you're too uptight, I suggest trying early mornings. *Really* early. For now, you can suck it up or go to the party like . . . that."

Ouch. Alessa gathered the tattered scraps of her dignity and kept walking.

"So, Talia," Kamaria said. "How did all this make it through Divorando without the Duo's protection?"

"You think we need *you* to protect us?" Talia scoffed. "That's cute."

Kamaria smiled, cocky as ever. "The rest of the world does. We're kind of a big deal."

"And yet here, you're nobody. We don't need you. We lock everything up, stay inside, and they fly right over us."

"You . . . hide?" Kamaria said.

Talia's knife was in her hand before Alessa even realized she was wearing one. "You calling us cowards?"

"Never." Kamaria sounded unusually earnest.

Talia lowered the dagger. "Good."

Saida coughed, drawing Talia's attention and averting bloodshed for the time being. "Apologies. We were taught—wrongly—that living off the sanctuary islands meant near-certain death. Kamaria was expressing her admiration."

Kamaria nodded vigorously. "Yeah. Admiration."

Talia bristled. "Do you see crops anywhere on the island? Wood buildings? Anything especially tasty?"

Kamaria looked Talia up and down but had the sense not to answer aloud.

Talia huffed a breath. "We leave nothing out to tempt them, they leave us alone. Simple."

"Well, I'm impressed," Saida said. "Surviving for so long *and* building a society? Incredible."

Talia's posture eased a bit. "Towels over there, baths through that door."

She left, and Alessa breathed a sigh of relief. She hadn't considered that "whatever it took" to win over the ghiotte might include getting naked in front of Dante's terrifying childhood sweetheart.

Kamaria sank against a wall. "I think I'm in love."

"*Really?*" Alessa couldn't keep the whine from her voice. "*That's* your perfect woman? Rude and violent?"

"Guess we both have a type, huh? Come hell or high water—sorry, shouldn't give Crollo ideas—I *will* win her over."

"People aren't conquests, Kamaria," Saida scolded. "And you've barely spoken to her."

"The gods handed me the ideal woman. Who am I to reject fate?"

Alessa wrinkled her nose. "She looks like she prefers stabbing to flirting."

"You're one to talk," Kamaria said. "How many times have you and Dante almost killed each other during your whirlwind romance?"

"We didn't *enjoy* it."

"If you say so."

Alessa shimmied out of her soiled clothing and wrapped herself in a towel. When she pushed open the door to the main room, though, she shrieked and almost dropped it.

"Oh, dear gods, I saw Kaleb's butt." She squeezed her eyes closed, but the image was burned on her brain.

"Naw, that was Adrick," Kamaria said.

"Even worse! Why aren't there *walls?*" *Not* two separate bathing rooms. Two changing rooms that opened onto *one* shared room with two pools divided by a half wall and columns much too slender to serve any real purpose. Judging from her brief peek at the closest pool, they weren't the only people there, either.

Kamaria cackled. "What a way to make friends. I love this place."

Saida laughed nervously. "A few steps farther and we'll have some cover. Eyes on the ground, ladies."

Kamaria cupped Alessa's elbow—clamped to her chest so she could cover her eyes without losing her towel—and clucked encouragingly. "Come, my prudish little ducklings. Follow me." She raised her voice. "Hey, Dante! No, don't worry, I won't let them walk into any walls."

"Don't *look* at him," Alessa hissed.

"Why not? He doesn't care."

Saida's giggles intensified.

"Okay, stop. Sit," Kamaria ordered.

Alessa dared to crack one eye and sat on the edge, checking with her peripheral vision that the half wall was, indeed, blocking the other pool. Not that it would stop anyone who walked over to it from seeing them over the top.

Two young women and an older woman with a child stared at them from the water.

"Sorry about my friends. We're new. Kamaria. Hi. Nice to meet you." Her towel hit the floor, and Kamaria sauntered down the steps with a muttered, "*Try* to be cool?" over her shoulder.

Saida and Alessa shared pinch-lipped looks, then Saida silently counted down from three.

They simultaneously shed their towels and scooted into the water, ducking so only their heads remained above the surface.

"Oooh, this feels amazing," Saida said.

Kamaria was already chatting with the two younger women.

Alessa rested her hand on her discarded towel in case it decided to wander off.

Dante washed quickly, keeping his injured shoulder toward the wall. He'd removed the stitches that morning, but the ridge of barely healed flesh left behind would raise questions he couldn't answer if any ghiotte spotted it.

He was the first one dressed and outside, smoothing his damp hair.

Talia was waiting impatiently. "Don't forget what I said. People need to know where your loyalties are. Especially tonight, you *have* to be ghiotte, first and foremost."

"I *am*." Dante's stomach twisted at the half-truth, but it wasn't the right time to tell her. He wasn't ready.

The day wasn't even finished, he'd already had a half dozen close calls, and now they were wading into the heart of ghiotte society.

The others emerged—Alessa's cheeks were very pink—and they set off.

People were everywhere on the piazza—dancing, kissing, performing gymnastic feats or cheering for someone who was, wrestling, arm punching, or whooping with laughter.

Talia walked backward to address the group as they approached the basilica. "Help yourself to whatever you want inside, but don't be rude. You're auditioning for the role of world's least annoying new neighbors. Don't mess it up."

A sudden (and otherwise inexplicable) gust of wind, which must have been Saida's nerves, extinguished one of the torches lighting their way, and Talia frowned.

Kamaria held up her palm. "Need a light?"

"No," Talia snapped. "We don't need magic to light a damn fire."

Kamaria dropped her hands. "Right."

Ciro hung back, looking uneasy. "I think I'll wait out here for a bit."

"Do you want me to stay with you?" Alessa asked him.

"No, no. You go ahead. I don't love loud noises or crowds."

Loud noises and crowds were . . . an understatement. Walking through the massive doors of the cathedral was like being sucked into a cyclone of color and sound and movement.

"Let me guess: That was the busiest time of day for the baths?" Dante shouted to be heard over the music, which seemed to be coming from musicians in each balcony with a tenuous commitment to playing the same song.

Talia didn't hide her smirk. "A little friendly hazing never hurt anyone. Sorry we don't have private spas or handmaidens for your pampered pets here."

He rolled his eyes. "They don't have handmaidens in the Cittadella."

"Servants?" Talia didn't break her stride as a young woman tumbled from the ceiling, controlling her descent with a ribbon of silken fabric twisted around her.

"Yes. Fine. They *do* have servants," he said, tracking another aerialist so he didn't get kicked.

"Hope you didn't get used to it."

"I was an employee. A temporary one, at that."

"Did you have a cute little uniform?" Talia teased. "A cubby with your name on it?"

"Enjoying yourself?"

"Always." Talia plucked two drinks from a passing tray, and

they waded farther into the crush of people. As they navigated their way through the bacchanalia, she pointed out Perduta's key players, giving him the rundown on key feuds, alliances, and power dynamics, the people he needed to know and those to avoid.

On the altar, the golden-haired chairman, Leo, lounged in one throne with a dark-haired woman in his lap and a blonde massaging his shoulders. Eyes glittering, Leo scanned the revelry before him like a predator with barely sated bloodlust—or another kind of lust—hunting for a worthy enough opponent. Or tempting prey.

His gaze landed on Dante, and the rumble of his low voice carried despite the noise. "Come here, new guy."

Dante waited a beat. Not a refusal, just long enough to show he was *choosing* to walk over, not snapping to follow an order.

Even a lone wolf recognized a pack leader when he saw one. Guys like Leo might enjoy making people take a knee, but they sure as hell didn't respect anyone who'd give it.

Baring sharp incisors, Leo gestured to the empty throne. "Sit."

Dante stepped forward, hoping he wasn't falling into a trap that would cause the first ghiotte uprising.

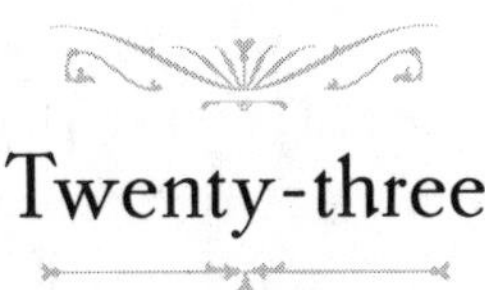

Twenty-three

Staring at Dante's back as he was swallowed by the crowd, Alessa tried not to feel as though he'd deliberately left her behind. Even though, obviously, he had.

The doors were thrown open to reveal a fever dream of noise and sound, thumping with music and pulsing with bodies in motion.

Saida plucked at her diaphanous pink skirts. "When they said 'party,' I was picturing something a little more formal."

Alessa had chosen a lacy blouse and aquamarine skirt from her meager selection; Kamaria was in her usual fawn-colored breeches and a low-cut tunic; and the boys had the eternal luxury of being able to wear dark slacks and light-colored button-down shirts to almost any event, so they fit in fairly well with the more fully dressed ghiotte. But there didn't seem to be a dress code. Or a requirement *for* clothing.

"Is that paint?" Adrick said under his breath.

A strapping young man swiveled his hips in time with the beat, wearing nothing but a scrap of fabric around his waist, unless you counted the red painted flames licking their way up his legs toward whatever it concealed.

"Did we die at Divorando without realizing?" Kamaria asked. "Are we in heaven?"

Alessa gaped at a girl swallowing a sword. "Do you think this is normal for them?"

"What?" Kamaria gave herself a little shake. "You mean hundreds of nearly invincible young people, many orphans, living in secret and on the run?" She waved at a girl posing atop the feet of a boy doing a one-handed handstand. "Yeah, this is pretty much what I would expect."

Around them, a group shrieked with laughter in a tumble of arms and legs

"They *are* all pretty young, aren't they?" Saida mused. "What's that about?"

Kamaria frowned in thought. "There's really no tactful way to ask, 'Do you kill your elderly or simply lock them up after dark?'"

"Let's not open with that question," Alessa said.

A man and woman in matching leather pants and vests greeted Adrick by holding out two blue glass bottles, speaking in unison. "You want?"

Adrick winked. "Depends what you're offering and if you come as a set."

The woman laughed. "For now, drinks. Welcome to Perduta."

They placed the bottles in his hands, blew matching kisses, and sauntered away.

"We are *not* on Saverio anymore." Adrick used his teeth to pull out one cork, then frowned around it as he realized he didn't have a free hand.

With an exasperated eye roll, Kaleb yanked it from his mouth and pocketed it.

"Aren't you going to run after Girl Dante?" Kaleb asked Kamaria as Adrick took a swig and passed it on to her.

She grinned and raised the bottle to her lips. "If she'd let me."

"Why does everyone like the stabby ones?" Kaleb asked. "Am I the only person who doesn't want to sleep with knives? You all need help."

Adrick uncorked the second bottle and took a swallow. "You're just jealous because if you spent the night with someone armed, you'd be dead by morning."

"Oh my gods, kiss already!" Kamaria hollered.

Kaleb glared murderously.

Adrick scoffed. "In his dreams."

"I'm going to find out what's happening in the dark recesses of this debauchery," Kaleb said with a bland smile.

"We're supposed to stay out of trouble," Adrick muttered.

"Boring." Kaleb set off toward a makeshift bar where a young man wearing what appeared to be some sort of chain mail and nothing else was pouring liquor directly into the open mouths of anyone who passed. With a sigh, Adrick trudged after him.

Kamaria took Alessa and Saida by the hands. "Come on, let's show these blessed warriors that we know how to have a good time."

"They certainly are . . . free with themselves, aren't they?" Saida asked as they skirted the margins of a roiling dance floor, where the pews had been dragged into forming a makeshift border.

The architects who'd designed the building as a testament to the gods probably wouldn't approve of the blatantly sensual dancing, but the ghiotte were so comfortable with their bodies, it didn't even feel rude to stare, and their natural physicality made them such ridiculously skilled dancers, it would take a strong person *not* to.

Kamaria sidled closer to Alessa. "Is there anything I should know about being with a ghiotte?"

"Like what?" Alessa followed Kamaria's gaze to where Dante and Talia stood on the far side. A spiky-haired girl in body paint crooked a finger at Talia, who demurred with a wide smile. So she *could* smile. That was reassuring.

"She's so much like Dante, you must have *some* advice," Kamaria said as the girl took Talia's hands and drew her onto the dance floor, where their bodies moved like twin flames.

Alessa frowned. "He was never *that* grumpy."

"You either have a very poor memory or love broke your emotional compass." Kamaria let out a sound that was almost a whimper as Talia glanced their way, eyes sharp despite her relaxed pose—head tipped up, throat bared, lips parted with the faintest hint of a smile. "She's messing with me, isn't she? You saw that, right?"

Saida sucked in a breath. "I did."

Kamaria exhaled loudly. "What do I *do?*"

"Try talking to her again?" Saida ventured.

Kamaria scoffed. "You don't fight fire by talking, you fight it with fire. Let's dance."

"Like *that?*" Alessa said.

"No, not like *that.* As much as I enjoy getting under Dante's skin, now that you're secret star-crossed-can't-touch-each-other lovers again it feels mean. Come with me so I can show off and prove I don't care that she's dancing with someone else."

"But you *do,*" Saida said. "Very much so."

"Yeah, but this is how you play the game."

Alessa pushed away thoughts of what the ghiotte might think and tried to emulate Kamaria's sensual hip movements.

She failed spectacularly.

Kamaria wiped tears of laughter from her eyes. "What are you *doing?*"

"They don't teach this kind of dancing in the Cittadella, and I wasn't invited to regular parties," Alessa said.

"Let your muscles go loose." Kamaria gripped Alessa's hips to guide her. "*Loose.* For Dea's sake, it's like watching a foal take its first steps."

"I have an idea." Alessa covered Kamaria's hands with her own. The moment their skin touched, she felt her movements shift into the sinuous swivel she'd been attempting.

"Damn, girl. Keep that up and I might fall in love with *you.*"

Though most partygoers pretended to ignore them, Alessa could practically see the news of their arrival rippling through the crowd. Her heart rate kicked up with every almost-glance their way, the subtle shift of bodies away from them.

Outsider. Enemy. Other. She didn't know exactly how the ghiotte quantified them, but it was all too familiar, the sensation of being unwanted carved so deeply into her bones it felt like banging a toe that was barely healed from the last time.

Alessa hadn't taken a drink, but the dance floor seemed to waver beneath her feet.

"I'm going to get some air," she said.

Wiping sweat from her forehead, she headed toward the side of the room where it was less dense, but a swarthy man with enormous muscles blocked her path. Scanning her from top to bottom, his lips curled in a sneer.

She met his stare without blinking. She had more than

enough practice facing strangers who looked at her with disgust. She wasn't going to break now.

He turned away with a dismissive huff, and Alessa kept going. She'd endured it before. She could again.

As she inched through the crush, her mind seemed to scatter in a dozen directions. Flashes of joy, excitement, anger, lust, and sadness blossomed and vanished, melding into a cacophony of emotion. She reached the wall and turned her back to lean against it. She was no closer to the door, but at least she had some breathing room.

It might have been another side effect of her strange sixth sense, or an audible shift in the crowd, but her attention snapped to the altar.

For some inexplicable reason, Dante was sitting in a throne beside Leo. A slinky young woman was serving them drinks, her enviably thick locks doing more to cover her than her dress—a generous description for a few strips of fabric—but Dante didn't seem to notice what must have been quite a view as she poured. Good man.

Both men appeared at ease, in the military sense of the word—alert, ready for action—but Alessa couldn't shake the sense that all their futures teetered in the balance.

Dante wasn't accustomed to making small talk with someone who had quite so much going on in his lap, but if Leo wasn't going to acknowledge the young woman gliding her hands across his chest, Dante wasn't about to.

Leo chuckled softly. "You like?"

It took Dante a second to realize he was talking about the throne. "Solid craftsmanship, but I'm not in the market."

Leo inclined his head. "Good to hear. Every few years a new kid gets it in his head to try and become king. It's damn tiring."

"I'm here for allies, not subjects."

It was the truth. Dante needed to win the guy over, not *beat* him, and that was a hell of a lot harder. He knew how to fight. He didn't know shit about politics.

"What *exactly* do you want from us, new guy?" Leo asked.

"To train with us, prepare for whatever Crollo is plotting."

"We never stop training. Never let down our guard. What makes you think we aren't already prepared?"

"It takes more than individual skills to make an army."

Leo stopped the woman kissing his neck with a light touch and reached for a bottle of ocher liquid. "Scottare. A Perduta specialty."

The brunette licked her wrist, and the blonde sprinkled it with black granules as Leo poured two glasses.

"The salt brings out the heat," Leo explained to Dante. "But you'll have to do your own. We share many things on Perduta, but Chiara and Vittoria are all mine." Leo took his time licking the salt off his lady's wrist and raised his glass. "Saluti."

"Saluti." Dante braced himself. Ghiotte liquor was bound to pack a punch.

It burned a trail down his throat, but it was a *nice* punch. Too many more and he'd be in for a rough night, though. After Divorando, he'd realized how much of his alcohol tolerance and fast recovery was thanks to his ghiotte healing powers. He didn't want to know what kind of hangover Crollo's nectar might deliver now, and he needed to keep his wits together.

Leo stood and gestured to the dance floor. As though he

had given a command, the dancers closest to the dais pulled back in one fluid movement, and for one confusing second, Dante thought Leo was asking him to dance.

His next words put *that* fear to rest.

"Weapon of choice?"

Twenty-four

The crowd was too thick to navigate without touching anyone, but Alessa dove in anyway. No one there was endangered by her powers. They were all Fonte or ghiotte, except for Adrick. And Dante. The space before the altar cleared as the closest dancers drew back, forming a dense wall of humanity she could barely get through.

"No throwing unless you want to take it outside," said Leo, as Dante drew his knives. "Winner draws second blood."

"Not first?" Dante said.

"Anyone can get lucky once." Leo saluted with one of his knives, and they began.

It was like being trapped in a repeat nightmare—Dante, surrounded by a hostile audience, staring down an opponent—but this was worse than the first time she'd seen him fight in the Barrel. He'd been a stranger then, and no one had been armed. And while she hadn't known he'd had powers that could save him that time, this time, she knew he *didn't*.

Most of the partygoers barely noted the knife fight about to start—another typical night in the land of the near-immortal—but someone shouted, "Anyone betting on the new guy?" and the nearest onlookers cheered like it was a game. Which it was, as far as they knew. What was a knife to someone who didn't fear a few stab wounds?

But Dante *wasn't* a ghiotte anymore. Because of her.

Leo circled, twirling his blade idly, then struck out like a viper. Close, but Dante held up his arm to show the crowd his uncut skin.

They dodged, parried, and slashed.

Alessa nearly screamed as a pack of oblivious dancers blocked her view. When she could see again, Leo was wiping blood from his cheek.

Second blood, Leo said. Dante had drawn first. Once more and he could end it without a scratch on him. But Dante's steps weren't as fast or as sure as usual.

Her gaze darted to the half-empty bottle between the two thrones. *Oh, please.*

One moment Dante was dancing back from a slash, the next he was shoved forward by an annoyed ghiotte who hadn't been paying attention.

He recovered, but not fast enough. Leo's next move cut through Dante's shirt, slicing him from one pectoral and down across his abdomen.

Alessa made a strangled sound as the torn edges of his shirt darkened like the edges of paper in a flame.

Dante didn't look down, merely nodded acknowledgment and kept going.

He couldn't tell how deep it was, didn't know how much his ripped shirt revealed, or how much he could bleed before it looked suspicious or he passed out, but one way or another, he needed to end this fight soon or everyone on Perduta would know he was a fraud.

His focus shrank to the man across from him. Leo was bigger, with a longer arm span, and he was probably stronger too, but more mass meant more to move, so Dante had the advantage when it came to speed.

Not much, but it would have to be enough.

Dante noted every shift of Leo's weight, every minute movement of his eyes.

Leo lunged. Dante dodged.

He had to keep Leo on the offensive, wait for him to strike, so he'd open himself up.

Leo was an attack dog, not a guard dog. He wouldn't wait long.

Dante held one of his daggers ready to slice, the other for stabbing. Leo's next move would decide which one.

Dante spun, barely slipping past the tip of Leo's knife, and jabbed the tip of his dagger into the meatiest part of Leo's shoulder.

Leo glanced down at the blossom of blood spreading across his sleeve. The music was still going, half the dance floor still full despite the battle a few feet away.

Leo stuck out a hand. "Good fight."

Dante shook it. "You too."

"Next time I won't go so easy on you." Leo grinned. "Enjoy your night. You won't have any trouble finding someone to celebrate with."

Celebrate. *Right.* By getting his ass out of there before he bled to death.

Alessa reached him as he stepped out of the melee of dancers.

"How bad is it?" she said softly.

"I don't know," he said, his lips barely moving. "But someone's gonna notice I'm still bleeding if I don't get out of here right now."

She walked in front of him, blocking anyone's view of his shirt, and they made their way through the crowd far too slowly for his nerves.

Dante kept his back straight and his expression neutral, even as warm wetness soaked the top of his pants. How much blood did a person even have?

Finally, they reached the door and he stepped into the fresh air, gulping shallow breaths so he wouldn't black out.

Around the side of the building, he stopped to pull up his shirt and check the damage. It wasn't deep enough to spill his guts, but that was about the only good news.

"Shit." He braced one hand against the wall. "What do we do now?"

Alessa's breath hissed out of her. "It's not spurting, so you haven't severed an artery. At least, I don't think so. If we can get you cleaned up and stitched without infection, you'll have a nasty scar, but you'll be okay. We can do this. I can do this. We need to apply pressure until the bleeding slows, then I'll get Adrick." She added her hands to his. "One of them must have seen, right? They'll come looking for us. Then we'll find something for a temporary bandage until we can get you out of here and stitch you up."

It wasn't Adrick who found them.

"What are you doing out here?" came Talia's voice. "You should be in there doing shots and taking the win."

Face tight with strain, Dante kept his voice casual. "Just cleaning up."

"Oh, please." Talia's footsteps came closer. "No one cares about blood here. Wear it with honor."

Alessa pressed harder, and a grunt of pain slipped from his lips. He needed to lie down. He needed bandages. He needed Talia to *leave.*

Alessa ducked to stay hidden, but the blood wouldn't stop. And neither did Talia.

"Seriously? You're with *her* right now?" Judging by Talia's expression, she'd jumped to the wrong conclusion. Which was still better than the truth.

"Give us a minute, will you?" Dante snapped.

Talia must have heard the fear behind his anger, because she didn't storm off. She leaned closer, eyes going wide. At Dante's blood-soaked shirt. Alessa's blood-covered hands. And a wound that any ghiotte would have been over with by now.

"Why aren't you healing?" Talia demanded. "What did she *do* to you?"

Dante replaced Alessa's hand with his own and turned to face Talia. If he moved slowly, he wasn't in immediate danger of bleeding out—a small win in a losing battle.

Talia wasn't a fool. There was no other explanation.

"I'm not a ghiotte," Dante said, bitterness burning hotter than his wound. "Not anymore."

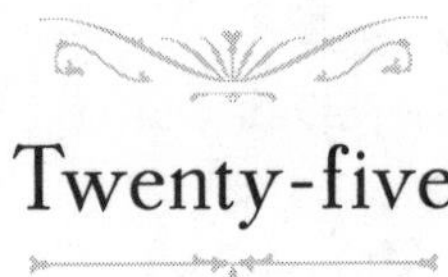

Twenty-five

Talia recoiled. From the truth. From him.

Dante took a shallow breath. "I made it sound like I *almost* died, but that was a lie. I *did*." *Cazza*. This was *not* the time to get dizzy. "Alessa kept a fragment of my powers, which was enough to bring my body back, but not my gift."

"You *broke* him?!" Talia spit at Alessa.

Alessa's breath hitched, but he knew she wouldn't cry. Not yet. He'd held her enough times when she'd broken down after a crisis had passed to know. And he'd do it again, if he survived this one.

"It's not her fault," he said. "If she hadn't tried, I'd be dead."

"People will flip out." Talia shuddered. "Even knowing it's possible . . ."

"You gonna tell them?" Dante held her gaze, daring her to look away.

"If I did, they'd think I lied about you. And *that* lie is not forgivable here."

He nodded. "Then we'll keep it quiet. If anyone finds out, I'll say you didn't know."

Talia's gaze slipped away. "Can't she try again? Just . . . put the rest of you back?"

His bitter laugh became a grimace. "Only Dea can fix this, and she's not listening."

Talia looked thoughtful. "Will you be able to train tomorrow?"

"No. He can't," Alessa cut in. "It's probably not life-threatening unless it gets infected, but he needs stitches and time to heal before he can do anything strenuous."

"You'll never make it through probation if you get found out." Talia looked around the piazza. "But everyone is here now. . . . Gods, this is *such* a bad idea."

"What idea?" Alessa asked.

"None of your business," Talia hissed.

Dante sighed. "Talia, please. We have a situation here."

Talia growled softly. "Meet me at the bathhouse in an hour. You won't die before then, will you?"

Dante frowned. "No, but—"

"Then *go*. I'll say you left with someone else. *Anyone* but her. And don't let anyone see you together or that you're still . . ."—she curled her lip—"*injured*."

Dante would have sighed, but he couldn't afford any unnecessary movements. Whatever Talia had planned wouldn't be enough. Even she didn't seem to think so.

They were officially screwed.

Alessa's legs were overcooked pasta by the time they neared the bathhouse.

Dante was becoming a dead weight as the blood loss and booze took full effect.

"Fuck," Dante slurred for the tenth time. "*Fuuuuuuuck.* One second faster and this wouldn't have happened. *One* second."

"It's going to be okay," Alessa wheezed. "Talia has a plan."

Dante snorted derisively. "Ghiotte don't know shit about healing wounds. Probably some tincture made of powdered chalk left over from the last time a regular person visited."

"Way to think positive." She stopped to breathe, unslinging Dante's arm from her shoulders.

He braced himself on the wall with a groan. "*Cazzo,* that hurts. *Fuck* me."

"I'd be delighted, but you're still bleeding and I'm sure it would kill you, so let's table that for now."

His laugh turned into a curse. "What time is it?"

"A little after midnight. Why?"

"Guess what?" He sounded oddly excited.

"What?" She rolled her shoulders back with a wince.

"It's our anniversary!" His grin was absurdly cute and entirely out of place while they were covered in blood, but she couldn't resist smiling back.

"Dante, love, if my math is correct—"

"You're good at math," he declared, as though it was fact.

"Am I?"

"Yes. I remember. You said you don't know how you know the answers but you always know them. Therefore, you're good at math."

"I'm not sure that's entirely accurate, but sure. Anyway, if my math *is* correct, we met about eight months ago, and I don't think *anyone* counts seven months and three weeks as an anniversary."

"Not from when we *met*. You don't count from when you *met*."

She shook her head. "Well, our first kiss was about a week and a half after that—"

"Two weeks." He held up two bloody fingers. "It was *two* weeks."

She pursed her lips so she wouldn't laugh. Or cry at how sweet it was that he remembered. "I'll take your word for it. But that's still seven months and a week. And the first time we, *you know,* was a few days after that. We *did* move fast, didn't we?"

He gave a small shrug. "It was the end of the world."

"Fair. But it's still not an anniversary. Even if you want to call seven months an anniversary—"

"For this, I do."

"Fine. But that would still be in a few days."

"Ah, ah, ah," he said, waving a finger. "Not a *kiss* anniversary. Not a *meet* anniversary. Not *that* anniversary."

She grabbed his wagging finger and pulled his arm around her shoulders again. "I give up. Which anniversary is it?"

He chuckled softly. "Our stabbiversary."

A laugh burst from her. "It is *not*. Is it?"

"It is! Ha! Ow." They reached the bathhouse at last, and Alessa managed to pull the door open without jostling Dante too much. "Seven months ago today—ow, *fuck* that hurts—I was dragging your loopy self back to the Cittadella. And look at us now."

She rubbed her temples with a weak laugh. "Can we *try* not to make this a regular thing?"

An hour later, Dante lay with his head in Alessa's lap in a damp corner of the bathhouse, his mood going dark. There was still no sign of Talia, and any numbing from the alcohol was long gone, leaving only throbbing pain where Leo's knife had split him.

If they had fetched Adrick, he could've been stitched up and resting at the house, but instead, they were drenched in blood on a cold damp floor.

At least Alessa was there, running her fingers through his hair and distracting him as best she could. He tried to focus on her touch and let the rest fall away.

Those were his favorite moments, the quiet ones. Not *literally* quiet—Alessa was rarely silent while awake—but the times when they weren't *doing* anything or talking about anything important. Just there, together.

He raised her hand to his mouth, speaking the words into her palm for safekeeping. "What if I can't do this?"

"You don't even know what she's planning."

"Not that. All of this. How am I supposed to turn them into an army when I'm not even one of them? I'm a fraud. A liar. I don't belong here."

"You belong with me," she said. "And that's where you are. And you can do anything."

He started to shake his head, but she held him still. "*We're* going to do this."

"What if we can't?"

"Then we'll go down together, fighting side by side." She trapped her lip between her teeth for a moment. "You once asked me what I wanted to do before Divorando. Your turn. What do *you* want to do before whatever's coming for us?"

He leered up at her, and she laughed again.

"Dream bigger. You have a second chance with your uncle

and Talia, an opportunity to finally get to know your people. You've been alone for so long."

"Not alone," he said. "Not anymore."

"You know what I mean. Maybe you could—I don't know—make friends? Find peace?"

He sighed deeply. "Why do you always try to make me be a good person?"

She bent to drop a kiss on his forehead. "Because I love you."

"Ti amo, luce mia," he whispered back.

They both jumped at the door slamming open.

Heat climbed Dante's neck as Alessa helped him stand, but they had bigger problems to deal with than what Talia might have overheard.

"I have *no* idea if this will work, but I brought clothes since yours are all bloody." Talia stalked over and tossed an armful of clothing at their feet, then pointed a dagger at Alessa. "If you *ever* breathe a word of this to anyone, I will cut your heart out and eat it, hear me?"

"Noted," Alessa said.

Dante winced for the five-hundredth time. "What *is* it?"

Talia pulled a large key from her pocket and gestured at the lone door on the far wall. "La Fonte di Guarigione, of course."

His last hope died. "That's not funny."

They already knew that Dea's gift of a source of healing was actually the ghiotte themselves, not some mythical fountain that had been created from an ancient mistranslation.

"I'm not joking," Talia said. "I guess Dea has a sense of humor, because after the first of us got banished because they thought we drank from a fountain that never existed, she blessed one of the baths here to augment our healing abilities—and you don't have to *drink* it. It can help a seriously injured ghiotte heal a bit faster, though, and using it regularly seems to slow aging—"

"I knew it," Alessa said, earning another glare from Talia.

"Probationary members aren't supposed to know about it until they're voted in, then there's a ceremonial baptism, but Papa has an extra key. Guard it with your life."

Dante caught it, his mind racing. "Will it give my powers back?"

Talia's mouth twisted. "I have no idea. It's ours. We don't let anyone else use it, so we don't know what effect it has on regular people. It might do nothing at all. Do me favor and don't track blood in the chamber." She curled her lip at Alessa. "You can both get cleaned up out here, but *you* don't get to use the *fontana*. It's for *us*, not people like you."

"Understood," Alessa said in the prim tone of voice she used to hide irritation.

"I'll keep watch outside," Talia said. "If anyone shows up, I'll say one of the new kids is a prude and I'm being *nice*. Good luck."

Dante grabbed Alessa's hand as Talia left. He'd need something to hold on to if this lifeline of hope snapped.

Squeezing once, as tightly as he could without hurting her, he took a breath and released her hand before peeling off his clothes and easing into the main bath.

The burn of salt water on raw flesh was enough to distract him from the sounds of Alessa splashing herself clean nearby. He was shaking when he stepped out and faced the chamber door. All those years of hating who he was, resenting the power he was born with, and now he *needed* it back.

For Alessa. For them.

For *himself*.

His hands shook as he slid the key into the ornate lock. The chamber within could have been in any luxury spa on Saverio if not for the unearthly blue glow of the water. Stone walls, marble floors, decorative pillars around a circular pool large enough for a dozen people, designed like an underwater amphitheater with descending stairs all around.

Alessa watched from the main room behind him, and he didn't have to look back to know she was holding her breath, too, as he stepped into the water.

Feet, knees, waist, chest. Barely stopping to suck in a breath, he submerged himself entirely, bright blue light undulating all around him.

He stayed below until his chest ached. Until his lungs screamed. Until he had no choice but to surface or drown.

Gasping, he shook his head. Blinked.

The world came back into focus.

His world came into focus. Clad only in a towel, Alessa hovered in the doorway, her hazel eyes enormous in her face as she stared. He couldn't bring himself to look at the gash on his chest, but he raised his arm. The cut was gone, no marks where he'd pulled out the stitches.

"One more." He went under again.

When he came up, he followed Alessa's gaze, but he could already feel it. The gash was healing.

His heart thudded painfully. The fountain had healed him, but had it *fixed* him? Hope was the most dangerous temptation.

He splashed over to the side of the pool and held out his hand, but Alessa wouldn't come closer.

"I'm scared," she said, hugging herself.

"So am I." He hauled himself from the water and walked over, hand outstretched. "We won't know until we try."

With a shaky breath, she placed her hand into his.

Nothing. No pain. Color flared in Alessa's cheeks, and the first hint of exultation buzzed in his veins.

"Now, the real test." He closed the gap between them until her towel rasped against him, her bare thighs warm against his. He pressed the first kiss to her lips, but she held back, her spine too stiff and lips too firm as she tried to rein in her passion so her power wouldn't take over.

But that was the *point*. It was *always* the point. And this time it was *really* the point. He had to know.

"Sei mia," he whispered. Slanting his mouth over hers, he teased until her lips grew pliant and soft.

His girl baffled him in many ways, but her body he understood. And he knew the instant she forgot about restraint. Her lips parted and she became liquid fire, melting into him.

Still no warning prickle at the base of his spine, no looming threat of pain.

Alessa was aflame with desire, and he *wasn't* suffering for it. *Finally*.

Their hands bumped as she unwrapped her towel, and he threw it across the room, deepening the kiss, heady with lust and relief and joy. She must have sensed it, begun to fully trust it, because her hands tangled in his hair as he gripped her waist, hoisting her up.

Keeping his arm between her and the cold wall, he pressed her back, murmuring, "Brava la mia ragazza," as she hugged him with her legs.

This Alessa was not the inexperienced girl of their first

time. She'd blossomed like a bud finally shown the light. *His* light.

She wasn't shy or timid, and she knew her body better now. He would have spent an eternity rediscovering every sensitive spot on her body, but she was, as always, impatient. Impulsive. And he loved her for it.

She hooked an arm around his neck, found him with her other hand, and he groaned a curse. Not very romantic. He'd do romance later. Next time. This time—his thoughts scattered. She was ready, *so* ready, and squirming against him.

He didn't have *much* control, but he taunted her—taunted himself—for one exquisite second, claiming her lips in a hard, deep kiss that had her begging—*Molto bella,* he loved it when she begged—and then. *Finally.*

Alessa cried out, her nails digging into his shoulders. He held still for a moment, savoring the homecoming of it, the ragged harmony of their breaths. But his stubborn, demanding girl couldn't wait, and she arched against him, gasping his name, hands flexing and grasping. Begging him to move.

Moving was good, too. He'd make it last next time. He'd treat her like a queen next time. Next time. This time—this time she was crying his name, her head thrown back, eyes squeezed shut, lips parted in a silent cry, and it was the most beautiful thing he'd seen in his whole wretched life.

He only had to hold on until—her nails dug into him and she went taut, sobbing his name again, and he groaned hers, the only word he could remember.

Maybe the only word he knew.

True love meant not dropping your beloved, and though Alessa could feel Dante trembling, she shivered in delight at the sensation of sliding against him until her toes touched the floor.

One hand braced on the wall above her, Dante bent to nuzzle her neck. "Vita mia."

She feathered kisses over his neck, his jaw. He tasted of salt and man and Dante, and if she'd had a way to capture the sound of his ragged breathing, she'd listen to it every night.

His cheek rubbed against hers, stubble rasping against her skin, and she held him as his shoulders shook. Running her fingers up and down his back, she whispered his name, on the verge of weeping from relief, love, and the joy of sharing pleasure, not pain, with him again.

He'd come back to her. He'd come back to himself.

She held him until the wave of emotion passed, murmuring phrases he'd taught her in the old language, terms of endearment that sounded like music when he used them but never came out right when she tried.

His ragged breath turned into laughter rumbling through his chest. "Your accent is still terrible. *No one* could be that bad unintentionally."

She slapped him lightly on the back. "I'm trying to be romantic."

"You love me." He drew back, grinning and unashamed of his wet cheeks.

She pretended to glare, but her face wouldn't cooperate. "I do. Amore mio."

"I can ignore the atrocious accent when you say that." He kissed her again before stepping away. "If Talia comes looking for us, I should probably have pants on."

"I get the feeling ghiotte don't really care about clothing. We may get to live your nudist life after all."

"Absolutely not. I'm a greedy bastard and I don't want anyone else to see you like I do." He tapped her on the ass. "Get dressed."

Talia was pacing in the foyer when Alessa followed Dante outside, smoothing her hair and trying not to look like someone who'd been doing what they'd been doing.

Dante, of course, was fully composed. He did it so effortlessly, too. It was disconcerting how easily he packed up his feelings sometimes. If he truly felt as strongly as she did, how could he hide it so easily?

She filed that thought away for another time.

Talia's gaze slid from Dante to Alessa's flushed cheeks and back. "Well?"

Alessa bit her tongue.

"It worked," Dante said, pulling up his shirt to show her his unmarked chest.

"Your powers came back?"

"Yup. Tested and made sure."

Talia blew out a breath. "How'd it feel?"

"Amazing."

Alessa bit her lip. *Surely,* he was messing with her *now.*

"You coming back to the party?" Talia opened the door.

"Nah." Dante scratched his neck. "Think I'll call it a night."

Talia looked like she wanted to say something, but she thought better of it, settling on a look of warning.

Alessa wouldn't let Talia ruin this moment. She had Dante back. She could touch him and be touched—her cheeks flared at the memory—even if they had to keep it a secret. She'd rather have stolen moments than none at all, and she never wanted to let go.

Dante must have felt the same, because he nodded to the

stairs when they reached the house. "We'll sleep under the stars. I've waited too long to let you go now."

"There are no doors."

"Then we'd better not waste time."

Dante tucked the bedrolls under one arm and reached out to steady her for the treacherous climb up the derelict stairs. Despite the dark, she trusted him completely.

He would never let her fall.

"Take my hand," he said.

And she did.

Twenty-six

DAYS UNTIL THE ECLIPSE: 20

Cradled in the crook of Dante's arm, Alessa traced each muscle with her fingertips as morning sunlight warmed their skin through gaps in the roof.

There. Right below his rib cage on the right side, his abdominal muscles flexed, slightly, when she drew the line between them.

He claimed he wasn't ticklish, but she was on a mission, hunting down every tiny twitch, memorizing his vulnerabilities for a future ambush that would prove him a liar.

"I was thinking," she said.

"Good for you." Dante patted her shoulder with a yawn.

Ah. His breathing stalled for a second when she ran her finger down the ridge of muscle where his hip met torso.

"Why do you think all of Dea's other gifts are granted at random but not the ghiotte's?"

"We're supposed to be her army," he said. "Wouldn't make sense to have little soldiers popping up all over the place."

"Every other power does." She shifted her attention to his

other side, but she'd be back. Any good investigation needed to be thorough, and she'd never been more dedicated to her studies.

"The Finestra is meant to be a leader, so Dea gives that power to someone who can lead. The Fonti . . . well, they're almost like a resource in some ways, so they don't need to grow up with others like them. She probably wanted us to pass skills down with each generation, so she kept it in families."

"Do ghiotte always pair up with other ghiotte, then?" she asked, *casually.*

Dante nudged her chin up with one finger. "Ask what you're asking."

So much for casual. She propped herself up on one elbow, letting her nightgown slip off her shoulder, but Dante wasn't deterred by the ploy to redirect his attention. He continued to study her face as his hand roamed.

Ah, well. She'd already failed at casual. "Do ghiotte ever choose to stay with someone who isn't one? I mean, are there rules about that sort of thing?"

"We don't even know if we'll live to see next month, and you're worrying about forever?" His smile went from teasing to tender at whatever he saw on her face. "I don't care about *rules.* I make my own choices. But if it makes you feel better, I've already met people with non-ghiotte partners, so even here, not everyone marries other ghiotte."

His lips twitched at the slight jerk of her head at the word "marries."

"Then what happens to their children? I mean . . . I don't . . . I'm not *asking* to have your babies, I'm just curious how this hereditary-gift thing works."

Dante cleared his throat. "Uh. Well. It's pretty simple. If a baby has a ghiotte parent, the baby is a ghiotte."

"Like, a half ghiotte?"

"No. A ghiotte."

Alessa scrunched her face in thought. "So they only take after the one parent?"

"If your mother can sing but your father's tone-deaf, and you have perfect pitch, aren't you still your father's child?"

"That's different."

"No, it isn't," Dante said firmly. "You are your parents' child whether you look more like one of them, or sound like the other, or whatever. People aren't broken into parts like that. If Tomo and Renata had a child, he wouldn't be half descended from Tomo's ancestors and half from Renata's. He would be one person, descended from both. It's addition, not division. A ghiotte's child is a ghiotte. Talia's mother wasn't, remember?"

"Then if other people have non-ghiotte partners, and there's no need to preserve the line or anything, why is it so terrible if anyone finds out we're together?"

"It's not *only* that you aren't a ghiotte. You're the *Finestra*." He tucked her hair behind her ear, running his thumb along her jawline. "On Saverio, you're a symbol of community and safety. Here you're a reminder that ghiotte were denied both."

"I *hate* being a symbol," she said. "Do you really think Talia hasn't figured out we're a couple?"

"No proof, no crime."

Alessa recoiled. "Oh, *lovely;* I'm a crime now."

His laughter rumbled through her. "I'll remind you it *was* a crime when we first got together, and I did the time for it."

She feathered kisses over his cheeks. "Was it worth it?"

In one swift motion, he rolled her beneath him. "I'd spend a hundred years in chains for one day with you."

Unlike Dante, Alessa *was* ticklish, and she yelped as Dante found the sensitive spot on the side of her rib cage.

"Don't think I can't tell what you're up to," he said, grinning at his victory. "I didn't stop to think, but are you using your powers enough to, you know, prevent things?"

She brushed a wayward curl off his forehead. "Between helping Saida dry laundry, lighting lanterns with Kamaria, and constantly blowing away the dust everyone keeps tracking inside, I'm quite confident I'm impregnable."

His lips twitched into a smile. "That's not what that word means."

"Of course it is. If you can't impregnate me, I'm impregnable." She rested her forehead on his breastbone, giddy with the satisfaction of having nothing between them.

"Mmm," he mused. "While I have no intention of impregnating you tonight—"

She pulled back to study his face. *"Tonight?"*

"Focus." His lips found the soft hollow behind her ear. "'Impregnable' means something you can't get inside, like a fortress."

"Oh, *no*. Lower the drawbridge, break down the walls—"

His palm swept up her thigh, and she forgot about coming up with a better metaphor.

"Found them!" Kamaria shouted from the doorway.

Dante buried his face in Alessa's hair with a groan. "Go *away*."

"Talia came looking for you, but we didn't even realize you'd come back last night."

Oh. Right. Talia.

Alessa reached for him with a drowsy yawn that almost

had him tell Kamaria to get lost—but no. He had a job to do. He also remembered how little he and Alessa were wearing.

"Uh. If she's still there, tell her I'll be down in a second." He gave Alessa a quick kiss and disentangled himself from the blankets to find his clothes. He could be back in her arms that night. Every night from now on. They'd still have to avoid each other during the daytime, but her nights were all his.

Determinedly ignoring Kamaria's wolf whistle, Dante walked out the door like a man reborn. Nothing could bring him down.

Until that moment, every step he'd taken on Perduta had been on broken ice, with only Talia's word to keep him from falling through. Now, after twenty years of being one kind of outcast or another, he was surrounded by his own kind and he didn't have to pretend to be something he wasn't. No more lying about who he was. No more worrying that a scratch or bruise might give him away.

The truth made him strong. Confident. Ready. Damn near invincible.

It was time to build an army.

Twenty-seven

Alessa descended the stairs as Blaise burst into the courtyard and leaped onto the bench with a grubby notebook held above his head. "Time for job assignments. We don't put up with slackers here. Everyone works, or they're out."

"What's *your* job?" Kaleb grumbled.

"Babysitter. Obviously." Blaise pulled a pencil from behind his ear. "Any of you have useful skills?"

Adrick cleared his throat. "I'm an apothecary and medic."

Blaise cocked his head. "A what?"

"I, uh, treat people who are ill or injured, set bones and . . . well, um . . ."

Blaise's expression was flat. "So, nothing *useful.*"

Adrick flushed. "Guess not."

"Have him clean chamber pots," Kaleb suggested.

"We have *sewers,*" Blaise said.

"Wait, I can bake," Adrick said. "Cakes, cookies, scones, pastries . . ." He ticked off a long list of decadent treats on his fingers.

"If you can make all that, they'll let you have whatever you want." Blaise wrote down *Curly: Kitchen.* "Who else?"

"I can cook, too, but my power is controlling wind," Saida said. "In case you need . . . um . . . linens dried?"

Blaise nodded. "Laundry."

Kaleb still looked miffed. "I can harness electricity."

"That stuff all broke ages ago," Blaise said. Adrick muttered something under his breath that sounded suspiciously like "shit shoveler" and Blaise checked his sheet. "Trash duty it is."

"Why do *I* get trash duty?" Kaleb said.

Blaise smirked. "Because I don't like you."

After sharing that he'd grown up in a fishing village, Ciro was told to report to a fishing vessel, while the girls were assigned to the communal laundry near the piazza.

Alessa wrinkled her nose. Dante was on a mission, and she was determined to be supportive. By being invisible.

He'd concealed his entire identity for years before meeting her. *She* had concealed their relationship from everyone until Divorando. This was no different.

Acting. That's all it was. Everyone had to *act* like Dante was their leader, he had to *act* like he wasn't in love with her, and she would *act* like they were mere allies.

They each had a role to play. She would do her part, too, even if that meant fighting from opposite ends of the battlefield.

"Where were you?" Talia asked when Dante caught up with her.

"Slept upstairs. Nice night. Figured I'd get some space."

She looked slightly suspicious but didn't press. "Turns out vanishing after beating Leo last night made people talk even more. By the end of the night, half the island thought you'd sliced him to the bone."

"That's good?"

"Obviously. Leo's a force, but you held your own." She nudged him with a grin. "Like I said, you were born for this."

Another surge of exultation knocked the wind out of him. He *had* been born for this. He *was* a ghiotte, and the one they'd follow into battle. He could finally show them exactly who he was and what he could do.

Talia paid for espresso in a bistro off the piazza, nodding to the other patrons but thankfully not dragging Dante through another round of introductions. "Some want to befriend you, others want to screw you, and the rest want a shot at you, but *everyone* wants to know you. And *that* means we can start recruiting."

She'd been busy the night before, and a dozen of her friends were waiting for them on the piazza. Not enough to win a war, but a start. Dante had met most of them, but Talia ran through names again, pairing each with a tagline about his or her skills: Jesse's uppercut would knock your teeth loose, Anya was the fastest sprinter in Perduta, Kira's flips defied gravity, Torin had a wicked roundhouse. . . .

"They're the best of the best," Talia declared. "If you can look past the fact that Jesse always 'forgets' to bring money for drinks, Anya insists on wearing clashing colors, and Maya bites. Don't call her short unless you want to lose a finger." Grinning, Talia shouted over a return volley of insults, "But *aside* from their glaring personality flaws, I'd trust them with my life."

Dante waited for her to continue, but everyone turned to look at him. Right. Leader.

"Uh, great. Let's get started, then. To create a unified force that will hold its ground and not run—" He held up a hand to stop their protests. "I know everyone here is brave. But I've seen battle-ready soldiers, some who'd trained for years, panic when scarabei attacked. We're going to need more than bravery. After we recruit, we'll need to *drill* until everyone's first instinct when hell breaks loose is to fall back on routine and not fall apart. It's the only way to keep as many of our side alive as possible."

The ring of faces was solemn, their enthusiasm snuffed like a pinched candlewick. Maybe he shouldn't have started his opening pitch with mass casualties.

Talia clapped him on the back. "Then we'd better get to work!"

Or not. With whoops and whistles, the ghiotte leapt to their feet, and Dante breathed a sigh of relief. He knew how to fight, but he had a lot to learn about leadership.

As the others held a quick and dirty strategy session, Dante pulled Talia aside. "Half the island was ready to stab me in the back a few days ago, and now they're all in?"

Talia's smile was exasperated. "You showed up with Saverio's holiest. Of course people were hostile. But *I* have been swearing up and down that you're family, so people are giving you a chance like they *would have* in the first place if you hadn't been such a dolt."

Dante scratched his chin. "Diplomacy's not really my thing."

Talia barked a laugh. "No kidding. When we were kids, we thought the strongest fighter wins every time, but in the real world, you need to be smart, too. Luckily, *I* know what I'm doing. You're welcome."

Talia's endorsement was like being handed an invitation to a family reunion and getting swarmed by a hundred cousins he'd never met. Her friends embraced him so quickly and enthusiastically it knocked him a bit off-balance. They acted as though he'd always been a part of their group, deferring to his judgment like he truly was the leader of an army that didn't yet exist.

It felt good. Really good. Almost *too* good after years of not caring what anyone thought of him.

For so long, he'd only known doors could be slammed in his face. He didn't quite know what to do now that they were thrown open for him.

Their new commanding officers set up an array of equipment in a highly visible area on the training grounds, loudly shit-talking each other as they did so to draw as much attention as possible and peppering Dante with leading questions about the threat to come.

In the short time since his arrival, Dante and Talia had dealt with a lot of new things, but *this* they knew. Tactics. Strategy. Competition.

It wasn't easy proving his mettle via wrestling, swordfighting, knife-throwing, and archery, while throwing around words like "inferno giant" as a lure for how "fun" it would be to fight the gods; but if they had to make a sales pitch, at least it came in the form of combat.

Dante accepted challenges all morning, half expecting to make enemies every time he won, but Talia wasn't kidding when she said the best way to make allies was to be the best at . . . well, anything, really.

And it worked. Bit by bit, ghiotte drifted over—alone, in pairs, then groups.

By midday, a pack of curious onlookers gathered, bombarding him with questions, suggestions, and arguments for why they each deserved to be first in line to face the toughest opponents.

The ghiotte who'd been raised in exile were full of questions about Dante's visions, Saverio, and all the gory details of Divorando, but they especially relished speculating about what horrors might be in store for them.

"Hope Crollo's not taking notes," Talia muttered after a few girls mused loudly about whether the gods could turn people inside out and make them wear their guts as skin.

The piazza buzzed with such excitement they might have been organizing a neighborhood sporting match rather than a war.

When the crowd grew too large to address everyone individually, Dante grudgingly took to the steps. He couldn't lead an army without a few speeches, but he'd barely said a sentence before a scuffle broke out between two ghiotte, laughing but swinging like they meant to kill each other. Crossing his arms, he waited for them to tire themselves out. He didn't join in the raucous cheering.

The first bout inspired another, and he sidestepped more swinging limbs.

Okay, so Dea's perfect soldiers weren't *exactly* a disciplined fighting force.

He finally had their attention, but they were a mess.

Twenty-eight

Alessa was determined not to complain—out loud, at least—but augmenting Kamaria and Saida's powers to dry linens and heat vats of washing water was hot, damp work, and it didn't feel anything like saving the world.

At the end of their shift, Alessa and the girls met Kaleb at the dining hall for lunch, where, despite a constant flow of arrivals, the tables around theirs remained empty.

Adrick circulated through the room with a basket of baked goods, his jokes and self-effacing charm garnering some smiles. His baked goods earned more.

Kaleb made a rude sound. "What's he doing? We're supposed to be lying low."

"*We're* the blessed ones, not him," Alessa said. If charm could be weaponized, Adrick had the best arsenal on their team.

"*They* don't know that," said Kaleb.

"He just told them," Alessa said.

Kaleb pointed his fork at her. "Is this a twin mind-reading thing? Can you feel each other's pain? If so, apologies in advance, because I have to step on your foot now."

Alessa scooted away. "It's not a *twin* thing. I saw him do the magic finger pop."

Kaleb's face went completely blank. "I'm afraid to ask what a magic finger pop is and how a sister would know such a thing."

Alessa let out a disgusted sound. "Like this." She showed him the sign for magic and explained how she and Adrick often inadvertently used fragments of signs, little hand motions or wrist twists most people probably didn't realize were anything but quirky gestures, which allowed her to read her brother better than other people.

Kaleb picked up his spoon. "Still odd, but I won't step on your foot."

Kamaria, dozing with her chin in her hands, slipped and barely caught herself before face-planting in her soup bowl. "Huh? What did I miss?"

"Freaky twin stuff," Kaleb said to Kamaria's confusion.

"Rolls? Ciabatta?" Adrick approached their table, a grin on his flour-dusted cheeks. "Baguettes are getting rave reviews."

Kaleb snatched one and ripped into it with his teeth.

"Uh-oh," Adrick said. "Someone's grumpy. Won't make friends with *that* attitude."

Alessa flinched at a burst of laughter from Dante's table.

"They really don't like us, do they?" Kamaria said.

Kaleb took another aggressive bite of bread. "Have I mentioned how much I *love* being shunned instead of living as a celebrated champion back home?"

"At least we're finally allowed out," Saida tried, but even she couldn't muster much positivity.

Alessa stood with a sigh. "We should get going before the rain starts."

She'd had enough experience as a social outcast back home. She didn't appreciate reprising the role for strangers in a hostile land.

Back at the house, Ciro had returned from his shift with a fresh catch and a sunburn. Everyone else took one look at his bucket of bug-eyed fish and forgot how to make eye contact, so Alessa offered to help him prepare it in the kitchen, which now had a table and chairs, thanks to Matteo's continued efforts.

Alessa chose the smallest and least squishy fish, while Ciro slapped a large one on the counter, then stood motionless, his knife suspended in the air.

"You *have* done this before, right?" Alessa said as the cat trotted into the kitchen, yowling and rubbing against her legs. "Deboned a fish?"

Ciro jerked to attention. "Of course. Having grown up in a fishing village, this is a thing I've done many times."

She shook her head. Sometimes he sounded as though he was playing a part and had forgotten to practice his lines.

Ciro brandished his knife as though the dead fish might attack at any moment. "I can't decide if it's miraculous that sacs of flesh and bones can do so much, or if it's a woefully disappointing attempt at creation."

Alessa laughed nervously. "I'm not sure I like the thought of being the gods' first draft."

"Who says we're the first?" Ciro sliced his fish down the middle, then gave her a questioning look. "Are you alright?"

Alessa tried for a smile, but it felt like a grimace. "Sometimes my thoughts feel like they're buzzing around like a swarm of angry bees."

"While my mind is alarmingly silent," he said. "Soft and

muted, like a heavy fog over my thoughts. It's often like I'm watching myself from behind a glass door, my mouth speaking words that aren't my own."

Ciro's blankness sounded preferable to holding her mind together by sheer force of will, but regardless of which was worse, they were undeniably different.

Ciro frowned at his knife. "You said you touched a scarabeo. I never did. Maybe we aren't suffering from the same thing at all."

"Or maybe Crollo is trying to sabotage us so we can't fight him."

"Perhaps." Ciro stiffened. "But if he is, Dea would have provided a solution, don't you think?"

According to the Verita, Saverio's holy text, Dea always provided. When Crollo devised Divorando, Dea created sanctuary islands and saviors to protect them. When Crollo sent fire, Dea sent rain. The gods gave and they took for their own inexplicable reasons, but for every challenge, a solution was offered.

If only they could figure out what it was this time.

Ciro's posture relaxed as he showed her how to clean and debone with deft movements. "Are you enjoying your new employment?"

"Laundry? Not especially." Alessa took a breath through her mouth. She might never be hungry again.

"Will you pursue another profession if you remain here?"

"I don't think that will be necessary." Alessa grabbed the cat as it leapt onto the counter and plopped it back on the floor.

Ciro gave the cat a stern look, tossing a small fish toward her. "An offering for your silence, beast."

The cat lurked beneath the table, watching them with unblinking eyes.

"But you're in love," Ciro said. "And his people are here. I presumed you would join him."

"I didn't peg you as a romantic, Ciro."

"He gave his life for you. Surely, you would do anything to stay together?"

Fiore launched another raid, and by the time they had defended their spoils, it would have felt silly to answer out loud.

Of course she'd do anything to be with Dante. She loved him. But he had fallen in love with her when he had no one else, and now he'd found his way back to his own kind, to people who cared about him.

Talia was a human pincushion, but it was clear she'd die for him, and Matteo seemed determined to find a way back into Dante's life, whether it be as his uncle, friend, or to fill the hole left by his father.

Alessa picked up Fiore and buried her face in the animal's soft fur. She had hoped she and Dante would make a life together on Saverio when it all was over, but he might want a different future now.

Twenty-nine

DAYS UNTIL THE ECLIPSE: 19

Alessa woke the following morning from a nightmare of drowning in blood surrounded by a thousand disembodied eyes. She longed for a warm, cozy pile of blankets or an overstuffed mattress, but she got a cold stone floor and the damp they couldn't keep out of the old building.

Dante was already gone. Only the faint scent of smoke and a memory of warmth at her back suggested he'd been there at all.

Through a gap in the curtains, the street outside looked murkier than her dreams. She was stiff and musty, but the thought of braving a walk to the bathhouse alone and disrobing without someone to guard the door—or at least stay nearby in case a stranger with bad intentions showed up—turned her stomach. She'd handled many frightening things in her life, but at least she'd been clothed for all of them.

She wasn't heartless enough to wake anyone else so early, but brothers didn't get the same consideration, and Adrick had to report to the kitchens soon anyway, so she nudged him awake and signed for him to follow her outside.

"Ivory tower made you into a real prude, huh?" Adrick stifled a yawn as they walked the fog-shrouded streets.

"Who would have thought that years of people cringing away from the sight of my bare skin might leave me a tad uncomfortable with nudity around strangers?"

"Speaking of nudity, Kamaria seemed to think you and Dante were, uh, *trading powers* the morning after the party, but I was under the impression that your activities were . . . ahem . . . limited by his lack *of* powers, and I have questions."

Alessa stifled a mortified laugh. "I don't ask you about *your* love life."

"Because you've never been a fan of tragedies." Adrick tripped on a loose cobblestone. "I'm not asking for *details*, and I was ready to credit you for reining in the old Finestra zippity-zap, but one of the cooks said that Leo guy nearly bisected Dante during a *knife fight*—not sure how I missed *that*—and he didn't look mortally wounded yesterday. In fact, I saw him get kicked in the face, and he *should* have had two black eyes by afternoon . . . so what's the deal?"

Alessa kept her head down, mentally counting cobblestones so he couldn't read her face. "Would you believe his powers spontaneously regenerated now that he's surrounded by other ghiotte?"

"I *might*, if you'd managed to say that without a question mark."

A guilty flush bloomed in her cheeks. "It's not my secret to tell. You'll have to resist your curiosity and be happy for me."

"Now *that's* a step too far," he said. "Fine, don't tell me anything, but I hope you know you can trust me with your secrets. I failed you once—or twice—before, but I'm not that person anymore."

"I know." It was a shock to realize she meant it without reservation. Over the past few months, Adrick had proven his desire to make amends, and for the first time since that horrible moment in the Cittadella's kitchen, she *did* fully trust him.

A spike of pain struck the base of her skull, and she gasped, grasping for Adrick's arm.

"Whoa." Adrick pulled her toward a stoop and helped her sit. "What's happening?"

She breathed through her nose until the vertigo passed. "Nothing. I'm fine."

Adrick blew a raspberry. "Cut the crap."

He was her brother. Her twin. The ties between them had frayed but never snapped. Even when Adrick had been horrible to her, she'd known that he still *loved* her. So she told him. About the voices, the dizzy spells, the awareness of things she shouldn't be able to sense, like the worry radiating off him, which she felt as sharply as her own.

"Please don't tell anyone. They'll be afraid of me again. I can't . . ." She pressed her knuckles to her mouth. "I've only had friends for a few months."

"I said I'd keep your secrets, didn't I?" Adrick sat beside her with a gusty exhale. "What are you going to do?"

She smiled weakly. "Hope the next battle with the gods fixes what the last one broke?"

Adrick rubbed her back. "You have some nerve trying to play both the hero *and* the villain while casting me in a supporting role yet again."

She hugged her knees to her chest. Her time playing the hero had ended with Divorando, and yet the gods kept writing. They'd chosen Dante for this chapter, and she didn't know what part was left for her.

The lover. The villain. Or the monster.

Thirty

If someone had asked Dante a year earlier what he thought about Saverio's "community before self" dogma, he would have scoffed. Had, in fact. Many times. And yet, eying the swarm of fun-seeking "warriors" Dea had sent him to find, he wasn't so sure those values weren't baked into him after all.

The ghiotte were all skilled and athletic—incredibly so—but they had no interest in working as a team, too focused on one-upping each other. Formations fell apart because everyone wanted to be in front, and they couldn't focus on anything for more than a few minutes before dissolving into chaos or shouts of "Watch this!"

They also had an annoying tendency to wander off in search of more entertaining activities. Dante spent half the time putting out fires—sometimes literally—and it was a constant struggle to keep their attention. If he'd known when he began working as Alessa's bodyguard that he, too, would someday have to turn a messy crew into a cohesive fighting unit, he would have taken notes.

Dante's days were consumed by combat drills, shifts at the

forge, and strategy sessions with his commanding officers. And thanks to the leaking roof, he could only look forward to a few fretful hours of sleep, crammed into the main room with everyone else.

It was too late for a visitor when he made his way back to the house after Blaise and Jesse dragged him out for a few rounds of beer. Slightly buzzed, his hackles didn't rise as fast as they might otherwise at the sight of someone standing outside, but he'd been successful at avoiding Matteo until now, and he wasn't sure he was ready to break the streak.

"Come stai?" Dante said in wary greeting.

"Bene," Matteo said with a nod. "I've been coming by to help fix the place up."

"I know."

"Talia says you go by Dante now? Your pa would've loved that. He always wanted it to be your first name, but your mama was so stubborn, he never stood a chance."

Dante let the silence stretch.

"I'd love to have you over for dinner sometime. Your friends, too, if they'd like. Just name the day." Matteo cleared his throat. "Look, I know you don't want to talk to me, but I need to say something."

"Then say it."

Matteo took a shaky breath. "If I'd thought there was any chance—any chance at all—that you might have survived, we *never* would've left. I swear."

"It's done. I'm over it."

"I doubt that." Matteo smiled tightly.

Dante glared past him at the deepening sky. "It's getting late."

"*Certo*. I'll get out of your way." Matteo turned, casting one last look over his shoulder, his expression too conflicted to interpret, and walked away.

Dante couldn't bring himself to go inside. There wasn't enough air.

When he was young, Matteo had seemed larger than life, a hero. But heroes weren't allowed to die. They definitely weren't allowed to let you down.

Alessa picked her way through the crowded floor of sleepers to the door and peered up at the roofline above. Even in the rainy darkness, she recognized those shoulders.

Tucking up her nightgown, she maneuvered around the puddles in the courtyard and picked her way past the waterfall coursing down the stairs to the front room she'd mentally claimed as theirs despite the gaping hole in the roof.

Dante was working to repair it. In the middle of the night. In the pouring rain.

"Do you ever sleep?" she said, crossing her arms against the chill.

Dante glanced down through the hole. "Can't sleep in a room full of people."

"You slept in pantries and barns for years."

"*Empty* pantries." He pulled a shingle free with a grunt. "*Empty* barns."

Something told her this wasn't about the crowded sleeping situation. Or at least not *only* about that.

"Come down and sit with me?" Alessa softened her voice so he'd think it was for her sake.

Dante lowered himself through the hole, and they wedged themselves into the driest corner of the room.

"You've made some progress," he said, staring up at the partially mended roof.

"That was mostly Matteo."

Dante's jaw clenched.

She took his hand in her lap, turning it over to trace the lines of his palm. "I think he knows you're avoiding him, but I'm not sure he understands why."

"What am I supposed to say? 'You left me'?" Dante shook his head with a bitter smile. "It's not even fair to be mad. He thought I was dead."

He always seemed to have an easier time talking when she didn't look straight at him, so she stared at the ground, rubbing his hand gently with her own, until he finally spoke again.

"When my aunt told me they were gone, it wrecked me," he said, the words halting. "But it was also a relief, in a horrible way. They hadn't *forgotten* me. They hadn't come because they *couldn't*. Only death could have kept them away." Dante closed his eyes. "Now that I know they were alive the whole time, I don't know how to stop being angry."

"You've forgiven Talia, though?"

"She was a kid. What could she have done?" Dante glared into the darkness. "Matteo was my hero. And when I needed saving, he wasn't there."

Alessa rested her head on his shoulder. Dante might not want to face his past, but the gods only knew what was coming for them, and she might not be there for him on the other side.

He deserved to face the fight of his life knowing he was loved and would never be left alone again.

Thirty-one

DAYS UNTIL THE ECLIPSE: 18

Three days after his powers were restored, Dante's recruitment drive was officially a success. Sort of. The ghiotte were terrific fighters but a *terrible* army.

Kira marched toward him, snapping a whip impatiently in the direction of the crooked rows of soldiers. People were already stepping out of line. "I'm ready to flay these slackers."

"Seriously." Blaise slung an arm over her shoulder, heedless of the danger. "It's like herding cats out there."

Jesse grunted in agreement, and the others nodded.

Dante rubbed his forehead. They were right. This wasn't working.

"We need to divide and conquer," he said. "Everyone, tell me your three greatest strengths. Physical, mental, whatever you can think of."

"How will that help?" Kira said. "I mean, I'm fast and I'm a good listener, but that's hardly going to win a war."

"It might," Dante said. "We'll need messengers to keep everyone informed during battle. Blaise, your imagination is, frankly, terrifying. Anything you come up with is bound to catch the other side off guard. You can run our ideas team. Jesse, people stop and listen when you do speak, so you can take charge of the front line fighters. Figure out who can handle more responsibility, then break them into squads. Make sure they know *why* you're picking them and pump their egos a bit while you're at it. Anya, identify the best archers and start mapping out prime locations around the city."

Kira raised her hand. "You're the general. Don't you tell everyone what to do?"

"I can't be everywhere at once," Dante said. "Besides, when it's time for battle, the troops will need to trust your leadership individually."

They managed to assign everyone a specialty by the middle of the afternoon, and his officers selected one or two responsible subordinates to assist each of them. Maybe now they could get things done without coming to him for every question.

Meanwhile, Talia was plotting her own mission. One he wanted no part of.

"How many times do I have to ask before you realize you're not getting out of coming over?" Talia said as they collected discarded weaponry at the end of the day.

"I'm not here for a family reunion." Dante yanked an arrow loose. "I have a job to do."

He should have known not to take his eyes off her. Talia's roundhouse buckled his knees, and he landed on his back with a thud. "Hey!"

She stared down at him. "If you're mad at Papa, tell him. Stop eating your feelings before you choke."

"Like you're one to talk?" He yanked her ankle out from

under her, dropping her on her ass. "I'm not dragging you back to Saverio for a heart-to-heart with your mom, am I?"

"I'd like to see you *try*." They lost the conversational thread for moment when she got him in a headlock. "She made a choice. Papa made a mistake. It's different."

Talia reluctantly let go as he tapped out.

"At least *you* got to leave *her*." Dante lay on the ground, catching his breath.

Talia sat back on her knees, looking annoyed at how quickly the match had ended. "Instead of her leaving *me*, you mean? Do you really think that feels any better?"

"Maybe it shouldn't, but it does."

"Dante, your parents *died*. They didn't leave you willingly."

"I know that," he said, his lips barely moving. Of course he knew that. His parents were murdered. They hadn't packed their bags and walked away from him. But it still felt like a betrayal, like they'd stepped through a doorway to somewhere he couldn't follow. And Matteo *had* walked away.

"But *we* left you," Talia said with a gusty exhale. "I'm sorry, Gabe."

He opened his mouth to correct her but stopped. Because she *was* talking to Gabe. He might have shed his old name, but that angry kid was still inside him, and *he* was the one who had to let go.

"There's nothing to forgive." Dante took a harsh breath. "I know you didn't mean to leave me behind." If the last part came out a bit strangled, Talia pretended not to notice.

She flopped on the ground beside him, rolling to her back to stare up at the sky. "Feelings are stupid."

He coughed a reluctant laugh. "Sure are."

"Even thinking you were dead, sailing away from Saverio

without you felt like slicing off a limb. I should have refused to leave."

"If you had, you probably would've been killed. That would have been worse."

Talia's snort turned into a laugh. "Aw, that's so sweet. I might get it tattooed on my ass—'You being killed probably would have been worse,'—a quote by Gabriele Dante Lucente."

He cracked a smile. "At least we lived to fight another day. There's no one I'd trust more to watch my back in a battle."

"Oh, please. You'll watch *my* back, because I'll be in front of you." She covered his face with her hands as though shielding him from an invisible threat. "You still need to talk to him, though."

Dante groaned. "How many feelings do you want me to have in one day?"

"Come on, it won't be that bad." She nudged him with her elbow, then again, harder, when he didn't react. "Are you really that big a coward?"

He shut his eyes. "Maybe."

She jabbed his ribs lightly with her fist, then again, laughing and threatening to put some force behind it.

"*Basta!*" He pinned her wrists with one hand.

"If I can deal with your magical menagerie, you can suck it up and talk to Papa."

She didn't get to play that card. No chance.

"*Are* you dealing with it?" he said. "Because we need to know how to fight together, and you have them doing grunt work. Sabotaging your own side in a war doesn't seem like 'dealing with it' to me."

Talia flopped around on the ground like an angry fish throwing a tantrum on land. "*Fine!* They can train with us, but no magic until they prove they can play by our rules. And keep them away from me."

"Good." He nodded decisively, not entirely sure whether he'd won or lost.

Jogging back toward the house, Dante shot a dirty look at the rumbling clouds. It *had* to be some kind of divine joke that the rain cleared every day and rushed back at dusk.

He stepped through the door and came face-to-face with Kaleb.

"It's been a week. When do we get to train?"

"Tomorrow." Dante said. He cast around for Alessa but saw no sign of her.

Kamaria pounced. "When do we get to—"

"Tomorrow!" Dodging another round of questions, Dante strode toward the kitchen, where he found Alessa on her hands and knees under a table that hadn't been there before. Reaching for something, she arched her back in a pose that wasn't meant for him but should have been.

He must have made an appreciative sound, because she sat up abruptly and smacked her head on the table.

"Sorry." He crouched to rub it for her, and she nearly bowled him over, burying her face in his shirt. Frowning, he rubbed her back as she clung to him.

"Hey," he said softly. "You okay?"

She nodded vigorously. "I've missed you."

He kissed the top of her head. "Me too."

"When do we start—"

"Tomorrow," he said with an exasperated laugh. "Talia agreed. Finally."

She pouted. "I was all ready to fuss at you."

Dante laughed. "You'd have to get in line."

Thirty-two

DAYS UNTIL THE ECLIPSE: 17

"You look like you're chewing glass," Alessa said mildly as Dante set up practice weaponry in an isolated corner of the training area. "Wondering how much lower Talia's estimation of us can go?"

Dante frowned. "Just keep your head down and avoid eye contact."

"Ah, yes," she said. "Because trying to avoid attention has *always* worked for me."

Shifting from foot to foot, Alessa eyed the target ten paces in front of her, daggers clutched in both hands. If she managed to send them in the right direction, she should be able to avoid impaling anyone.

She flipped one and caught it neatly, the only trick she had. It probably looked less impressive the tenth time, but she'd been standing there too long to casually walk away now.

After casting a surreptitious glance around in hopes none of the ghiotte were paying attention, Alessa drew one hand back. "Go *that* way."

Dagger number one arced high and plummeted halfway to its destination, the tip planting itself in the seam between two cobblestones and vibrating like a murderous flower.

She pointedly ignored a muffled snort from the other side of the invisible line separating them from the ghiotte forces.

Dante moved his wrist in a slow version of the flick she'd been attempting. "Like this."

That's what she *thought* she'd been doing, but clearly not.

Deep breath. Aim, inhale, and fling.

It didn't *quite* hit the target, but it might have sliced a sliver off the top.

He took her hand and held it longer than strictly necessary before repeating the motion. "Try again."

This time, her knife flew as though it had a mind of its own and planted itself dead center.

Alessa stifled a victory squeal. "That wasn't me at all, was it?"

"First impressions," Dante grumbled.

"You're supposed to be *coaching* me, not tricking everyone into thinking I'm gifted like you." Infuriating, really, how easy it was to do with his skills. If she didn't love him so much, she'd hate him for it.

She was proud of herself for taking the moral high ground but abandoned it with haste when Talia sauntered toward the targets.

"Remember what I said about your wrist," Dante said.

"Remind me?" Alessa said through gritted teeth.

He kept a professional distance as he took her hand again and moved it in the precise motion he'd shown her before.

Alessa focused on stealing his powers. She could work on true skill development when Talia wasn't sizing her up.

• • •

Hundreds of ghiotte watching his friends and Alessa in action, up close, *without* their magic, had Dante regretting a number of life choices.

He'd been so focused on finding the ghiotte and winning their trust, he'd completely forgotten to keep up the Saverians' battle training, and now they were the focus of a *lot* of unfriendly attention.

Talia's friends and his new recruits may have agreed to work with him, but that didn't mean their support was *unconditional.*

Dante wanted to stand guard over Alessa all day—hell, he'd prefer to lock her in a tower where no one could see her—but he'd only draw more attention by hovering, and he could wreck all his progress *and* paint a target on her back by revealing their relationship to the wrong people.

With her hair braided, dressed in a flowing white tunic and soft blue leggings, Alessa looked sweet and innocent. She was tougher than she looked, but she *looked* like bait.

If he wasn't careful, the ghiotte would eat her alive.

Thirty-three

DAYS UNTIL THE ECLIPSE: 15

Two days later, Alessa lowered her bow with a sigh at another cheer from the far side of the training field.

There was nothing quite like being surrounded by Dea's army of super-soldiers to make a girl feel wholly inadequate, and after another day of watching the ghiotte fight, throw knives, and shoot arrows effortlessly, Alessa could almost believe they would *enjoy* a war with the gods.

Kamaria stabbed at an imaginary opponent. "Why are we even here if we can't practice with the actual army?"

"We're the entertainment," Kaleb said.

"Nah, we're the common enemy they bond over," Adrick chimed in.

Alessa craned her neck to see what Dante was doing with a row of archers nearby. She *knew* why he had to, but it still sat heavy in her gut how easily he ignored them. *Her.* No point lying to herself. It stung how easily he ignored *her.*

He avoided her in public, but he found his way back to her at night. Granted, she was usually asleep, and he slipped out before she woke in the morning, but he did come back. She held on to that.

Once he'd earned everyone's trust, they wouldn't have to hide their relationship anymore

Hopefully. Or they'd complete their mission and Saverio would be waiting for them with open arms.

Or . . . they'd all die and Crollo would wipe out humanity.

Fine, she wasn't doing a *spectacular* job of being positive at the moment.

"Adrick, you have to *thrust,* not poke the sky," Dante called out.

Alessa's surge of excitement at seeing him jog toward them was downright embarrassing.

"Kaleb, keep your shield up or he's going to chop your arm off." Dante stopped in front of Alessa, and her traitorous heart did another flip. *Pathetic.*

She raised her bow and lined up the shot. "Talia's letting you cross the invisible line?"

"She's running combat drills in the basilica." Dante trapped his lip between his teeth, eyes sparkling with mischief. "Figured I'd see how the outcasts were doing. Draw your elbow out, not down."

He stepped behind her, placing one hand on her hip to adjust her posture, his other arm coming around the other side to fix her grip.

Heat rose in her cheeks. "I thought you weren't supposed to come near me."

"I've been helping other people all day." His breath ruffled the flyaway curls by her ear. "Now I'm helping you."

His fingertips skimmed the bare skin above her waistband, and her knees went wobbly.

"Please tell me you haven't been 'coaching' other people like this." She turned her head slightly, and the scruff of his chin rasped against her cheek.

"Not like *this*," he said, easing closer. Hand over hers, they drew back the bowstring together.

Zing. The arrow struck, quivering, in the target.

Alessa's next inhale stretched the limits of her leather vest, making her modest cleavage swell above the top.

Dante's breath went ragged. "Mi fai impazzire."

"I don't know what that means," she said. "But if you want to maintain the illusion that we're merely colleagues, you should probably let go."

"It *means* if I step away right now, there will *be* no illusion." His voice was rough despite his amusement.

Alessa tilted her hips back, silently gloating at his frustrated grunt.

"Stop moving and shoot the arrow before I rip that damn vest off," he muttered.

She drew back quicker than she meant to and jabbed her elbow into his sternum.

"Ow," he said with a laugh. "That's one way to deal with it."

"Ahem," she said. Talia was glaring from the basilica steps. "We're being watched."

Dante stepped back, hands clasped in front of himself.

"Keep practicing." His voice was so curt her whole body tensed. "Kamaria, do you remember *anything* I taught you?"

Kamaria flipped him off as he walked away.

Saida's smile was coy. "You two are adorable. He loves you so much."

Kamaria snorted. "That wasn't love, that was lust."

Saida's eyes went wide and she gave the other girl a loaded look.

Kamaria hastily backtracked. "I'm not saying he *doesn't* love her, just that—never mind. Sorry. Ignore me."

"It's okay." Alessa reached back to fix her braid, which had already begun to fall apart before Dante mussed it further. "I know what you meant."

She nocked another arrow and raised her bow again. If only she could lift her mood as easily. One minute he was *her* Dante, teasing and smoldering, the next, a stranger, steely with indifference. As effortless as swapping one hat for another.

It was unsettling how easily he did that.

"Swords," Talia said, with no explanation.

"Spears," Dante responded, without asking for one. Following the conversations volleyed back and forth across the dining room table was like tracking six jugglers at once.

Kira spoke up around a mouthful of bread. "Flaming arrows."

"Axes." Talia made squeezing motions with her hands. "Those things with balls at each end of a chain."

Everyone at the table looked at Dante again. "Um . . . daggers?"

Talia shook her head. "Too small. Horses?"

Dante cleaned his plate with a crust of bread. "For what? I don't understand what we're doing."

Talia gave him an exasperated look. "Planning our arsenal."

Jesse grabbed an armful of bottles from the counter and began passing them out. "We have no idea what Crollo might throw at us, so we need to be prepared for anything."

"We have to think big to defeat hellspawn." Blaise used a

fork to mime swordplay. "The biggest swords ever made. Or something double-ended with grips in the middle, so you can spin it. Wait, how about a long blade on one side and a scythe on the other? Stab one, pull back, lop off another head in one move."

"Or accidentally rip out your own guts," Talia said. "We don't need to invent *new* weaponry. We just need everything we can think of that would be useful."

Blaise began sliding beers across the table. "What about, like, burning oil, or traps? Oooh, trebuchets!"

Talia knocked the cap off her bottle. "Do *you* know how to make a trebuchet?"

"Someone must." Blaise chugged his drink like he'd never seen liquid in his life. "What about a mace? That's what they call clubs with spikes on them, right?"

Dante could feel Alessa's presence across the dining hall like a hand on the back of his neck. It had been brutal enough when he couldn't get close to her, but now that he was physically able to do so and never had the opportunity, some primal instinct growled at him to trek across the room and throw her over his shoulder, mission be damned.

While she'd been away on Altari, he'd been able to distract himself because she was gone, but now she was *right there*, and his concentration was consumed by the effort of pretending not to care.

Talia hadn't pushed him about their connection again, so as far as she knew for *sure*, Alessa was just one of his team, but under her suspicious eye, he couldn't even risk a lingering glance, which was an impossible ask when Alessa was wandering around in that vest.

Plenty of the other girls wore similar attire, including

Talia, but it wasn't the same. Not to him, at least. Talia was a weapon, honed for a purpose, all sharp edges and deceptively lean muscles. On Talia, a leather vest made sense. It was practical, durable.

On Alessa, the rich warm leather laced tight across her chest was like a bittersweet chocolate truffle with a creamy center, every curve all the more delicious for the contrast.

"Explosives!" Blaise slammed the table, rattling glasses.

With a cough, Dante pulled his attention back to the task at hand. Some general he was turning out to be. Couldn't even stay focused on preparing for a holy war.

Dante pulled out his notepad, wrote ARSENAL in capital letters at the top, and stared until his eyes went unfocused. He needed to pull it together.

When all this was over, he'd have to find a hobby or he'd end up following Alessa around like a lovesick puppy. Maybe he could pick up an instrument and write song lyrics with her dirty jokes. Or take up sketching and map out the constellation of tiny freckles across the bridge of her nose. But a sketch couldn't capture the flecks of green and gold in her irises, or the full three-dimensional perfection of her. *Sculpting.* Yeah, then he could pose her however he liked, shape his favorite curves out of marble. Sculpting would require *lots* of research. Serious business, art.

From the corner of his eye, he saw Alessa returning her dishes.

Grabbing his own empty plate, he stood. "I need to finish something at the forge. Strategy session first thing tomorrow?"

Talia waved him off without looking, too busy explaining to Blaise why high-proof alcohol would be a terrible liquid for lighting on fire, as it would explode and kill their own soldiers before it could touch their enemies.

Dante knew the back alleys well enough to intercept Alessa a block over. When he hissed her name, she whirled, fists up in a defensive pose—good girl—but her expression lit up as she saw who it was.

He reached for her hand. "Come with me."

The roiling clouds had cleared the streets, but he stopped to check every intersection, leading her farther off the beaten path to the outskirts of the city, where the buildings were rougher and uninhabited.

The clouds opened, and they ran toward a covered bridge ahead, laughing as they tumbled inside the meager shelter.

Her tongue darted out to wet her lower lip, but he didn't kiss her right away. There was something so vulnerable and honest about her like this—barefaced, rivulets of water tracing serpentine lines across her skin. She was so beautiful it hurt to look at her, like a physical ache in his chest.

Her warmth soaked through the layers of wet fabric as he pulled her close, but she pushed back. "You're poking me."

"You've never complained before," he said with a laugh.

She gripped the knives on either side of his waist. "Sharp. Ow. Danger poke."

"They're *sheathed.*" He cut her off with another kiss before she could voice the inevitable joke, his hands working to unfasten his knives. She accepted them, looking appropriately smug. He never took them off for anything but sleep, and he certainly never handed them over to someone else. His knives were almost a part of him, and she was the only one with a claim to either.

"I like you this way," Alessa murmured against his lips.

"Desperate?" He sucked a raindrop off her neck, ego thrumming with satisfaction at how long it took her to remember there was a question in need of answering. Few things were powerful enough to stop Alessa from talking, but *he* was.

"That too," she said, more breath than words. "But more that I finally know what you're thinking sometimes. I had enough of guessing before you accepted that you love me."

He pulled her tighter, forcing her to tilt her chin to look up at him. "A bold claim," he said, grinning down at her.

"Just because you only say it in a language I don't *speak*, doesn't mean you haven't said it," she said, jabbing him in the side with a finger. "And you can't take it back."

Words were overrated. He could worship her better without speaking. Even the crackle of lightning didn't deter him.

Until he realized it *wasn't* lightning raising the hair on the back of his neck.

"We should get back," he said, his pulse spiking.

"Why?" Alessa twined her arms around his neck.

He huffed a laugh. "Lightning. And I, uh, just remembered something I have to . . . do. I'll meet you back at the house."

He gave her a quick kiss and bolted. Heart thudding, he rounded the first corner before realizing he'd left his knives. For the first time in years, he was unarmed when he needed them most. Panic surging, he searched the ground for the first sharp object he could find—a shard of a broken bottle.

He ran it across the pad of his thumb. The rain washed away his blood as fast as it welled, which made it easy to see how long it took before the cut began to close.

Dante broke into a run, heart pounding as fast as his footsteps. His powers *couldn't* vanish again. He refused to let the possibility take root.

He was *not* going back.

Pressed close to the buildings to avoid the worst of the rain, Alessa saw no sign of lightning as she wandered through the outskirts of the city.

She reached an area where regular folk lived above family businesses, like the street where she had grown up, and as though she'd conjured the memory of home into a physical thing, a puff of warm air smelling of flour, butter, and yeast rushed to meet her.

"Alessa?" At the sound of her name, she blinked a few times to be sure she hadn't conjured Adrick, too, but he was real, outlined in the light of an open doorway. "What are you doing? Get in here before you get washed into the bay."

Wiping her face—futile with the downpour—she followed him through the back entrance to the dining hall kitchens. Her sense of direction was so poor she'd walked all that way only to end up behind the building where she'd started.

"There." He handed her a stack of cookies so tall she needed to use both hands. "You look like you want to stab someone, and now you can't. Why are you moping in the rain?"

It *was* hard to hold on to her indignation with a mouth full of sugar. "I was walking back to the house with Dante when he suddenly *remembered* something he had to do and just . . . ran away."

"Without his daggers?" Adrick swiped an apron from a peg on the wall and tossed it to her. "Strange. Well, the guy's never exactly been an open book. The mysterious grumpy thing's part of his appeal, no?"

Alessa rolled her eyes. "If I wanted a bad attitude and lack of transparency I would have fallen for Kaleb."

"Ugh," Adrick said. "Kaleb in the family? I'd rather eat glass."

"Why do you hate each other so much?"

"Trust me, you don't want the whole ugly story."

"I absolutely do." Alessa put down the remaining cookies and picked up a rolling pin. "Nothing cheers me faster than hearing how your life is a mess."

"You asked for it." Adrick grabbed two rolling pins and held them up like the ends of an invisible scroll. "Scene one: Enter, stage left, the most handsome and charming fourteen-year-old Saverio's ever seen, abandoned by his twin sister when the gods chose her for eternal glory, leaving him with twice the chores and a devastating suspicion that the gods had considered them both and chose *not him*."

Alessa spread a thin layer of flour across her work surface with an amused smile.

Adrick plopped a ball of dough in front of her. "So one day, this older kid—rich, popular—starts being friendly, and it felt good to be singled out, you know? Then it came time for you to pick your first Fonte, and everyone starts talking about who will be the chosen one's chosen one. I realized my new *friend* is a candidate. He never *actually* liked me; he was just using me to get to you."

Alessa settled into the familiar rhythm of rolling and folding, rolling and folding. "That explains why you don't like *Kaleb*, not *his* level of hostility toward you."

Adrick grimaced. "He may have overheard me saying something less than kind after your second Fonte died."

Alessa's mouth dropped open. "You insulted *Ilsi?*"

"I was talking about you, actually, but Kaleb assumed I was referring to him, and I didn't correct him."

"What did you say about *me?*"

Adrick rubbed his floury hands together. "I'm not going to come out of this story looking very good."

"You tried to kill me. It can't get much worse."

"Don't be so sure." Adrick laughed nervously. "Please remember this was a long time ago, and my bruised ego was speaking, all right? I . . . sort of implied that the gods don't bless the best people, but rather the most expendable." He cringed. "I *might* have said you could tell by looking at how often the gods choose the less impressive child in a family."

"*Wow.*"

"I *know.* I'm *sorry.*" Adrick clasped his floury hands in front of his face. "It was mean and petty and untrue."

"Let me get this straight. You were feeling jealous of me so you proclaimed the gods only bless the family losers? You saw how his parents treated him at the gala."

"Indeed." Adrick worked the dough a little harder than necessary. "I have a gift for hitting sore spots."

"Why don't you tell him you were talking about me?"

"That might've worked at the time—two brats bonding over resentment toward our illustrious siblings—but Kaleb's quite fond of you now, so that wouldn't help."

"Adrick, he didn't even know you were my brother. Someone mentioned the shop a few weeks before Divorando, and he was very surprised to find out I was a Paladino."

"Really?" Adrick's forehead creased. "Well, it's too late now."

"I forgave you for slipping me poison. Kaleb might be more forgiving than you give him credit for. Especially if you grovel."

Adrick looked mortally affronted. "I'd rather drink poison myself."

Dante felt like the world's biggest creep, lurking in the bathhouse for hours.

Half of Perduta had decided it was the perfect time to relax in the waters, so despite his crackling nerves, he had to act casual, lounging with his elbows propped on the side of the pool.

Alone. Fully nude.

Exchanging nods with ghiotte he'd met, dodging eye contact with those he hadn't, and feigning a studious interest in the ceiling tiles, frescoes, stained-glass windows, anything but the couples flirting and kissing—at least he hoped they were only kissing.

Aside from a few curious glances, most ignored him, until Leo arrived with his girlfriends. Chiara and Vittoria cast coy looks at Dante as they slid into the water.

Dante glowered at a mosaic on the ceiling as the girls giggled and played with each other's hair. The more he scowled, the more they preened.

Leo glared as though daring him to lust after them, but if this was a trap, he would be disappointed. Dante had never been less interested in power plays, and he didn't want the guy's companions or his throne. He *wanted* them to *leave*.

Dante rolled his fingers across the tile. Maybe if he closed his eyes for a minute, Leo would give up.

The tingle could have been a nearby lightning strike. Or maybe Alessa had been extra charged up. He felt wrong blaming her, even in his own head, even if it was better than the alternative.

But the test cut on his hand was a faint line now, and it should have been *gone.*

He clutched the key in his fist like it was the key to salvation.

Dante didn't mean to doze, but when his eyes opened, he was alone in the bathhouse.

A quick glance at one of the windows high on the wall told him it must be close to dawn, which would leave plenty of time to get in and out before anyone showed up. After all, who woke before the sun to walk across town for a bath?

Someday, he'd stop underestimating his own bad luck.

In the fontana chamber, he dunked himself quickly, then again for good measure, dressed and listened to be sure the main room was empty before opening the door to leave. He didn't see Adrick standing by the changing-room entrance until too late.

Dante smoothed his expression. "What are you doing here?"

"I have to get to the kitchens early." Adrick cocked his head. "Where'd you go last night?"

"Talia needed help with something." He stepped away, trying to draw Adrick's attention from the door and what it concealed.

Adrick's eyes narrowed. "Does Alessa know you're having naked meetings with another girl?"

"What? No, not here. Earlier." Dante opened it just long enough for Adrick to peek inside, then slammed the door shut and locked it. "See? Empty."

"Then why did you lock the door?"

Dante pocketed the key. "None of your business."

"If you're keeping something from my sister, it *is* my business, and I'll tell her."

Dante gave him a withering look. "You *could* plant ideas in her head, but I think you've hurt her enough already, don't you?"

He left, squashing a rush of guilt at Adrick's stricken expression. Maybe that would convince him to leave it alone.

Dante walked away, scratching at his palm with his thumbnail.

He couldn't risk checking in any way that might leave a mark, but he couldn't shake the fear that his powers were already fading again. Maybe it just took a few visits to the fontana to lock it in. He could do that.

He'd return the next day. And the next, if needed. Twice a day, even. As often as it took. It would stick. It had to.

Dante's skin was still damp and warm from the water, but goosebumps rose on his arms as he stepped out of the building.

He slowed, picking his steps carefully and perking his ears for any sound.

There was something . . . wrong . . . with the air. Or the scent. Something he couldn't put his finger on, an animalistic sense prodding him to keep moving, to keep his back to the wall, because something was coming.

The troops wouldn't arrive for hours, but he headed for the armory anyway. Nothing dulled a sense of danger like a machete in one hand and a sword in the other. Might as well use the energy coursing through his veins to burn through a workout.

As he crossed the silent piazza, his neck prickled with warning at the echo of footsteps on stone.

"You couldn't sleep either?" Talia crossed it toward him, glancing around nervously. "I've been up for hours."

Dai nemici mi guardo io, ma dagli amici mi guardi Dea.

Ridiculous. Talia wasn't a threat. But Dante's nerves pulled tighter.

"What's up with the light?" Talia said.

The *light*. That was it. There was something wrong with the light.

Dante looked up through the thinning fog. Above them, the moon hung heavy in the sky, enormous and scarlet red, as though the gods had dipped it in blood, a silent reminder that time was running out.

"What's white turns red then black . . ." Dante muttered.

He had two weeks left to turn the ghiotte into the greatest army of all time or die trying.

Thirty-four

DAYS UNTIL THE ECLIPSE: 14

Alessa pulled Dante's daggers and holster from her bag as she walked across the training ground. He hadn't returned the night before, but there he was, looking surly and wearing the same clothes as he'd worn the day before.

"You forgot these." She tossed them to him.

Thanks," he muttered, fastening the belt.

"I hope you had fun wherever you ran off to."

"Sorry." His gaze slid toward her, then away. "I had a thing to do."

"Well, that clears it up." Her pride wouldn't allow her to press him about his strange behavior where anyone might overhear, but he had better have a good explanation ready for when she did.

In the armory, Alessa chose a light sword and gave it a gentle test swing. A good weight, nice balance. Perfect for jabbing at imaginary enemies to work off a foul mood.

"You know how to sword fight?" Talia called out.

"Not as well as you." Alessa looked around for someone to save her. Anyone.

"I'd like to see that." Talia gestured toward an open training area.

"Fine," Alessa said. It wasn't like she was having such a great day she couldn't risk ruining it.

They took their positions and she raised her sword with a sigh.

"Hold on a second." Dante strode between them to adjust Alessa's grip on the handle. "You've got this," he whispered.

"Do I, though?" A generous person would say she whispered back, but it was more of a squeak. He was supposed to *save* her, not give her a pep talk.

Dante's hand slid higher, his fingers wrapping around her bare wrist. "Yup. Take it."

She'd never wanted to turn down an offer so badly, but she refused to die before getting answers, so she took his powers. Reluctantly. She focused on drawing as much into herself as she could in one pull, like drinking an entire glass of water through a straw.

"Are you going to keep grabbing me every few minutes?" she muttered through clenched teeth.

Dante's expression didn't change. "When you feel it fading, drop something. I'll hand it to you."

It was unclear how many times one could drop an object midfight without raising suspicions, but Alessa took inventory of anything on her person that could be dropped: a hair tie, a shoe could fall off, she could trip and fall. Easy enough; she did that all the time.

The first clang of steel woke her battle training, and she stopped thinking of anything beyond her footwork, her blade, and her opponent. She suspected Talia wasn't giving it her all, but the girl didn't go easy on her, either, and within minutes, sweat dewed their skin.

When she began to falter, Dante called out, "Talia, show me that move again?"

Talia rolled her eyes but stopped to re-create a spinning thrust with which she'd nearly punctured Alessa's kneecap.

"Again, but slower. Watch what she does there," Dante said, clapping Alessa on the shoulder. Pointing with one hand, his other slid to the back of her neck, and she exhaled in relief as her bank of stolen talent filled.

Alessa held her own. Onlookers gathered, but she didn't let them distract her. Stubbornly, she kept going, even after Dante's powers ran dry.

The third time they locked blades, Talia stepped back. "Stalemate. Not bad, princess."

"You should see her with a bow," Dante said casually. "Won my respect."

He may or may not have been impressed on his first day in the Cittadella, but it *had* been the first time he'd looked at her like she might be more than a pathetic, spoiled girl.

"So impressed you almost stabbed me?" Alessa said. Might as well play to her audience.

"I thought you *did* stab the Finestra," Talia said to Dante. "That was my favorite part of your introductory speech."

Dante gave Talia a look of gentle reproach. "The first time was a close call. Second time was real."

Talia snorted derisively. "Slow learner."

Dante pinned her with a glare. "Cut it out."

Alessa took one look at Talia's shocked expression and hastily made her escape.

The roof was finally finished, and Matteo must have enlisted half the city to carry a house's worth of furniture inside.

Alessa sat on the bed, eying the walls and waiting for inspiration. If Dante chose *this* of all days to stay out late with friends instead of coming back to her . . . She stood with a flounce.

She would be happy for him. His timing was atrocious, but she *would*.

She would *try*.

Their room wasn't luxurious, with drafts leaking through the boards propped over the remaining holes, and it still didn't have a door, but Alessa found a woven rug to soften their footsteps, and Matteo had brought sconces, so it was cozy.

Humming to drown out Kaleb and Adrick's excessively noisy furniture assembly from the next room, Alessa gathered up a blanket and climbed the ladder Matteo had left behind.

Dante stepped inside and dropped his satchel. "Aw, piccola you decorated."

"I wanted *my* room to feel cozy." Alessa began wedging the corners of the blanket into the cracks above the doorframe to make it drape like a curtain.

"*Your* room? Ay, you wound me." A smile played on his lips as he admired her work. Or her legs. Dante's fingers found the hem a few inches above her knee. "Is this my shirt?"

"I stole it," she said primly, but she couldn't fight a shiver at his touch. "I hardly ever get you to myself these days, so I figured I could wear you at least. I'd almost forgotten what you look like."

"I'm sorry," Dante said, more earnest than usual. "Really. I am. It's a lot of pressure when everyone is counting on you to save the world, you know?"

She stepped down. "Lucky for you, I do. But if you *ever* drag me into the rain, kiss me dizzy, then run away from me again, I swear to Dea, I'll—"

Dante grasped her waist and kissed her like a drowning man who'd found his last breath of air.

When he broke the kiss, Alessa swayed slightly. "Well. Glad we got that sorted out."

The makeshift blanket door fell to the floor. Grumbling, she bent to pick it up, then stilled at the sight of a lacy scrap peeking from Dante's bag.

She would *not* get jealous. She was not the jealous type. At least she didn't think she was. The ugly knot around her lungs begged to differ.

Tugging it free, she stood, dangling the lacy thing from one finger. "What's this?"

He looked up. "I don't know."

Blink. *Don't react.*

Oh, screw that. She fired it at him like a slingshot. "You're supposed to come up with something better than 'I don't know'!"

Laughing, he caught it. "I really don't know. I saw it in the clothing swap and grabbed it for you."

"For *me*."

"Obviously." He tapped her nose. "But you're cute when you're jealous."

"I'm not jealous." She pretended to nip at his thumb, but he wasn't deterred, running it across her cheekbone.

"Sure you aren't. Anyway, I have no idea what it's supposed

to be, but I'd really like to watch you try to figure it out, and if you can't, I'll enjoy taking it off."

"We're going to need a door for that."

Dante swiped the fallen blanket from the floor and began vigorously stuffing the edges into cracks above the door.

"It never ends," she grumbled at another loud bang. "Kaleb's been stuffing himself with Adrick's pastries, but they *still* don't get along." Abruptly, the yelling from the other side of the wall stopped, and Alessa froze. "Oh, gods. They killed each other."

Dante made a face she couldn't interpret. "They didn't—"

"One of them is dead and I can't decide who I want it to be!"

Adrick and Kaleb's room didn't have a door, either, and she skittered to a halt outside. Kaleb had Adrick pinned to the wall, his hand fisted in Adrick's shirt. No blood yet. She'd made it in time. She was about to yell at them to knock it off when something about the fierce look in Kaleb's eyes stopped her.

Dante's arm hooked her waist, and her last glimpse as he threw her over his shoulder wasn't Kaleb knocking Adrick's teeth out, but—

"No," she said, trying to get free. "No, no, no! That is *not* happening."

Dante tossed her on their bed, caging her with his arms when she tried to climb out. "Leave them alone. You aren't even dressed, and I highly doubt you want to see what comes next."

"But they hate each other!"

Dante relaxed his grip a trifle. "Hate and lust are close cousins."

"That's . . . That's *not* . . . They can't."

"Alessa, it's none of our business."

"He's my *brother*. And he's my *Fonte*."

Dante's lips twitched. "I'll remind you, you're sleeping with your bodyguard."

"Not the point. He's *mine*."

Dante stilled. "Who?"

"Adrick!"

"He's your brother, not your property."

"Still. A sister should know these things." There it was. The crux of it. She hadn't known Adrick as fully as she thought she had. In her mind, he'd been her brother, not entirely a person in his own right. And she'd never thought to ask what kind of person he fancied. She'd been so wrapped up in her own struggles, she'd barely spared a thought on what he wanted, who he dated, or much about his personal life at all, and she hadn't even realized it.

Now he was pressed against a wall, nose-to-nose, locked in a fierce grip and staring into the eyes of—*Kaleb?* She shook herself. No. It was too much.

"They hate each other," she repeated, weaker this time.

Dante kicked his shoes off. "I remember when we weren't too fond of each other, either."

"That was different," Alessa said. "I wasn't married to your sister."

Dante scrunched his face in thought. "Not sure that's the right comparison. And I don't have a sister."

"If you did, I'd have to kiss her now."

"I'm *confident* that's not the right comparison."

"Oh, gods, is Talia the equivalent? Do I have to kiss Talia?"

"*Please* don't kiss Talia."

"Would that make you jealous?"

Dante blinked. "Honestly, yes. But also, she'd probably slit your throat."

Despite his ominous premonition, Dante didn't register the footsteps coming down the hallway until it was too late.

"I knew it!" Talia scorched Dante with the kind of look that used to have him cupping his balls and keeping his back to the wall, braced for the inevitable knee to the groin or elbow to the kidney. This time he deserved it, so after pulling on his clothes and chasing her down the street, he kept his hands at his side.

All things considered, he got off easy.

Talia grabbed his collar, yanking his head down to hiss in his face. "She's the *Finestra*!"

"I'm aware." Dante pulled free, smoothing his shirt to avoid meeting her eyes.

"And you're, what? Her guard dog? Her pet? Her *whore*?"

"Hey!" he snapped. "Watch it."

Talia made a sound somewhere between a sob and a scream. "I *told* you to stay away from her!"

"No, you *told* me not to let anyone know about us, and you're about to blow that secret wide open."

"Unbelievable." Talia reined in her temper just enough to lower her voice. "She's the figurehead of the church! The one that declared us monsters. The entire reason we needed a refuge from their crusade. The church that hates us. *That* church."

"She's not like that."

"It doesn't matter what *she's like*." Talia made a sound of disgust. "She's the leader of the whole damn thing. You can't honestly think she sees you as her equal."

He clenched his jaw. "You don't know her."

"I know *you*. Or at least I thought I did." Talia closed her eyes for a moment and inhaled deeply. "You lied to me."

"I didn't *lie*." Dante pushed aside the memory of his powers blanking out. He hadn't told her that, either, but it hadn't happened again. He hadn't *let* it happen again.

"Cut the bullshit."

"Fine, I didn't *lie*, but I let you believe something that wasn't true."

Talia looked more hurt than angry now, so his balls were safe for the moment, but he knew better than to try to escape while she was still riled up.

"Give me a chance to plead my case, at least?" he said. "I'll buy you dinner."

Talia was still grumbling an hour later, glaring at him from across a small round table in a closet-sized bàcaro. He'd burned through a few coins already in his crusade to mellow her mood with cicchetti.

"Any number of ghiotte would happily warm your bed, but you just *had* to plunder the Cittadella's treasure room," Talia said, spearing a meatball with a skewer. "Let me guess, she's magic between the sheets, too?"

"It's not like that."

"Oh, gods, *please* don't tell me you've convinced yourself you're in *love*."

He didn't answer, but he didn't blink, either.

"Till death do you part?" Talia smiled grimly. "That's what Papa thought, too."

"I'm sorry about your mom, but—"

"Spare me the pity. She taught me a lesson. Family means the people who understand you, who have skin in the game."

"And sometimes we choose them."

Talia shook her head in disbelief. "She stole your powers and *killed* you. Family doesn't do that."

Dante rolled his eyes. "She didn't *kill* me. She let me save her life. And she didn't want me to. I saw it on her face when she realized what I was trying to do. Believe me. But she was the only one who could save everyone else, so she didn't fight it."

"Then she's a fool."

"No. She did her job. She let me save her so she could save everyone else. She was brave enough to live with the guilt of that. I don't know if I could make that choice."

"I still don't understand why you'd help Saverio anyway," Talia said. "Those people drove our people out and killed your parents. Why would you give your life to save those assholes?"

"I didn't." He held her gaze. "I did it to save *her*."

Thirty-five

DAYS UNTIL THE ECLIPSE: 13

Alessa's primary goal for the remainder of her time on Perduta was to dodge a confrontation with Talia. Her second goal was to avoid making a ninny of herself in front of the greatest fighters the world had ever seen.

The Saverians and ghiotte were finally training together, rather than in the general proximity of each other, and she waited for Dante's signal, poised on the balls of her feet.

Adrick raised his fists with a sigh. "Just punch me in the face and get it over with."

"You have to *try*."

"Why? I'm shit at fighting. I'll be dead before the eclipse is over."

Alessa tapped his side with a gentle roundhouse, and Adrick pantomimed a dramatic death scene, sprawling on the stones with his tongue hanging out of his mouth.

Kaleb grappled with Blaise, losing fast. Sparks danced across Kaleb's fingertips, but Alessa made a motion like cutting her throat that earned a deadly glare in response.

The non-ghiotte contingent had been strategizing and practicing with powers on their own, but they hadn't been given the go-ahead to use their powers within sight of the ghiotte yet, and they certainly didn't have permission to use them *on* the ghiotte.

On Alessa's other side, Talia glared at Kamaria. "Stop *smiling*. You shouldn't be happy that I'm about to kick your ass."

"If I'm going to go down, I'll do so with a smile on my face," Kamaria said with a wink. "You want to go down scowling, that's on you."

Talia's grin was feline and terrifying. "Sweetheart, *I* am not the one going down."

"Great. I've been waiting for you to make a move." Kamaria said with a smirk.

"You aren't ready for my moves," Talia said. "Hope you stretched this morning."

"Sweet of you to worry, but this isn't my first time."

It wasn't unusual for Alessa to hear innuendo where there was none, but she genuinely couldn't tell whether Kamaria and Talia were doing this on purpose or not.

Talia scoffed. "Big talk for Saverian royalty."

"Oh, yeah, I'm a spoiled brat, and you're the rebel bitch. Whatever roles you're into."

As long as it kept Talia distracted, Alessa wouldn't complain.

It didn't. Talia cornered her in the armory at the end of the day.

Extremely uninterested in a confrontation while surrounded by so many sharp objects, Alessa moved too fast in her haste to escape—never a good idea for the eternally clumsy. Her palm struck a battle-ax and split open like one of Ciro's fish.

"That doesn't look good." Talia watched the blood leak between Alessa's fingers. "How long will it take to get over that?"

Alessa fought a gag. "Do you really have no idea how regular healing works, or do you just enjoy treating us like a novelty show?"

"I actually have no idea." Talia leaned in. "That's pretty deep, though. At least a day, right?"

Alessa pressed harder, stomach churning. She wasn't afraid of blood in general, but the *spurting* was revolting. "More like weeks, but I can heal myself if you get Dante."

Talia stared harder. "You mean *he* can heal you."

Alessa stopped walking when her vision went black. "Could you please get him before I pass out?"

"If you can use *his* powers, you can use mine."

Alessa had never heard a more hostile offer in her life. "I assumed you'd rather I bleed to death."

Talia shrugged. "You *killed* my best friend. Wouldn't you? But as someone with a motive, I probably shouldn't be the last person seen with you before you bleed out."

"This feels like an important conversation, but if I don't find Dante or some bandages, I'm not sure I'll remain conscious long enough to finish it."

Talia thrust out her hand like a dare. Alessa steeled herself. The last thing she needed was to lose control and wallop Talia with her powers. She'd probably retaliate by killing her out of reflex.

Talia inhaled sharply at Alessa's first touch, but she didn't pull away until the wound healed completely.

"Huh." Talia dropped her hand like it was made of filth. "It's almost like you're one of us. But you aren't."

"You've made that very clear."

Talia dropped the fake smirk. "Then let's be honest. I don't like you. Not for him."

Alessa considered her words carefully. "Would you make it this hard if I were someone else, or is it just the Finestra thing?"

Talia almost smiled. "Why shouldn't it be hard? It's not all bathhouses and parties here, you know. In the winter, it gets cold. And we get hungry. You wouldn't last a year before you started crying for your fancy island."

"You don't know me."

Talia laughed. "No, but I know how this story goes. Cute guy, dangerous secrets. He's a challenge. You work your way into his confidence and he falls for you, but deep down, you know relationships that starts under that kind of circumstance never last. And when the excitement is gone, you'll realize everything you have to give up to keep him. My mom was just like you. Infatuated with her ghiotte husband until his little *problem* made life too hard, then she cut us loose."

Alessa wavered. How many times had she told herself Dante would get used to public life, that he'd enjoy himself once he adjusted? He'd never been entirely comfortable in her world, and now she wasn't welcome in his.

"Dante deserves the best." Talia held her gaze so intently Alessa fought not to look away. She *was* good for Dante. But the *best?* She'd never felt like the best at anything in her life.

She realized too late that Talia was studying the play of emotions across her face.

Talia raised her sword and touched it to Alessa's chest. "If you *ever* break his heart, I will break every bone in your body *and* your heart. And I *don't* mean metaphorically."

Thirty-six

DAYS UNTIL THE ECLIPSE: 10

By the middle of their second week on Perduta, Dante had successfully organized the ghiotte into specialized units, and his subordinates were finally stepping up without coming to him for everything.

The Saverians even held their own during training drills. They didn't *win* matches, but they didn't embarrass themselves, and they'd have their powers for the real battle. And, despite a few close calls, Dante kept Talia from "accidentally" murdering Alessa on the training field.

"I'm going to throttle my father if he tries another round of 'Twenty Questions About Dante,'" Talia said, dogging his footsteps as he mapped out the day's training exercise. "You can't avoid him forever."

"Get in formation," Dante said. With ten days remaining before the attack, he didn't have time for social calls, no matter how insistent Talia—and Alessa, oddly enough—were about him meeting with Matteo.

Scanning a row of archers, Dante counted in his head. One

group was short, and after his struggle to establish the importance of attendance and reliability, he couldn't let them slip now.

Talia stepped in front of him. "Dinner. Tomorrow."

He pointed at an empty spot. "Formation. Now."

He found the missing archer sitting behind a half-built armory shelter. Tall but skinny, the kid couldn't have been over thirteen, and his expression wavered between dread and belligerence as his general approached.

"What's going on?" Dante said.

"Nothing," the kid muttered.

"Your name's Jakob, right? What's the problem?"

The kid swallowed. "I don't *want* to fight the gods."

Dante nodded slowly. "Fair enough."

"Aren't you going to call me a coward?"

"No," Dante said. "If I didn't *have* to fight them, I wouldn't want to, either."

The kid scoffed. "Yeah, right. I heard what you said in the basilica. You almost died saving a whole island. I bet you've never even been scared."

Dante blew out a breath. "I wish that was true, but I *was* scared that day. Hell, I'm scared now."

The kid's eyes widened. "Nuh-uh. You're like a hero. Heroes don't get scared."

"You've got it backward. You can't be a hero *without* being scared." Dante crouched. "Courage doesn't mean you aren't afraid, it means you *are* and do it anyway. Think about it. What's heroic about doing something that *doesn't* scare you?"

Jakob mulled that over. "I guess so. . . ."

"If someone you love was in danger, and the only way to help them meant risking your life, what would you do?"

Jakob shrugged one shoulder. "I hope I'd do it."

"That's all you can do—hope that when the moment comes, you do the right thing. You don't have to enter battle without fear. In fact, I'm more worried about those who do. They get reckless, make sloppy choices that endanger everyone around them. Fighters who want to stay alive—who want *everyone* to stay alive—those are who we need."

The kid frowned in thought.

"See, that's the difference between us and Crollo," Dante said. "He doesn't care who lives or dies next week. We do. We're fighting to stay alive. That gives us the upper hand. Being afraid can make you a *better* fighter."

"You really think so?"

"I have enough fighters who want to prove how tough they are. What I *need* are people willing to do the work that's less flashy, the stuff that keeps everyone else alive—replenishing weapons, building barricades, seeing who needs backup and when. Can you help me with that?"

The kid nodded quickly. "My sister's one of the fastest sprinters on the island. She's little and not so strong compared to some of the guys, but you can hardly see her when she runs."

"Perfect. Round up the fastest kids you can find and meet me here first thing tomorrow. Kira could use more messengers, and we could all use help replenishing ammunitions."

Dante left Jakob with a proud smile on his face, and headed back to his post. Everyone was still in their places, but there was a shift in the air.

Leo strutted through the middle of his carefully arranged formation.

"I've decided to fight," Leo said. "Your little army can take the day off."

"You can't dismiss my troops," Dante said.

"Why not?"

"Because you can't fight the invasion alone. You know that, right?" Dante waited . . . for nothing, apparently. "You can fight *with* us if you're ready to be a part of a *unit,* but if not, I have to ask you to leave."

Leo smirked. "I've beaten a dozen ghiotte bare-handed. I'll take an army at my back—why not—but we both know wars aren't won by the people huddling behind barricades."

Dante's expression tightened. "Those people *huddling* behind the barricades have shown up for training every day, brave enough to face a war with the gods. Where have *you* been?"

Leo's expression grew dark. "I took it easy on you last time, but you're getting on my nerves."

Dante's thumbs slipped off his daggers. He wasn't doing this. Not today. "You're an excellent fighter, Leo, and we could use your help, but if you're not interested in being a team player, you'll have to leave. I have to get back to work."

Leo's eyes narrowed. "You're turning down a challenge?"

Dante sighed. "Yeah, I guess I am."

Leo's smirk faltered. "You can't do that."

Dante shrugged. "I just did. I don't have time for pointless exhibitions, and fighting each other won't help win this war."

Kamaria snorted a laugh.

Leo leveled his gaze on her. "The *lady* wants a challenge. What's your weapon of choice?"

Kamaria spread her arms and her hands burst into flames. "I *am* the weapon."

"No magic!" Talia snapped.

"Why? Because you're all too scared to fight us for *real?*"

Kamaria's flames grew brighter. "Let *us* use our powers, or send us home."

"Oh, *no;* does it tickle?" Leo taunted her. "Cute party trick."

"Kamaria," Dante warned. Too late.

Her eyes narrowed, a whip of fire snapped through the air, and flames sizzled down Leo's front.

He looked down, unconcerned, at the fire burning away his clothing like dry brush.

With slow movements, Leo patted at his hips and crotch to douse the flames before the final scraps went up in smoke.

His clothes in tatters, skin red and blistered—but healing fast—he tipped his head to one side. Then the other.

He raised his chin to stare directly at Kamaria. And began to laugh.

Excitement crackled through the ranks at the prospect of a true challenge, but warriors primed for battle were dangerous. Warriors accustomed to unnatural strength and healing abilities, even more so.

"The Saverians are *not* ghiotte." Dante put as much gravity into his voice as he could. "Do *not* forget that. If you cause real damage to any one of them, you'll answer to *me*. We can't win a war by brute force alone, but we *can* hurt our own side, so be *smart*. Strategic. Precise. Careful. *No* casualties. Understood?"

"Thanks, Dante," Kamaria said with an edge of irritation. "And *we* will also be sure not to cause too much damage with our super-powerful magical gifts."

Talia snickered.

Kamaria's expression turned arch. "Don't get cocky, sweetheart. We repelled an entire swarm of bloodthirsty scarabei after they flew over you, remember?"

Talia pounced and knocked her to the ground. Straddling the taller girl, Talia held Kamaria's neck with one hand, the other drawn back in a fist. "Don't call me sweetheart."

"Do it, and don't make it quick." Kamaria spun a wreath of fire and hovered it above her head, holding her hands in a prayer pose.

Talia unclenched her fist with an exasperated groan. "Do you take *anything* seriously?"

"Two things, actually." Kamaria's fiery halo vanished. "Love and war."

"Talia, get over here," Dante said. This was no time for flirting.

While the Saverians huddled for a strategy session, Adrick arranged sconces around Alessa, Kamaria, and Saida, and another set around Ciro and Kaleb.

Dante followed and nudged them farther out. When their "fortress" was arranged to his liking, Dante strode from one regiment of ghiotte to the next, shooting dark looks at those most prone to recklessness.

If anyone accidentally wounded Alessa or one of his friends, the ghiotte would bend their rules about the fontana, or he'd change their rules at knifepoint.

With Divorando, his duty had been perfectly aligned with his instincts. Alessa protected Saverio; he protected *her*. But this time he was the leader of an army, not her bodyguard. His duty was to watch, critique, and coach, not guard her, even if it went against every instinct to sic hundreds of ghiotte on her.

Torches flared, fire snapped, and electricity crackled.

Saida took Alessa's hand, and a wall of rolling air knocked half of the front line off their feet.

The fallen ghiotte helped each other up, looking a bit abashed.

Leo raised a fist. "Again!"

When Dante called it a day, they'd tallied forty-two injuries—none life-threatening, because the injured were ghiotte—two barricades scorched to ash, and one trebuchet in need of serious repairs, but Alessa and the Saverians were fine, and everyone was smiling, almost drunk on exhilaration after an epic day of training.

Far from being repelled by the Saverians' powers, his army reveled in the novelty, taking their formations to new heights, with acrobatic feats and a level of coordination he hadn't dared to dream they'd ever master.

Alessa and Ciro had both been spectacular, Alessa more so. Dante was biased, sure, but Alessa also had experience using multiple powers at once, while Ciro hadn't mastered the art of combining them for the flaming tornadoes and electrical storms Alessa conjured.

But even a historic mock battle couldn't deter Talia. She wasn't a dog with a bone, she was a wolf with a rabbit.

"I'm not *inviting* you, I'm *telling* you," she said. "You're coming to dinner *tomorrow.*"

He heaved a sigh. "And I told you, I *can't* tomorrow."

"Oh, yeah? What plans do you have that are so important?"

He was running out of excuses, but he had one ready this time. "It's Alessa's birthday."

Talia muttered something rude under her breath. "Fine, then the day after."

"Fine," Dante said. "I'm bringing Alessa."

Talia's nostrils flared. "*Why?*"

"I'm not hiding our relationship forever," he said. "You were right that people needed to know me first. Now they do. It seems like *you're* the one who can't deal with it at this point."

Talia glared harder. "I'm not the only one who hasn't forgotten history. We'll use their magic to fight this war, but then that's it. Gates closed. Outsiders *out*."

"Would you kick me out, too?" Dante asked. "Vote against me because of a girl you barely know?"

Talia's scowl deepened, but they both knew she wouldn't.

"I get why you don't want to trust her, but you should," he said. "Alessa was willing to keep my secret before anything happened between us, and she's a *good* person. Too good for me. Believe me, I tried to scare her off."

"Yeah, I bet," Talia said. "Playing hard to get just makes someone more desirable."

"Is that your strategy?" Dante tipped his head toward where Kamaria was making a group of ghiotte laugh with an impression of Kaleb being scared by the cat.

"*I'm* not foolish enough to fall for an islander," Talia said. She didn't look away, though. "It's a waste of time. I mean, you like it here, right? You think the *Finestra* will give up her fancy life if you decide to stay? How *do* you see this little love story ending?"

"We're facing Crollo in a little more than a week. I'll worry about that first."

The worst part wasn't Talia's cynicism, but the niggling

worry that she might be right. Even after a dozen visits to the fontana, Dante's powers only held a few days, and they waned faster the more he used them, whether by healing from injuries or being with Alessa. If he left Perduta, it would only be a matter of time before they were gone entirely.

The only way he could be with Alessa was for her to *want* to stay on Perduta, and Talia wasn't helping.

He stopped to face her. "Will you give her a chance?" he said quietly. "Please? For me?"

Talia looked like she'd rather eat shoe leather. "I'll *try*."

Thirty-seven

DAYS UNTIL THE ECLIPSE: 9

Matteo had been a bit *too* efficient at fixing up the house, and the addition of working plumbing meant Dante no longer had an excuse to visit the bathhouse, so he'd made a habit of sneaking out while Alessa slept.

No easy feat, as she tended to fall asleep wrapped around him, and he had to wage a war of willpower to leave her warm embrace.

Dante stifled a yawn as he jogged through the misty streets for a while, attempting to burn off the anxious energy running beneath his skin on his way to the bathhouse.

Adrick was waiting outside. "I knew it."

"Did you follow me?" Dante demanded.

"No," Adrick said. "But I'm here, and so are you. And Alessa isn't. So you're secretly visiting a bathhouse when we have bathing facilities at the house, which means you're meeting someone behind my sister's back, or that chamber isn't just for bathing. So what is it? Are you running around behind my sister's back, or is there something magical about the water in there?"

Dante had no good options. Revealing the truth meant betraying Talia's trust, but he couldn't let Adrick tell Alessa a lie that would break her heart.

"It's not for you," Dante said.

Hurt flashed across Adrick's face. "I wasn't asking for *myself*."

"Then why do you care?"

"I just want to know."

"You figured it out. Now forget you ever asked."

"But . . . if your powers came back, why are you still going in there?"

"Let it *go*, Adrick." Dante's words came out harsher than he'd intended.

Something shifted in Adrick's expression. "Does Alessa know?"

"Of course. She was there when it fixed me."

"Does she know it *wears off*?"

Dante raised a finger. "Don't even think about telling her."

"She deserves to know the truth," Adrick said. "If this means you can't—"

Dante cut him off. "We're facing a war with the *gods*. Everyone has to trust that I'm fit to lead this army, and the last thing Alessa needs now is to worry about our future when we don't even know if we'll live through it."

"You can't keep it from her forever."

"I *won't*."

As night fell outside their villa, Dante pulled a scarf from his pocket with a flourish, earning a very wary look from Alessa.

"Trust me," he said, laughter warming his voice.

Blindfolded, she clung to Dante's arm as he led her down

the street. The house around the corner was smaller and boarded up, but structurally sound, overlooking one of the larger canals and a rooftop deck with view of the city.

"Watch your step," he warned before she reached the stairs, but she still bumped her toe on the first step. He swung her into his arms, smiling at her squeak of surprise. "I'm not going to drop you. Have a little faith."

The air shifted from musty to crisp as they reached the top, and Dante lowered Alessa to her feet. Lanterns lit the space with a warm glow, illuminating an array of colorful blankets and pillows, and a makeshift table displaying an impressive array of baked goods.

"Tanti auguri," he said, loosening the scarf to fall around her neck.

Alessa spun in a slow circle to take in the rooftop deck, lit by a hundred candles, blankets and throw pillows scattered beneath a ceiling of stars. "How did you do all this?"

"Saida helped. She went a bit overboard with the baking, but it's your birthday. I wanted something special. And I got you a real present. Nothing lethal this time."

Alessa unwrapped the glittering gown and matching eye mask and clapped her hands in excitement. "Oh, it's stunning!"

"Saida helped with that too." In truth, Saida lobbied for a more modest dress but the slinky, low-backed gown was made of a silky fabric that would highlight Alessa's curves, and he knew how tired she was of covering up. She deserved the kind of dress that would give the judgy old farts of Saverio heart spasms, and he was thirsting to see her in it.

"The party before the vote is a masquerade," Dante said. "So people can vote anonymously."

Alessa tore her gaze from the dress. "How are you feeling about the vote?"

He shrugged one shoulder.

It should count for something that he'd won dozens of challenges, made friends, and amassed an army. But the thought of standing before his people while they debated whether they wanted him or not turned his stomach. Besides, even if they did vote him in, it wouldn't lessen the blow if Alessa decided not to stay.

Alessa stroked the dress with a happy little sound. "Thank you," she said with a coy smile. "I can't imagine a more perfect celebration."

"Hey, there—" he said as she began unbuttoning his shirt, trailing kisses as she worked her way down. "It's *your* birthday, not mine. . . ."

She looked up at him. "Don't *I* get to choose my present?"

When she put it *that* way . . .

Some time later, he remembered the questions he needed to ask.

"Tell me something," he said, as they gazed up at the stars. "If you could have anything you wanted, what would the rest of your life look like? The Cittadella? Galas and ball gowns every day?"

Her laugh was apologetic. "I earned that celebration. But no, that's not my dream."

"Tell me, then."

Alessa considered. "I used to have this ritual to calm myself. I'd imagine sitting outside a little house at sunset, waiting for someone returning in a boat. I never pictured the details of that person, because they were just holding a place for who, I *hoped*, would be a real person someday. It got more detailed over time, though, like someone crept into my head each night to fill it in. A window planter full of herbs I forgot to label so every harvest is an adventure, a fat cat sleeping in the sun, lemon trees nearby so I can make soaps like Nonna. And I don't remember when it changed, but now I can't picture it without knowing it's you."

He could imagine it so easily, the cozy cottage littered with remnants of Alessa's abandoned hobbies—half-finished paintings, tubs of glass beads, and misshapen crocheted potholders—the herbs in window boxes, and a cat drowsing on the sun-dappled floor.

He could imagine coming home to her.

"Your dream is a cluttered house on the water, a garden, and . . . me?" he asked.

"Give me a cozy little house, a cat to snuggle, and your obnoxiously handsome face on the other side of the breakfast table, and my life is complete."

He rubbed a thumb over the back of her hand. "What if you could have all that, but it was here instead of Saverio?"

Her grip slackened, and he waited for her to ask why. To force him to say it, but she didn't. "Could I still go back for visits?"

He nodded, unable to speak.

She spoke slowly, carefully. "Then if you decided to stay, I'd stay."

"Could you be happy, though? Even without the galas and ball gowns?"

Her smile was wistful. "Of course. I don't want the party to *be* my life. The dream is what remains when the party's over."

Thirty-eight

DAYS UNTIL THE ECLIPSE: 8

When Talia answered the door the following evening, Alessa nearly pulled an about-face, but she wasn't there for Talia. She was there for Dante.

Matteo stepped out of the kitchen wearing an apron, and Dante moved as though he was going to reach for Alessa's hand but clenched his into a fist instead.

"Zio," he said with a sharp nod.

Matteo dusted his hands on the front of his apron. "Lupetto."

Alessa mentally kicked herself for not studying the old language faster, but if she was interpreting Talia's expression correctly—no guarantee there—they'd taken a step in the right direction.

Matteo approached, arms wide. Dante stiffened but didn't pull away, and after a moment, he returned his uncle's embrace.

Alessa had to look away from the naked emotion on Matteo's face and accidentally met Talia's gaze as the other girl looked away from whatever she saw on Dante's. They'd probably both seen more of each other's hearts in one brief moment than either was prepared for. Talia had her faults, but she loved her father and Dante, and she wanted them to make peace, too. For that, Alessa could forgive her almost anything.

Matteo let go with a hearty pat. "Make yourself at home. Natalia, come set the table."

Talia hovered near Dante as through she was standing guard. "In a minute."

"Pronto, cara."

Alessa had lived through some tense meals, but none compared with sitting beside a silent Dante, across from a scowling Talia, while Matteo fought valiantly to engage in small talk.

"This looks wonderful," Alessa said when Matteo brought out dessert.

"His mother used to make this for every birthday," Matteo said softly. "It seemed fitting."

"You must give me the recipe, then," Alessa said. "Our friend Saida is working on a collection of traditional family dishes. I'm sure she would love to include one of Dante's."

Dante didn't look up from his plate. He'd never contributed to Saida's anthology, either because he didn't know any family recipes or hadn't wanted to dig up the memories they came with.

Eventually, Matteo stood, squaring his shoulders, and invited Dante to accompany him to his study. The tension left in their wake was thick enough to cut with a knife.

Talia glared, tapping her spoon against her saucer in a rap, rap, rap that felt like a tiny nail moving incrementally deeper into the base of Alessa's skull.

She lifted her cup without drinking. A single drop of

coffee would be more than her nerves could take. Deep breath. Another. She tried to let her mind drift, visualize it freed from the prison of her head.

Mutterings skittered across her mind, words she didn't know. She put her cup down too fast, splashing her skirt.

Talia looked over at the clatter. "Our coffee not good enough for you?"

"It's lovely. I'm just clumsy."

Were the mutterings Talia's words? Her thoughts?

"Sorry about your fancy skirts."

Alessa's head throbbed like it might crack in half, and Talia's sarcasm was the last straw. "I get it, Talia. You're not like other girls. Congratulations."

"Excuse me?" Talia asked.

Alessa dabbed at the spill, but it wasn't coming out without a good soak. "I'm not a super tough soldier, and I cry when people are mean, and I like pretty dresses and makeup, and I don't care if you think that's frivolous. And honestly, I like the parades and parties too. After years of isolation, people smile and wave at me now, and I like it."

Talia's eyes narrowed. "I don't hate dresses and makeup."

"That's the part we're focusing on?"

"Just making it clear."

Alessa threw her napkin on the table and stood. "I give up. I don't care if you like me or not."

"It's about time you fought back." Talia took a swig of her drink.

Alessa held in a growl. "I've been trying to be nice to you."

Talia shrugged. "Why? Nice is cowardly. I don't trust anyone who won't defend themselves or the people they love."

"What is that supposed to mean?"

"It means, Finestra, that centuries of hatred don't vanish overnight. If Dante returns to the outside world, he'll never be safe. People will say things. They'll turn on him the next time they need someone to blame. He will always be a target, and as his friend—no, his family—I need to know the people he cares about won't brush it off or let them do it."

Fine. So this was the moment. Alessa took a deep breath. "My parents didn't speak to me for five years. The church told them they no longer had a daughter and they just . . . accepted it. Saverio turned against me, my guards tried to kill me, my advisors debated whether to assassinate me, and my brother urged me to drink poison. I've worked really hard to forgive, but I will never forget how people turned their backs on me. And I would never do that to him or let anyone treat him like that again. No matter what."

Talia's voice lost its edge. "He's happy here."

"I know," Alessa said softly. "And I know you aren't thrilled that I'm in his life, but believe it or not, I'm grateful you are. No matter what happens, I never want him to be alone again."

"He won't be," Talia said.

Alessa had to reach for the table as her vision went dark. She had to get out of there. "I have to go. Tell Dante I had a headache."

Talia followed her to the door. "Will you stay with him if he decides not to return to Saverio?"

Alessa had no idea what would happen in a few weeks. "If I can."

"It's not a hard question," Talia said. "What are you willing to sacrifice so Dante can be happy?"

Alessa steadied her footing. "Anything."

Talia's focus tightened. "Even him?"

Dante strolled the perimeter of Matteo's study, examining the handmade shelves full of knickknacks—some he remembered and others he'd never seen.

"I tried to salvage as much as I could," Matteo said. You're welcome to anything you'd like. You should have something special for the vote tomorrow."

Dante ran his fingertips over a hand-carved wooden ship he used to play with on the beach. Beside it, a lopsided clay jar had once held a bouquet of wilted wildflowers he'd picked for Talia, shriveled leaves gone sickly sweet as they rotted because she refused to throw them away, even after laughing in his face for the gift.

Matteo inhaled and held it for a moment. "You have every right to be angry at me."

"I'm not," Dante said. Matteo just looked at him. Dante rolled his words around for a while, but they didn't come out any less sharp. "Fine. I *am* angry. But I don't want to be."

"Sometimes anger protects us until we're ready to move on. I'll be here whenever that day comes." Matteo opened a cabinet and withdrew a package wrapped in paper. "Your parents' portraits. I was afraid they would fade, so I kept them out of the sun. They belong with you."

Dante accepted the package but didn't unwrap them. The first time he saw his parents' faces again, he wanted to be alone. Or maybe with Alessa. But not here. Not a guest in someone else's house where he'd have to face them afterward.

"I'll give you a minute alone," Matteo said. The door closed behind him with a soft *snick*.

A glint of light caught Dante's eye. A set of rings in a dish on Matteo's shelf.

For the space of one breath, his heart ceased to beat. It just . . . stalled for a moment.

His parents' wedding rings. He picked them up with weak fingers. Turned them over in his palm. He'd seen his mother polishing hers once and caught sight of lettering inside. He had asked her what it said, but she'd only smiled and told him it was a secret. She would show him when he was grown. When he fell in love. When he was old enough to understand such things.

"Love is a peculiar magic," she'd said. "Because it makes you strong but also delicate."

It had sounded absurd at the time. A person could be strong or delicate. Not both.

He understood better now.

Love itself might be strong, but loving made you vulnerable.

When he returned to the sitting room, the rings safely tucked in his pocket, Talia was alone. "Your girl left early. Said she had a headache."

More likely she'd fled Talia's hostility. Regardless, Dante seized the excuse to leave.

He walked slowly, covering the portraits with his jacket to protect them from the light rain, then sat on the stairs of the house for a while before he found the courage to open them.

He'd never said it to anyone, not even Alessa, but he'd begun to worry he'd forget his parents entirely. Or worse, that he'd already made things up, filled the missing parts with falsehoods, but the first glimpse of his parents' faces hurt less than he expected. His memories had held true, if a bit blurred. His father *did* look like him, eerily so, but his father's smile was wider and warmer, like someone who expected joy. A man who believed the best of everyone.

His mother's was more subtle. She had been serious, observant, slower to warm up, but with a subtle, sly sense of humor. His chest ached for every joke he would have committed to memory if he'd known the end was near.

The night thickened as he stared at their faces until the raw parts weren't so raw and he could pack it all away again, lighter than before. He wrapped them carefully and jogged up the stairs. Alessa would want to see them.

But when he reached their rooms, the bed where she should have been waiting for him was empty.

Alessa woke as though stepping off a ledge into nothingness.

She wasn't curled up beside Dante in bed. Or even inside. She was on her hands and knees in a garden, shivering in the pounding rain. Shaking, she pushed back to kneel and swiped hair from her face with bloody hands. Dirt was caked beneath her nails, like she'd clawed her way out of a shallow grave. Terror shot through her.

On either side of a gated park, broken windows leered down from crumbling buildings.

She tried to stand. Stumbled. Righted herself and ran.

A canal. A bridge. She was still on Perduta, but in a part she'd never seen before. She didn't even know if she was going the right way.

Something clamped over her shoulders, and a scream ripped from her throat.

"Hey, it's me! It's *me*." Dante, gripping her shoulders. "What are you doing out here?"

Her teeth chattered. "I got lost."

Dante's face shadowed. "What happened to your hands?"

"I . . . tripped. You know how clumsy I am."

Dante draped his jacket over her shoulders. "Come on, you're soaked."

Back at the house, Alessa made a show of wringing out her hair, joking about her terrible sense of direction.

She hoped he'd believe her shivers were from a chill. In bed, she snuggled close to him, afraid to close her eyes.

The darkness inside her was growing, and she had no idea what would be left of her when it finished.

Thirty-nine

DAYS UNTIL THE ECLIPSE: 7

The next evening, everyone else left for the masquerade before the vote, but Alessa and Dante dawdled, cuddling and talking about silly things, neither venturing to touch on anything serious. She smiled and feigned calm, and he did the same as the hours ticked down.

"It's not too late for body paint," Alessa joked as she watched Dante get dressed. "Mastra Pasquale's lessons could finally come in handy."

Tonight, Perduta would decide if he was granted permanent residency. A road diverged ahead. In one direction, Saverio, where Dante had never felt truly at home. In the other, Perduta, where he was embraced but she would always be outside looking in. There were other paths concealed by the shadow of uncertainty, but she wouldn't tread those yet, not even in her imagination.

A few more days. She could hold herself together for a few more days. If—when—Dante's army of ghiotte defeated

Crollo's minions once and for all, Dea would reward them. She had to.

Crollo destroyed and Dea saved. And yet, hope was a lantern growing dimmer each day.

The silvery blue dress Dante had bought slipped across her skin like water as they walked in silence, hands clasped, until the basilica gleamed ahead, spilling music into the night, and she pulled free. The formal vote would be held within, but the evening's revelry was outside on the piazza. Most of the revelers' faces were concealed by masks, some horrifying, some stunning, but she still recognized their closest allies gathered around a bonfire.

As they crossed the piazza toward them, Dante rested a hand on Alessa's back to guide her through the crowd. He made no attempt to keep his distance. After weeks of hiding their relationship, the change was wonderful, but his proximity made it harder to hide how she was falling apart.

Saida bounced over, grinning beneath her mask, and Dante went to find refreshments while Saida gushed about how well everyone was getting along and how wonderful it was to see some team bonding at last. Even Ciro seemed relaxed and happy to be there.

Caught in the penumbra between firelight and night, Kaleb laughed at something Adrick said, a genuine sound that was nothing like his usual sardonic chuckle. Maybe there was hope for them yet.

Dante returned, but Kamaria snagged a glass of wine from his hand before he reached Alessa. Frowning slightly, he turned around, presumably to fetch a replacement.

"Sorry, but I need to borrow her," Kamaria said, looping an arm through Saida's.

Left on her own, Alessa scanned the crowd, attempting to appear relaxed and entirely unperturbed, as any normal person would be upon finding themselves alone in the middle of a party. Definitely not like someone fighting to hold her brain together as it attempted to unravel.

The minds all around pulsed against hers, vibrating Alessa's skull until her jaw ached from clenching her teeth. No matter what, she would stay by Dante's side.

A handsome young man near Talia turned his gaze on Alessa. "Buonasera, princess."

"There are no princesses on Saverio," Alessa said.

"I know a princess when I see one." His tone was so flirtatious she couldn't help smiling. "Talia, introduce me?"

Talia flicked a glance at Alessa. "Finestra."

"Should've known you were the wrong person to ask." The boy extended a hand to Alessa. "Dario."

"Alessa." Her powers were under control, so she obliged.

Dario turned over their clasped hands, studying hers. "Hmm. I expected something a bit more interesting to happen."

Alessa laughed. "I can only magnify someone *else*'s powers or skills."

He raised her hand for a courtly, if prolonged, kiss. "What *kinds* of skills?"

"Almost anything. I can heal like a ghiotte if I touch one of you while injured, my voice could bring you to tears while I'm holding hands with a singer, and I fight like the best after touching a skilled fighter." Talia's head snapped up at that. Oops.

Dario smirked. "I have been praised for my *skills*. Does that mean if we were together, you'd be even more talented at my favorite pastimes?"

Alessa took her hand back. "Flattering, but I'm—"

"Taken." Dante's arm slipped around her shoulders.

This felt dangerous, but a frisson of delight danced over Alessa's skin anyway.

Dante met Talia's murderous glare without apology. "I've been sparring with him all week. Dario, are you going to turn on me now that you know Alessa's my girl?"

Dario pretended to consider. "Saverio's elite has been screwing us for years. About time one of us returned the favor."

"Careful," Dante warned.

Dario chuckled. "Afraid I'm going to steal her?"

"I'd like to see you try." Dante raised his glass.

After checking to be sure her mask was firmly in place for anyone nearby who wasn't as relaxed about outsiders, Alessa dared to slide her arm around Dante's waist.

"Isn't anyone single in this fine-looking group?" Dario said, loud enough to be heard from a distance. Saida fluttered her fingers, and he sauntered over to charm her instead.

Dante pulled Alessa closer as Talia turned on her heel and strode away.

The night darkened and the music swelled. Blaise broke into a series of flips, shouting for people to join in. Saida shimmied circles around Dario, and Kira coaxed Ciro into a dance, throwing sidelong glances at the blacksmith. Judging from Ciro's slightly alarmed expression, he'd be relieved once he figured out he was merely jealousy bait.

Blaise reached the final crescendo of his dance and slid to a stop, urging his audience to applaud as the final notes of the song rang through the air.

Kamaria crossed the impromptu dance floor toward a

surly Talia. "We're supposed to be bringing these two factions together. Will you dance with the enemy or are you too scared?"

Talia pursed her lips for a long moment. "One dance. Don't read too much into it."

Kamaria grinned triumphantly and tugged Talia into her arms, dipping her with a flourish that drew catcalls.

Dante eased Alessa back into the shadows as the music transitioned into something low and sweet. His voice was so soft she could barely hear, but she saw the request on his lips and felt it in his hands.

She was weary of holding herself together. For this moment, she had to trust she could let go without dropping everything.

She let her consciousness expand, riding the swells of joy like jumping waves on the beach. She could find her way back, tethered to Dante's warmth. Anchored by his love. By his arms around her. By his voice as he sang in her ear, a song she didn't know in a language she was only beginning to understand. She didn't need to know the words to know what it meant, or to feel what he felt. She closed her eyes, extinguishing one sense to heighten the others, and let herself get lost in him for as long as she could.

Hugged by the heat from the fire against her back and Dante's heat against her chest, Alessa let go of her fears. And she forgot them, entirely, when his hands found their way into her hair, which had come loose from its tie and fallen around her shoulders.

At the boom of a gong, the music ceased, and the warm, hazy veil of peace evaporated. Alessa shuddered as her mind was barraged by thoughts and emotions again.

"You cold?" Dante asked, already shrugging out of his jacket to drape it over her shoulders.

On the steps of the basilica, Nova stood in crimson robes. "Let the voting begin."

Dante radiated calm confidence, but his thumb lightly caressed the curve of Alessa's spine the same way he rubbed the handle of his blades when he was tense.

She had become his comfort object, and she didn't know whether to cry from joy or sadness. His blades would never fail him, but she might.

"Good luck," Alessa whispered, stepping away.

The other ghiotte began walking toward the building, but Dante grabbed her hand. "Take off your mask."

She cast a nervous glance around. "Now?"

"If they don't want me because of you, then they shouldn't vote for me." He untied the strings and placed the mask in her hand, then tipped her face up for a long, slow kiss no one could miss.

Alessa held his gaze as they parted. She didn't want to know if Dante's kiss was drawing stares or judgment. All those years of being shunned, an outcast, and he gambled it all for her. Tears pricked her eyes as he reluctantly let go.

It was time. Kamaria whooped and Kaleb thumped Dante on the back, bringing a reluctant smile to his face as he joined the rest of the ghiotte headed for the basilica.

The doors closed behind him with a resounding clang that rattled Alessa's head.

It was almost funny how they were *so* worried about concealing their super-secret rituals, while she was fighting *not* to hear the myriad thoughts within.

One of Leo's girlfriends, the light-haired woman named

Chiara, was among those left outside, talking to another couple. Interesting. For all Leo's barbed comments about outsiders, it seemed he was also involved with a non-ghiotte.

Kamaria swaggered over to Chiara and her friends. "Where's the after-party?"

A brief pause, then Chiara smiled back. "My place."

Saida skipped over to join them, but Alessa waved off their invitation, and Ciro must have exhausted his tolerance for socializing because he was halfway across the piazza already.

"You want company?" Adrick asked Alessa.

"No, I'm fine," she assured him. "Go enjoy your night." She would rather curl up in bed to wait for Dante's return.

Kaleb and Adrick left together, and she started the slow walk home. With most of Perduta gathered inside the basilica, the cobblestone streets were dark and empty, and the silence soothed her throbbing mind like ice on a bruise.

She shoved her hands into the pockets of Dante's jacket, and her fingertips hit something hard. Metal, smooth and rigid, like the cold, hard, carapace of the scarabeo that triggered the dark power now taking over her.

Crollo destroyed, and Dea saved.

Alessa's fingers closed around the metal key to the fontana.

If Crollo was harming Dea's chosen saviors, Dea would provide a solution.

Or maybe she already had.

Dea must have been so disappointed in her. A lifetime of stories about a mythical fountain of healing, and it had still taken Alessa weeks after learning about a *real* one to put the pieces together.

Most of Perduta was at the vote, so Alessa's path to the fontana was clear.

Her hands shook as she hastened to unlock the chamber.

The water in the fontana rippled in silvery blue like her gown. Grasping the hem so it wouldn't get wet, Alessa crouched by the edge of the pool and extended her hand, holding it above the surface.

According to Talia, the fontana wasn't for her. But Dea had chosen Alessa, and Dea had created the fontana.

Two conflicting powers warred inside her. The dark and the light.

One urged her forward and the other commanded her to turn back.

The light won.

With a fortifying breath, she plunged her hand into the fontana.

Forty

Dante was only a little nervous as he stood on the altar waiting for Nova to call the vote. The basilica was full to bursting, and the feathers, body paint, and glitter should have watered down the solemnity of the occasion, but that *was* Perduta: a messy, chaotic family where loyalty reigned and propriety was scoffed at.

Dante understood them. He was them.

In the end, it was almost too easy. Nearly every attendee raised their hand with a chorus of "ayes," and Dante exhaled fully for the first time he could remember.

He'd visited the fontana that morning, so he extended his hand without fear when Leo held out a jewel-encrusted dagger to slice the heel of Dante's palm while Nova performed the same ritual on Talia and Matteo.

"Even as we bleed, we heal," Nova proclaimed. "As we are banished from their cities, we build our own. They sought to break us, but we remain unbroken. Dea blessed us as protectors, and her blessing protects us. And soon, we shall complete the mission she gave us by protecting the world."

They let blood pool in their palms until it dripped into the chalice below, then raised their hands aloft for all to witness. Fresh blood from unbroken skin, a symbol of who they were and what they had endured.

Dante strode to the register on the altar and signed his name. He wished his parents' signatures could be there, too. They would be proud of him. They would be happy.

Leo bowed his head in a gesture of respect that rippled across the crowd. "At midnight, you'll be baptized in our sacred waters and face tomorrow renewed."

Fitting. The fontana had brought back his powers, given him the right to belong here. What better way to honor his coronation?

His powers might not be permanent, but they worked when he needed them most. His hand, perfect and whole once more, was his badge, his key, to this life. The life where he could lead an army, save the day, and get the girl.

He might never be a full ghiotte again, but he could live like one.

He could have it all, as long as he had the fontana.

Forty-one

The ceiling of the bathhouse came into focus as Alessa reached for her throbbing head. Her hand came away bloodied. She must have slipped and fallen on her way to bathe. Except she was fully dressed. And sopping wet.

She sat up with a groan. The door to the fontana chamber hung drunkenly from one hinge, as though torn off by massive hands. Beyond it, the faint blue glow was gone.

As she squinted to see inside, tattered memories flickered through her mind:

Creeping through the bathhouse, key in hand.

Touching her fingers to the surface of the pool.

A tremor. Ripples. The walls rattling. The ground shaking.

The world going dark.

"Alessa?" Adrick's frantic voice echoed off the stone. He froze in the entrance to the baths, his jaw falling open. "What happened?"

She found her feet as he ran over. "I don't know. I barely touched it."

Tearing his eyes from the destruction, Adrick checked her

over with quick movements. "Superficial. Heads wounds always bleed a lot, but you'll be okay."

Together, they took in the darkened room. It looked as though a massive fist had punched the columns surrounding the pool, sending chunks of marble into the fontana, which had split down the middle.

"Damn, Lessa. What have you done?"

Her legs shook. "It was an accident."

"It was a *mistake*, Alessa. Not an accident. You chose to go in there." Adrick took an involuntary step back. "They'll never forgive you."

A wave of nausea stole her breath. "Do you even know what was in there?"

"Yeah. I do. *Did*. Did it work, at least?"

She closed her eyes. The buzz in the back of her mind came into focus, breaking into muddled mutterings. The jumbled internal monologues of a group of people getting closer.

"No," she said, her heart sinking. "No, it didn't work."

She wasn't better. The fontana hadn't been powerful enough to banish the darkness inside her. Instead, her darkness had been powerful enough to destroy the light.

The voices were getting louder, more distinct. In minutes, they'd arrive and they would find . . . this.

Alessa's heart lurched as the door opened, but it was only Kaleb, holding a towel. His confused gaze darted between Adrick and Alessa. "You brought your sister?"

"Get out," Adrick snapped, and Kaleb's head jerked as though he'd been slapped.

"What the hell happened to that door? Is she bleeding?" Kaleb asked.

"Broken holy fountain and we don't have time to explain," Adrick said. "Alessa, go. Now."

Too late. Voices, and not in her head this time.

Adrick rolled his shoulders back. "Okay, new plan. Tell them I did it."

"*No*," Alessa said. "They'll execute you."

"The world needs you, not me. Dante just publicly claimed you in front of everyone. If they find out you destroyed their magic fountain, everything will fall apart. So the story is . . . I stole the key from Dante, you tried to stop me and you fell."

The voices grew louder. Talia, Leo, Nova . . . They were in the foyer, and in a moment, they would reach the door to the bathing chamber. There was no way out.

Alessa's mind raced, searching for a solution that didn't exist. Dante was a part of this world now, and he had tied his fate to hers the moment he kissed her in front of everyone. Her mistake would either be a noose around Adrick's neck . . . or Dante's.

Adrick's hand shook as he pushed back his hair. "Just tell Mama and Papa the truth, please? If I'm going to die a villain, I want them to be proud of me at least."

Dante stepped through the door, his brow furrowing at the sight of the disheveled trio. "Alessa? What are you—"

Blood snaked down Alessa's neck from a wound he couldn't see.

White-hot rage coursed through Dante's veins. If someone had done this to her— No, vengeance could wait. His focus narrowed to a point. She was hurt and scared and he needed to get to her.

"What happened?" He crossed the room in long strides. He was supposed to keep her safe. His arrival should have *made* her feel safe, but she looked *more* frightened to see him. His rage curdled into something worse. She was afraid of *him?*

Dante took her chin. Gently, he turned her head to see for himself. His neck tingled as her gift drew from his, and her scalp began knitting together.

She was okay. She was safe. His frantic heartbeat began to slow as he ran his fingers over her skull, her neck, making absolutely sure.

"It's my fault," said Adrick. "She tried to stop me. We struggled, and she fell—"

"Struggled?" Dante whirled on him.

Alessa grabbed Dante's arm. "No, there was no struggle! I slipped."

A look passed between the siblings that Dante couldn't decipher.

Matteo, Leo, Nova, and Talia entered, red robes as striking against the tiles as Alessa's spilled blood, and their horrified gazes locked on something behind Dante.

A memory tickled the back of his mind. A door that should be closed, open.

No. *Broken.*

Dante turned, reaching as though to catch something before it fell. But there was no catching the tumbled bricks, no stopping the cracked basin from emptying.

The fontana that gave back his powers, that had *been* restoring them all this time, his only hope . . . destroyed.

Forty-two

Dante shoved Adrick against the wall. "What have you done?"

"He didn't even know what it was!" Alessa cried.

"Yes, he did." Dante's voice turned brittle. "He knew *exactly* what it was, and he ruined it anyway. That's what *he does.*"

"Adrick would never do something like that on purpose," Kaleb said quietly.

"He just admitted it," Dante snarled. "You wanted to become something more than you were meant to be and damn the consequences."

"You figured me out," Adrick said, voice flat. "I wanted to be special, but the gods found me lacking yet again."

"You betrayed the people we came to ally with. You betrayed *me.*" Dante shoved Adrick again. "Tell me why I shouldn't kill you."

Adrick didn't fight back, arms tight at his side, even as his eyes began to water.

Dante knew what anger tasted like. Righteous fury, sharp and clean. The hot, dense burn of vengeance. A grudge, dark and smoldering. But this was different. *This* was the choking kind of anger, thick and rancid, sour with recrimination. Because he'd let this happen.

He'd known who Adrick was since the first day they met. Adrick tried to poison Alessa. Adrick publicly exposed Dante as a ghiotte. Adrick had made it perfectly clear he couldn't be trusted. But he was Alessa's brother. So, despite knowing better, Dante had given him another chance.

Look where that got them.

"Release him so he can plead his case," Leo said. "How did you know about the fontana, boy?"

Dante waited a moment longer before yanking his hand back.

Adrick slid to the floor, gasping. "I guessed. I grew up hearing about the legend of the Fonte di Guarigione, so when I found a locked door, I got curious. I stole a key."

"From whom?" Nova said. "Only a handful of citizens even have a key."

Talia kept her gaze trained on the floor.

"I've been working on their house," said Matteo. "I must have dropped mine. As his sponsor—"

Nova cut him off. "You *were* his sponsor, Matteo. But he came here with a ghiotte and that ghiotte is now one of us. Signor Lucente, do you have anything to say in defense of this boy?"

"No."

"Will anyone speak on his behalf?"

"I will," said Matteo.

Dante held his fury in check while Matteo argued that Adrick's treachery shouldn't be held against the rest of the Saverians. Like the ghiotte, they were blessed, too, all victims of a petty human's envy. Adrick alone was a mere mortal.

Not a Fonte. Not a Finestra. Not a ghiotte.

Every time Matteo repeated it, Dante felt the blow.

The last of Dea's blessed water trickled through the shattered marble floors, absorbed into whatever lay beneath the foundation. Dante fought the urge to drop to his knees and chase the dregs, to lick every drop from the floor, but the magic was gone.

Guilty.

It was unanimous. Dante heard Alessa's muffled sob, but he didn't look at her. She didn't yet understand what her brother had done.

"On Perduta, we let the aggrieved party decide the punishment," Leo said. "Dante, the decision is yours."

Dante looked down at Adrick's bowed head.

Alessa believed in forgiveness.

She forgave Tomo and Renata for plotting against her.

She forgave her parents for turning their backs on her.

She had forgiven Adrick for trying to poison her.

She didn't know her brother had stolen their future.

Dante stood tall. "I'll do it myself."

"Wait!" Alessa's confession caught in her throat as Adrick met her eyes with a silent warning. For good measure, he signed a quick "No."

She had done this. *She* had fractured the fragile peace between two groups who needed each other to prevent the end of the world as they knew it. One impulsive decision might have damned them all.

"Alessa, *go*." Dante's eyes were cold. No warmth, no love. Not even anger. Just cold.

Kaleb took Alessa's arm. "Come on. We can only make it worse."

He was right. Her brother had already accepted the responsibility for her crime. If she tried to take it back, she'd take Dante down with her. So she left. She hated it, but she left.

Kaleb held Alessa's arm in a vise grip the entire way to the house, staring straight ahead as though looking at her would make him sick. "Adrick tried to get you killed, so now you're returning the favor?"

Shame buckled her knees. "They can't execute him. They *can't*. Dante won't do it."

She simply couldn't live in a world where that happened. Where *she* let it happen.

Kaleb kicked the gate closed behind him, blocking her escape.

"Don't," he snapped. "You've done enough. We have to trust Dante. He's never let us down before." With a heavy sigh, Kaleb climbed the stairs, leaving Alessa alone with her guilt.

Adrick's life was on the line because of her, and it had all been for nothing.

She was still a monster. Still a killer. And now a traitor, too.

The balcony was as close as she could get to the gods, and she needed them to hear her now.

Below, the city was dark and quiet, no torches or mob descending. Yet. She grasped at hope as she idly stroked Fiore's fur. If only she could absorb some feline skills. Cats cheated death and landed on their feet, while Alessa killed and stumbled her way through life.

Fear clawed up her throat. She had to know.

Like unspooling a ball of thread in a dark and cluttered room, she followed a path she couldn't see to where others' consciousness met her own. Kaleb's pulsing fear, sleepy rumblings from Saida and Kamaria, past a blankness from Ciro, who must be an exceptionally deep sleeper. Her mind roamed until it snagged.

She sifted through fragments of feelings, bits of sound, until she caught a glimpse through Dante's eyes of Adrick, his face drawn and haggard, standing in a boat with his hands bound.

A violent shove overboard.

Alessa's mind snapped shut against the pain.

He'd done it.

He'd actually done it.

Dante had killed her brother.

Forty-three

Dante held Adrick's life in his hands, and he wanted to crush it.

Adrick sat in the prow of the boat, head high like a noble martyr instead of the conniving thief he truly was.

"You just couldn't stand it, could you?" Dante put down the oars and stood, bracing his feet for balance. "The gods didn't bless you because you're weak and you don't *deserve* it."

"Is that why you haven't told Alessa about losing your powers?" Adrick said calmly. "Our minds can be cruel, can't they, convincing us we're less than because we don't have what someone else does?"

"We *aren't* the same." Dante grabbed him by the collar, twisting it tight. "I *had* powers. Now, thanks to you, I have nothing. *Nothing!*"

Adrick's stare was unapologetic. "If you still think your powers are the most important thing in the world, I feel sorry for you."

Dante chucked Adrick over the side. If he drowned, so be it.

Adrick floundered, struggling to keep his head above water

without the use of his hands. Gasping, he finally got his feet beneath him in the shallows.

"Get out of my sight," Dante growled. "If I ever see you again, I'll put a knife through your heart."

Matteo and Talia were waiting by the dock when Dante rowed back to Perduta.

"Word is spreading fast," Matteo said as Dante tied up the boat. "People are mad, but we already have healing powers. It'll be fine."

Dante gave the knot one last tug. It would *never* be fine. They had no *idea*.

Matteo gripped Dante's shoulder. "Son—"

"I'm not your son." Dante jerked away. "And I'm not a ghiotte anymore. My powers will be gone in a few days, and so will I."

Talia's face blanched. Matteo's mouth took on a grim line. Dante walked away.

There was no point lying. It was over.

With every passing minute, he would be a little bit less. Less ghiotte. Less a leader. Less himself. Less his parents' son. And less of what Alessa needed him to be.

He would face the gods as a mere mortal. He probably wouldn't survive, and if he did, he'd be left with nothing. No future with Alessa on Saverio. No future with the ghiotte on Perduta. Every time he reached for more, the gods ripped it away.

He flung open the basilica doors, kicking aside discarded bottles and scraps of clothing. He wanted to tear apart the thrones on the altar, smash every window until his knuckles were shredded skin and fractured bone.

But he couldn't. His powers were a finite resource now.

Acrobatic silks dangled from the ceiling, languidly swaying in the gloom as he climbed the stairs to the highest balcony.

For years he'd turned his back on society, choosing to starve instead of beg for scraps. Then Alessa made him believe life could be different, and he'd gorged himself on everything he wasn't meant to have—love, friendship, respect. Now, he'd suffer all the more for knowing the taste. He should have kept his head down and his feet in the dirt where he belonged.

"You look like you could use a friend right now." Matteo hoisted himself up to sit on the railing with the strength of a younger man. Maybe he'd regularly visited the fontana before its destruction. Maybe he, too, would be a little bit less in the days to come. A cruel, bitter part of Dante hoped so.

"We aren't friends." Dante clenched his fists. "Leave me alone."

"Sorry, but no. You aren't getting rid of me." Matteo held his arms out. "Go on, hit me if it will make you feel better. It can't hurt any more than my own regrets."

"I'm not going to *hit* you," Dante said, even though he *wanted* to.

"Then talk to me," Matteo said, soft and earnest.

"I *can't*."

"Why not? You think I'm gonna run?"

Dante said nothing.

Matteo rubbed his jaw. "I know you're mad, and some of that is my fault, but it's gonna eat you alive if you don't let it out."

"What do you want me to say?" Dante snapped. "You *left* me! Years locked up, waiting for you to save me, and you weren't even *looking*."

Matteo took a shaky breath. "And I'll regret that the rest of my life."

"*Why?* Why didn't you look for me?" Dante demanded. His

life was imploding, and none of this mattered, but somehow it still did, and he needed to understand *why*. Why everyone always left.

Matteo spoke into the grim dark. "Your father was like a brother to me. I'd never loved anyone else like that until you and Talia were born. When I heard what happened, I came running. . . . Losing him like that, it was like the world cracked in half. And all I could think about was how much he loved his son, and what you must have suffered. I didn't think you could still be alive, and I couldn't bear to see you like that, too."

Dante could barely breathe past the pressure on his chest.

Matteo's knuckles were white on the railing. "I was scared and grieving and too angry to think, but that's no excuse. I should never have left without making sure. I will *never* forgive myself for leaving you to go through that alone. I was a coward and I failed you."

Hearing his own bitter thoughts aloud took the fight out of Dante. Not the anger—that still festered—just the desire to lash out.

"As soon as the battle is over, I'm leaving," Dante finally said. "I don't belong here."

"Bullshit. Everyone voted. You're official." Matteo wouldn't let Dante shrug it off. "It's up to you whether to tell people or not, but you're one of us, and if anyone disagrees, screw them. You're our family. And if you leave, I'll be right behind you."

Dante dropped his head in his hands. He was so tired. Of holding it all together, of carrying it alone, working so hard just to hold on to something—anything.

Matteo's arm came around his shoulders. "It's going to be all right."

Dante took a long drag of cool air. Maybe it would. Maybe it wouldn't.

But maybe he wouldn't have to do it alone.

Dante's never-ending night wasn't over, though. Alessa would be waiting.

His reflexes were dulled by exhaustion, dread, and guilt, so Kaleb avoided an untimely death when he jumped out as soon as Dante stepped into the courtyard.

"He's exiled, not dead." Dante sheathed his blades and shouldered past.

He had to tell Alessa everything.

He didn't want to tell her anything.

He'd saved her brother but lied about his powers being restored. He loved her, but they only had a few days left together. He had no idea how that math worked out.

Alessa was sitting on the balcony off their room, but she stood when he entered. She waited for him to speak with her heart in her eyes. Soon to be broken. By him. Like everything else.

He couldn't cut her free. He wasn't strong enough. He could only tell her the truth and make her do it for him.

First things first. Her brother was alive. He'd given her that, at least.

"I let Adrick go."

He shouldn't have let her throw herself into his arms.

He should have held her at arms length until he told her the rest.

Instead, he kissed her. Because he was selfish, and he wanted one more night with her before she learned the truth—that she'd given up her chance at happily ever after the moment she fell in love with him.

One more night of Alessa believing he was her hero.

Forty-four

Alessa fought the urge to cry as Dante fell asleep with his face buried in the crook of her neck, the warm huff of his breath tickling her skin. She should have confessed.

Her breath faltered, catching in her throat. She forced herself to release, exhale.

In and out.

Out and in.

All she'd ever wanted was a quiet life cluttered with simple joys. A house near the ocean, bare toes in the sand and fingers twined together, teasing and laughing over inside jokes.

Instead, she got a destiny built of battles and war, trauma and loss, and now *another* apocalypse.

She smoothed Dante's hair with a light hand. It wasn't fair. But she got to love him, and that was too precious to be fair. Carefully tucking the ends of the blanket down, she watched him sleep, aching with love for her beautiful, broken man.

Dea, I swear, I will chase you to the very ends of the afterworld if you hurt him again. Please, let him have peace.

Fiore curled up at the foot of the bed, rumbling reassurance, but guilt sat like a boulder on Alessa's chest.

Dante had slept with one eye open for years, not trusting anyone, and for good reason. Now he lowered his defenses and slept in her arms when she was the most dangerous of all.

He was the one person who had never been afraid of her. But he should be.

For one impulsive moment in the heat of battle, she had reached for a demon, and she would forever suffer for taking a power she wasn't meant to have. A mere touch of her hand had destroyed one of Dea's gifts. What else would it ruin?

The Finestra was meant to be a window to the divine, lighting the world. *She* was a portal to darkness.

She slept fitfully, wracked by guilt and dread.

When dawn struck the window, she rolled out of bed. If she didn't put some distance between herself and Dante she might do something foolish like shake him awake and blurt out the ugly truth. If he knew she was broken, corrupted, that something ugly lived within her, he might never look at her the same way.

She was pacing the main room, counting her steps, when Kaleb trudged in. Hair mussed, shadows under his eyes, he looked as miserable as she felt.

"Adrick was *exiled,*" Kaleb said, anxiously rolling a cork in his hand. "The gods are going to pummel us in a matter of days, and your brother's wandering around the Continent with no protection."

Alessa shushed him. "Crollo is coming *here*. Adrick's safer on the Continent."

"You're making excuses."

Her temper snapped. "You've spent months saying I was wrong to forgive Adrick, that he hadn't made up for what he did. Now he's finally done so and you're mad at me for *letting* him?"

"Adrick deserves better than to have his friends think he's a villain. He did the right thing. Now it's your turn."

"What's going on?" Saida asked, peering into the main room with Kamaria.

"Ask her." Kaleb shot Alessa a loaded look and crossed his arms to wait.

Alessa's heart sank. They would hate her. Fear her.

"I . . ." Alessa stuttered. "I . . . did something bad."

Telling the truth may have been right, but she felt horrible when they stared in horrified silence after her confession. If only she'd never touched that blasted fountain. She'd already lost her brother, now she'd lose her friends, and next she'd lose Dante.

Kamaria stood with a huff. "I know you missed out on some key friendship years, Alessa, but friends tell each other stuff. Especially when they're in trouble."

Alessa blinked back tears. "I'm sorry."

Saida walked over with such determination that Alessa flinched before the girl's arms came around her. "We're just upset that you didn't tell us."

Alessa gave her a weak smile. "You can help me figure out how to tell Dante."

Kaleb straightened at a faint rumble, growing louder. "What the—"

With a clang, the gate flew open and a mob flowed into the courtyard.

Forty-five

DAYS BEFORE THE ECLIPSE: 6

Dante didn't sleep with his knives anymore. He might have to change that.

Lurching awake, his first thought was to shield Alessa from the ambush, but she was nowhere to be found, and a grinning Blaise and Jesse had him by the arms.

Dante cursed and strained to throw them off. He wasn't even awake yet, the assholes.

"Don't bother resisting," shouted Blaise. "You're outnumbered, and we aren't afraid to fight dirty."

After a brief scuffle, Blaise and Jesse half carried, half dragged him out of the room. Hands grabbed at Dante, carrying him toward the stairs, and the wave swept him away.

"Sorry!" Blaise shouted back at the house. "It's a tradition! We won't rough him up too bad!"

Dante had fallen asleep dreading telling Alessa everything, and now he couldn't.

An hour later, the brief moment of gratitude was long

forgotten. Dante sat on the edge of the grand canal, arms crossed. He could practically feel his powers fading.

"Jump, jump, jump!" The pack of ghiotte chanted from the water while Blaise struck a pose atop the bridge before swan-diving into the wide canal.

Surfacing, Blaise spit an arc of water. "You're up, General Ghiotte!"

Jesse bounced on his toes, preparing to do a back flip. "And nothing boring either. Get up here, fearless leader."

Dante had already completed his obligatory coronation jump, and he was over it. He couldn't take another minute of this.

"Enough." He got to his feet. "We have work to do."

Jesse made a rude sound. "It's a rest day."

Dante flicked a hand toward the sky. "There's no time to *rest*. Get your squadrons ready."

A chorus of groans followed, but he'd rather pull out his fingernails with pliers than hear one more person say he was the toughest ghiotte of all time.

"Dante, hey, wait for me." Blaise jogged along behind him. "I was thinking we could prepare different types of ammunition for the catapults based on possible threats, like flammable bundles if the baddies are beasts, water boluses if they're fire monsters, or even bees!"

Dante pinched the bridge of his nose. "Bees?"

"Yeah, beehives! Smoke them out and keep them wrapped until they're loaded, then bam, bee explosion!" Blaise arced one hand like an object soaring through the air and clapped it with his other.

Bee explosion. As though an undisciplined crew of show-offs wasn't enough to deal with, Blaise wanted them swarmed by insects during battle. "I don't—"

Blaise interrupted, caught up in a flurry of ideas. "What about a moat of alcohol around the basilica, waiting for a match and boom! Booby traps inside the building so the only way in is from the rooftop! Or, how about strings tied to the doors and if they're opened, knives fall from the ceiling?"

Dante couldn't hide his exasperation. "We need more *discipline*, not chaos."

Someone had returned from a supply run and left a dozen crates full of lemons baking in the sun in the middle of the training area. The squad of younger ghiotte in charge of assembling barricades could use the wood for building, but for now, they were an annoying obstacle in the middle of everything. Dante dragged a few out of the way while his army trickled in, before abandoning the effort. There were too many.

The Saverians were the last to arrive, and Dante glared while they found their spots.

"Sheesh," Kamaria said. "We're not the ones who carried you out of bed."

Dante paced from one end of the piazza to the other, scrutinizing the troops and barking orders. The archers weren't shooting straight enough, the sword fighters were a chaotic mess, and Blaise's trebuchet team spent more time fantasizing about fun shit they could throw than actually manning their weapons.

Midway through the morning, one young ghiotte nearly severed his battle partner's arm, and Dante blew up.

"Are you trying to win this war for the other side?" Dante snatched the boy's sword and pointed it at him. "Get out until you learn some damn sense!"

The injured girl looked more alarmed by Dante's anger than the blood spurting from her bicep.

Talia crossed the piazza toward Dante like someone approaching a nest of angry hornets. "Everything okay over here?"

"Perfect." Dante threw the sword to the ground. "Kamaria, you ready with that fire whip?"

"Ready as ever." Kamaria snapped a lick of flame toward Alessa.

"Stop screwing around," Dante snapped. "This isn't a magic show, it's war."

Kamaria snuffed the flame, looking like the fire had leapt into her eyes. "A war we'll lose if our leader keeps throwing tantrums."

Dante turned away, his scowl deepening.

Kamaria's hand darted into the nearest crate to grab a lemon, and it struck the side of Dante's head with a splat.

The piazza went deadly silent.

Talia grabbed Dante's arm before he could retaliate. "You need a time out."

He shook her off and walked away without a backward glance.

They were better off without him.

Turning into the nearest alley, Dante pressed his clenched fist against a wall until the rough stone threatened to slice his skin. He could feel Talia behind him, knew she'd start talking if he looked over. So he didn't. It didn't stop her for long.

"What is *wrong* with you today?" she said at last. "I thought you came here to build an army, not rip it apart."

"They're all yours," he muttered.

"Aw, my very own army?" Talia teased. "It's not even my birthday."

"You heard what I said last night." Dante crossed her arms. "This is the part where you kick my ass for lying."

"No," Talia said. "This is when I say I'm sorry."

"For *what?*" His words came out in an exasperated huff.

"I've been riding your ass about everything—your friends, your relationship—of course you didn't think you could talk to me. But I don't care if you have powers. I mean, I *do,* because it's awful to have that taken from you, but it doesn't change who you are."

He glowered at the water.

It did, though. Without his powers, he didn't deserve to lead an army of ghiotte. And he didn't deserve Alessa. For the longest time he'd thought being a ghiotte was why he had no right *to* be with her, but it was the only reason he ever *could.*

Talia wouldn't understand that his identity, his sense of self, everything he wanted and needed, had been snatched away. That he must have done something wrong if Dea didn't love him enough to give it back. He wasn't . . . enough.

"So you have to be a little more careful." Talia nudged him. "If it makes you feel better, I can pull more punches—"

"Don't you dare."

She laughed. "I guess I won't feel too bad about taking a swing at someone who's *only* a super-skilled fighter and not a super-skilled fighter with healing powers. No matter what, you're still *you.*"

"It's not just that." He dropped his chin to his forearms. "Without my powers, I can't *be* with Alessa."

"Why?" Talia made a face. "She have a thing for ghiotte?"

Without delving into the details, he told her the basics.

Talia grimaced. "Well, shit."

"Yeah." He blew out a breath. "Try not to celebrate too loudly."

"Her powers will move onto someone else eventually, right?"

"Supposedly, but we're living in unprecedented times here."

"You think she'll bail when she finds out?"

"No. That's the problem. I *don't* think she will."

"So end it, then. Set her free and stay here. You'll find someone else."

"I don't *want* to find someone else." The mere thought of pushing Alessa away, even for her own good, felt like plunging into an abyss with no bottom.

"All wounds heal eventually."

"Except those that kill you."

"You aren't dead yet. Decision time." Talia stepped closer, tipping her chin up defiantly in a clear challenge, even if he didn't know what she was daring him to do. "Are you going to do it or not?"

His brows furrowed. "Do *what?*" He didn't have time to figure it out before Talia made her move.

Leaning in, she pressed her lips to his.

Alessa's stomach refused to unclench. Dante's anger was usually an internal, quiet, thing. She'd never seen him lose control like that. But Talia had run off after him, so Alessa took over for the missing generals, giving orders, correcting anyone who put a toe out of formation, and scanning for weaknesses in their defensive lines. She did it well, too.

The ghiotte barely managed to conceal their surprise. While the ghiotte drilled, Alessa and Ciro ran through hypothetical scenarios for which Fonti powers would be most useful, and which could be combined effectively: Any threat with enough water to douse Kamaria's fire would mean she was out and Kaleb or Saida were in. Anything alive—man, beast, or monster made of flesh—Kaleb's electricity had the most potential for incapacitating them.

Working in tandem, Kamaria and Saida could create fire tornadoes, waves of scorching hot air or burning embers, and they had barrels of water positioned around the piazza which, if their own side was able to clear the space, could be used to flood the ground so Alessa could augment Kaleb's powers to electrify anything standing on it, as long as their own side had enough warning. Ghiotte healing powers weren't guaranteed protection against death, so this would only work if their own side could clear the area first, or they were desperate enough to risk the collateral damage. But she wouldn't think about that.

Alessa didn't expect Talia and Dante to be gone so long.

When the last group finished their part of the drill, Alessa called a break for lunch and set out to find them.

Near the wide main canal, she heard their voices before she saw them. Picking up her pace, she turned a corner and froze.

Sneaking up on Dante had never gone well for her.

She never learned.

If Talia had punched him, Dante would have been prepared. He didn't have a defense maneuver for a *kiss*.

Thoughts flashed through his mind. His body froze.

Talia wasn't subtle. Never had been. When he dodged a topic of conversation, she knocked his feet out from under him. When he teased, she teased back.

She was challenging him again. *Choose*, the kiss said. Your old life or a new life here. Choose Alessa and watch her light dim every passing day. Or walk away and salvage a different life, in a new world, without her.

Talia leaned back. "Well, that answers *one* question at least."

Dante blinked, still trying to catch up. "Which question is that?"

"I'm *definitely* not into guys."

"Glad I could help you sort that out."

She patted his shoulder. "If there *was* a guy in the world for me, it would be you. But . . . Niente. I'd prefer to *never* repeat that."

"Um. Ouch?" It wasn't like he'd been any more enthusiastic about it, but still. "What just happened?"

"You needed a shove."

Dante shook his head. "Then why didn't you shove me?"

Talia shrugged. "I dunno. You're having a romance dilemma so I came up with a romance maneuver. Your turn: Even if it's not me—and it's *not me*—do you think you could be happy here, maybe find someone else, eventually?"

Dante closed his eyes. "No. I love her."

Talia sighed. "Yeah, I can tell."

He dropped his head in his hands. "What do I do?"

"You fight like hell so you both survive. If her powers don't go away after that, you tell her you want to be with her, but you want her to be happy even more. Then you let her go."

He'd die a hundred times to save Alessa. He was strong enough for *that*. He wasn't strong enough to give her up.

Sacrificing his life for Alessa's had been the easiest decision he'd ever made.

But sacrifice *her*? Not for the world.

Forty-six

Alessa wanted to rip them apart, to challenge Talia to a duel that she would certainly lose. She wanted to be angry, to take refuge in the fury of a woman scorned.

Instead, she backed away on silent feet and made her way to the water's edge, thoughts swirling like the sea in a tempest.

When she'd told Talia to make sure Dante wasn't alone, she meant *after*. Not now. They might only have a few days left together and she wasn't ready to lose those, too.

Dante loved her. He *did*. He *would* choose her.

She pressed a fist to her chest.

But maybe he shouldn't.

With every passing hour, her mind fractured more. She had no idea if she'd even make it to Crollo's judgment day, much less survive to see what was left after it ended.

Crollo had her in his grasp, and she couldn't escape. Without a miracle, she wouldn't live long enough to see the world they saved . . . or lost.

But Dante wasn't a prize to be fought over. And she wanted him to be happy, with or without her. Her chest squeezed at the thought of her little house on the beach, the sight of Dante silhouetted against the sunset as he rowed home . . . to someone else.

It would hurt. It *did* hurt. But she couldn't fight for him if she wasn't going to be there when the fight was over. She stared over the water, rolling the sharp blade of anger and betrayal around until the edges rubbed off.

She'd been holding onto the hope that by defeating Crollo, the darkness inside her might die, too. She'd never imagined Dante wouldn't be there to hold her hand if it didn't.

Dante found Alessa by the water's edge, staring out at nothing.

"I need to tell you something," Dante said.

"I already know." Alessa's voice was flat, emotionless.

"How—" No. Not important right now. Somehow, she knew about the fontana. She knew his powers were finite.

"I want you to be happy." Her breath hitched. "Even if it's without me."

No. *No.* A heart-sized hole opened in his chest. He hadn't even had the chance to ask her to stay, and she was leaving.

"You don't know what will happen after the battle," he said. "Don't give up on us yet."

"I'm not giving up on anything." Alessa sniffed. "You have every right to choose a future without me."

"Wait. *What* is it that you know?" He held very still, certain that saying the wrong thing would make an already precarious situation even worse.

"I know you kissed Talia." Her lower lip trembled. "I'm not angry. If that's what you needed to do to figure out your feelings, then . . . I'm glad."

"I'm not. I didn't. That's not—" Dear gods, he'd managed

to find the *one* way to make things even worse, burying one betrayal with the next by kissing another girl.

"It's okay." Alessa's hands twisted, and he felt the squeeze in his chest, like she was wringing the air from his lungs. "If you love her—"

Her forgiveness should have been a relief, but he only felt worse. "No. *No.* I don't want that, and I know how I feel about you. How I'll *always* feel about you. I don't love Talia. I mean, I *do* love her, but I'm not *in* love with her."

"But you could be."

"No," he said, harsher this time. "I couldn't. Not even if I wanted to. And I don't. It's always been you. You're all I want. The rest of the world can burn for all I care. I *need* you to know that. Never doubt that. Anything else, but not that."

"Then what is it?" She touched his hand, lightly at first, then pulled it between her own. "Are you alright?"

"No, I'm not. I lied to you." Dante's voice shook. "The fontana didn't work."

She gave her head a little shake. "Of course it doesn't work. It was destroyed."

"I mean, it didn't fix me. Not permanently. I kept going back, hoping it would last, but . . . it didn't." He pulled in a breath as though the air was fighting him. "I'm not a ghiotte. It was just the fontana. And now it's gone, and in a few days I won't have my powers anymore. I won't be able to touch you."

Her face went pale and she swayed. "It's my fault."

"No." Dante steadied her. "You had no idea what Adrick was going to do."

"It wasn't Adrick. He was lying to protect me."

Dante's grip went slack.

"I'm supposed to be Dea's chosen." The words tumbled from her lips. "I thought Talia was just being mean when she said the fontana wasn't for me, like everything else, and then I had the key, and it seemed like a sign."

Dante shook his head. "*You* took the key? Why?"

"I thought—" She stopped to gasp a breath. "I thought it would fix me."

"*Fix* you?"

Alessa's voice got higher and faster as the truth spilled out. He could barely grasp one word at a time, but like the mechanism inside a lock, the pieces began to click into place.

Alessa was still hearing things.

Blacking out.

The incident with Diwata hadn't been a one-time thing.

She had been getting worse all this time. Something was harming her right now, and he couldn't protect her, even while he held her in his arms.

She gasped for breath. "I can't make it stop. I've tried and tried, but it's getting worse."

Panic choked him. He couldn't fight an enemy inside her head.

"Breathe, cara." He pulled her to his chest, holding her as tight as he could without hurting her. "Per favore, piccola. Just breathe."

He felt sick. She'd been frightened, and he hadn't even noticed. He'd been too busy hiding the truth about his powers from her to see what was happening to her. He'd let her suffer alone.

"I ruined *everything*," she sobbed.

"Hush," he murmured into her hair. "If I'd known, I would have tossed you in the damn fountain myself."

"You should be angry. I stole your powers again."

"Cara mia," Dante whispered. "If we start keeping score of who has hurt who in this relationship, we're going to need an entire library full of ledgers. Let it go. It's done." He tipped her face up, smoothing away the tears. "Why didn't you tell me?"

Her hands fluttered against him like a moth against a lantern. "I was afraid you'd see me differently if you knew I was . . . broken. When you look at me, I feel as close to perfect as I ever have. I didn't want to lose that."

It knocked the wind out of him. Alessa had concealed her sickness while he hid the loss of his powers, both driven by fear that if they were fully seen, they'd be found lacking.

"You'll always be perfect to me," he said.

She hiccupped a sad laugh. "Then you *must* be in love, because I collect personality flaws like trophies."

He hugged her again for a very long time, and she wiped her tears before they headed back.

"I'm going to let Talia take over," Dante said.

"Hand over command?" Alessa stopped in her tracks. "Why?"

"They think I'm one of them, and I'm not."

Alessa gripped his chin to force him to look her in the eyes. "Gabriele Dante Lucente, you listen to me. The child of a ghiotte is a *ghiotte*. You can't change the definition of a word to make yourself feel like an outsider when you aren't."

It would take no effort to escape, but if she was so determined to hold his attention, he would let her.

"You *are* the child of ghiotte. You've lived your life as one. You've benefited from your gift and suffered greatly for it, too. With or without your powers, you built this army. You organized and delegated and turned a bunch of rebels into one unified fighting force."

"Their lives are on the line. They deserve to have the best leader."

Alessa looked mulish. "No one could be better than you."

"Oh, yeah, and why is that?"

He expected her to say something about his fighting skills, but she surprised him yet again.

"Because you see the potential in people."

He scoffed. "You aren't serious."

"You try *really* hard not to, but you do. You see people's strengths. You don't accept any less than the best from yourself, and that makes people want to live up to it and make you proud. That's powerful. That army isn't following you because you're the strongest or the toughest—maybe they did at first, but that's not why they stuck around. They know anything you expect from them, you expect more from yourself, and they trust you."

Dante gestured in the vague direction of the piazza. "There are dozens of ghiotte out there who can fight just as well as I can and *they* all have ghiotte powers."

"So? You say you love me despite my flaws, but you won't give yourself half as much grace. You don't have to be *perfect* for people to respect you, Dante." She arched a brow in challenge.

He gazed down at her, his perfectly imperfect girl. The stubborn set to her jaw, the notch in her ear from a long-ago assassination attempt that led her to hire him as her bodyguard, her convoluted metaphors, odd quirks, and messy mistakes—her million tiny imperfections were his favorite part, because they were all his.

It was so easy to see when he looked at her, and yet he didn't expect the same for himself. He had to be the strongest, fastest, toughest, or he didn't expect anyone to give him half a chance.

He didn't love her because she was *perfect*, and she'd only fallen for him *after* his mess came into the light.

Maybe he didn't have to be perfect, but he did have to tell the truth.

He'd justified his secrecy as protecting her, but it hadn't protected anything. It only led to misery, the destruction of the fontana, and Adrick's banishment.

He was done pretending. The world could take him as he was, or not at all.

Eyes followed Dante as he crossed the piazza to stand by the stack of crates.

He cleared his throat, but he didn't need to.

No one was wandering off or roughhousing or cracking jokes. His squadron leaders stood tall in front of their regiments, ready to protect their homes, their world, and their lives. They would fight and fight well, because of him.

He'd built this, one day and one soldier at a time. Even after his unforgivable behavior, they were united. He had done the job and done it well. No one could take that away.

Dante pulled a lemon from the top of the heap and held it up so everyone could see. "Are these spoken for?"

"They got left out in the sun," Blaise said. "They aren't even worth juicing."

"Good." Dante tossed it, underhand, to one of the young ghiotte he'd yelled at earlier. "Go ahead. Take a shot. I deserve it."

The boy looked around, shrugged, and stepped up.

The lemon smacked into Dante's chest with a juicy splat.

"Who's next?" Dante said, unperturbed. "I've been an ass to pretty much all of you today. Surely someone else wants payback."

Blaise skipped over to the crate. "No need to ask me twice." He squeezed until the rind split and juice ran through his fingers, then wound up and took aim. "Hold *real* still."

A moment later, Dante wiped juice from his eyes and addressed the troops. "I'm sorry. You volunteered to fight with me, not get treated like shit. It won't happen again."

The bonds he'd forged might break, but *he* wouldn't.

Dante cleared his throat. "I was born Gabriele Dante Lucente, son of Ludovico and Emma, a ghiotte, like all of you. I grew up in the shadows, knowing we were different, that we were never safe and we might never *be* safe. I'm honored that you've welcomed me into your community, and even more that you let me lead you this far."

He glanced down, took a deep breath. "I was born with the powers of a ghiotte, but I lost them. During Divorando, I died. Temporarily. I wish I could pretend it was because I was defending some noble cause, but the truth is . . ." He cracked a smile. "I did it for a girl."

Confused glances, a few hesitant chuckles.

"Alessa brought me back, but it turns out resurrection comes with side effects. My powers were gone, and I spent months recovering as slowly as any non-ghiotte would. I'm not one of you anymore. Not truly. And by the time Crollo attacks, I won't be at all."

A sea of unreadable stares looked back at him.

"So now you know. The guy you've been following isn't the strongest or the hardest to kill. Probably the opposite. Talia will be an incredible commander, and I'd still like to stay and fight with you . . . if you'll have me."

Talia walked over to stand beside him, his second-in-command and battle partner, always. Dante steeled himself to accept their silent verdict and walk away.

Leo raised a hand. "You're saying we should respect you *less* because you're taking a *bigger* risk? Seems pretty brave to me."

Someone shouted, "Plus we'll know anything that doesn't kill you *definitely* won't kill us!"

Dante shook his head with a smile as the ribbing escalated. He didn't feel especially brave. Just determined.

"Told you." Talia clapped him on the shoulder. "Now that we've settled that, can we get back to work?" With her boot, she tipped a crate over, sending lemons rolling across the cobblestones. "Ammunition. Break into teams and whoever is the least juicy at the end is the winner."

"Saverians versus ghiotte?" Dante asked.

"Naw, then we'd have both generals on our side." She kicked over another crate.

"Hey!" shouted Kamaria. "Dante's ours."

Dante swallowed a lump in his throat. They all knew the truth, yet they claimed him anyway. "Let's mix the groups this time. Ciro, Kaleb, and Kamaria with Blaise and Kira's squadrons. Alessa and Saida with Talia and Jesse."

Talia squinted at Dante, a smile toying on her lips. "And you, Dante? Which team are you on?"

Dante hefted a crate onto his shoulder. "Both. I'll provide backup for whoever needs me most."

His fight would be harder for playing both sides, but he'd always relished a challenge.

Alessa watched him with a proud smile.

Perhaps she was right, and he didn't have to be invincible or without fault to lead. To belong. He might not be invulnerable or unscathed, unscarred or perfect, but he was still whole.

Maybe the cracks in his walls weren't the first sign of collapse, but the only way to let in the light.

Forty-seven

In nineteen years of life, Alessa had never made a throw worth bragging about, but she had a perfect shot and for once, she wouldn't miss.

"Jesse?" she asked the taciturn giant as they neared their team's barricade. "How good is your aim?"

"Incredible," he said.

"Excellent. Mind if I touch your arm for a moment?"

Jesse shrugged, entirely unconcerned with the odd question.

Alessa skimmed a bit of his skill using her powers, lined up the shot, and a soggy lemon thwacked Talia in the forehead.

The other girl looked up with a glare. "We're on the *same* side."

"When I said I didn't want Dante to be *alone*, I wasn't actually *offering* him to you." If Alessa's tone was a little prissy, that seemed justified.

"Oh. That." Talia sucked her teeth. "I guess I owe you an apology."

"You *think* so?" Alessa said, leaning heavily on the sarcasm.

Talia shrugged. "In retrospect, there may have been better

ways to get him to stop whining and make some decisions. I guess I could have used . . . words. Or something."

Alessa chucked another lemon.

Talia knocked it away. "If it helps, neither of us enjoyed it."

"Good," Alessa said. Somehow, in all their encounters, Alessa hadn't realized that she was taller than Talia. Not by much, but a little. Talia was so fierce and intimidating she gave the impression of taking up more space than she actually did.

Talia looked like she was chewing nails. "I also *probably* shouldn't have been so awful to you all this time, but you didn't exactly make it easy on me. Gods above, the *Finestra*? I mean, come on."

"How much of it was because you care about him versus how much you hate everything I stand for?"

"Hmmm," Talia mused. "Eighty/twenty?"

Alessa nodded. "Fine. Then I forgive you eighty percent. You do realize I don't have control over the other twenty percent, right?"

Talia ground her teeth together. "That's why I'm *apologizing.*"

Alessa's lips twitched. "Will it cause permanent damage?"

"I'm starting to get what he sees in you."

A shout from the far end of the piazza caught their attention. Blaise and Jesse were creeping up on Dante, undeterred by his warning shout of "Don't even think about it!"

From his vantage point, Dante couldn't see the group of officers coming at him from the other side.

Talia cupped her hand around her mouth and yelled something that made his face go comically blank for a moment before he got tackled from behind.

"What did you say?" Alessa said. "He looked appalled."

Talia's smile vanished. "Why? You gonna defend his honor?"

"No, not at all," Alessa said. "I'd like to memorize it in case the opportunity ever presents itself."

"Gira che ti rigira; il cetriolo va in culo all'ortolano." Bemused, Talia repeated it slower when Alessa didn't get it the first time.

"The cucumber . . . goes . . ." Alessa arched her eyebrows.

"You get the idea." Talia smirked. "I told him he'd be screwed either way."

"I don't remember that one in his book of proverbs."

"The one from his mom? He used to carry that thing everywhere."

"He still does," Alessa said. "Well, he *did*. He gave it to me as a wedding present."

Shock flashed across Talia's face.

"Not *our* wedding." Alessa pointed at Kaleb, who had just slipped on a lemon while crossing the piazza and landed on his rear. "Technically, I'm married to him. Divine pairing stuff."

"Huh," said Talia. "I thought he was into the blond guy who wrecked the fontana."

Alessa grimaced. "My brother."

"Wait, your brother and your ordained spouse—"

Alessa raised a hand to cut that off, offering Talia her most haughtily prim expression. "I do *not* ask questions I'd prefer not to know the answers to."

Talia chuckled. "The Cittadella trained you well."

"They certainly *tried*. Etiquette, weaponry, history, fine arts, ballroom dancing—that was difficult with the deadly skin situation—and yet, they got a Finestra who scared the kitchen staff, snickered at the naked statues, and smuggled a ghiotte into the Finestra's suite."

Talia's lips twitched with suppressed laughter. "How *did* you get some random guy into the Cittadella?"

"The rules say the Duo can hire their own security, so I sneaked out one night and bullied Dante into the job."

Talia gave her a skeptical look. "You threatened him?"

"Worse." Alessa winced. "I cried."

Talia made a disgusted face.

"When the fate of the world is on the line, you use any weapon you have."

"He loves you." Talia tried to hold on to her scowl but couldn't maintain it.

"I know," Alessa said, not intending for it to sound like an apology, though it came out that way. "And you're his best friend. I'm not trying to take that away from you."

Talia sighed heavily. "You *promise* you're not going to break his heart?"

Alessa's own heart sank into her stomach. "I'll try my best, but we're going to war. Anything could happen."

Talia waved a dismissive hand. "Dante's the best fighter I've seen, and you're the Finestra. Dea *chose* you. We're going to win."

"Winning doesn't mean they'll let us both live." Alessa dropped all pretense, meeting Talia's gaze with no mask. "If things go wrong, he's going to need you."

Blaise was supervising the loading of lemons onto a trebuchet when Dante walked up, and he eyed Dante's approach with wariness.

"Sorry about earlier," Dante said. "But I could use your ability to think outside the box."

Blaise sat back on his heels. "No bees?"

"Let's hold off on the bees, but I'll give you the day tomorrow to write up a report identifying and fortifying any routes in or out of the basilica that we might have missed." Anything to utilize Blaise's unique skill set without having insects dropped on the soldiers.

An ear-splitting whistle from the opposing forces put everyone on alert, and Dante backed up to watch the show. Alessa and Saida launched the first assault, flinging a whirling storm of fruit toward Leo, who flipped with swords in both hands, butchering the cloud of flying lemons in a spray of juice and pulp.

Ciro and Kamaria retaliated with their ghiotte teammates at their heels, and the battle was on.

Under attack from all sides, he spun, speared, and battled his fruit nemeses with all the skill and determination he'd train on a swarm of scarabei.

A week ago, he would have been frustrated, seeing only disorder in the chaos, but Leo and his team of bruisers executed the transition from a frontal assault to loop around, dispatching lemons with their battle axes and scythes without touching anything else, while Blaise's crew pounded their opponents with a fruity barrage, and Kira's runners ducked and wove through the melee without a drop of juice on them.

Each unit assessed, adjusted, and worked in tandem, like a flock of birds riding the wind.

Kira's runners remained in the lead as the piazza became a citrus massacre, stones littered with lemon carcasses and smashed crates, but Dante would have one hell of a time judging who'd lost.

Their mock battle crescendoed to a chaotic finale and everyone forgot entirely about winning and teams, turning on whomever they wanted to instead.

Dante spied Talia and Alessa gathering ammunition for an

ambush, so he was ready when they began chucking lemons his way. His sword flashed, and two halves of a lemon flew wide.

He caught the last one midair, crushed it, and whipped it toward Alessa.

She'd anticipated his move—he suspected her high five with Talia a minute earlier had been a sneaky attempt to boost her evasive skills—so she dodged the first round, but while some of Dante's ghiotte traits might not have been permanent, his fighting skills were woven through every fiber of his being, and he had the upper hand.

Alessa shrieked as a particularly juicy fruit smacked her on the chest.

"Oh, you'll pay for that," she said as pulp slid beneath her neckline, sure to wreak sticky havoc beneath her blouse.

Lemons in each hand, she sprinted after him.

Dante bolted, still clutching his sword. "I've seen you throw. You won't hit me."

"Then why are you running?" she shouted.

He dodged another attacker. "Because you'll shove it down my pants instead."

Lemons flew all around them, speared by arrows, split by swords, impaled by daggers. Everyone was sticky, shrieking with laughter and occasionally cursing at stinging eyes.

Dante slowed as Alessa laughed too hard to keep up—not that she stood a chance of catching him in the first place—when Talia flung a mushy lemon into Kamaria's face.

Kamaria retaliated by scooping up an armful and chasing her around the piazza, wedging one down the back of her shirt before Talia pulled a knife on her.

Dante crept up behind Alessa, rolling a lemon in one hand, and she yelped when he squeezed it over her head. Laughing, they wrestled over the last of his fruit arsenal.

Blaise tore off his shirt and ran past them toward the bank where the piazza met the bay. "Last one in is a rotten lemon!"

The army followed, hooting and hopping as they ran, kicking off shoes and discarding clothing on the ground as they went.

The piazza rang with the echoes of shouts and squeals from the water, but Dante caught Alessa's arm so she wouldn't follow.

"What are you—" she started to say.

He tugged her hand and they ran together toward an empty building off a side street he'd walked past that morning.

He opened the door, pulling her inside. "I'm stealing you for myself."

Their days were numbered, and he would memorize it all. Every sound, scent, and taste, every last touch. They pulled at each other's clothing, both sticky and sweet and tart all at once.

He wanted to promise her they'd never be apart. That they would both survive whatever was coming and live happily ever after. But a promise he couldn't keep was as good as a lie, and he'd never lie to her again.

Instead, he would love her enough for a lifetime with whatever time they had left.

He'd faced death once, accepted it as the price for Alessa's life. He didn't want to die now. He'd never wanted to live more. He had to survive, and they had to win, so she could have her happily ever after.

Their happily ever after.

Maybe he deserved one, too.

Whatever the gods had planned for them, that's what he'd be fighting for.

His lips found the curve of her neck. "Please," he murmured. Just please.

She clutched at him, his name on her lips a plea for salvation. He'd kneel at her altar and pray for their lives.

She smelled like home, of citrus and salt and the wildest beach on Saverio's farthest shore.

His love, who tasted like lemons kissed by the sea.

One last burst of sunshine before the storm.

Forty-eight

DAYS UNTIL THE ECLIPSE: 5

Drip. Drip. Drip.

Someone was saying Alessa's name. She willed herself to follow the voice, but it got more difficult to find her way back each time she drifted.

She knew she was standing in a room, but the details were ethereal, wisps and colors that only looked like solid stone.

Except she couldn't walk through stone.

She certainly couldn't watch the rain drip down the roof while she was inside. Yet she *was* inside.

If she tried very hard, she could feel the floor beneath her feet. A little more, and she could hear the voice again.

Focus, Alessa.

The floor was solid beneath her feet. The evening breeze from the balcony was cool and damp. The voice calling to her was a promise of warmth and safety.

A little more concentration, and she could hear the words he spoke again.

"Alessa?" Dante sounded as though it was at least the third

time he'd said it, his voice tinged with concern, but not panic. He'd coaxed her back too many times now to worry. Or at least too many times to let his worry show.

Another blink, and she was confident she was wholly back within herself. For now.

"Sorry?" She pinned a vague smile in place and turned to face the bed.

He'd pushed up on one elbow, a crease between his brows. "What's so interesting out there?"

The drip of rain, nature's metronome. The beating hearts in other rooms. The people eating and talking and dreaming in nearby buildings. How thin and frail the tether was between her soul and her body.

"Nothing," she said. "Nothing important." She padded across the room to climb in bed beside him. "What happens if we win but Dea still doesn't take my powers away or give yours back?"

Dante rested his chin on the top of her head. "Dea can fix it, if she chooses to."

"Which means she's choosing not to."

"If we beat Crollo, the game's over. No more Finestra needed. She can make it go away."

She held her breath for a moment. "Or we'll lose, and all my powers, both good and bad, will die with me."

"Don't say that." His arms tightened around her. "Don't even think it."

"I had to. Just once. I've been trying so hard not to think about it, but holding so much fear inside me all the time only gives it more power."

"I hope Crollo himself shows up to this fight," Dante said with a scowl. "I'll take him down myself for hurting you."

"That's the attitude." She snuggled closer, breathing him in and tucking away the memory as though she could take it along to wherever the gods planned to send her next. "You'll lead us to victory, and Dea will fix me and bless you with your powers as thanks for proving her point."

"Right," Dante said softly. "Just like that."

The days remaining before the battle were slipping away like sand through an hourglass, and their secrets had all been spilled, for better or worse.

Talia had been quite disturbed to hear that Alessa could hear people's thoughts, which raised interesting questions about what, exactly, Talia had been thinking about Alessa all along, but it was probably best for both their sakes that Alessa hadn't tried too hard to glean the specifics.

Dante's soldiers didn't treat him any differently, but he'd finally become as careful with his own safety as he was with Alessa's, supervising instead of battling during training, calling on others to demonstrate the more dangerous maneuvers, and trusting his officers to do their part without diving into the fray.

Unlike the rest of the ghiotte warriors, he wouldn't have unlimited healing power to call on when the battle arrived, so he conserved it like the gift it was.

Mostly. He was careful to avoid wasting any of his abilities on unnecessary injuries, but he indulged in any opportunity for tender kisses and fierce embraces with Alessa.

With her tenuous hold on her mind weakening and Dante's powers dwindling, every shared moment was infinitely precious and equally fraught. Each time felt like the last. And worse, a tiny frightened voice in the back of Alessa's mind warned that every kiss made him easier to kill.

Someone knocked, and Dante rolled over to cross the room and open the door.

She could only partially see Matteo past him, but the older man looked grim. "There's been a development. Nova and Leo need to speak with you."

Dante seemed wholly unconcerned that he was shirtless and disheveled as he left with Matteo. Alessa followed, reminding herself that their relationship wasn't a secret anymore.

Leo and his girlfriends were in the courtyard with Nova and Talia. Chiara's cheeks were streaked with tears, her hands bound and held by Vittoria, whose face was solemn.

Leo's words sounded dragged from his throat. "Chiara woke under some sort of spell, tried to strangle Vittoria, then attacked me when I pulled them apart. Took us at least five minutes to snap her out of it."

"She's not the only one," Nova added. "We're hearing from others that their non-ghiotte family members had similar episodes. Thankfully, no one was killed. You said this happened to someone on your island? What *is* this?"

Alessa's blood ran cold. Crollo. It had to be.

Dante must have come to the same conclusion. He spoke gently to Chiara. "Do you remember anything?"

Chiara shivered. "Blood. Darkness. And silence. Like all the sound had been sucked out of the world. And then I woke up and . . ." She stifled a sob. "I would never hurt either of them on purpose. *Never.*"

"We know," Dante said softly. "That wasn't *you*. That was Crollo reminding us that he's coming. He wants us on edge, afraid of each other. He wants us to turn on each other so we prove him right. I'm surprised he waited this long."

Alessa hugged herself. He hadn't, though. Crollo had been toying with her and Ciro for weeks.

"What do we *do?*" Leo demanded. "We can't have people getting attacked in their sleep, but I *won't* lock her up—"

Dante raised his hands. "Of course not. We don't want *anyone* locked up."

"We should evacuate anyone who won't be fighting," Matteo said. "Children, elderly, non-ghiotte family members. They'll be safer away from the battle, and Crollo will have no reason to use them against us if we're separated."

A muscle ticked in Leo's jaw. "There's an old monastery about a mile inland. Walls as thick as anything here on Perduta and space underground where they can shelter during the battle. They'll need plenty of food, blankets, whatever medical things they could possibly need."

"I'll organize it," Matteo suggested, earning a grateful smile from Nova. "We have limited boats and a lot of people to move. I'll need to start first thing in the morning, with carte blanche to raid the supplies."

"Take anything you need." Leo looped an arm around Chiara's shoulders and pulled her close. She nodded bravely, and Vittoria's eyes glistened with tears.

"No time to waste," said Nova, motioning for the trio to go ahead of them.

Dante jerked a nod at Matteo, and the two men stepped aside to speak privately.

"Well, there's an unexpected silver lining," Talia said under her breath. "Crollo made a huge mistake messing with Leo's girls. He really *will* take on the whole invasion now."

Alessa shivered. Crollo didn't make mistakes. He made offensive maneuvers. And he wasn't subtle with his warnings. If Dante had one weakness, it was *her*.

Talia glanced down as Alessa grabbed her wrist, then back at her face.

Alessa spoke fast. "If you think, at any point, that I'm a danger to our side, I need you to take me out."

"What?" Talia gaped.

"Please," Alessa said. "Dante won't do it. I need to know someone will."

Forty-nine

DAYS UNTIL THE ECLIPSE: 1

One day left. The barricades were ready, the troops were getting one last rest, and Dante was going over plans with Talia yet again. His most recent visions hinted at a water arrival, so their front line would be positioned on the edge of the city facing the bay. Whatever was coming, he'd be among the first to greet it.

In a normal war, they might not be so confident about when and where their enemies would attack, but Crollo and Dea wanted this fight. They would be there.

Talia moved their unit markers across the map to positions where they'd have the best vantage point: archers on the rooftops; trebuchets on the perimeter; foot soldiers in formation on the piazza in front of the basilica, and more manning every palazzo.

They had barricades to protect shelters, fortified hideyholes, and maze-like arrangements the fighters had memorized and practiced attacking from inside, and Blaise had turned his terrifying creativity into a labyrinth of traps constructed around and within the basilica. They had anything and everything an army might want.

Except for an inkling of what they would actually be facing.

Alessa crossed the room to their strategy table. "I shouldn't be with you during battle."

"What are you talking about? We need your powers." Dante glanced at Talia for backup, but she wouldn't meet his eye.

"I'll still fight." Alessa clasped her hands in front of her. "But I don't know what this power might do to me during the battle. If Crollo *is* causing it, Ciro and I might both be part of his plan to sabotage our side. We have to split up."

"No," Dante said, out of pure reflex. He couldn't protect her if they were apart.

"It's too dangerous," Alessa said. "*I* am too dangerous."

"She's right," Talia said. "*You're* the leader. You need to be able to lead without worrying about her or what she might do when your back is turned."

He dropped his diagrams on the table. "The messengers can only move so fast. Crollo's minions could pick us off one by one and we wouldn't even realize it until it was too late."

"I can help with that," Alessa said. "I don't know *why* I can hear other people's thoughts, but I might as well use it. Put me in a central location, and I'll relay messages to runners so they can update everyone else more efficiently."

"Alessa's team can start at the basilica," Talia said, moving another marker. "She'll have a great view of the action and her powers work just as well from a distance."

"It's a good plan," Alessa said. "Plus I can conserve my powers by not needing them for self-defense, only offense." She didn't speak the rest, but he knew what she meant. Every use of her powers made her weaker and more prone to dizzy spells. Whatever Crollo had done to her, it was progressing too fast already.

With Alessa's newfound ability to skip through other people's thoughts, she could glean real-time information about how each unit was doing—what they saw, what they needed. Their own hive mind. But she would be on the other end of the battlefield. He wouldn't know if she was safe, if she lived or died. Fear clawed its way up his throat.

"I'll stay with her," Talia said. "I'll be damned if you win this battle only to get your heart broken." She arched a brow at his hesitation. "Don't you trust me? I know your plans as well as you do. We'd have two generals, one on each end. My team will take the Basilica, and if it's breached, I'll guard her with my life."

Alessa and Talia exchanged a loaded look. Of course they'd finally bond over conspiring against him.

He jerked a nod. "All right. What's our plan, then?"

Talia swapped out their markers without hesitation. "You're on point, here. Alessa and two of the Fonti can be in this tower, Ciro and the rest over here, with guards and runners assigned to each unit. Kira's messengers have practiced both ground and rooftop routes."

Dante perused the map, memorizing the new positions. "From that vantage, with Alessa's powers, you'll have more real-time information than anyone else. If you have to make any strategic decisions for the whole, just do it."

Now two the people he loved would be out of reach when the fighting began.

Whatever came for them would have to get through him first.

Fifty

THE DAY OF THE ECLIPSE

Even in her most dire predictions, Alessa had assumed they would be able to *see* the eclipse that would mark the beginning of Crollo's assault. Instead, the piazza below the basilica was shrouded in fog.

From a small room overlooking the piazza, Alessa squinted at the murky sky, trying to gauge any shift in the lighting.

Talia stood watch at the railing outside, one hand on the hilt of her sword, the other raised to shield her eyes despite the lack of glare. The distant clink of armor punctuated the nervous rasp of their breathing.

Behind Alessa, Kaleb and Saida held their fear in check, waiting to offer their hands and their powers. Ciro and Kamaria were in the opposite tower, and she reached for their minds every few moments, frustrated again by Ciro's naturally opaque thoughts. Kamaria resonated like a plucked guitar string, mentally vibrating with anticipation, poised and ready for Ciro to channel her fire into all sorts of spectacular defensive magic

It was difficult not to seek Dante with her mind, to rest in his mental stillness, but this was not the time for respite. First, they had to survive. Win.

She felt him anyway, the hum of anticipation beneath his watchful readiness.

Dante wasn't twitchy with nerves like she was. His emotions didn't swing wildly like a pendulum. He was ready. Prepared. With every passing moment, he settled deeper into his focus.

The gods may have chosen her to fight as a warrior, but they created him to *be* one.

Her nerves drew increasingly taut, energy building inside her body until she felt like a bottle of prosecco about to pop its cork, and she resorted to fiddling with anything and everything she could get her hands on to release some of the pressure.

Her fingertips fluttered and tapped against her side, her weight shifting from foot to foot and back again, and she kept having to remind herself to finish the breaths that she forgot to complete, holding the air inside her lungs as though she could conserve it for later.

When her anxiety grew unbearable, she reached for the rings dangling from the delicate chain around her neck.

The night before, Dante had entrusted her with his parents' wedding rings, the enduring symbol of their devotion, and, she hoped, a token for luck that their own love story would have a happier ending.

They couldn't end the battle until it began, though, and she had no idea what was going on above the clouds.

With a steadying breath, Alessa grasped the open doorframe and pulled herself up to step out onto the roof, which spanned the length of the building.

The first rumble of thunder made everyone flinch, fearing what the sound might herald, but the wan glow of the sun through the cloud cover hadn't vanished yet.

And so they waited. And watched.

For the space of a breath, maybe two, the world went dark, and a faint corona shone through the cloud cover like a tarnished halo.

The skies opened, releasing a torrent of rain. Pounding the roof, the piazza, water sheeted so thick Alessa could barely tell when the eclipse ended.

Whatever was about to attack, they would be fighting it blind.

Below, the ghiotte standing guard in front of the basilica braced against the pounding, but they held their weapons at the ready.

Alessa reached for Saida's hand, concentrated, and sent a burst of wind just beyond the soldiers, pushing the rain outward like blowing a bubble, to clear their line of sight.

No massive claws or buzzing wings. No thunderous footsteps or fire and brimstone.

Only rain.

She let the wind die.

"What's happening?" Kaleb shouted over the rush of rain.

"Nothing!" Talia shouted. "The troops are still standing by the water. No one has moved."

Alessa stretched her senses, reaching for some hint of what was beyond, searching for any minds or sign of life beside their own forces.

She found . . . emptiness. A void so vast and deep it wasn't a mere absence of thought, but a voracious abyss. Her mind instinctively recoiled as though she had looked down to realize she was skirting the margins of a pit.

Whatever it was, the emptiness felt like the *opposite* of thought rather than a *lack* of it.

She pushed deeper, feeling beyond the invisible wall of nothingness.

Screams. Exploding inside her head. Torn from her mouth.

She clapped her hands over her ears—futile, as her mind, not her ears, were under assault—and dropped to her knees.

Nothing existed but terror.

And then came the pain.

Screaming.

Screaming.

Screaming.

Fifty-one

Dante squinted through the downpour at the bay. Still nothing. Rain beat on his shoulders and weighed down his clothing.

"You see anything?" he asked Leo.

Leo shook his head and wiped his face again. There was still nothing to fight. No fire and brimstone. No herds of monsters or swarms of scarabei. Nothing but open water churned so rough by the storm it appeared to be boiling.

He blinked. Or . . . something? A tiny flicker of movement where the stone edge of the piazza dropped off into the open water of the bay.

He shouted for his fighters to ready their weapons, but they already had. They had *been* ready and waiting for long enough.

Something slithered up from the water, serpentine and pale, tendrils creeping over the rim of the stone ledge where Perduta's grand piazza met the bay.

On another day, a peaceful day, he would have assumed it was a dangling rope waiting to tie up a fishing skiff.

But not today.

Dante stared harder, straining to make out the details of Crollo's first menace.

Snakes—no. Fingers. Gripping the edge of the ground.

His heart rate ramped up. Slow and steady. No sudden moves. Analyze, then fight.

A figure pulled itself out of the water, unfolding and stretching into the shape of a person. Another. Then more. Until a row of enemy soldiers stood shoulder to shoulder.

They looked human but stood like statues. No weapons. Unmoving.

"Nice try," Dante muttered. He wasn't about to step into an ambush. Crollo's minions might appear nonthreatening, but for all he knew, they were demons who could spit flames.

Their ranks grew, row after row, only moving to step forward when another line crawled from the bay. Hundreds of blank faces, devoid of humanity, of individual thought.

The empty eyes from his visions came to life before him. If the rest of his premonitions came true, the piazza would soon be drowning in blood.

His troops waited for his command.

Time to find out whose blood it would be.

Over the pounding rain, Dante heard the sharp intake of a thousand breaths behind him as the front row of Crollo's army bared their teeth.

"Now!" Propelled forward by the guttural scream of his army at his heels, Dante charged.

His first swing severed a head from a body. His next cut a form off at the knees.

Later, his stomach would turn at how his blade squelched through flesh, the crack of steel against bone. Not now. Now, he wouldn't think about the wet thud of severed limbs or the hot blood and cold rain splashing his legs.

War meant death.

Kill or being killed.

His blade hissed through the air, tracing arcs of bloody water.

Just like slicing lemons on a hot day

Fifty-two

Alessa's skull was about to shatter.

So much terror. So much pain.

So many minds, crying out for help as they tried but failed to stop their bodies from hurtling into the fray where the ghiotte army carved a path through their ranks.

She felt every spear crunching through a breastbone to stop a heart. Each severed limb. Each life abruptly ended.

It had to stop.

"*Stop!*" Her own scream snapped her back into the moment.

She was kneeling on the roof of the basilica, wet stone beneath her hands and knees.

With a sword at her throat.

"Don't move!" The whites of Talia's eyes matched her bloodless cheeks. "I'll do it!"

"Wait. Don't kill me." Pain throbbed in Alessa's temples, the beat of desperate minds begging for help. "We have to stop the fighting."

"Stop the fighting?" Saida repeated.

"Crollo is tricking us again," Alessa said. "Kira, tell Dante the soldiers need to retreat. Now."

Kira looked to Talia for confirmation.

Talia kept the sword trained on Alessa. "You're sabotaging our side by calling him off?"

Kira peered over the edge. "They're climbing the walls. Do I go or not?"

Talia wavered.

Something slammed into Alessa's back, throwing her to the floor. Boots and clawed fingers battered her, ripping at her hair, gouging her arms—

Talia wrenched the sneering man off Alessa and thrust the sword through his belly.

Saida's wind blasted past them, and a man teetered on the ledge, muscles locked.

His eyes cleared and the person within returned to his body, only to fall. . . .

Alessa slowly stood on shaking legs. "We can't fight our way through this. They aren't soldiers. Or monsters."

Dante didn't have to look around to know his army was glorious.

He could *feel* them in action. Dea's perfect soldiers had waited a thousand years for this fight.

They had perfected every step, practiced maneuvers so many times they could have worked together blindfolded.

A pack of Crollo's soldiers cornered him but he felt no fear. Fear could only grab hold in moments between combat, when he stopped moving. And he never stopped moving.

Blood and rain.

Sweat and gore.

Stab and sever.

His body took over, training and instinct carrying him through. He fought, drenched in crimson with the proof of his kills. A tide of red washed over the cobblestones.

Two of Crollo's men—if one could call them men—came from both sides, snarling. He ducked and spun out of their path, leaping over half-submerged bodies to get to the next fight and make more.

A flash of movement in the corner of his eye. He leaned into the spin, letting his momentum carry him a step farther as he extended his sword arm to whistle toward—

Large eyes. Chubby face. Short stature.

Throwing himself to one side, he twisted so his blade wouldn't complete the turn. He slid across the wet stones, scrabbling to regain his footing, as the child hissed in fury.

A heartbeat later and Dante would have sliced her tiny body in half. Demon or not, he couldn't.

Crollo was a sick monster, making his demons look like children.

Swallowing bile, Dante ran in the opposite direction. There were countless others left to fight.

The demons showed no emotion but pure rage until they suffered a mortal blow. Then they screamed. Their death cries rattled his bones. They sounded too human. Too real.

It was worse when they looked familiar. Like the one who fell to his knees after Dante stabbed him in the heart, who looked like the stablemaster from the inn. Or the severed head with tangled black hair that stared up at him from eyes that looked like one of the sailors on Ciro's ship.

Bitter cold washed over Dante.

Crollo wouldn't . . . He couldn't have.

Dante had to stop running so he didn't retch.

Crollo's army didn't look like people.

They *were* people.

Another child sprinted past, nearly in range of the archers atop the basilica. Dante grabbed the child by the back of her shirt and hauled the spitting, flailing body into the air.

"Fall back!" Dante shouted. "Fall back! Get inside and barricade the doors!"

His movements hindered by the effort of holding the squirming kid aloft, Dante ran, dodging and ducking, shouting orders at his confused troops.

He saw their hesitation.

They were supposed to be fighting, and they were.

They were supposed to be winning.

And they were.

Leo roared and battled on, his axe cutting a swath through their enemies.

"Fall back!" Dante shouted, his voice hoarse with desperation. "That's an order!"

The ghiotte had always known how to fight. He was about to learn whether they'd learned to trust him.

If not, there was no telling how many innocent people would die.

Fifty-three

The world below was a crimson blur.

Two women crawled over the ledge and toward Alessa. Kaleb's electricity crackled and one screamed, her lightning-wrapped limbs convulsing. A streak of fire shot toward the other from the archers on the roof behind them.

They kept coming. From all sides, too many to escape. Alessa had no choice. She reached for Saida's hand and blew the intruders over the railing.

Her breath caught in a sob. "Get inside. Block the windows!"

They scrambled through, grabbing at the nearest furniture to make a barricade.

"Adrick!" Kaleb shouted.

Alessa was too stunned to back away as her brother clambered over the sill, his face blank and empty. "Adrick, don't—"

He lunged, knocking her over. His hands wrapped around her neck and squeezed.

Alessa fought, thrashing, her powers sparking to life while her lungs screamed.

A moment. A lifetime. An eternity searching his eyes for

any sign that the soul within could take over before he killed her.

Her vision went black.

The heavy doors of the palazzo slammed shut behind Dante.

Still holding the rabid child, he scanned the building packed with confused warriors. "I need a rope."

With a muttered apology, he lowered the child, pinning her skinny arms behind her with one hand while a soldier walked over with a length of rope and bound her hands, then legs.

"Stick her in a corner somewhere," Dante said. Blood dripped from his sword, puddling on the floor.

Wide-eyed, drenched, bloody, and baffled, his troops waited for answers.

They'd prepared for a war, not a retreat.

"What is this?" Jesse asked, eying the snarling child. "What are they?"

"People," Dante gasped. "They're just people."

"Who cares what they are?" Leo said. "We should be out there fighting, not *hiding*."

"Crollo has them under some kind of spell," Dante said. "He's making them fight."

Leo scoffed. "Nah. Crollo just thinks you're too soft to fight something that looks like people. I'm not falling for it."

"I'm not afraid to fight anything or anyone that *wants* to kill me," Dante said. "But not if Crollo's *making* them do it. I recognized some of them, and I don't know what's going on, but they weren't like this before. Don't you think it's odd how they don't seem human until we kill them, and then they scream like . . . like us?"

An impact rattled the doors. Bodies, throwing themselves against the metal in a *thump, thump, thump,* like the erratic beat of a failing heart.

"But *why?*" Jesse said. "Why would Crollo want us to kill regular people?"

"I don't know," Dante said. The question rang in his ears. *Why?*

Divorando had begun as a challenge for humanity. A chance to prove that Dea's love was justified, a test of their collective strength and ability to work together in order to ward off their own destruction. With every Divorando, the Finestra and Fonte, backed by their army, fought to prove that humanity was worth saving.

Now they faced their final challenge . . . and it was to massacre their own? It made no sense. It was all wrong.

"Heads up!" Kira swung through the tower window, clambering down the rope to the floor. "I have a message from the base. Dante, you need to get over there right now."

Ten minutes into the war, and Dante was being called to leave his post.

Leo shoved past him. "People, monster, beast. I don't care what they are as long as they die."

Dante ordered the front line to hold the doors. "We're here to prove we're *better* than Crollo says we are. We can't do that by slaughtering innocents."

The team manning the barricade refused to lift it for him, so Leo grabbed the massive beam of wood on his own, grunting with the effort.

"What if I'm right, Leo?" Dante said. "What if they *are* just people being controlled and forced to fight us? What if they're just like Chiara?"

Cruel, but it was his best shot.

Leo stopped, hands clenched around the barricade.

Dante had his attention, and he'd make it count. "Do you think she's out there right now? Will you send your people out there to kill her, Leo? If you're the first one to see her, will you do it? How about *me*? Can I—"

With a roar, Leo dropped the beam and barreled toward Dante.

Dante held his ground. He didn't raise his sword.

Leo wanted a fight, but if Dante gave it to him, he'd lose the war.

Leo slowed, reaching for his axe . . . then stopped, chest heaving.

Dante held his gaze with no anger. "We don't need to kill to win, Leo. We win by keeping our people alive."

Leo lowered his weapon. "Go. Find out how to end this."

Dante grabbed the rope and motioned for Jesse to step up and take his place. "Hold the line, but don't kill anyone unless you have to. Just hold them off as long as you can."

They needed to stall. He had to figure out the catch.

Crollo wanted a *war*. They had prepared to give him one. This was all wrong.

If the god of chaos sought to prove that humans were selfish and violent, slaughtering an army of innocents would only prove him right. Even if they *won*, they'd lose.

It had to be some kind of test, but what did Dea want them to *do*?

The rope was slick with rain, sending him sliding back down a handspan, his palms burning. From below, a crash as the doors fell, then shouts. Jaw clenched, he fought to keep his eyes on the window above and kept climbing.

Dante followed Kira across the roofline, one hand on his weapon, the other out for balance, his gaze darting from the narrow route ahead to the swarm on the piazza below.

He did his best to keep up, but Kira had been practicing her route across the rooftops for days. Like a goat, she leapt from one building to the next, landing so lightly she made no sound, her steps so quick she seemed to fly.

A fall from such a height would kill anyone, even a ghiotte at his peak, which he was not, but Dante ignored the slippery rain and kept going.

Mindless and fearless, their attackers threw themselves against the basilica. Others scaled the sides, smashing their way through the stained glass.

Alessa was in there. He'd left her inside, and it was under siege.

Heart lodged in his throat, he yelled for Kira to run faster.

He dug in for a surge of speed—

And slammed onto his belly, the impact knocking the air from his lungs.

Kill or be killed. He looked back long enough to be sure it wasn't someone he knew, then slashed the woman's arm off. He wanted to look away as she fell, but she wasn't alone.

Hands—so many hands—gripped the edges of the roof, clambering over the sides, their vacant eyes locked on him.

He got his feet under him. "Keep going!" he yelled to Kira between labored breaths.

Two more rooftops. Three dozen more strides. One leap. He had to keep going. He had to make it inside before they did.

Gathering his strength, he launched himself after Kira—

And fell.

Kicking at whatever had grabbed him, he clawed at the roof as the weight of whoever—whatever—was latched onto his foot dragged him down, but his fingers couldn't hold.

He plummeted toward the ground below.

Fifty-four

Alessa had often heard that a person's life flashed before their eyes when they faced death, but she'd always assumed that if it ever happened to her, she would witness the moments through her *own* memories.

Instead, as her brother crushed her airways, she saw her life through his.

A girl, too old for childish nightmares, begging to sleep on her brother's floor because she felt safer near him.

Thirteen, wide-eyed and pink-cheeked with delight as horns blew and banners waved for her confirmation parade through the streets of Saverio, seen from the back of a cheering crowd on the day she became Finestra and Adrick was no longer allowed to call her his sister.

An older version of herself in the Cittadella gardens, dressed in black and hiccupping with laughter despite tears streaming down her cheeks, while Adrick danced a jig and sang sea shanties to lift her spirits after the funeral for Emer, her first Fonte.

Standing in the darkened Cittadella kitchens, raw horror on her face as he handed her a bottle of poison, his own vision wavering as his eyes swam with tears.

Her cheeks dusted with flour as he coaxed a smile from her in the Perduta kitchens after Dante left her in the rain.

The will to live and love for her brother warred with her powers.

At any other time in her years as Finestra, she wouldn't have had a choice. Her powers would have taken his life before he could end hers, but every expenditure of magic over the past few weeks had taken a little more of her strength, weakening her body and her magic.

Her fingers grew numb and clumsy as she strained to pry his ruthless hands off her neck.

Stars were born and died in her vision. The darkness was closing in too fast to stop him.

And then, with a wrench, Adrick's weight was gone. Air rushed back into her lungs.

Gasping and retching, Alessa pushed up on one elbow.

Kaleb had slammed Adrick against the wall. Adrick snarled and snapped his teeth.

Talia was subduing yet another rabid invader as Saida fought to repel others with her unaugmented powers.

Alessa needed to get to her, to help before they were all overcome.

But Kaleb's knife was in his hand. Her brother was in a frenzy that couldn't be stopped.

"Wake up!" Kaleb shouted, his voice cracking. "Dammit, Adrick, snap out of it!" He fought, pleading and sobbing between grunts of effort. His lightning shivered across Adrick's skin but did nothing to stop his violent thrashing.

Alessa clutched her chest and found it hot and wet. She was bleeding. Somehow, in the melee, one of her attackers had landed a strike and she hadn't even had time to register the pain.

Talia dispatched another attacker and dropped to kneel beside Alessa and take her hand so Alessa could draw from her healing powers.

"*Wake up!*" Kaleb bared his teeth as tears streamed down his face. "I swear to Dea, if you make me kill you I will *never* forgive you!"

Adrick—or what had once been Adrick—slammed his head into Kaleb's cheek.

Kaleb cursed, his lightning crackling brighter.

Adrick's entire body twitched, but he showed no sign of stopping or waking.

Talia let go of Alessa and pushed Saida aside to kick a young woman who was trying to clamber inside. "Knock him out already or—"

"I can't! I'd stop his heart!" Kaleb's face twisted with anguish.

Adrick's eyes were empty as his mouth snarled.

Talia adjusted her grip on her sword.

"Please don't," Alessa begged.

Talia readied for a strike. "Move out of the way."

Kaleb dropped his weapon instead. Plunging his fingers into Adrick's hair to hold him still, he gave Adrick another shove, another, over and over, then stopped abruptly. And kissed him, hard, on the mouth.

Alessa held her breath.

Talia froze.

Adrick's thrashing stopped.

After a long, breathless moment, Kaleb pulled back, gasping.

Adrick blinked. Again. His expression was shocked, confused, but he was *there*.

"Sweet Dea," Kaleb choked out. "You absolute dick."

"I couldn't stop," Adrick breathed. "I couldn't make it stop."

Talia recovered from her surprise, shouting for Saida and Alessa to drag a table over so she could barricade the window.

Kaleb's head fell to Adrick's shoulder. "I thought I was going to have to kill you."

Adrick gripped his shoulders. "If that happens again, do it. I mean it. If it comes down to you or me, take me out."

Kamaria stumbled through the doorway. "What the hell is going on? Ciro went rogue and disappeared; there are lunatics climbing through the windows; the ghiotte have retreated; and—*Adrick?*"

Adrick waved weakly.

"He was tranced," Kaleb said. "Like all those people out there."

Kamaria gaped. "What? How did you snap him out of it?"

"I—I kissed him," Kaleb said, sounding surprised by his own confession. "It always works in the fairy tales."

Kamaria groaned. "We can't kiss *all* of them!"

If it weren't for the last flicker of Dante's ghiotte healing powers—which he swore he felt blink out the moment he landed—and the bodies crushed beneath him, he would have died on impact.

Instead, he heaved himself off the pile of entranced fighters, weaponless aside from his daggers. Grimacing against the pain of a few broken ribs and a twisted ankle, at least, he limped away.

Blaise had barricaded and booby-trapped the ground level

entrances to the basilica, leaving only the highest windows for access to Kira's runners, and Dante had fallen short of reaching the roof, landing in one of the alleys to the side of the building instead.

The basilica was close enough that he could throw a dagger and hit it, but he'd need to get through hundreds of entranced fighters to find another way in.

The rain was as much a godsend as a curse, cutting visibility down to the span of a few strides in either direction, but there were still too many of them to avoid.

The mob was ferocious, fueled only by anger. Without the ghiotte actively fighting back, they had begun attacking their own as well as their enemies. It took a minute before they noticed Dante in their midst.

Then a woman hissed.

As quickly as he dodged one pack, another spotted him and came running, snapping and shrieking, determined to rip him apart. He stabbed and punched, aiming for vulnerable spots that weren't fatal first. Hopefully.

At this rate, he'd never make it.

Splashing through the murky water, Dante tripped over a body and nearly fell.

A bolt of agony shot up his leg from his damaged ankle.

At his feet lay Dario, the cocky flirt who had hit on Alessa, staring with sightless eyes. Well. Parts of Dario. How many others had already joined him in death?

Someone roared, and Dante whirled, cursing, as Leo barreled into the swarm. His battle axe was discarded, his only weapons his fists, knocking people aside and drawing the attention of the rest.

"Go!" Leo shouted at Dante. "I'll hold them off."

One man pounced on Leo's back, another lunging for his feet. He reared back with a primal scream, shaking them off like a dog shedding water, and Dante thought for one moment that Leo might actually emerge victorious, but then the man stilled.

"Chiara!" Leo yelled.

He knocked attackers aside as he waded through the throng, until his arms closed around a smaller figure within the mob, and the tide of entranced fighters engulfed them.

Dante fixed his sights on the basilica ahead so he wouldn't see the wave of death drag Leo under.

Fifty-five

Alessa wasn't proud of how loudly she shrieked when Blaise swung through the window.

"Well, hello again," he said with a grin, holding on to the top of the frame. "Why am I sitting on the roof while you hog all the fun down here?"

Talia flicked a rude gesture at him. "What happened to your boiling oil and tar? You're supposed to keep the basilica from getting breached in the first place."

"There are a *lot* of them out there," Blaise said with a shrug. "I left Jakob in charge of the flaming arrows, and they're reloading the oil now, but when I saw one of those nasties heading inside after you, I thought I'd check in. I guess you took care of him, huh?" He glanced around the mess with a confused frown.

Adrick gave a weak wave. "That was me. I'm better now."

Blaise looked even more confused. Probably because Adrick was supposedly executed or banished by Dante. There wasn't time to explain.

In the middle of the chaos in her head, a blank silence throbbed. A muffled absence of thought that Alessa had noticed a dozen times before.

It wasn't a void. It was a shield.

She traced it to the source. Ciro was sitting on the altar. Waiting. And he wasn't alone.

Alessa reached for the door. "Ciro is being controlled by Crollo and he's waiting for me on the altar. I need to get there."

"We can't," Talia said. "Blaise booby-trapped the whole place."

"I *have* to. It's the only way to stop this massacre," Alessa said. "Blaise, can you get us down there?"

Blaise pulled up to his full height. "I'm the only one who can."

Talia waved her sword at him. "Then let's do it! Go, go, go!"

Alessa learned an entire new vocabulary from Talia's expletives when they reached Blaise's first masterpiece—a trip wire that dumped molten cooking oil from the ceiling—but it wasn't nearly as alarming as the staircase turned into a pit of spikes.

With his help, they made it down to the next staircase.

Talia pinched the bridge of her nose. "Blaise, is there anything else?"

"Nope," Blaise said.

It looked clear enough, but Alessa didn't trust it.

"Look, I'll show you." Blaise stepped down first.

A sharp whistle through the air was their only warning.

Three spears impaled Blaise against an ancient wall tapestry.

"Oh, right," he said with a gurgle. "I forgot that one."

Alessa gulped air, trying not to vomit. One spear was through Blaise's right arm, another through his middle, and the third was just below his heart. At least, she hoped it was below.

"Don't move." Adrick held up a hand. "Just *don't* move,

Blaise. Hold his legs so he doesn't fall. They're barbed, and if he moves, his heart could be punctured."

"Help me!" Talia dropped her sword and lunged to support Blaise's weight.

Kamaria and Kaleb held Blaise's arms, Saida his legs, preventing him from sliding any farther.

"Okay, we can do this," Adrick said. "He's a ghiotte. They're really hard to kill. Just don't let him move."

Blood dribbled from Blaise's mouth as he smiled. "Pretty cool, though. Didn't see that one coming. Am I gonna die?"

"No," Talia said. "Stop talking and conserve your strength."

"I must be your best friend *now*," Blaise gasped. "I can't die as your second-best friend, so you have to say it."

"Then I'm definitely not saying it, because you aren't allowed to die. Now shut up and let us keep you alive."

Glass shattered somewhere below and the entire building rumbled as though being shaken by giant hands. Alessa braced herself on the wall, afraid she'd fall into Blaise, while the others fought for balance without letting go of the wounded boy. The shaking subsided.

"I don't know what that was, but it wasn't one of my traps," Blaise mumbled.

Alessa hovered, unsure what to do. Blaise would die if they left him, but *everyone* would die if she didn't find Ciro and stop this battle.

Talia shot Alessa a pained look. "Go on. Tell Dante I'm sorry I couldn't stay with you, but I have to—"

"I know," Alessa said. "Take care of Blaise. I'll be fine."

A bold lie, but the darkness within her was as likely to be her undoing as any outside threat, and the only one who could fix that was waiting for her on the altar.

"Hang in there, Blaise," Alessa said to the boy, who curled his fingers in a weak thumbs-up, only to get yelled at by Talia again for moving.

With a silent plea to Dea to protect Blaise and the rest of her friends, Alessa ran.

The small side door of the basilica was ajar, its locking mechanism dislodged by the quakes. Dante dragged it open, lurched inside, then pulled it closed and bolted it shut.

Alessa had to be alive. She had to.

He shouted her name, then Talia's, too frantic for caution. The enemy was already swarming the exterior. It was too late to hide.

His boots squeaked on the wet floor, an irregular shuffle and thump as he limped along.

He held his daggers lightly, ears pricked for any sound of movement.

Footsteps. On the stairs. A stifled cry of pain. He'd know the sound of Alessa anywhere.

He reached the bottom as she turned the last corner, clinging to the railing as though she couldn't hold herself upright. Her front was stained with blood, but her eyes lit with relief and she fell into his arms. Together, they tumbled into the shadows.

"You're injured," he said.

"Talia healed most of it. But my mind is getting worse," she said through gritted teeth. "I feel like I have to *hold on* just to stay here."

He scanned her from head to toe, noting the tension around her eyes, the paleness in her cheeks. He wanted to carry her away, to leave the battlefield behind and run, but the only way to end this once and for all was to keep going.

One more day. One more battle. If they won Dea's bet, the goddess would have to *fix* her.

"This wasn't the plan," Dante said, looping an arm around her waist. "This wasn't what we prepared for. Those people out there aren't monsters."

"I know. It has something to do with Ciro," Alessa said with a labored breath. "He abandoned his team. I *saw* him on the altar. I think he's working with Crollo."

Their footsteps echoed through the hollow space as they made their way, slowly and painfully, farther inside.

If Dante hadn't already known the gods were playing tricks on them, the interior of the basilica would have tipped him off. A massive tree had grown through the stone behind the altar, with moss spreading outward from the stones dislodged by its reclamation of human space.

A crack ran down the aisle, and insects scurried through the sandy earth beneath. Rainwater dripped through fissures in the walls, puddling on the floor, and gold tiles from the ceiling plinked to the ground.

In the center of it all, Ciro smiled placidly from Leo's throne, as though he wasn't in an ancient decaying cathedral under assault from a swarm of murderous hypnotized people.

Dante stepped forward, ready to attack.

Ciro burst into flames.

Shielding Alessa, Dante braced for the heat, but the blaze vanished as quickly as it flared.

When the dazzling burst of light faded enough for Dante to see again, Ciro was standing on a heap of smoldering ash, all that remained of the throne, his body and clothing unsinged.

A human working for a god couldn't do that. Only a god could.

Alessa shuddered, holding tight to Dante. Now she knew why she couldn't read Ciro's mind.

"Why are you doing this?" Alessa asked. "Why are you making those people fight against us?"

Ciro—Crollo—frowned. "It's getting a bit tedious, all these millennia of the same battle, over and over. Yet my dearest still insists you can overcome your flaws, so I agreed to one last wager."

"Starting without me?" Soft footsteps came from the nave. Diwata, smiling beatifically and carrying . . . the cat? "We can't settle the fate of humanity without the jury, now can we?"

"*Dea,*" Dante said softly.

Diwata—*Dea*—smiled proudly. "I was a little disappointed you didn't figure it out earlier."

"What happened to the real Ciro and Diwata?" Alessa asked. Talia's healing gift hadn't had time to take full effect, and the ominous cold spreading to her limbs didn't bode well.

"Oh, they're still here." Dea nuzzled Fiore's head. "We're merely borrowing them to communicate with you. Felines can't emulate human speech, though she was a very good observer, weren't you, precious?"

Crollo tutted affectionately. "We said no interfering."

"And I *didn't.*" Dea touched her fingers to her chest. "But you got to watch up close. It seemed only fair I could, too."

Either Alessa was hallucinating, or Dea and Crollo in human form were bickering on the altar of an ancient cathedral, and Dea had just admitted to possessing their cat.

Alessa's mind grew fuzzy around the edges as the pain sharpened. She sank to one knee.

"What's happening to her?" Dante demanded.

Dea steepled her fingers. "As I tried to tell you, we are all made up of lights. By taking the scarabeo's power during Divorando, Alessa set off a chain reaction that has been severing the bonds between her own sparks and releasing her light, bit by bit, to return to the universe." Dea bent to set down the cat. "The scarabei are a collective, created to be one, to work together with no awareness of themselves as individuals. As you might say, they have no . . . soul. They are a void, meant only to consume, absorb, take—they do not create order, but chaos."

"You're a *goddess,*" Dante said. "You create worlds. You can stop it."

"Indeed, if that's what the two of you decide."

"*After* hearing the terms." Crollo patted the remaining throne beside him. "Come, dearest."

"We don't need to hear anything," Dante cut in. "Just stop this from killing her."

"You see?" Crollo smirked at Dea.

Dea tutted at him as she sat. "They haven't heard their options."

With a sigh, Crollo continued. "We've been going about this wrong for ages by giving you challenges that required you to work together. What has it proven, besides that you humans can put aside your petty grievances every once and a while. It wasn't the battles that made my point. It was the fallow years between, when people grew tired of virtue and turned to violence, time and time again. In my quest to break you, I gave you a common enemy when I should have let you destroy yourselves.

"You told me to raise an army, so I did," Dante said. "Give us the real enemies and let us end this."

Crollo chuckled. "Truly, it's adorable. You honestly thought you'd end the debate that has haunted your species for a millennia with some . . . kicking and punching? Apologies. I shouldn't laugh. My mistake all those centuries ago was in allowing you to *fight* to prove my point."

"If you don't want a war, what *do* you want from us?" Dante growled.

"*I* want you to end this," Crollo said. "Show us who humans really are, and put the debate to rest for good."

"Enough with the riddles," Dante said. "What does that *mean?*"

Alessa had a sickening suspicion.

"They even turned on the ghiotte I created to *protect* them," Dea said mournfully. "But you're all here now, and you two can end this bloodshed with a word. Those people out there will return to their right minds, no more aggressive than before, and it will all be over if you both agree to the price."

"What price?" Alessa said, remaining upright by sheer force of will.

Dea pointed at Alessa. "Your life for theirs."

Crollo addressed Dante. "And you must agree to let her die."

Fifty-six

Dante launched himself at the altar.

Ciro—*Crollo*—flicked a hand, and Dante's momentum stopped. He hovered, frozen midair as though trapped in glass.

"Oh no, boy," Crollo said. "This is not the moment when you slay a god."

Through clenched teeth, Dante wheezed with what little air was left in his lungs.

Crollo's smile was cold. "I was here before you, and I'll be here after you are gone. There is nothing you or any other mortal can do to hurt me. If you destroy this human body, I'll simply choose another. Makes no difference to me. I could even take *yours*."

Dante grunted, the cords of his neck standing out as he tried to move *anything*. His hands, his eyes. His lungs screamed for air.

"Stop struggling, and I'll release you," Crollo said. "She doesn't have much time left. Do you really want to waste it?"

Dante forced himself still.

Crollo waited a beat, then Dante fell to his knees, too

air-starved to do anything but heave one labored breath after another.

"That's better," Crollo said. "Where were we?"

"My life?" Alessa asked. "Only mine?"

"*No,*" Dante choked out.

Alessa helped him to his feet. "Why me? What does that prove?"

"From the very start," Dea said, "I have been trying to prove that humans are better than my dearest believes. We chose the two of you to argue our points. He doesn't believe you'll have the courage to accept your own death."

Crollo cut in. "And even if you do, he will never agree to condone your sacrifice."

Alessa held tighter. "And if we do agree?"

Dante stepped in front of her. "We don't."

Crollo smiled. "Then the war will continue, your ghiotte will inevitably win the battle of a lifetime, and the two of you get to live happily ever after."

Alessa clutched Dante's hand. "Because the ghiotte will keep fighting until they've slain everyone else."

Crollo shrugged. "Every decision comes with consequences."

Dea smiled. "I *am* betting on you. If you both agree to let the darkness set Alessa free, this war—all wars, unless you create your own—will end the moment she crosses the final threshold. Forever. No more Divorando, no more interference from us. Humans of every kind can live on, unhindered by our machinations. It all depends on you."

"But I die," Alessa said.

"*No,*" Dante repeated, louder this time. It was out of the question. The gods could demand anything else, anything at all, but they couldn't have her.

"Yes." Dea ignored Dante and responded to Alessa. "As you have cleverly figured out already, you have been walking toward the light for a while now. All you must do is agree to continue these last few steps into the unknown."

"*Or*," Crollo said, sounding annoyed, "you choose to live, we undo the damage done by the scarabei, and the war continues."

The ghiotte were made for this. Dante had prepared and trained and armed them for *this*. They would win. Most would survive. Perduta would stand, but the rest of humanity . . .

Dante hardened his heart. The world had beat him down for years, and it could burn for all he cared. Alessa was better than any of those people.

She tried to step forward. "All I have to do is agree to die?"

"*No*," Dante growled. "Give us another option."

There had to be another choice. Any choice but this.

The world shook.

Alessa's face went as white as bone, and her fingers dug into his hand.

The trebuchets. The ghiotte had waited long enough. They were fighting back again.

"Let's give them a moment to discuss." Dea reached for Crollo's hand, and the duo strolled down the aisle, fading like words on a printed page left in the sun. They were still there, still visible, but silent and translucent.

Alessa whimpered. It hurt. Everything hurt.

"Sit. Don't exert yourself. We have to think." Heedless of his own injuries, Dante carried her to the altar.

"There's nothing to think about," she said. "They gave their terms. Countless lives for mine." All those people, hypnotized and trapped within their own minds as Adrick had been, forced to face the greatest warriors the world had ever known.

The ghiotte had trained to kill, not take prisoners. And even if they could restrain without killing, those innocent people would be locked into their torment forever.

Her neighbors. Her parents. Crollo would just keep sending them. Every second that passed meant more deaths.

"I have to do this, Dante," she said. "We have no other choice."

"No. No." He shook his head, repeating the refusal again and again, and the anguish in his eyes hurt her more than any pain in her body ever could.

For weeks, she'd felt the life leach out of her. She'd had time to face the very real possibility that she was never meant to walk away from their war with the gods.

But she'd concealed it. Dante hadn't known what was happening to her until recently, and even after she told him the truth about the darkness spreading within her, she hadn't let him see how bad it really was. Now he was left with no time to make an impossible decision, and every passing minute while he debated would mean more bloodshed outside the basilica doors.

She would finally get to be the hero, but not by winning a battle. By accepting defeat.

And Dante got to raise an army only to have no enemy to fight. Instead, he would have to lose someone he loved in order to stop the war he'd come for.

It was masterful but cruel, how they knew to demand the payment that would hurt the most.

She'd always suspected the gods had a twisted sense of humor.

"We have to agree to their terms." She took his face in her hands. "If we don't, *all* of those people will die."

"But *you* won't." His voice cracked. "I'll challenge Crollo. We can fight this."

"We'll lose if we try," Alessa said. "You heard Crollo. Every Divorando for a millennia was child's play. One word and we can put an end to centuries of attacks and save everyone. No more Finestre, no more Divorando. No more war."

Dante crushed her hand in his grip. "There has to be another way."

"Why would there be?" Alessa said with a bitter laugh. "This is their final test. Crollo doesn't think I'm brave enough, and he doesn't think you're selfless enough to let me go."

"I'm not," Dante said through gritted teeth.

But he was. He always had been. Dante was the one who saved little girls from bullies and rescued cats from riggings, who took a job he didn't want from a stranger he didn't like because she cried in an alley wearing a necklace of bruises.

Crollo had given Dante an army and told him to fight, to raze the world in the name of love, but Crollo didn't understand what love truly was any more than he understood who Dante really was. Love wasn't a greedy, selfish thing, and Dante was the most selfless person she knew.

"I'm so sorry." Alessa reached up to touch Dante's cheek. "You have to let me be the hero this time."

Fifty-seven

Agony cut through Dante like a sword drawn from the forge.

He was supposed to *fight*. He was meant to battle the gods and *protect* the people he loved, not sacrifice them.

All he had to do was say no, and they could be together.

Forever.

Alessa could have her house on the beach. They'd live to see a new world, explore new lands, swim in the bluest seas, sleep under the stars, and kiss atop mountains.

Happily ever after.

Crollo offered Dante everything he'd ever wanted—to live surrounded by his people, with his love and their friends, a chance to live in a paradise of their own creation, where there was no more hatred and no more wars. . . .

He could have it all.

And everyone else would become ash and soil, a new world built from their bones.

Crollo would spend eternity gloating that he'd been right about people all along, that they were as selfish as he'd always known, all because Dante chose his love over the world.

Dea knew what Dante knew: that if he refused, Alessa would never be happy again, consumed by grief, knowing what her life had cost.

The only thing worse than holding her as her life leached from her body would be a lifetime watching guilt eat her from the inside.

Someone screamed outside. A person, snapped out of the trance by their death throes.

"Dante, please." Alessa was crying now. "I love you, and I'd rather die in your arms than live anywhere else."

If the gods looked inside his heart at that moment, they would see the ugly truth—that any decision he made would be no act of sacrifice, no testament to humanity's selflessness or noble gift from his broken soul to the world.

"Ti amo, luce mia," he said. "I'll write it down on every scrap of paper, carve it into the walls, tattoo it on my skin. I love you. I'll always love you."

He had to let her go.

For her.

Because he loved her.

Each word scraped his throat raw like a hundred blades. "I agree."

Fifty-eight

The priests lied. The gods were cruel, not merciful.

Crollo pursed his lips with a long-suffering sigh at Dante's declaration. "Congratulations, my dear. Looks like you may win, yet again. What a tedious bore."

God or not, Dante would have ripped him to pieces if it didn't mean letting go of Alessa. He wouldn't let her go, not even for revenge.

"If he caves before she's gone, be sure to let me know so I can gloat." Crollo swept a bow to Dea, and the incandescent light that was the god of chaos blinked out.

Ciro's body, callously worn as a costume and discarded, crumpled to the floor.

Dea's face was so beautifully sad that anyone else's heart would have broken, but not Dante. Not now. Grief was for later.

Right now, he was pain and rage. "I did everything you wanted, and still you punish me."

"I know it must feel that way," Dea said. "I promise you, this was never meant to be a punishment. You got the chance to love and be loved, and now your love will save the world. That's a gift."

The cruelest gift imaginable, because even now, as the fabric of Dante's world tore in half, he still wouldn't give back a minute of his time with Alessa.

He drank in every rasp of her breath, each flicker of eyelash. He counted the freckles on her nose, memorized the specks of green and gold in her eyes, the whorl of her ear and the faint pink of her lips.

Every detail he collected was like stuffing his pockets with shards of glass to cut himself on in the future.

Someday, after she was gone, every memory would draw new blood, and he would welcome it.

Alessa would die. And he would suffer.

He brushed the dark hair from her forehead, and she smiled weakly as her eyes closed again.

He should've carried her upstairs, found a quiet corner overlooking the fading murals near a window so she could see the world outside. But his legs were weak, his arms as heavy as his heart.

Alessa's breath stuttered. She was still alive, still warm in his arms and fighting to remain conscious, but she was fading quickly.

Angry bruises peeked from beneath her clothing, evidence of injuries beneath her skin he couldn't heal.

"Would you like your powers back?" Dea asked. "That was part of the bargain, I'm afraid, but you never lost your gift. It's connected to you in a way that would have torn the rest of you asunder. We merely . . . locked it away."

"Does *her* power still work?" he asked.

"Yes, but—"

"Then I want mine."

Alessa had agreed to die. He had agreed to let her. They had spoken the words aloud. Their half of this vicious bargain was fulfilled. If his powers healed her despite it all, who could say they had broken their word?

Hope made him lightheaded.

Dea flicked her fingers in Dante's direction and the throbbing in his ribs and ankle vanished. The sudden loss of pain he had already forgotten about felt like background noise abruptly cut off.

He didn't listen to what Dea said next, didn't spare her another thought as he bowed his head to Alessa's face.

So still, so fragile. He pressed a kiss to her lips, murmured to her, begging and pleading for whatever was left of her power to take from him and save her one last time.

And bit by bit, he grew more certain that it was working. Warmth against his mouth, the faintest rush of breath.

He dared to lift his head. Watched her.

Waited.

And waited.

Her pulse was strong, the last of her wounds healed. Even the color returned to her skin, but she didn't open her eyes.

"I'm sorry," Dea said. "You can heal her body, but your gift can't call back her soul. Souls are fickle things, you see."

Dante's face fell. "Then take it back. I don't want my powers if I can't save her."

"You'll live a long and healthy life."

"I don't want that, either."

"I know you're angry. You've given so much, and I keep asking more, but you will save them all, you know. It's what she wants."

"You brought *me* back. I was gone and you brought me back to life, so do it for her."

"*She* called you back. She held onto enough of your soul to lure the rest back into your body. All the blessed have the ability to trade their light. To share. A Finestra is given more . . . room, shall we say. For regular mortals, there is no trade. That's why it is so painful when one of my children tries to use their power on one without a gift to give, because they take light but cannot return it and simply drain the other's."

"Give her my light, then."

"That wouldn't work. There is a threshold of how much of her soul, her energy if you will, must exist together in order to call it back."

"What happens to it . . . when she's gone?" Dante asked quietly.

"Once there aren't enough to hold on to each other, they simply . . . let go," Dea said. "Like escaping gravity to return from whence they came. None created and none destroyed, only energy changing from one form to another. Perhaps it will comfort you to *see* that she isn't leaving for some other place; she's merely returning to the universe."

Alessa began to glitter with what appeared to be tiny gems—no, flickers of light, like minuscule flames too small to make out.

One glowing mote escaped the outline of Alessa's form and drifted into the air, joining a diffuse cloud of others that had already left.

"It's always easier to find your way with more light," Dea said. The goddess glowed so brightly she seemed to *be* light made solid, illuminating the cavernous space.

Dante, too, was lit with a constellation of light. But his stayed in place, confined by the margins of his body.

Alessa's light kept slipping away. Her life diffusing as the bonds released, and each flicker of *her* floated farther from the rest. Farther from him.

Dea strolled closer to get a better look. "Isn't it beautiful?"

Beautiful, she said.

It was *beautiful* how Alessa's light returned to the universe.

But Dante didn't want to share her, not even with all of creation.

She was his, always his.

He yearned to breathe her in, to hold his breath forever, but her light went right through him, as futile as trying to hold on to the sea.

One breath.

Another.

Hers. His. The same.

The world would know her as the girl who saved them.

But she would be gone.

Life without Alessa stretched before him, and Dante knew one thing for certain: With every step he took until the day he died, he'd hope and pray that one of her sparks passed through him.

Fifty-nine

The world went silent.

Perhaps because she was dying or because the battle had ceased and taken the horrible sounds of death with it. Either way, Alessa embraced it. The quiet allowed her to concentrate on the feel of Dante's arms cradling her, his hands holding hers.

He was arguing with Dea. Of course he was. He wouldn't let her go without a fight.

But some fights were unwinnable.

Twice now she had been a party to saving the world. The first time taught her how hollow it was to become a savior when winning meant losing someone you loved. But she'd only had to suffer that pain for a matter of hours. He would have it for the rest of his life.

A dull ache sat in her chest, but everywhere she looked, there was light.

The ceiling of the basilica gleamed with gold tiles, meticulously applied long ago by someone whose name was lost to history. It was all the more beautiful for the places where tiles had been lost over the centuries. Dark specks amongst the glimmer, like a universe full of stars turned inside out.

Weak sunlight highlighted a shroud of dusty air, shimmering from the water dripping from broken windows, and coaxed the amber from Dante's dark eyes.

Her awareness flitted like the dust motes, darting from one point to the next across what she now knew to be the liberated fragments of her soul.

How strange to be in her own body and also outside it, watching herself and her love and the world beyond from all angles, all sides, at once.

She was a hero, at last. And she wasn't alone. She wasn't afraid. She was in loving arms, and she could see it all.

She could hear Dante's voice, the tender words he said in every language he knew—the old, the new, those spoken and those told through touch. If the future beyond the veil allowed for memories, she hoped to hold on to this one.

Some part of her rested in Dante's arms, savoring his sweet words, relishing every touch. Another part of her drifted through the people beyond the basilica, feeling their pain, their sadness, their relief.

She saw Kira running to Jesse and the exquisite joy of their embrace.

She heard Vittoria weeping over Leo's battered body where he'd fallen to shield Chiara.

She felt Crollo's pawns returning to their bodies, relieved and horrified, crushed to discover the many who never would.

They aren't gone, she wanted to tell them. *They're all around you.* But that wasn't enough. Knowing their loved ones were still there, but scattered and untouchable, might dull the pain of loss, but it wouldn't heal the absence.

Still, she wanted Dante to know. She tried to curl her fingers around his, but she couldn't feel them anymore. Or much of her physical form, for that matter. She had the vague sense of pressure where Dante's body touched hers, could feel the tears drying on her cheeks, but little more.

Time didn't stop, but it fragmented like sunlight through a prism, bisected into every shade of the rainbow, each beam of light a different color of her life.

The red flare of courage when she'd stopped playing the part of Finestra and embraced being herself instead.

A bright orange sunset rising over the Cittadella.

Vivid yellow summer afternoons beneath the lemon trees at her grandparents' house.

New friendships, bright green and hopeful like the first seedlings of springtime.

The deep purple of dusk and bedtime stories by a hearth burning low.

And the cerulean blue of a secluded beach framed by high cliffs—her safe harbor.

Together, the myriad colors illuminated her existence from the beginning to the end, and Dea was right. It was beautiful.

Everywhere, there was light. And for as long as there was anyone alive to look for her, she would be there, too, in the shimmer on the ocean, an arc of color in the sky after rain, or the gleam of stars to light their way.

No matter how lonely, no one was truly alone.

Sixty

The rain hadn't ebbed, pouring from the heavens as though determined to drown the city once and for all. Good. It could swallow the city and drown him, too.

Dante gritted his teeth so he wouldn't scream for the gods to make it stop, to take it back and let him keep her. He had made a promise. He would keep it, even if it killed him.

The flickers of Alessa's soul slipped free in silence, but he heard each one like the ticking of a clock.

One.

Another.

Each carried her closer to a threshold he could not cross.

A stronger man would have tried to hide his grief, buried his pain to let her die in peace, but Dante wasn't strong enough. He clutched her to his chest, pressed his cheek to hers, telling her in every language he knew, everything he'd ever felt or wanted to say and not known how or not been brave enough to do so.

He knew the moment she left him behind. There was a

sudden chill in the air and a lightness to her body that stole the warmth from his bones.

A ragged sob tore from his chest.

He yearned for the war to rage on, for the basilica to fall and crush him beneath the weight of history, to bury him with Alessa right then and there, so their stories would end together and he wouldn't have to summon the strength to take another breath.

"I'm so proud of you," Dea said to Dante. Her light began to dim. Not float away, like Alessa's, but like sunlight in the evening, or the moon behind a cloud. "Do apologize to Diwata on my behalf when she wakes."

The aftermath of battle rose beyond the open doors of the basilica, clamoring for Dante's attention, but he refused to give it.

They were on their own now.

He was on his own.

Adrick entered, covered in blood, and choked on a sob.

Dante didn't care how Alessa's brother had returned. It was right that he'd be there now.

Someone laid a hand on Dante's shoulder.

Someone told him they were sorry.

Someone sat beside him.

"I'm here," Matteo said. "Come, let me help—" He reached as though to help Dante stand.

"No." Dante pulled Alessa tighter to his chest. He wouldn't leave her alone.

"I understand," Matteo said.

Alessa's hand slipped and fell, limp at her side. Matteo picked it up and gently placed it back across her chest. His own hand glittered with emerald light. As he patted her hand in place, one light flashed gold amongst his, quivering as though undecided where it belonged.

Dante's powers had done their job and healed Alessa's body, but it wasn't her body that needed healing now.

Something plucked at his thoughts.

"When they trade their powers, it's like a dance, with their lights moving to fill the empty spaces left behind."

Kaleb. Kamaria. Saida. Alessa had used their gifts often. Every time she had taken their powers—or so she'd thought—she hadn't known it *was* borrowing.

Sharing implied they'd get something back.

And they had. At least, that's what Diwata had said, and Dante could only hope that Dea had been speaking through her then, too.

All that time, they had been swapping each other's light.

Lights that were drawn to each other. Like gravity.

Everyone who had ever shared their gifts with Alessa might still hold a bit of her light.

And if they did, maybe they, too, could give it back.

Sixty-one

Dante shouted for someone to open the doors.

Dea's gifts were scattered in all directions, and he needed them all to make this work.

He needed to round up every Fonti and rouse Ciro and Diwata, too.

Alessa had used her powers to stop Diwata during that fateful attack on Naming Day, and Alessa and Ciro had attempted to find out what would happen if they used each other's powers—it turned out, not much at all, but the effort might have led to a swap nonetheless.

He barely glanced up, afraid if he took his eyes off Alessa's face, she would leave him for good.

Somewhere within himself he held on to a few precious sparks of her life, and he urged those to hold fast to the rest.

From the periphery of his vision, he caught glimpses beyond the open doors, the dazed and bloodied people milling about the piazza, weeping, dying, grateful to be alive. Ghiotte ran from one fallen body to the next, checking for signs of life.

Kamaria ran toward the altar, her face going white at the sight of Alessa lying lifeless in Dante's arms. "No. Oh, no."

"It's not over yet," Dante said. Wake Ciro and Diwata. I need all of you."

Kamaria knelt to pat Diwata's cheeks.

"Hang on a little longer." Dante ran his fingers along Alessa's jaw, her cheeks, brushing kisses on her eyelids, her lips. "I'll sing to you every night," he promised. "I'll never laugh at your accent again. You can beat me at whatever challenge you'd like. Please don't leave me."

He could barely see her face in the cursed dark, only the dwindling glimmers that were left of her.

Ciro stood, reaching for a very pale Diwata, and together they made their way toward the altar.

Dante couldn't tell how many ghiotte gathered behind them, but he sensed the room filling.

Shuffling footsteps, a small sob. Bloodied and tear-streaked, Saida hobbled toward the altar.

"Her powers," Dante said. "Every time you shared your powers, you took a bit of her, too. She needs it back."

Looking confused, devastated, and skeptical in turn, they trusted him anyway.

Saida was first, laying her hand on Alessa's as Dante cradled her. Saida gasped, looking around in wonder. "The lights," she said.

Kaleb joined them next and he too, could see the lights as soon as his skin touched Alessa's arm.

Then Kamaria, followed by Ciro and Diwata.

Alessa's face hadn't changed.

She still breathed, but she didn't wake.

Her light was still fading.

It wasn't enough.

She was still limp in his arms, her remaining glimmers of light so sparse and dim compared to everyone else.

He could see Alessa's golden specks floating within the others gathered around, the glimmers of a few within himself. But it simply wasn't enough. They stayed where they were, or within other people, instead of returning to Alessa.

"Does she know how to turn it around?" Kaleb said quietly. "Her power only works in one direction, right?"

"Dea's gifts divided must be united

In order to turn the tide

Choose to fight or choose to die

Lest what is loved be vanished."

Dea had granted them three gifts. The finestra, the fonti . . . and the source of healing that so many had assumed was a fountain for centuries, but they had been wrong.

The ghiotte were Dea's third gift.

Once divided, Dea's gifts must be united in order to turn the tide.

He shouted again, summoning his soldiers closer. A wall of bloodied, dirty warriors stepped forward. The closest reached out to touch Alessa, the rest pressing closer to form a tight ring around their huddle. He didn't know if their touch would help, but it couldn't hurt, and he felt their support like a bracing grip.

Dante stared, his eyes stinging from the strain of not blinking.

The tide . . . was turning.

A few lights shifted closer to Alessa like curious fireflies afraid to land.

The others seemed to vibrate in the air.

They still hadn't reached the critical threshold Dea had told him was needed to draw her lights back together. They didn't have enough.

Nina and Josef were a continent away. There was no one else.

It wasn't enough.

He had tried, but even knowing how to save her, he couldn't.

A figure ran toward them.

For one confused moment, he thought it was an attack, moving to cover Alessa, but Talia gave him a look of utter exasperation.

"Me," she said. "Alessa said you'd need me."

Dante had no idea what she was talking about.

Talia nudged him over, just enough to wedge into their little huddle, and slapped her hand on Alessa's forehead.

"Was that necessary?" Dante said.

Talia swallowed, nervous. "I really hope so."

Dante's breath stalled in his chest.

Yes. Yes, it was.

The moment Talia's skin touched Alessa's forehead, the movement of lights shifted perceptibly, flickers slowing their drift, then halting.

And now moving back toward them.

Toward Alessa.

Into Alessa.

Until she glowed as bright as any of them.

And then a little brighter.

Dante watched in amazement, and then a wince as flickers of gold, then red, orange, blue, and green moved into her from those gathered around her.

Soon Alessa was lit with shimmering gold dotted with flashes of color.

The cold stone of the altar ceased to exist, and all Dante saw was Alessa's face and the glitter of a thousand stars.

She was surrounded by love, safe and cherished in his arms, her hand clasped in his, and he wouldn't let go.

She was his light, as he was hers.

And now his light would guide her home.

"Come back to me, luce mia," Dante whispered.

Alessa opened her eyes.

Epilogue

SIX MONTHS LATER

The lettering on the sign was a touch crooked, with some letters too large and others too small, but it fit perfectly with the mismatched decor and unassuming ambiance of the cozy little inn on the shore.

The Last Finestra offered a home away from home for any travelers passing by.

There weren't many yet, but that would change.

The new establishment had hosted the first batch of guests a week earlier, when a few brave souls from Saverio traveled to the far side of the peninsula in hopes of spotting a glimpse of the mysterious ghiotte island off the shore, where the final battle for humanity had been won.

Most people didn't know about the gods' true final test, and the ghiotte accepted credit for defeating Crollo once and for all.

Perduta was still invitation-only, but a number of ghiotte had chosen to migrate off the island and claim homes in the shoreside town slowly being rebuilt around the inn.

Visitors knew to treat them with respect . . . or else.

It wasn't easy to advertise the presence of an inn so far from most other populated areas, but the property overlooked the shore, and the owners lit a fire outside every evening, just in case a ship passed by. Soon enough, rumor would spread about where the famous Fonti liked to visit.

Even with empty rooms most nights, they frequently had a full table.

Matteo had set up his own carpentry shop down the road, and he stopped by nearly every day, offering to repair things around the house or asking Dante for help with one thing or another, whatever it took to claim some time together.

Talia stopped by for supper at least once a week, sometimes with Blaise in tow, and Kamaria, who had decided to stick around Perduta, often happened to pop in those nights, which was purely a coincidence, surely.

Alessa could hear Adrick and Kaleb bickering affectionately before they rounded the corner, luggage and gifts in hand, so she was only slightly caught off guard when Adrick hauled her off the ground for a bear hug that squished every last breath from her lungs.

"And one from Mama and Papa," he said with another squeeze. "And Nonna and Nonno."

Alessa squirmed to get free before she suffocated, but she couldn't wipe the grin from her face.

Behind Adrick, Kaleb's arms were full of luggage and gifts.

"Next time we're hosting you at the Barrel," he said. "I worked miracles to class up the place and Adrick doesn't appreciate half of my improvements."

Adrick gave his sister one last rib-cracking squeeze and put her back on her feet. "You wouldn't recognize it. And we don't even need a bouncer because Sparky over there just makes a little light show whenever patrons need a reminder to stay in line." He reached back and Kaleb handed him a package which he presented to Alessa. "For you. Nonna says hello."

Alessa didn't need to open it to recognize the scent of Nonna's lemon salt scrub, but she held it to her nose and took a deep breath anyway.

"You two are the first to arrive, so pick whichever room you'd like," she said, shooing them toward the building.

Dusk was falling fast, so she kicked off her shoes and walked toward the water.

Kneeling on the sand with a smile, she breathed a flame to life in her palm and brought it close to the kindling until it caught.

A puff of wind, also hers, fanned the nascent flames higher, and she sat back on her heels to admire her handiwork.

Dea's parting gifts came in handy in small ways that delighted her daily.

Not echoes or scars, but gifts of her own, a bouquet of talents. Souvenirs from every trade she'd ever made.

She even got to keep a wisp of the ghiotte healing power, which came in handy every time she bumped her hip on the corner of a table or stubbed her toe while walking barefoot in the yard to feed the chickens.

The gentle shushing of waves broke behind her, followed by splashing and the scrape of a boat being pulled onto the sand.

Alessa stood and turned, shielding her eyes against the setting sun's reflection off the waves to watch the silhouette outlined in orange and gold striding her way with the day's catch tossed over one shoulder.

Fiore yowled, nearly tripping Dante by weaving frantic figure eights between his feet until he tossed a small fish onto the grass, grumbling about placating the menace.

They performed the same ritual every day, yet he still let Fiore doze on his lap every evening.

Alessa waited, a smile playing on her lips, until he stopped before her, his broad shoulders blocking the glare so she could see his face.

"I still can't believe you kidnapped Dea's cat," Dante said with an exasperated sigh.

Alessa took his hands. "I didn't *kidnap* her. She wanted to come with us. She loves you. And you promised me a house on the beach with a cat and chickens."

"That she keeps chasing away. And it isn't a house, it's an inn."

"It's a home. Close enough."

"Yeah, well, we've populated the entire Continent with chickens by now, and I haven't eaten a fresh egg in weeks. *Cara,* that cat is a demon."

"A goddess, actually." Alessa stepped into Dante's arms, sliding her hands around his bare waist, heedless of the seawater dappling the golden skin of his torso.

He bent to nuzzle her neck. "You don't think Dea still pops into her head, do you? She's always *watching* us."

Alessa laughed as Dante's scruff tickled her. "I think Dea can see whatever she wants, whenever she wants, without needing to possess a cat. And besides, I have no secrets. She already knows I'm in love with you."

She felt him smile against her collarbone.

"And you're in love with me," she said. His answer was to kiss her again, which she broke with an indignant laugh. "You're supposed to *say* it."

"Sì. Ti amo molto, tesoro."

"No. Say you *love me.*"

"You love me."

She laughed, slapping him lightly on the chest. "You're impossible! Why won't you say it?"

"I say it all the time."

"In the *old* language. Why never any other way?"

"Because it makes you laugh." He kissed one corner of her mouth, then the other. "And because I have better ways to tell you how much you mean to me. Ti adoro, luce mia."

She went soft, leaning into his embrace.

No more funerals.

No more wars.

Just a mischievous cat, hot sand beneath her toes, the sun setting over a perfect beach, and a hand to hold.

Happily ever after.

Acknowledgments

Everyone warns authors about the second book, but I still wasn't prepared for the challenge, and I owe my eternal thanks to so many people for helping me through it.

My wonderful agent, Chelsea Eberly. Words can't express my gratitude for your unwavering support through the million panicked texts, late-night emails, and rambling phone calls. There's no one else I'd rather have on the other end of the line when I'm melodramatically crying in the rain. You're a true MVP.

My editor, Vicki Lame, for your enduring confidence that I could, in fact, pull this off, even when I was convinced otherwise, and the entire team at Wednesday Books for your patience as I figured out how to write a sequel during a global crisis while navigating debut year angst, and eighteen months without childcare: Vanessa Aguirre, Sara Goodman, Eileen Rothschild, Michelle McMillian, Lena Shekhter, Anne Newgarden, Meghan Harrington, Alexis Neuville, Eric Meyer, Meryl Gross, Brant Janeway, and to Kerri Resnick and Kemi Mai for the gorgeous cover art that perfectly captures the story within these pages.

My deepest thanks to my publishing teams worldwide and the incredible translators who have gone above and beyond to bring this story to readers around the world. To Molly Powell, and my team at Hodderscape, Lydia Blagden, and Sangutan for their work on the UK covers, everyone at Fairyloot, and the many brilliant artists who have made my authorial dreams come true.

Emily Taylor, my debut buddy and fellow data nerd, Ayana Gray for being an absolute gem of a human, Lauren Blackwood, my co-mentor and editor sister, Natalie Crown for all the voice messages, Lyla Lawless, who's been there from the very start, and the very best mentees turned friends turned colleagues, Lyssa Mia Smith and Sophie Clark.

Thank you to Sibley Johns, Ron Harris, and everyone at WriterHouse. Joanna and Rachel, Alice, Naomi, Christine, Jess, Meghann, Lolly, Alyse, Nicole, my Dunova boys (you're actually reading my book?!), and every friend who has showed up and cheered me on. Monica, Emma, and Diletta, thank you for all the Italian help and cheers to continued adventures.

Hannah Teachout and Kristie Smeltzer, I can't even begin to thank you for all the brainstorming, note-card sessions, and pep talks.

Rajani LaRocca, Andrea Contos, Anna Rae Mercier, and the rest of my Pitchwars cohort, the 2022 Debuts and 2K22s, and my No Excuses crew: Eliza, Melody, Ryan, Brook, Jeff, Kristine, Erin, Margie, and Lisa.

To Kel, Kailey, Mike, Cody, Andi, Flannery, and every bookseller who has shared their enthusiasm, thank you from the bottom of my heart.

To Autumn, Sunny, and Molly. I feel her light every time I

hear from readers who found solace in the passages about love and grief woven through these books. Always in my heart.

Of course, none of this would have been possible without my amazing family. My parents, my wonderful in-laws, and Brian, Cora, and Lyla. I love you all so very much.

And lastly, thank you to the readers. Your love and enthusiasm has been absolutely incredible. Thank you for giving me a chance, and for loving this story as much as I do.